ABOUT THIS BOOK

These imaginary memoirs record with engaging warmth and humour the life of one Horace Ignatius Jay, a Victorian railway servant whom in 1874 was catapulted by promotion into his first appointment as stationmaster. The story begins with his arrival, encumbered by luggage and doubts, at his station on the South Exmoor Railway, a privately capitalized branchline deep in rural Devon.

In *Spook Comes To Stay* (the first book in the series) events reveal how important was the role of the 19th. Century stationmaster in the social and economic life of his community, for Jay finds himself at the beck and call of a feudal squire, a philanthropic titled baron, the local vicar, and a retired brigadier. Equally manipulative are his staff who, together with the artful peasants in the district, drag Jay into a livelong struggle to maintain the upper hand. In this struggle, Jay is hampered by a dark secret; that he does not know how to operate the telegraph apparatus. Indeed, he is as intimidated by the Morse key as any 20th. Century man ever was by the computer keyboard.

But although countless mysteries torment Jay, such as the disappearing lamp oil, the hog pudding that would not be eaten, and the adorable 'belle in white lace', not to mention the rumour that no stationmaster before him has lasted more than twelve months, Jay's ingenuity grows by degrees until his survival looks possible. But then turmoil returns on a grander scale, in the shape of the London and South Western Railway Company preparing to take over the line.

The reader is invited to enjoy the beautiful scenery, to come to know the colourful characters, and to loiter among the nooks and crannies which the men (and in this case one woman) of our bygone railways knew. Through Stationmaster Jay's memoirs one may observe the very nuts and bolts with which early railwaymen attempted to overpower nature, and the ease with which nature overpowered the railwaymen.

An apt analogy would be to say that *The Memoirs of H. I. Jay* are themselves a train journey, not by a modern express flashing through the countryside to deliver its passengers to an important destination, but by a slow, steam hauled ensemble of vintage rollingstock snaking along a pretty branchline.

Since such an intimate account of life in the service of a mid-Victorian railway company has yet to be unearthed, if indeed one exists, *The Memoirs of H. I. Jay* with all its places and characters, including Stationmaster Jay's great-grandson, are of necessity fictitious. The name Michael Jay serves merely as a pen name for the author.

It would have been easy to 'grow' these tales from a seed of truth, an odd paragraph found in an archive somewhere, and thereby claim that the book is based on true stories, but such resort is as unnecessary as it is beguiling. The author claims no more than that the records have been consulted to ensure that events maintain true fidelity to the times they portray, alloyed here and there with much humour.

This is not to say that any trade-off between humour and authenticity is required in the portrayal of railway history. Railway companies were the first large scale employer to offer genuine career prospects to the simple unskilled man, particularly in rural areas, and for this reason the unsuspecting railway employee often accepted promotion which placed him beyond his limitations. Such is why railway history is so rich a source of comedy and tragedy.

You will find that each book in the series, indeed each chapter in each book, traces a multiplicity of overlapping sub-plots which jockey for one's attention as they flesh out the chaos and romance of Horace Ignatius Jay's life. However, these fragments of ephemera, although linked by cause and effect, are animated by the wand of imagination in such a way that each book may be enjoyed independently of the others.

Of course, greater enjoyment will be derived from reading the entire series, for it chronicles Stationmaster Jay's precarious career from the moment he becomes a full-time stationmaster, to the day he marries the mysterious 'belle in white lace', and continues until the arrival of his first son. Whereupon, incidentally, the troubled gentleman discovers the riddle of his existence.

In the struggle between the new stationmaster and his artful staff, Book One reveals who gains the upper hand. It also introduces the setting which, despite being a sleepy independent branchline in Devonshire, is one of mounting upheaval as progress gathers pace in Britain's darkest age of railway accidents. No sooner does Horace Jay set foot upon the bucolic corner of England which is to become his home, than the tendrils of turmoil begin to coil around his feet.

Finally, one learns from the memoirs that Horace Ignatius Jay is given to attacks. These, however, are best explained in the Foreword by his great-grandson, Michael Jay.

The South Exmoor Railway Company

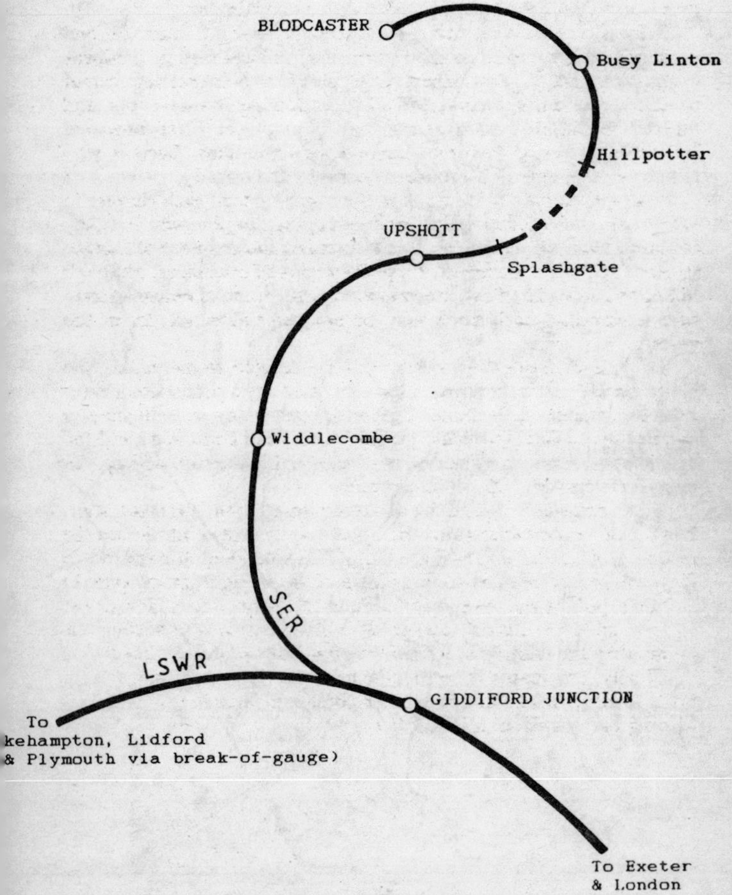

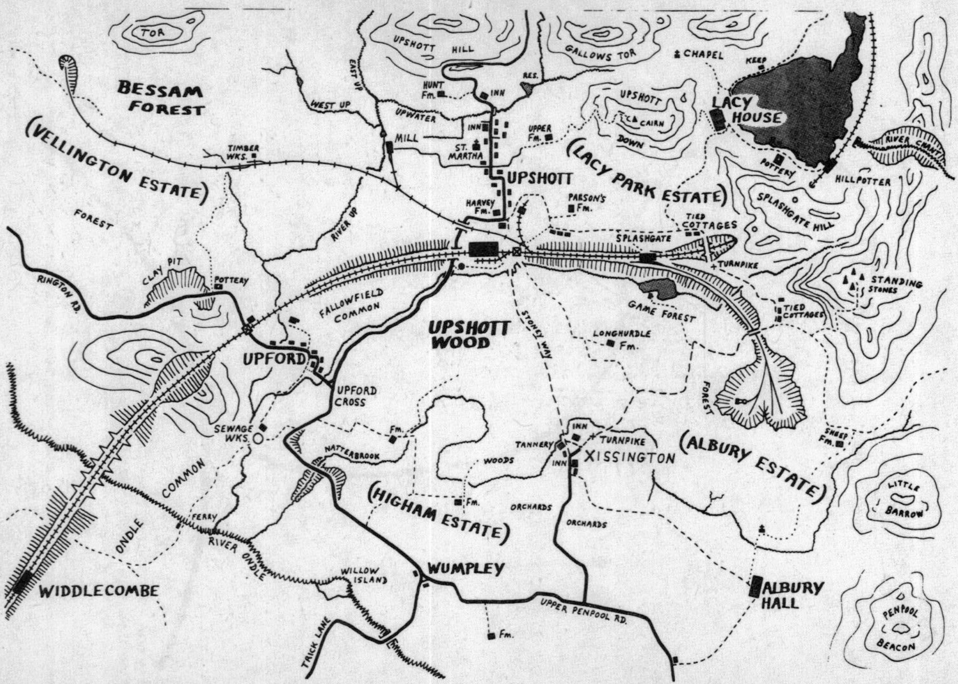
TOR
UPSHOTT HILL
GALLOWS TOR
CHAPEL
KEEP
BESSAM FOREST
WEST UP
EAST UP
HUNT Fm.
INN
RES.
UPSHOTT CAIRN DOWN
LACY HOUSE
UPWATER
MILL
INN
ST. MARTHA
UPPER Fm.
RIVER CHANT
(VELLINGTON ESTATE)
TIMBER WKS.
UPSHOTT
(LACY PARK ESTATE)
POTTERY
HILLPOTTER
SPLASHGATE HILL
HARVEY Fm.
PARSON'S Fm.
TIED COTTAGES
FOREST
RIVER UP
SPLASHGATE
TURNPIKE
STANDING STONES
CLAY PIT
POTTERY
RINGTON RD.
FALLOWFIELD COMMON
GAME FOREST
TIED COTTAGES
UPSHOTT WOOD
STONEY WAY
LONGHURDLE Fm.
UPFORD
UPFORD CROSS
FOREST
SEWAGE WKS.
Fm.
INN
TANNERY
TURNPIKE
XISSINGTON
(ALBURY ESTATE)
SHEEP Fm.
NATTERBROOK
WOODS
INN
COMMON
(HIGHAM ESTATE)
Fm.
ORCHARDS
ORCHARDS
LITTLE BARROW
ONDLE
FERRY
RIVER ONDLE
WILLOW ISLAND
WUMPLEY
ALBURY HALL
WIDDLECOMBE
UPPER PENPOOL RD.
Fm.
TRICK LANE
PENPOOL BEACON

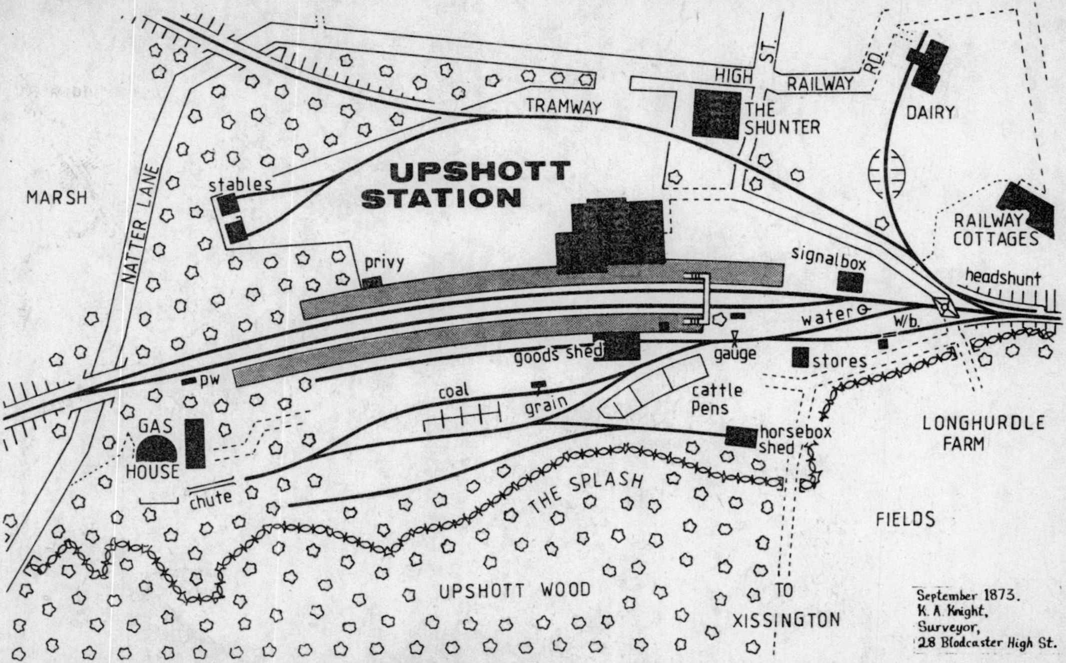
UPSHOTT
STATION
MARSH
NATTER LANE
stables
TRAMWAY
HIGH
ST.
RAILWAY
RD.
THE
SHUNTER
DAIRY
RAILWAY
COTTAGES
privy
signalbox
headshunt
water
W/b.
goods shed
gauge
stores
pw
coal
grain
cattle
Pens
horsebox
shed
GAS
HOUSE
chute
THE SPLASH
LONGHURDLE
FARM
FIELDS
UPSHOTT WOOD
TO
XISSINGTON
September 1873.
K. A. Knight,
Surveyor,
28 Blodcaster High St.

The Memoirs Of H. I. Jay:
Spook Comes To Stay

Michael Jay

STORMLAMP

Fiction.

First impression, published (in Great Britain) by Stormlamp 1990

British Library C.I.P. Data
Jay, Michael, 1949-
The memoirs of H. I. Jay : Spook comes to stay.
I. Title
823'.914 [F]

ISBN 0-9515354-0-4

Stormlamp,
P.O. Box 984, Bournemouth BH16 6YE

Stormlamp is the publishing imprint of Michael Abbott.

Typeset for Stormlamp by Saxon Printing Ltd, Derby.
Printed and bound in Great Britain by
Courier International Ltd, Tiptree, Essex
Marketed and distributed by Ruskin Book Services Ltd., Adam House, 56-58 Birmingham Road, Kidderminster, Worcestershire, DY10 2SA.

Cover picture:
Upshott Station 1874. Based on a photograph of 'the first train entering Shanklin Station' (Isle of Wight) supplied courtesy of R. E. Brinton. Stationmaster Jay and overlay artwork by Anthony King.

To my wife, Yvonne, who is my banking engine on life's steep gradients.

Also to the Swanage Railway, which exudes all the amiable charm one expects of a country branchline. Often are its sights and sounds the ink in my pen.

And finally, with apologies to the editorial staff of *Steam Railway* magazine who, of course, never found Splashgate Tunnel.

CONTENTS

Foreword

Where have all the branchlines gone?

It is a curious fact that while Third World countries aspire to develop and expand their rail networks, as indeed do our European partners, we in Britain, having invented the revered road of iron and subsequently built the greatest railway infrastructure on Earth, have since the 1950's been dismantling ours. At one time, over 21,000 miles of permanent way served our 800 mile long island, forming the backbone of steel which allowed Great Britain to become the 'workshop of the world'.

Then came Dr. Beeching who, in the 1960's, prescribed the tearing up of 5,000 route miles of railway and the closure of 2,350 stations, thereby condemning Britain to a future of waste and pollution. Heavy goods vehicles too large for our roads, and bumper-to-bumper crawls of frustrated motorists have now made a misnomer of the term 'rush hour'.

Why railway nostalgia?

Perhaps the suddenness with which the rails vanished from our island is to blame for the sense of loss which has persisted now for over a quarter of a century. If, as in the days before anaesthetics, the swiftness of the Doctor's cut was intended to rob the amputee of the time to protest, then it worked. But, equally, it rendered the bereft of limb too little time to adjust to a life without that hitherto commonplace form of mobility, the local branchline.

Railway nostalgia, therefore, is probably a kind of psychological scar on the collective mind of the generation robbed, the physical scar being that ubiquity of abandoned bridges, embankments, tunnels and cuttings which criss-cross our countryside to this day. Only when the last mile of disused railway trackbed has become a bypass, the last wayside station an industrial estate, and the last nostalgic old fool a memory himself, will the romanticizing end.

Restoration, a grass routes industry

Perhaps the romanticizing will never end. There are, in 1990, sixty restored steam railways (one-hundred-and-twenty including the narrow gauge lines) totalling about three-hundred-and-fifty route miles of railway reopened against all the odds, like severed limbs growing back again. Also in Britain, there are well over one thousand steam locomotives in preservation, the majority of which are in working order or approaching it.

So many decayed wrecks have been towed away from scrapyards to be transformed into gleaming, steaming, living examples of railway history that they now form a leisure industry which has the power to enthrall children, astonish parents, and moisten the eyes of grandparents to whom childhood is suddenly only yesterday. The collective mileage of Britain's atmospherically restored branchlines, over which these halitous workhorses haul their vintage rollingstock, is increasing annually.

Why should a cumbersome boiler on wheels hauling a rake of draughty old-fashioned carriages with liveries variously described as 'blood and custard', 'plum and spilt milk' and 'chocolate and cream' attract swarms of spectators, while at the same time an Inter-City 125 passing at speed does not? And why is the public so enchanted by volunteer operated railways which recreate the sleepy branchline era, an era in which stations were sleepy, and eventually closed, precisely because the public preferred to gaze at them affectionately than to take trains from them?

What of the lines we shall never see again?

Walk the course of a dismantled railway and you will, if industrial history stirs your blood, become acquainted with melancholy. Here you will find the forlorn signal post lacking a semaphore arm, the enjungled stone bridge of a stoutness and visual appeal which has outlasted some of London's trendiest concrete by one-hundred years, and the drunken telegraph pole cobwebbed with broken lines of communication. Also, you will hear the haunting drone of the wind passing through a once bustling railway station from which will have begun journeys of a lifetime, and at which will have ended tearful domestic sagas.

As you stand on the overgrown platform from which has receded the human tide of sad farewells and joyous reunions, you shall defy the wind's lonely call to occlude the imagined thunder of a passing express. Above all, you will come to know how reluctant to succumb to oblivion is an abandoned railway.

Gone but not forgotten, the SER

When recently I strolled the trackbed of the old

South Exmoor Railway in Devon, to experience what union I might with my great grandfather, I discovered more than historical relics. I discovered how alarmingly transparent, to the receptive mind, is the membrane of time which separates us from our forebears.

Many of the clues to the fact that the path I trod had been the course of a branchline railway were painfully obvious. I stubbed my toe on a half-buried gradient post, was obstructed by the dank arch of a bridge fenced off to make a pig sty, and lost my footing in a rain-filled sleeper indentation. Then I found myself on a dizzying viaduct defiantly traversing a wooded valley scoured by a fast flowing river. Usage of the graceful Exmoor Stone structure, which had once been celebrated as the hallmark of progress in the district, was now confined to easing the step of the occasional rambler, its fate in the hands of conservationists.

Further on I peered through a gorse bush and discovered a rotting goods van which had been parted from its wheels to accommodate a coterie of chickens. To circumvent the reverberating coop, I climbed over a stout wooden stile made of old railway sleepers, and passed a cottage garden bounded by a redundant pair of level crossing gates.

A considerable stretch of the route appeared, at a glance, to be no more than a farm track. However, on an embankment I noticed iridescent pieces of clinker lying among the stones, and looking about me I calculated that no farmer ever built such a solid earthwork merely to drive his cattle from one field to another.

Moreover, I could feel in the air the presence of the past. The experienced railway explorer, it must be said, senses as much as he sees, including the indelible mark a railway leaves upon the atmosphere of a place. The most rational sentimentalist will imagine he can smell the residual sulphur of a steam locomotive where rails have not existed in decades.

Harmless fantasy? Of course. But I would submit that an apparition is not.

The riddle of Stationmaster Jay

On this walk along the old SER did I witness, perhaps even precipitate, an extraordinary event, an event which I now believe to have been a communion of my great grandfather's subconscious making. Of this I shall reveal more later. First allow me to tell you about the memoirs you have before you, for these are a communion of my great grandfather's conscious making, his intention being to rob oblivion of the South Exmoor Railway.

The tales you are about to read describe everyday life in the service of a mid-Victorian railway company, mediating, in the process, detailed portraits of the characters encountered. They are the gift of *Horace Ignatius Jay*, one of the branchline's principal stationmasters. Towards his journey's end (he died in 1902) Horace Jay committed his recollections to paper so that his beloved railway might be remembered as it was at the height of its prosperity rather than in the state of calculated decline prior to its closure in 1966.

Quite how Horace Jay foresaw the closure of the South Exmoor Railway, which took place sixty-four years after his death, one cannot begin to imagine, but it seems he did! The following verse, written in his own copperplate handwriting, was found inside the cover of his works:

DAWN OF THIS CENTURY, PRAY BE MY DUSK

This my era, this my age,
Steam, not muscle, turn this page,
And want drive the peasant from the farmland raw,
To the wheel, the crucible, and factory floor.

Forge and hardship, street and row,
River of white hot metal flow,
And run through the valley to set rock hard,
In rail, and junction, and marshalling yard.

Not my era, not my age,
Oil, not steam, turn this page,
Great ferris wheels of greed revolve,
Around machines that act, machines that solve.

Methinks they'll say in this century bold,
When scarce it is more than halfway old,
That the steel which once in this valley shone,
Has been, has done its job, has gone.

That there was a discarnate element to Horace Ignatius Jay, an element which he himself did not understand, becomes apparent with careful reading of 'the memoirs'. Throughout his service on the railway, perhaps even throughout his entire life, Jay seems to have been the subject of recurring metaphysical disturbances which one might loosely interpret as premonitions. These disturbances, if they have been recounted accurately, seem to indicate a temporal and spiritual consciousness not always in conjunction.

Whilst it is certain that my great grandfather did not intend his memoirs to be a vehicle for describing these inexplicable events, they do. And since, therefore, one should not treat his recollections as a catalogue of clues to the unknown, to a tantalizing extent they are.

A stark apparition

And now to my own extraordinary experience. About two weeks before my walk along the railway, fate, imponent of the inevitable that it is, had unearthed my great grandfather's memoirs and delivered them to me by way of a bequeathal. Having blown the dust from them, and delved into their brittle, yellow pages, I had been transported to the all pervading stillness of rural England in 1874 when not one motorcar or aeroplane existed on Earth. There I had discovered Horace Ignatius Jay accepting his appointment as master of a valleyside railway station situated midway along a locally capitalized line soon to be absorbed into the London and South Western Railway.

I had been enthralled from the very first tale, and had lived vicariously in the Nineteenth Century for as long as my forebear's pen would allow. It was after this, with the sounds of the Twentieth Century flooding back to my ears, that I had felt the compulsion to walk the course of the old South Exmoor Railway in search of the past.

On this pilgrimage did I learn that whilst a glimpse of the future may be a chilling experience to a Victorian stationmaster, to the Twentieth Century person being glimpsed, it is positively alarming. Having reached the station house in which my great-grandfather had lived and worked for so many years, and which, incidentally, survives to this day as the headquarters of a road haulage company, I relaxed on a grassy knoll to eat my pack-lunch. It was while repasting here, intoxicated by the sun's warmth and nature's chorus of birds and insects, that I experienced a fleeting embrace with a spirit so kindred that the passing of one-hundred years could not prevent it.

First my wristwatch went haywire, driven into a blur as if by a silent, oozing stream of impulses. Then it stopped abruptly, and I heard the tinkle of a cowbell. At this point I thought I was dreaming, yet, with wide-awake awareness, I sensed that something peculiar was happening. I looked up and was confronted with a most vivid and uncanny spectre. On the short length of platform still intact at the station house there appeared an incongruous top-hatted figure. At first I was apprehensive, but the apparition brought with it a wave of warmth and reassurance, and somehow I knew I was witnessing my great grandfather.

Dream or reality, and I leave you to judge which, it was as if the present time had become a mere image cast upon canvas, and that this canvas had been stretched to a frail, misty membrane through which could be seen the past.

With my thoughts reeling and my head swimming, I left my half-eaten sandwiches and walked towards the platform to test the reality of the vision. And as I drew near, I noticed that the stationmaster was holding a fobwatch in his hand, as if expecting a train.

Although I came close enough to my forebear to speak with him, no words were exchanged, for he did not see me, and shock had usurped me of my voice. Instead, the Victorian gentleman blinked, surveyed with disdain the serried ranks of parked motorcars and motorcycles which have slain this country's tranquillity, and slipped his timepiece back in its pocket. He was, I believe, suspended partly in my time, and I partly in his.

Suddenly the stationmaster was staring down at me with as much alarm as I was staring back at him, and I felt compelled to call out. But my voice was drowned by a startling shriek. I turned and found a train bearing down on me, its whistle blowing, its bearded engine driver wide-eyed with disbelief. In panic I turned towards the platform and reached out for my great grandfather's hand to pull me to safety, but defiantly the phantom faded away. So too did the train, its thunderous presence having lasted no more than a second. My heart was jumping with disbelief. No. It was jumping with belief!

If this was a dream, then all my senses had conspired to deceive me in a way I would not have believed possible. For when that locomotive appeared, not only did I hear its brakes grinding, I felt the ground tremble, and I tasted its swirling, acrid fumes.

After the incident I found myself once again sitting on the grassy knoll, gazing pensively at the crumbling platform. A profound sadness had overcome me; a feeling that I had been left behind, much as if I had missed the last train of the day, the train that had only just missed me.

About this time, a jet aeroplane was ripping through the sky, and not until it had become a distant and angry speck did I hear the new silence of the Twentieth Century, its threshold being the relentless rumble of a trunk road in the foot of the valley, the impatient buzz of a chain-saw felling trees for a new development, and the symphony of lawn-mowers in concert at a nearby housing estate.

Also I noticed a cloud of diesel fumes billowing upwards from a truck bursting into life on the premises of the road haulage company, and it made me realize that Stationmaster Jay belonged to an age when freight travelled on rails, not on people's doorsteps. When industrial pollution, though never welcome, was mere grime, not invisible, deadly poison. Jay had returned to a time when only by the firebox and the boiler could man unleash the forces of nature, when substances of such diabolical potency as plutonium, dioxin and chlorofluorocarbons were undreamed of.

In the hope that this freak yet wonderful moment was not lost, I tried to follow my great grandfather, to see how the station yard looked before being turned into an industrial estate. Along the edge of the estate was a neatly planted row of silver birch trees rustling in the breeze, and I allowed their sibilations to become the approach of an early steam locomotive. Also I allowed the slamming of car doors to become the slamming of railway carriage doors along a busy platform, and willed my wristwatch to go into that blur again. But, alas, I remained a prisoner of the present, frenetic age.

Nevertheless, through *The Memoirs of H. I. Jay*, the Victorian stationmaster and I do still meet occasionally.

Michael Jay

CHAPTER ONE

IN AT THE DEEP END

I reported for duty on a fine Monday morning in June 1874, having arrived at Upshott Station by the 5.05am Mail Train. The former stationmaster, Mr. Mildenhew, had vacated his rooms above the station to meet me on Platform One. He insisted on a formal handing down of the books and keys with a solemnity engineered to sober me to my new post, but it was a ceremony I scarcely required. Then, with a glance at his silver pocket-watch, he reminded me that I had but half-an-hour to unpack my trunk, don my top-hat and frock-coat, and receive the 6.45am Market Goods train.

Mr. Mildenhew's next gesture filled me with sadness. He handed me his company timepiece stoically, with the intention of declaring that I had inherited it with the job, and faltered. Betrayed by a tear, and quite unable to speak, he shook my hand lingeringly and turned away, leaving me with the suspicion that he had intended to warn me about something.

I found my South Exmoor Railway Company uniform both comfortable and discriminating. The proximity of steam locomotives necessitated a predominance of black, but this serviceable colour rendered all the more relief to the company crest. The railway had been capitalized jointly by the business community and landed aristocracy along its course, and a very striking company crest had been distilled equitably from the shareholders' coats of arms, such as that of the Lacy family of

Upshott itself. Every uniform bore this crest embroidered in gold and cherry thread by the mother of a junior member of staff.

I oversaw the arrival of a young horse rider returning a single-line baton to the signalbox. This peculiar practise I shall describe later because it characterized most aptly this oddly run little railway. Having seen to it that the boy's horse was watered and stabled properly, I took a pinch of snuff and spent a few minutes anticipating the arrival of the Market Goods. Realizing that I needed to acquaint myself with the station's layout and details, I patrolled the platforms and imbibed the cool moist air of Devonshire in the early morning.

In my solitude I puzzled at Mr. Mildenhew's reluctance to introduce me to the staff. Whilst I could appreciate that many of them would be indisposed to muster at this time, it would have been gracious of the fellow to summon the Booking Clerk and Senior Porter, if not the Switchman. Instead, the erstwhile stationmaster had deposited his trunk in the Parcels Office for safe keeping and wandered away forlornly towards the village, presumably to bid old friends farewell. Attached to his trunk was a company pass to travel on the first passenger train of the day, and so it was that I knew he would return in time for the 7.47am Giddiford Junction train.

Despite his terse conduct, I felt sure that Mr. Mildenhew was actually of a kindly disposition. Indeed I saw much of myself in him. Like me, he had received little formal education and had seized upon the opportunity to better himself, unhampered by the barriers of social class, that the railways provided. This relatively new vocation could, given time, reward the determined and self-disciplined equally with the privileged. As in my case, Upshott Station had been Mr. Mildenhew's first permanent appointment after serving as a relief manager, he for the London Brighton and South Coast Railway, and I for the nearby London and South Western. The LSWR had customarily provided the South Exmoor Railway with relief managers, so I was already partially familiar with this beautiful valley and its railway.

A man of about my own calibre, Mr. Mildenhew had been dismissed for incompetence, and it was this aspect of his fate which worried me. You see, it was not a railway ethic to offer an employee a second chance of promotion once he had declined an earlier one, even if that employee had declined out of genuine concern that the nature of the promotion would place him beyond his limitations. In plain English, you either took every opportunity to elevate yourself or you were a dead duck. The result of this admirable precept was that the typical railway employee stopped seeking promotion only when he found himself out of his depth.

Now, a cunning relief manager could defer the knottier problems until the return of the full-time incumbent, but when poor Mr. Mildenhew had become the latter he discovered that he simply could not balance the books in the long term. Since the company did not indulge in reappointing over-stretched stationmasters, Mr. Mildenhew was not leaving Upshott for a less demanding railway position. He was leaving the railway community for ever, and probably would never hold a salaried position again.

To my aunt's advice 'think positively' I had long since added 'and deport one's self with due bearing'. Mindful of this, I squared my shoulders and forbade myself to think about Mr. Mildenhew. I also determined to gather my staff for a formal introduction at the approach of Noon, when no traffic was due.

* * *

From the top of the wooden footbridge connecting Platforms One and Two I surveyed the tranquil and reassuring scene that was Upshott Station, which nestled halfway up the north slope of Ondle Valley. The station house had been constructed in stone hewn from nearby Splashgate Quarry, and the base of its salmon pink walls had yielded to dappled mosses, its grey slate roof to bright yellow lichens. As if inspired by architectural megalomania, the little square building was top heavy with mock Tudor chimneys reaching impudently for the sky, yet remained dwarfed by the tribe of hills surrounding it. For here it was nature, not man, which determined the skyline. The moorland's natural steeples were founded in emerald, climbed through levels of wind-scorched heather, and aspired in naked granite. Today the sky above these peaks was calm and friendly, a pastel blue.

The station, although serving a single-line railway, had three platforms. Platforms One and Two enclosed a crossing loop which allowed 'up' and 'down' trains to pass each other in opposite directions, and Platform Three was a small half-length platform for handling parcels and goods. There was, as one would expect, a goods shed and sidings including a small grain dock, weighbridge, and horsebox shelter. Upshott had no engine house, but on the forecourt were stables for two shunting horses, and boxes for riding horses and carriage teams.

This peaceful morning there were but two sounds on the wind; the station cock crowing from the signalbox steps, and the punctuating crunch of a local fuel merchant filling his handcart in the coal siding. A viaduct carrying the railway across the River Ondle could be seen rising from a lake of mist in the streaky eoan light, like a giant pink comb left in the silver hair of dawn. But soon the innocent peacefulness of this day's youth would be gone, for my senses were about to be caressed by the approach of a train: a plume of steam rising from that viaduct, the asthmatic beat of a locomotive engaging the harsh incline through Upford Cutting.

The addition of an early 'down' goods train on Mondays, this being Market Day in Blodcaster, was giving rise to increased activity around the station. Local farmers and drovers were arriving with their reluctant livestock in tow, warily traversing the level crossing to reach the cattle-pens.

The Goods Clerk, a fellow by the name of Phillips, emerged to rule over the loading and documentation of these noisome creatures. The plaintive bleeting of black-headed sheep and the bellowing of disgruntled longhorn cattle grew to a comical symphony of protest during the boarding operation, but the clamour ceased abruptly once this was over, and the hapless creatures awaited in restless silence their next trauma. This would come in the form of some very rough shunting, for the schedule allowed the locomotive crew of the Market Goods train just thirty minutes to marshal and entrain the miscellany of wagons strung out along Upshott's grassy sidings.

All around me, preparations were in hand to dispatch the community's produce. On Platform Three, the half-length platform, a pair of ventilated vans were being loaded judiciously with watercress and edible mushrooms from Hunt Farm. Rabbit carcasses were heaped everywhere, and parcels marked 'fragile', which contained pottery from Bessam, were being weighed on the platform scales. Smell was always a prominent feature of mixed goods going to market. Stirred into the station yard's own unctuous graveolence was the fragrance of greenhouse fruits, the musty odour of those snow white mushrooms, the starch waft of local lace, and the pepper of freshly dipped livestock.

On the Dairy Siding a stout company dray-horse snorted as it struggled to shunt a flat-truck loaded with milk churns from the north side of the 'running' line to the south side, but its hooves were denied adhesion by the dew on the sleepers. However, the Horse Superintendent had no time to be sympathetic towards the beast, and applied the crop. For looking down on him impatiently from the signalbox was the Switchman awaiting completion of the manoeuvre so that he could swing the crossing gates in favour of the approaching train. Elaborate mechanical linkages had been laid underground to allow the Switchman, or 'Signalman' as he was now officially known, to swing the gates remotely by turning a handwheel inside his box.

A few minutes later, after the horse-drawn dairy truck had been parked behind some other flat-trucks on the weighbridge loop, the Market Goods could be heard descending the far side of the valley. The Signalman set the handwheel spinning and, with a wild, hesitant swing, the frail level crossing gates clattered across the cobbled road which served the station yard. Next, to permit the train to enter the station, the Signalman pulled a lever to set the Down disc signal to 'clear'. This disc, located on a forty-foot post at the far end of Platform One, rang out like a cracked bell as the distant and elusive rhythm of the approaching steam locomotive grew in urgency to become the beat of a Zulu drum.

Railways, by means of their electric telegraph circuits, had forced upon our nation the concept of universal time. Prior to 'Railway Time', itself synchronized daily with Greenwich Mean Time, the further east was an English town or village the more advanced would its inhabitants set their clocks. I was proud to be a part of the continuum of railway life which fermented such progress, and with pride I watched my station run itself like clockwork beneath the footbridge. I need hardly point out, however, that my couch of aloofness did not last.

The scent of straw yielded to the stink of sulphur as a Beattie designed 2-4-0WT locomotive named '*Briggs*', the WT meaning Well-Tank, rolled into Platform One with its steam whistle shrieking. Smiling benignly, I descended the footbridge steps to take the single-line baton from its driver and hand it to Signalman Hales. Outshopped in olive green and black, a South Exmoor Railway locomotive made a pleasing sight at the head of a rake of SER passenger carriages of pale green and white livery, but the same engine formed a somewhat less tidy spectacle hauling a jumble of private-owner goods wagons.

Mr. Wheeler, the Booking Clerk, approached

me with a sly grin, but before speaking he waited for *Briggs* to be uncoupled and steamed away to the South Siding.

"You shouldn't 'ave let them pigs on, Mr. Jay," he said with the gravity of a juvenile, and pointed to a Board of Trade bulletin pasted to my office window.

Mr. Wheeler was several inches shorter than myself, so for reasons of dignity I maintained my gaze upon *Briggs* in the station yard. Enwreathed in steam, the doughty engine was reversing to entrain Upshott's rake of cattle trucks. Further, I made no reply to the clerk's uninvited remark. I wanted to see how he would respond to my authority.

"Swine fever hereabouts," he explained, calculating that this snippet of information would alarm me.

It did. I looked at Mr. Wheeler, and then at my window. I had been given no advance warning of any such outbreak, but I could see that the Board of Trade bulletin was current. So I thanked my Booking Clerk for bringing the matter to my attention, and set off immediately for the marshalling yard, this being known broadly as the South Siding. I was puzzled by Mr. Wheeler's warning, I must say, because I did not recall seeing any pigs. I summoned the Goods Clerk.

"Which of these vans contains pigs?" I queried him.

"None sir," he replied, somewhat bemused. "It would be an offence to transport pigs. There's been a case of swine fever in the district."

"I know," I said brusquely. "However, Mr. Wheeler assures me that we have a consignment of pigs aboard. As the Goods Clerk, Mr. Phillips, I expect you to know of their whereabouts. Have you no docket for pigs?"

The studious Mr. Phillips examined his papers and became increasingly irritated as *Briggs* jolted the trucks behind him for coupling together.

"If Jack Wheeler says we have pigs, then we have pigs," he fussed. "Jack misses nothing. We will inspect the vans together, Mr. Jay. It is not uncommon for breeders to smuggle their livestock aboard a train during a ban. Many local farmers rely on Market Day for much needed cash."

The pigs obligingly began to snort, and we identified their location quickly. They had been squeezed in with a consignment of sheep.

"Whose pigs might these be?" I asked Mr. Phillips. "Defying a Board of Trade quarantine order is a serious offence." The Goods Clerk appeared to be troubled. "Well? Out with it Mr. Phillips, if you please."

"There is only one local pig breeder who would go this far," he said, having counted a total of one dozen swine, "and that is Smethwick of Longhurdle Farm."

"Get the pigs back in a pen, Mr. Phillips," I instructed the clerk. "It will be a sporting affair with these stupid sheep in the same van, but we shall have sufficient time. I will ask the engine driver to work Platform Three first."

I noticed Mr. Wheeler listening from the foot of the animal ramp.

"The Giddiford baton rider is away on time," he called out unnecessarily, the purpose being to justify his presence. Mr. Wheeler now pinched a pig's rump. "Pity about these 'ogs. They're fine and plump," he said. I raised an eyebrow. "I'll get ol' Smethwick back 'ere then, Mr. Jay, shall I?" he changed the subject quickly. "I know a short cut yonder."

Mr. Wheeler scurried off past the horse-box shed and across a stream at the back of the sidings. Mr. Phillips and I began separating the pigs from the sheep and guiding them down the ramp.

"Handle Farmer Smethwick carefully," the clerk warned me. "That man has a propensity towards violence."

By the appointed time of 7.15am Upshott's contribution to Blodcaster Market had been entrained for departure, and the unwanted pigs were assembled in a pen for their owner's collection. *Briggs*, having been to the water tower, was dribbling spillage from its footplate like a salivating dog as it barked into life, and suffused moist, grey breath over the trucks it was heaving into motion. The sulphurous concoction oozing from the engine's chimney also swept across the platforms, causing a disorientating swirl. Having decided to give this, my first departure from Upshott, the 'right away' personally, I held a handkerchief to my face and raised my arm in the air.

The loosely coupled cattle-trucks and goods vans jostled each other clangorously as the locomotive lost its footing briefly on the rising gradient, causing the ground to tremble, but, with the businesslike rumble of freight under way, the goods vehicles were soon thrusting in and out of the steamy fog with gathering pace. I watched the train until the sound of its locomotive had faded to a distant thudding, and then switched my gaze anxiously towards the pigs. Soon I was gazing even more anxiously at the woods beyond the South Siding. Mr. Wheeler was nowhere to be seen, and of this Farmer Smethwick, I was yet acquainted only with his ugly reputation.

CHAPTER TWO

THE TELEGRAPH NIGHTMARE BEGINS

With a salaried staff of three, and a wages staff of fourteen including the gangers, memorizing all the names in the staff manifest had taken me some time. But, having done so, I now knew which employee held each position in my station, and was therefore able to recall instantly the name of the person wearing any variant of uniform I encountered. This simple artifice had my staff wondering if they had been appointed a telepathic stationmaster. Tipping my top-hat, I introduced myself to the Senior Porter whom, by the aforesaid means, I knew to be Humphrey Milsom.

"I would think your name is Milsom," I declared.

"Delighted to make your acquaintance," the ageing porter responded courteously, raising an eyebrow.

After a little introductory conversation, I braced myself and said: "Mr. Milsom, doubtless there are matters outstanding here at Upshott of which I should be cognisant, but which your erstwhile stationmaster seems reluctant to enumerate. Therefore, I should like everyone to assemble in the Booking Hall at ten minutes to Noon for the purpose of a formal introduction. Perhaps you would care to promulgate my wish."

Mr. Milsom stared at me blankly, as if I had addressed him in a foreign language.

I know that my vocabulary did, on occasions,

startle simple porters, so I assumed this to be the difficulty. Naturally it was not my desire to confuse anyone. My turn of phrase was merely the result of having had, since childhood, an insatiable appetite for reading. However, I did tease Mr. Milsom by not re-phrasing my request. Indeed, I preserved silence upon the matter and awaited his reply with a probing stare.

"Certainly, Sir," the porter agreed eventually, like a slot machine in which the penny is weighed before dropping.

Humphrey Milsom was a portly fellow, close to retirement, and not looking forward to being cast aside by the railway. This was not surprising because in the days before the working classes could afford to participate in pension schemes, retirement, in the true sense of the word, was an unattainable luxury. Humphrey, therefore, had made up his mind to enjoy to the full his remaining days upon the railway before returning to the land.

The company cap, a peaked 'pork pie' affair, endowed Humphrey with a jolly visage, rather like that of an approachable uncle at a children's party. In reply to my request for a noon mustering, he stroked his argent moustache and advised me with a smooth, almost songful voice:

"I doubt you'll catch the gangers at that time of day, Sir."

"Mr. Milsom," I smiled. "I believe I described the introduction as 'formal'. I shall address the gangers separately. It is my experience that permanent way men do not have a constructive effect upon such occasions. In the meantime, I would appreciate a resumé of affairs generally. I observe that Platform Two has been partly excavated."

"Arr, it be a time of great upheaval on the South

Exmoor, Mr. Jay, as you probably know. Matter of fact, we've a gang of workmen arrivin' on the 12.32pm. Tis all for to do with standardizin' the platform heights to two-and-a-half-foot above rail level, as I understand it."

"These workmen are coming to re-lay Platform Two?" I queried him.

"Not exactly, Sir. They're intendin' to dig up this 'ere platform also."

Mr. Milsom pointed to a pair of telegraph wires traversing the yard, and chortled mischievously. "While we be on the subject of change, Mr. Jay, the telegraph's been installed for some months now, but still no one at Upshott knows how to operate the blessed thing. The apparatus chatters like teeth in December, but it don't mean a thing to anyone here. Head Office aint too pleased. Between e, me, and the fence post, I reckons it were the last straw for old Mildenhew. At Headquarters they be after more enlightened stationmasters such as your good self, Mr. Jay, there bein' so much change on the horizon."

Mr. Milsom's cavalier remark filled me with horror. You see, I knew as little about telegraph codes as no doubt did he, but I had allowed Head Office to assume otherwise. To conserve my air of authority, by way of a few knowing nods I encouraged Mr. Milsom to share Head Office's misconception, and determined to learn about the strange cyphers later. Little did I know that my Senior Porter was concealing a shameful secret of his own, one which would cost him his job were it to be revealed, but this is another story.

"Arr, old Mr. Mildenhew were nothin' short of perplexed by the telegraph," Mr. Milsom reflected wistfully. "One mornin', in sheer desperation, he took hold of the code book and locked himself in the Telegraph Room. Spent the entire day fiddlin' with the apparatus tryin' to receive a message, he did."

"And did he receive anything that made sense?" I asked, wondering if this method would suit me.

"Not as I recall, Sir. He received an electric shock, but that made no sense at all. They tells I the electricity has to be what they calls 'high voltage' for to make it travel down all those miles of wire. T'aint natural if you asks I. Medallin' with nature, tis. An electrical current comes all the way from Giddiford, and then goes back again via Mr. Mildenhew? I just hope the poor gentleman's still a Christian. Well, I suppose someone has to pay the price for makin' the world a faster place."

Mr. Milsom dealt me a mawkish smile and grunted to indicate his satisfaction at now serving a stationmaster accomplished in telegraphy. "Now, Sir, what else be there? Ah yes! Word has it we'll soon be biddin' them disc signals farewell. We'm gunna get semaphores at last."

"The semaphore system is scarcely new," I concurred heavily.

"Tis all for to do with the impendin' absorption into the London and South Western," he said distantly. "They wants to take over a workin' railway, not a museum of antiquity."

"Quite. Now, is there anything else I should know about?" I asked dismissively, confident that there was not. A gust of wind had set the Waiting Room sign squeaking and, with my teeth on edge, I was anxious to move away.

"There be the disappearin' lamp oil," Mr. Milsom chirped brightly, as if the matter would cheer me up. "Course, Mr. Turner will tell e all about that. Oh, and I nearly forgot. We'm got another cider war loomin' betwixt the Highams and the Alburys. Tis a great thing if e be a ganger with a long thirst and a short pocket, but often as not these skirmishes turn nasty. Between e, me, and the fence post Mr. Jay, as Stationmaster of Upshott, e'll find that out, probably to your cost. The railway gets to be the battle-ground, e see. Last season a torch were put to a Company horse-box."

"Good Lord!" I winced. "Were there any horses in it?"

"Heaven forbid, no Sir. Only barrels of costards! Twer a splendid growin' season for apples, twer, and we ran out of wagons to ship the blighters."

I resolved that no such felony would take place during my aegis.

Where is the Booking Clerk?, I wondered. The pigs were mounting each other and squealing piercingly. Next there would be a claim against the company for damage to livestock. Suddenly I realized that Mr. Milsom was still talking to me.

"When the London and South Western absorbs the South Exmoor," he said, pointing a stubby finger at the railway track, "them old wrought iron rails is a comin' up, so Mr. Mildenhew told I. We'm a gettin' steel'uns! There be a twenty mile-an-hour limit on them metals down there, not that anyone takes any notice of it. An I reckons that the timetable won't be worth the paper tis printed on when they begins upgradin' all this permanent way. Why, we'm got seventy pound rails set in light-weight cast-iron chairs runnin' the whole ten mile. Her's all got to come up." Mr. Milsom paused to think. "I knows progress be the thing of the future, and we ought to look forward to it, Mr. Jay, but I prefers to look back on it myself. Bein' around at the time aint good for e. Still, there b'aint no stoppin' the mighty London and South Western Railway Company."

"Not so mighty that it can do battle without allies, Mr. Milsom," I enlightened the fellow. "Especially against broad gauge companies like the South Devon and the Great Western Railway. The South Exmoor is afforded much leverage by being an enclave of preferred gauge railway in broad gauge territory. We are what those seven-foot gauge companies derisively call 'narrow' gauge, you know."

"I knows that, Mr. Jay. I knows that. But if they calls us narrow, what calls they the two-foot gauge mineral lines like old Albury's?" Humphrey asked. "This gauge business do confuse I more than a mite."

Having no answer to the porter's question, I continued on the subject of passenger carrying railways.

"The mixed gauge metals at Giddiford are not the property of the London and South Western," I said. "They are leased from the Exeter and Crediton Railway. Indeed, four-foot eight-and-a-half-inch gauge progress towards Plymouth is bedevilled with legal jiggery-pokery. As I understand it, this 'all-powerful' London and South Western of yours must curry favour not only with the Exeter and Crediton Railway, but with the Bristol and Exeter too. We have the Devon and Cornwall Company, not the London and South Western, to thank for the preferred gauge line to Okehampton and for conquering the wilds of Dartmoor to Lidford. Only when the Lidford extension has been completed by the Devon and Cornwall, in about six months time, will the

London and South Western step in and purchase the line. What say you to that, Mr. Milsom? We shall have yet another break-of-gauge, this time with the South Devon's broad gauge Launceston branch! The railways hereabouts are a tangle."

I paused to ponder my own curious destiny in this great railway conflict. Having terminated my employment with the expansionist London and South Western Company, I was about to be handed back to it like an item of lost property. I broadened my Senior Porter's knowledge of railway politics a little further.

"The truth of the matter is this, Mr. Milsom. Parliament is holding the London and South Western Railway Company to its agreement with the Great Western. To wit, that it shall not encroach upon the latter's territory in the south-western peninsular. Not surprisingly, the London and South Western Company has come to regret this foolhardy undertaking, and now seeks to circumvent it by colluding with broad gauge companies eager to convert to the more popular gauge. The scheme entails pursuading broad gauge companies not bound by any such demarcation agreement to lay a third rail along their lines to Devonport and Plymouth Friary."

I realized by my colleague's silence on the matter that I had ruined his respect for the London and South Western Railway Company. At this point we found ourselves wandering towards the pen of pigs, and a tacit mutual feeling that nothing so mundane as railway matters should be allowed to spoil this pleasant morning compelled us to change the subject.

"Those are fine porkies," Mr. Milsom observed with a twinkle in his eye. "Her'll be too bad if the

Inspectorate requires their destruction. A terrible waste. Don't e agree, Mr. Jay?"

"They are all accounted for, Mr. Milsom," I warned the porter. "If they are to be destroyed, then they shall be. Ay, and by Mr. Smethwick, lamentable though that may be. The carcase meat shall not be spirited away to a railway employee's table."

"No Sir."

I changed the subject again, lest I hear an improper suggestion. To have had my authority compromised so soon would have been inexcusable.

"According to today's Traffic Book, the 7.45am is bringing down from London a private horse-carriage, the property of one Lawrence Albury," I revealed. "The conveyance is a somewhat splendid cabriolet, I am told, so I want it set down on its own wheels without incurring so much as a scratch or finger mark. The price of it I dare not enquire. However, having said that, I am bound to add that we shall need to uncouple it promptly. The timetable allows precious little latitude for such operations, and I do not wish to see the passenger train delayed. For a branchline, the South Exmoor enjoys an enviable timekeeping tradition, and one which I expect every man, however humble his role, to maintain. Most rural railways are infernally slow, do you not agree, Mr. Milsom?"

"Indeed," Mr. Milsom chortled proudly, and then, eyeing me deedily, added: "I'm afraid old Mr. Mildenhew experienced a lot of trouble with Squire Lawrence Albury. The Alburys did not welcome the comin' of the railway, and almost prevented its construction. The Lacy family, upon whose estate stands the village proper, were entirely in favour of the line, of course. Indeed, it were Lacy money and influence that got the Act through Parliament, and it were the re-surveyin' of the line through Lacy property that ultimately defeated Squire Albury. He be a mean and unreasonable man, Mr. Jay. The earthworks on the new route nearly bankrupted the company before the line were completed. There'd have been no need for a six-hundred yard tunnel if..."

"I am familiar with the history of this line," I interrupted Mr. Milsom. However, Upshott's font of local knowledge was not to be stemmed.

"Squire Albury wouldn't allow the railway to take the easy route across his land," he continued. "But even so, now her's built and runnin', the crafty ol' weasel has expanded his quarryin' business and laid a two-foot gauge mineral line out to meet her at Splashgate. The hypocrite sells Splashgate stone to builders as far afield as Lincolnshire now, via the very railways he claims to despise. What's more, he has the nerve to complain that the South Exmoor brings unwanted strangers into the valley."

"Disrespect for one's superiors is unbecoming," I warned Mr. Milsom.

"Well Sir," he replied complacently. "With respect to e, if Squire Albury be an example of 'superior' I be glad to stay inferior. Now, supposin' I tell e we be a ganger short, Mr. Jay. Ol' Albury's gamekeeper shot him in the foot. Pure vindictiveness if you asks I. The ganger had made it back to the railway line when the shots were fired. E can't expect gangers not to poach, no more than e can expect 'em to stop a quaffin' cider. Tis a pity the railway runs hard by the Albury Estate, that's all I can say."

"I am not surprised to hear of your malevolent Mr. Albury," I replied absent-mindedly, adding: "Upshott is a beautiful place. In my experience beauty is like ointment, there is invariably a fly in it. Nevertheless, we must remember that this fly is superior."

As we tarried by the pig pen, I sensed Mr. Milsom rocking inwardly with laughter.

"How far away is this Longhurdle farm?" I asked, seeing no sign of either Wheeler or Smethwick.

"Well now," answered Mr. Milsom, "funny enough it be on the dreaded Albury Estate, which might account for Farmer Smethwick's sour demeanour. Tis about half a mile down the track over the stream there. Jack should have returned b'now, right enough. But we must count our blessin's, Mr. Jay, for I've heard no shots from Smethwick's scattergun."

I gazed upon the sloping furrows of the Albury Estate but saw nothing stir, save the odd swooping peewit and a peppering of crows. To make use of the time, I taxed my Senior Porter a little further on a matter to which he had alluded earlier and, in the interest of a cordial relationship, decided to address him by his Christian name.

"Humphrey, pray tell me more about this disappearing lamp oil," I asked. Humphrey cleared his throat to speak, but before he could say anything I noticed that the Stores Clerk was in his hut. "Perhaps I should have a word with Mr Turner whilst I am on this side of the track," I interrupted.

"Arr, 'twould be a waste of time, Mr. Jay," Humphrey rattled. "Tis best if I asks Tom to see e tomorrow, I reckons."

"Come now, Humphrey. How might a stationmaster be wasting his time consulting his Stores Clerk?" I levied.

Mr. Milsom hesitated before replying.

"Quite easily, Sir. Tom Turner be goin' through one of his 'sleepy' spells. You'll get a quicker uptake on him tomorrow. Tis not the dullard's fault, Sir. Word has it the moon takes him."

"The moon?" I roared. "Sleepy spells have nothing to do with the moon, dear fellow. Has Mr. Turner ever visited the tropics?"

To avoid an argument, my Senior Porter changed the subject briskly.

"Talkin' of tomorrow," he said, although I could recall no mention of it. "we'm a gettin' a surprise arrival by an unexpected train."

"Mmm?" I quavered melodically, perplexed by this enigmatic reverse in our conversation.

"Between e, me, and the fence post, Mr. Jay," Mr. Milsom continued, "our top brass be entertainin' bigwigs from the London and South Western Railway tomorrow. Arr, they be a payin' our line a visit, right enough. But the pity of it is, they b'aint told no one they'm a comin'." I stared at Mr. Milsom blankly. If the visit was a secret then how did he know about it? I decided that the porter was baiting me and so did not respond. "Percival Hiscox told I," Mr. Milsom added at last, revealing his source of information. "Driver Hiscox has got connections in the company hierarchy. Perhaps e can discover more by eavesdroppin' on the telegraph, Mr. Jay?"

By now I was becoming familiar with Mr. Milsom's use of the word 'e' when he meant 'you' but his habit of lingering on the word 'telegraph' disturbed me. I nodded grimly and made off towards Platform One.

CHAPTER THREE

THREATS FROM A PIG FARMER

I had no need to introduce myself to Driver Hiscox. We were acquainted. He was a dedicated footplateman and, like me, an ex London and South Western employee. It was widely believed that Mr. Hiscox had assisted Joseph Locke in firing up The Rocket in preparation for the Liverpool-Manchester Railway's inaugural service nearly forty-five years earlier. I refer, of course, to the same Joseph Locke who had been a pupil of George Stephenson, and who had gone on to become the London and South Western's Chief Engineer.

Percival Hiscox was too modest a man to boast of past associations, and so his humble silence upon the matter was taken to be confirmation. He certainly had been an engineman during railway infancy and, because of this, had become one of the 'kings of speed' without first having had to serve as a cleaner and fitter. Dark horse or not, old Hiscox was a man of his word, and known personally to directors on the boards of both the SER and the LSWR.

I tarried awhile on the lower steps of the footbridge and surveyed the vegetable garden surrounding the signalbox. Mr. Hales was to be congratulated on his lineside plot, for it was usually only the two-trains-a-day signalman who found time to cultivate so much. A dozen or so rows of sprouts had been freshly earthed up, next to which some carrot tops and lettuces were breaking through the rich red soil, and beyond the signalbox was a goat tethered to a stake. The beast's tugging had created a circle of baize-short grass blemished only by the tall clumps of hemp-nettle for which it had no taste.

In further evidence of Mr. Hales's beaverlike nature, sundry bicycle machines were propped against the signalbox steps. Manifestly these were awaiting repair. From his vantage point in the box, Mr. Hales acknowledged with a proud smile my interest in his activities. He had noticed me studying a row of strange plants.

"Are these love apples per chance?" I called up to him.

As a boy I had been made to eat them boiled with honey, and had found them quite beastly.

A commotion prevented Mr. Hales from replying. Mr. Wheeler had sprinted out from behind the Weighbridge Office and was trying to warn me of something, and a dozen or so chickens which had been pecking quietly upon the railway track were now squawking and running amok. Farmer Smethwick appeared, and began waving his crook angrily at the clerk, whose patronizing attempts to calm the farmer would have angered a saint. I watched the antagonists circle the grain shed and come to rest gesticulating at each other across the pen of pigs.

Curiously, Mr. Hales ignored the fracas as if it were an everyday occurrence, and stepped out onto the signalbox balcony to continue our conversation.

"That's right, Mr. Jay," he called down. "Tomatoes! You shall have one or two when they are formed."

"Thank you," I replied with a sickly grin.

"Everyone hereabouts calls me Ivor," the Signalman informed me, and retreated to his levers.

My attention was drawn to further uproar from the cattle pens, where now I saw Farmer Smethwick marching towards me with his colour as high as that of a ripe plum. He grunted with each step he took, as if it were a kick in the stomach, and seemed unaware of Jack Wheeler following him skittishly at a safe distance. Mr. Wheeler froze in horror as Smethwick and I met nose-to-nose, whereupon the pig breeder's gritty voice began boring harshly into my ears. Yet for all his volume, the farmer could not articulate himself with any degree of clarity. Indeed, he spoke with the incoherent slowness of a drunkard.

Trying to understand the rustic, I cocked an ear and listened intently, indicating with my hand that I wished him to lower his voice. In defiance his voice grew louder and adopted a hostile and threatening tone. I narrowed my eyes upon the cove meanly and said nothing.

The farmer, whose greasy black hair lay across his sweaty forehead in warlike spikes, peered at me with half closed eyes as if doubting my credentials. Not to be intimidated, I maintained my stern posture and still tongue.

It was then that I caught sight of a woman behaving strangely on Platform One. She was gazing pensively at the sky, and I found myself staring across Smethwick's shoulder at her. This was quite the most adorable woman I had ever seen. My own age, or thereabouts, she had wavy blonde hair and big china-blue eyes which distance could do nothing to diminish. A most charming outfit completed the apparition. Her powder-blue dress, shaped most fashionably by a large bustle, was flounce-trimmed in peach to match her bonnet, and all was festooned majestically with fine lace offering but the merest hue of white.

The delectable woman turned and smiled at me, but my attention was drawn away by Jack Wheeler signalling wildly. The code my Booking Clerk was transmitting in the flailing of his arms might just as well have been Morse, for I was quite unable to decipher it, so I returned my attention to the attractive woman.

The pig breeder introduced himself to me a second time, in another attempt to register his presence, and then stared at me knowingly. He fancied, I suspect, that sooner or later I would be shocked to attention by his name. Twice was he disappointed, though, for again my eyes refocussed involuntarily on the platform behind him. Unfortunately it was now deserted.

I sighed yearningly and went into a trance, supposing that the woman had been a fantasy. But then, if she had been just a figment of my imagination, why did I detect the lingering fragrance of perfume abroad? No. She was real. And I knew that I must discover who she was. The problem was that her elusive scent was my only clue.

Before I could gather my thoughts upon the matter, the fetor of an irritated pig farmer supplanted the whiff of heaven which had been stirring my senses.

"My name is Smethwick," the grating voice recited yet again, still louder, causing reverberations upon the station house wall. The delivery came back at me like a plucked wire. Thrice now had this magic password 'Smethwick' failed to invoke terror, and so, reluctantly, the pig farmer resorted to that time-honoured alternative mode of communication, civil dialogue.

"Why are my pigs still here?," he said. "I have a buyer expecting them in Blodcaster."

"Well, Mr. Smethwick," I replied stoutly, "the company is not at liberty to convey your pigs out of the district until the Swine Fever alert is over. So I advise you to remove your livestock forthwith."

Somewhere beneath Smethwick's tufted and untidy beard was a chin. It lifted with hastily gathered pride, and I could see that the fellow was loth to co-operate in a matter of such inconvenience to himself. Mere thought of it intensified his feverish anger until glistening beads of perspiration had gathered upon his moustache like settling gnats. With menace flickering in his cold, grey eyes, and the stench of his livelihood turning my stomach, I took one precautionary step backwards. It was not wise to stand close to a man who was probably infested with lice.

"Swine Fever be damned," the farmer railed me. "Stationmaster Mildenhew would have known better than to accuse me, a Smethwick, of taking sick stock to market. Just who do you think you are?"

"Horace Ignatius Jay," I replied loftily, after an annoyed pause.

Smethwick produced a company docket and staggered forward. I stepped back again. Smethwick staggered forward once more, and I stepped back once more. A bystander would have thought that I was teaching a local farmer the minuet. Presently Smethwick tired of the game and, after a moment's libration, became bent with defeat. In a pathetic final protest, as if having missed a rare opportunity to raise much needed cash, his voice punctured the stillness of the station.

"But I have a buyer!" he cried.

Heads turned as the farmer's forlorn voice rasped through the air like a crow taking shot, and on an impulse of pity I expressed a hint of sympathy for his predicament. Quite a mistake. The contemptuous fellow boiled visibly at my charity and spat in the direction of my boots.

"This docket constitutes an agreement, and you have reneged on it," he warned me. "You'll pay for this, Jay. I've a long memory."

Thus discharged of his venom, the cove collected his crook and stormed off.

Just as soon as there was a respectable distance between us, I hailed him a few home truths.

"You have advanced no monies to the company, Smethwick, and I have no doubt that you were warned that your ticket might be rescinded. Own up, Sir. You have attempted to break the law. Take your pigs and go, and next time see to it that you are sober when conducting business."

It appeared that my last remark was uncalled for. The pig breeder turned abruptly and glared at me with furious astonishment, his colour rising as quickly as Jack Wheeler's was draining, and all in a silence so intense that one could hear Smethwick's bronchial wheeze twenty yards away. One also heard the crinkle of the nullified docket being stuffed inside the farmer's waistcoat pocket, a gesture intended to imply that the matter was not yet over. For one moment I thought that the farmer was going to seek revenge there and then. But, instead, he lowered his tired eyes, as if concluding that men such as he were the victims of a middle class conspiracy, and turned unsteadily towards the pens.

I watched Smethwick drive his pigs over the bridge into Stoney Way, and wondered what I had said to devastate the fellow so.

"You shouldn't 'ave said that, Mr. Jay," Mr. Wheeler confided ruefully. "You shouldn't 'ave told 'im 'e was drunk."

"Why ever not, Mr. Wheeler? The scoundrel is manifestly intoxicated."

"No 'e isn't. I was trying to warn you," Mr. Wheeler came back. "Smethwick's got something wrong with 'is 'ead, Mr. Jay." These words of advice were delivered with a series of compulsive winks which lasted until seized by a slanted frown. The clerk went on to explain: "It's like this, Mr. Jay. Smethwick's wife ran off with a mariner, and ever since then Squire Albury's been trying to drive the cuckold off 'is estate with unfair tithes. As a result, 'e 'as gone a bit demented. Folks reckon 'e tried to 'ang 'imself. But 'e didn't succeed."

"This much I can see for myself" I said.

"Anyway, 'e weren't drunk, Mr. Jay," the clerk continued. "If I 'adn't been watching, 'e would 'ave gone for you like a rabid dog. I've seen 'im bite people. Especially when accused of drinking."

This was indeed a pitiful tale, and I found myself in need of a more soothing sight than Wheeler's face twitching as if troubled by flies. My eyes wandered towards Platform One, but the woman in lace had not returned. *Who is she?* I wondered.

CHAPTER FOUR

TIMBER, SEWAGE, AND SQUIRE TROUBLES

I checked my timepiece, something which I was unable to do without being reminded of Mr. Mildenhew. It was 7.40am, and the former stationmaster was collecting his luggage from the Parcels Office. Upon leaving the Parcels Office, Mr. Mildenhew crossed the footbridge to Platform Two and took up a waxwork pose at the far end. The porters' boy, barely able to drag his former master's weighty trunks, struggled across the footbridge behind him and stationed himself obediently at his side.

At this time, two trains were due simultaneously, one bound for Blodcaster, the other bound for Giddiford Junction, and consequently the travelling public had imported its colourful presence to both platforms. Since Upshott Station provided the only crossing loop on the South Exmoor Railway, the remainder of the enterprise being single line, the station was unique in having separate 'up' and 'down' platforms. At Giddiford Junction, the southern terminus of the branch, the railway occupied a single bay platform, and at Blodcaster, the northern terminus, a second platform was only now under construction.

With regard to the adorable woman whose brief presence had graced my station, for the time being, tracing her would have to wait. For I could hear the thudding of the 'down' train among the hills, and it heralded my first test as Stationmaster. Had the runaway commercial success of the South Exmoor Railway been anticipated by its founders it would have been laid from end to end as a double line railway to avoid traffic congestion, but because it had not, some horrifying practises were necessary, such as the one I was about to co-ordinate.

You see, the only way the Monday morning Timber Train could be found a path, that is to say, squeezed into the timetable, was by attaching it to the rear of the 'down' passenger train. This amalgamation of rollingstock was hazardous even by the standards of the day, and it required a peace-shattering trio of locomotives to bring it as far as Upshott; two at the head of the train, and a third pushing the timber trucks at the rear.

For the benefit of the reader who is unfamiliar with railway nomenclature, the leading locomotive in such an arrangement is called the 'pilot' engine, the one behind it, the 'train' engine, and the locomotive at the rear of the train, the 'banker'. This configuration was not entirely safe in the days before continuous vacuum brakes.

Presently I heard the precarious ensemble climbing the ruling gradient out of Widdlecombe Viaduct.

With the arrival of the Giddiford train in the opposite direction a few minutes later, the effluvia of no less than four steam engines at once would befog the station. This weekly event, although brief, made many a mainline station look tranquil by comparison, and it reflected the South Exmoor's imperspicuous style of management. You see, most rural branchlines made do with just one locomotive. But then, most rural branchlines had neither the freight spurs to service, which usually resulted in undercapitalization, nor the telling gradients with which to do battle.

Goods trucks attached to the rear of a passenger train were known as 'swingers', and so many swingers were there on the 7.46am each Monday that, when the train came to a halt, they overhung the platform and the crossing loop points by several yards, or so I had been warned, and thereby obstructed the departure of the Giddiford train.

As Stationmaster, it would be my duty to have the pilot engine uncoupled and parked in a siding, have the timber trucks at the rear uncoupled from the passenger rake so that the passenger train could be taken on to Blodcaster by the train engine, and then have the banker push the goods rake forward into Platform One. This final manoeuvre would clear the loop points to allow the 'up' passenger train to leave Platform Two for Giddiford Junction. Now, if this operation sounds complicated, it is because it was! Once over with, however, a more leisurely pace could be adopted for dealing with the Timber Train proper.

In due course the dread mixed train arrived, but, alas, it concealed within its thunderous envelope of smoke and steam a nasty shock.

As you undoubtedly know, troubles, like wolves, hunt their prey in packs, and this day my scent had been well and truly picked up. For, alas, the mixed passenger and timber train included Squire Lawrence Albury's private cabriolet. But the conveyance was not aboard one of the swingers as one might have expected. No Sir! When the veil of smoke lifted, to my utter dismay, I discovered it strapped to a flat-truck sandwiched between the train engine and the leading passenger carriage.

Verily my heart sank at sight of this mobile conundrum, and my stomach churned at the prospect of having to deal with it in the short time available. However, on my first day at Upshott I was not going to be the cause of a logjam, delay, or worse still, an accident, so I took a deep breath and moved in. It was no help that an extremely unpleasant smell had pervaded the station.

Mr. Wheeler took up beside me as the ungainly train convulsed to a halt, and hearkened reverently to the rumble of three boilers heaving with pressure.

"What is that foul smell?" I queried him. "It is unforgivable to expect fare-paying passengers to abide it."

"That's the price of sanity," the clerk enlightened me with a facial twitch. "The smell comes from the new sewage farm down at Upford. One of the spreaders told me in The Pheasant yesterday that microbes make that smell, Mr. Jay. Microbes are so small, you can't see them, yet they can raise a stench fit to curl your nose, and no one knows why they do it. All the same, the spreader reckons we're lucky to 'ave sanity in Upshott, and we're to thank the Lord for it. Lord Lacy, that is. E's what they call a phil... phalinthro... philampro..." Wheeler gave up trying to say philanthropist and continued: "There's parts of London don't 'ave it yet."

"I know all about the new sewage works, Mr. Wheeler, and I fully appreciate the value of sanitation. My mother died of cholera when I was eighteen months old. What I want to know about is that ghastly stink, and presently it most strongly resembles a conspiracy. Mr. Milsom claims he cannot even smell it! If, as you claim, the smell is emanating from the new Pasteur works, then how do you suppose it is getting here? By one of our trains? There is not so much as a whiffle of air, Mr. Wheeler."

"Oh, it don't need wind to get about, Mr. Jay. It's what they call organic. Microbes are organic, see? They can turn anything they like into manure for the farmers."

Jack Wheeler was a woolly minded individual, but the key to the matter lay in his use of the word 'manure', for I recalled seeing the London and South Western convey such sullage to farms for application on the land. More significantly, Mr. Hales's vegetables were uncommonly verdant, and his plot of land curiously fertile given the meagre upland soil found elsewhere in the district.

"I shall look into the matter," I told Wheeler, and dismissed him.

With the arrival of the Giddiford train, Mr. Hales signalled me to commence shunting operations, and I was now confident that I could execute these with minimal fuss. Upon my specific instruction, the first uncoupling was made between the rake of passenger carriages and the flat-truck carrying Squire Albury's new cabriolet. Still coupled together, the two leading locomotives now took the cabriolet to the headshunt and waited there for further instructions. In due course I had one of these locomotives return to the passenger train in readiness to take it on to Blodcaster. This, I thought, was a clever first move, and ought to provide the key to unlocking the rest of the shunting puzzle, but my stratagem was impaired from the very start by one simple oversight.

My inevitable downfall was heralded by Mr. Wheeler tapping me on the shoulder with a pantomime exuberance fast becoming familiar to me me.

"Albury's coachman is 'ere, bearing gifts," he confided through walnut teeth.

Lawrence Albury's emissary handed me a muslin bag.

"Mr. Albury trusts his new carriage will reach him in pristine condition," he smoothed dutifully.

I accepted the gift and, peering inside the bag, replied:

"Please convey my thanks to Mr. Albury, along with my assurance that his magnificent cabriolet has, and will, come to no harm."

The bag contained a plucked goose.

Gifts to the stationmaster were common currency at this time, although I believe the custom did not survive the turn of the century.

After my optimistic exchange with the coachman I expected him to leave but, instead, he took to a platform bench and settled. Unperturbed, I ordered the uncoupling of the passenger carriages from the timber trucks and gave the Blodcaster train its 'right away'. So far, so good. Events were running only one minute late.

As a point of interest, you might like to know that it was not common practise to 'right away' a 'down' train before an 'up' train, but on this occasion a break with railway tradition was unavoidable.

While I was waving the Timber Train into Platform One, Mr. Wheeler tugged at my arm impishly.

Now, you must understand that my Booking Clerk was a foxy fellow. He had a mat of tight curly hair and, in his eye, ever the twinkle of mischief. When he grinned, and that was often, it was either because something unwholesome had occurred, or was about to.

"Mr. Jay, Sir," he whispered in my ear, "Tom Turner and me 'ave devised a scheme to catch the lamp oil thief."

From what I had heard, I could not imagine sleepy Tom Turner catching a dead fish in a beer pot.

"Not now, Mr. Wheeler," I retorted. "Can you not see I am busy?"

"But Sir, we need your permission to go about it," he plagued me.

Because I knew Jack Wheeler had something of a reputation as a trapper, with a wry grin I gave him the permission he sought. This was a naive and foolish act by a green stationmaster who had not yet learned that Mr. Wheeler always waited until his superiors were too busy to pay attention before seeking permission to go about a dodgy enterprise.

"Be careful what you get up to Jack," I cautioned the clerk with a wink. "Burglars are not hares."

Mr. Wheeler was visibly flattered that I should call him by his Christian name, and began blinking wildly. His face shrank to a bunch of wrinkles and then expanded to a wide, bewildered grin. I had witnessed this malady before. Jack Wheeler, it seemed, had a full facial tick. He scuttled away to the Ticket Office to assist Mr. Milsom.

Once the banking engine had pushed the empty timber trucks forward to Platform One, various signals and points were set to 'right away' the 'up' passenger train. The locomotive's shrill whistle of departure turned heads and spawned a string of echoes which tootled among the hills like a shepherd's flute, and the train's boxlike carriages clattered and swayed onto Fallowfield Embankment. Soon the 'up' train was but a smear of steam on the highway crossing at Rington Road, poised to plunge into the precipitous Upford Cutting.

Now, I had been nurturing the hope that I could steal a few minutes to enquire of my staff the identity of the 'belle in white lace', as I had come to think of her, but I was thwarted by a wizened old lady whose eyesight, it seemed, was too poor to read the train times. Truth be known she was illiterate, like most of the simple souls hereabouts, but I played along. Having intercepted me with a wave of her parasol, the old lady thrust a copy of *Bradshaw's Universal Timetable* into my hand and insisted that I read it aloud. All of it! Explaining that this was impractical, I delved into the appropriate section for her and drew breath to speak. But before I could be of any assistance, a series of impatient whistles sounded from the Dairy Siding. I had forgotten about the pilot engine.

"The driver is awaiting instructions to deal with that private horse-carriage, Mr. Jay," Ivor Hales told me in one of his rare excursions from the signalbox.

I referred the old lady to Humphrey Milsom and trudged across the ballast to the locomotive in question. This was Number 205 *'Lacy'*, a Beattie 2-4-0WT on extended lease from the London and South Western. The driver, a stocky fellow with red hair and an 'explosion' of a beard, was scratching his head through a tam o' shanter and staring at me quizzically. It was as if he knew instinctively that I had overlooked something obvious, and I felt a rising sense of unease.

I approached the footplate and smiled up innocently.

Although I witnessed no facial movement, from somewhere beneath that flaming bush upon the driver's jaw came a clipped Highland voice asking:

"Have ye no crane?"

My collar tightened and I was struck dumb. Having served only in large stations, I had assumed that a crane was to hand. It simply had not occurred to me that Upshott Station might have no yard crane suitable for unloading a valuable private conveyance.

My memory now jolted, I recalled that in such circumstances on the SER it was customary to request in advance a mobile crane which resided at Giddiford. Had I done this, the crane would have arrived behind the very item of cargo it was required to lift.

"I shall be back in one minute," I told the incredulous driver.

Upon returning to Platform One, Lawrence Albury's coachman apprehended me. I crossed my fingers that his fractious master did not require the cabriolet immediately.

"Mr. Albury requires his new carriage immediately," the servant told me anxiously. "My master has important calls to make this morning."

I turned my head and saw in the station forecourt a team of fine white horses waiting to be harnessed.

"The conveyance cannot be made available immediately," I told him bluntly, knowing that I was inconveniencing the valley's second-most powerful family, and certainly its most hostile. "We do not have a crane with which to unload it from the flat-truck." My candour disarmed the coachman briefly.

"Well, surely you can requisition one by telegraph?" he suggested with begrudging civility.

"This I have done," I bluffed, and shied away from the coachman's suspicious squint.

Since his arrival, the coachman had been watching me like a sparrow-hawk. He knew that I had not entered the Telegraph Room, but such was the mystique of railway communications that he did not challenge me. As luck would have it, *Lacy's* driver began tooting his whistle again, the locomotive being required to perform many duties this morning, so I exploited the distraction and slipped away.

"A pretty state of affairs, I must say!" the coachman called after me.

Had I anticipated the need of a crane, even belatedly, I could have asked Driver Hiscox to deliver a written requisition to Headquarters upon his arrival at Giddiford, but it was too late now. Hiscox's 'up' train had gone several minutes ago.

As if to mock me, the two bright new telegraph wires above my head began to twang. They were playing host to a band of rooks. The birds, it seemed, could find greater use for the telegraph system than I.

The next 'up' train that could convey my request for a crane was not until 10.48am, in another three hours. But in any event, no matter how I made that request, and even assuming that the mobile crane was available, the earliest 'down' train by which it could be delivered to Upshott was the 1.08pm passenger. This was far too late to avoid a conflict with Squire Albury. The best I could do now was to give my requisition to the driver of the next 'up' train, surreptitiously if I wanted to keep my job, and put telegraphy tuition at the top of my list of priorities. But, alas, this plan did not rid me of my immediate embarrassment.

"One o' Clock is far too late, Mr. Jay," the coachman insisted. "My master will not countenance such a delay. I think you do not appreciate Mr. Albury's influence in the district."

Just now I hearkened to the whistle of a locomotive a mile or so distant, and at sight of a plume of steam rising from Upford Cutting, I summoned Jack Wheeler.

"The Giddiford train seems to have stopped on the line," I queried him.

"She'll be at Fallowfield Crossing," he confirmed. "'iscox often stops 'er there to take on pottery from Bessam."

Upon hearing of this unofficial activity I was momentarily taken aback, but I recovered quickly, broke away, and marched over to the porters' boy who was weeding a flower bed nearby.

"Diggory," I commanded him loudly. "I want you to take a horse from the company stables and ride down to the 'up' train with a message to pass on to the Giddiford Yard Superintendent. Hurry boy, you must catch the train whilst it stands at Fallowfield Crossing."

While the lad was saddling a horse, I scribbled out a note requesting urgent use of the mobile crane, suggesting that it be dispatched to Upshott at once using any motive power available. '*The customer is extremely important*', I added.

The boy took my note, engaged the stirrup, and looked down at me quizzically.

"You want me to ride up to the 'down' train," he confirmed erroneously, pulling his sluggish mount in a circle. I fancy he was being impertinent.

"Well may you act the fool, lad, but this is an emergency," I berated him. "You will ride down to the 'up' train."

Truth to tell, I was amused by my Junior Porter's pun, but I contained my mirth lest he be encouraged to overstep the mark habitually.

At sight of Diggory galloping along the edge of the railway towards Fallowfield, my spirits were lifted wonderfully.

I returned to the coachman, whose colourful green tunic piped in gold was something of a focal point on the now deserted platform, and reassured him that everything possible was being done to release his master's conveyance. He removed his black plush top-hat and mopped his brow nervously, then rounded on me.

"Nevertheless this is quite inexcusable," he snarled. "Quite unprecedented. My master simply will not countenance a delay. He requires his new carriage immediately, not in one hour's time."

Had not the platforms been bounded by picket fencing, and furnished lavishly with such obstructions as decorative seats and lamps, I might have considered discharging the cabriolet laterally onto one of them. But given that they were so cluttered, I could think of nothing useful to suggest. Jack Wheeler came forward with an idea.

"There's a big crane up at Bessam Forest," he proffered.

"For lifting logs," I retorted with a degree of irritation. "It is merely a log hoist, as I recall. Hardly suitable for setting down a highly burnished carriage."

"But if we use copious sacking and broad leather straps we can get 'er on the ground inside twenty minutes, and without a scratch," Wheeler insisted.

"Twenty minutes!" The coachman seized upon this estimate. "That will do... just! Please, go ahead with your plan Sir. Go ahead immediately."

The coachman donned his top-hat proudly, having adjusted its silk cockade by an imperceptible degree.

I felt uneasy about this solution, but took comfort from the fact that Squire Albury's personal coachman had sanctioned it. Mr. Wheeler reminded me of another important point.

"Squire Albury 'as a foul temper, Mr. Jay. I've seen 'im lash out at folk with 'is riding crop."

"Perhaps your idea is workable," I concurred. "But in all earnest, Jack, that cabriolet must not receive the slightest score."

"I know that, Mr. Jay," Wheeler responded with a twitch of the face.

I took a deep breath, and in an act of supreme blind faith, gave the nod. Jack Wheeler bounded across to *Lacy*, scrambled aboard the footplate, and elbowed the driver and fireman aside. He now raised his arm wildly and swung it forward as if leading a cavalry charge against the Ashantis. Jack Wheeler's vocabulary did not stretch to such polite phrases as 'driver, would you please propel this flat-truck to Bessam for me.'

"Precisely where is this crane?" the coachman enquired.

"Across the marsh," I told him. "It is served by a light duty tramway running two or three miles into the forest. The spur branches off at the Dairy Siding over there, traverses the station forecourt, crosses the swamp, and climbs up to a logging station where they operate a steam saw and other machinery. Now, I think it is of the first moment that you lead your horses up to Bessam, in readiness to bring the carriage back to the road. In the meantime I will prepare the documents for your signature. May I suggest that you follow the sawyers' trail."

I left the coachman to his preparations and hurried through the Booking Hall to the forecourt. Here I found Jack Wheeler opening the tramway gates for *Lacy*. Jack's face lengthened at my approach.

"You are quite safe, Jack. I have not come to deprive you of your footplate ride," I said. "But did we not speak of sack-cloth and straps?"

Mr. Wheeler blushed like a fine old port and scurried away to the Stores hut to get the items he had forgotten. The locomotive driver hissed with exasperation, shut off *Lacy's* regulator, and applied the hand-brake. *Lacy*, having crept forward onto the forecourt tramrails, squealed to a halt. Preparing the engine for its climb into the forest, the fireman shovelled coal into the four corners of the firebox, taking care to spread the fuel evenly across the firebed. Meanwhile the Driver, scratching his head through his tam o' shanter, stared down at me enigmatically. It was some while before he broke the uncomfortable silence which had developed between us.

"Ef yeer gunny wetness thess event, yeel be needeng a steff drenk," he announced with a wry grin.

The Scotchman produced a costrel, removed the cork with a squeak and a pop, and offered it to me.

I had no use for a cork, so I gave it back to him. At this he grinned broadly and offered me the vessel itself. I must say that I was quite tempted by the aroma of a mature malt whisky, but declined demonstratively. Company regulations forbade the drinking of intoxicating liquors whilst on duty, particularly by locomotive drivers. Apparently this driver considered himself to be above the rules. Not only did he carry liquor at his hip, he felt free to offer it to stationmasters! I was singularly distracted.

"I have no intention of witnessing the unloading of this conveyance," I informed the Scotchman defensively. "I wish only to be notified when the deed is done. Once you have propelled the cabriolet to the logging station you will come back here and collect the timber empties. I want Platform One cleared as soon as possible. After that you may go about your normal shunting duties on the tramway. I will take responsibility for your lateness."

"Aye, ye will," the driver quipped emphatically, and opened *Lacy's* cylinder cocks. The deafening hiss which followed drowned all further conversation.

CHAPTER FIVE

UP ON THE FOOTBRIDGE

Whilst crossing the line, via the footbridge, I chanced upon Humphrey Milsom lumbering in the opposite direction carrying a stack of pigeon baskets.

"Ah, Mr. Milsom... Humphrey!" I serenaded my Senior Porter, and offered him some assistance. "Per chance you did not see the woman on Platform One earlier this morning? Did you? It was just after the departure of the Market Goods?"

"I did not, Sir," he replied with a baffled gaze.

"She was wearing a good deal of lace... white lace," I added anxiously.

"Missed her did e?"

"I believe she wished to speak to me, but I was engaged at the time," I said, and added with a pinch of indifference: "Never mind. It does not matter."

Humphrey's face contorted.

"It don't worry e then?" he quizzed me. "You know? About Albury's private carriage. Her won't look pretty with gashes in her where they'm sunk grapplin' hooks, yon at Bessam."

"Humphrey, the reason why a railway station has a stationmaster," I explained, "is not because the company expects anyone to control its staff, it is so that there is someone to pillory when things go awry."

Humphrey chortled unsympathetically, and continued: "Even if Jack don't wreck that cabriolet, her'll get plastered with mud. Arr, and also those fine white horses. After last night's deluge, Mr. Jay, ol' sawyers' trail will be a morass."

Mr. Milsom was right, of course, and I began to wonder if I had taken leave of my senses. Truth to tell, my superior calm was no more than a well practised illusion.

"If necessary, we will wash the carriage down with hot water from *Lacy's* slack pipe," I advised Humphrey, donning the mask of an optimist.

"Talkin' of *Lacy*, they'm got trouble with her."

I had noticed that conversations with simple countryfolk tended to lack focus, and that Mr. Milsom was no exception. Having lost my thread, I prompted the porter to continue with his digression.

"Trouble?" I enquired.

"Stickin' safety valve, by all accounts, Mr. Jay. Her aint blowing off all the excess pressure, so tis said. I never heard a boiler groan like it. Apart from my misses when rain be due, course."

I yielded a long and feckless sigh. This turned into a gasp when the significance of Humphrey's warning registered.

"Saints preserve us!" I jumped. "A sticking safety valve is the most dangerous fault a steam engine can develop. Are you sure the footplatemen have not been tampering with it? I have heard that these men sometimes screw down the knurled nut to increase boiler pressure on a difficult run. This is quite against the rules, you know, and extremely dangerous. It increaseses the pressure beyond the boiler's designed limits."

"I knows that, Mr. Jay, but it aint bin done here," Humphrey advised me. "*Lacy* don't have the Salter type valve, e see. Her be tamper-proof."

"Well, if the safety valve really is sticking, the

crew should throw out the fire at once and have the locomotive towed back to Giddiford," I said.

"Not Driver MacGregor," the porter wheezed. "He be too stubborn to admit anythin's wrong."

"Driver MacGregor, is it?" I mumbled, handing Humphrey back his pigeon baskets. The porter struggled away with the feathered gossipers warbling noisily.

I remained on the footbridge to take an overview of the station. Beneath me, simmering quietly at Platform One, was the engine that had banked the mixed passenger and timber train, this being a visitor from the London and South Western Railway. In front of the visiting locomotive was a rake of goods vans, and in front of the goods vans were the empty timber trucks waiting to be returned to the logging station.

The axle loading of the LSWR four-coupled locomotive was too high for the lightly constructed tramway, and so, having no work to do, the footplate crew had settled themselves upon the wheel-splasher to play cards. Beyond the marsh, rising from the dense patchwork of deciduous trees which cloaked the lower slopes of Bessam Tor, was *Lacy's* column of steam pinpointing its place of toil in the Forest.

On my left I could see the River Ondle meandering like a silver sash through the valley's turquoise haze, and on my right I could see the village of Upshott manifesting itself bashfully through a plush canopy of chestnuts and oaks. At a glance, the village appeared to be no more than an assortment of sagging stone roofs, but with more careful observation one could see the display window of the pork butcher, and the candlemaker's shop, and the occasional passing of a cart along the High Street.

Upshott nestled on a hillside shelf which afforded it breathtaking views to the south-west, and to the north-east was a dappled backdrop of tors, three in all, the lower slopes of which were dissected by residences and smallholdings adjoining Upshott High Street. Here the eye was beckoned to dwell upon the Norman tower of an Eleventh Century church, the parish church of St. Martha, its three bells being noted throughout the district for their pleasant timbre. Beyond the upper end of the village, the High Street climbed still higher to become the Blodcaster Road and, after a writhing struggle to scale some precipitous terrain, meandered its way into the windy pass between Upshott Down and Upshott Hill.

This morning, with the ever wheeling peewits of Ondle Valley piercing the air with their reedy call above the fallow fields of the lower region, and the lowing of cattle floating mournfully through the gentle stillness as they grazed in the luscious meadows by the watermill, I felt at peace with the world. I turned and looked east, from which direction a still more mesmeric sound was emanating. High on the meagre slopes of Splashgate Hill, sparsely dotted sheep were bleating with a haunting loneliness which invoked in me the most strange and idle thoughts.

I could not help but wonder what purpose all this beauty served, this undulating veneer of bucolic bliss, save to induce in one's soul an inexplicable yearning. I use the words 'veneer' and 'inexplicable' because, as far as the peasant community was concerned, life here was hard.

Perhaps my leaning towards the melancholy side

of life had something to do with my upbringing. With no brothers, no sisters, and no parents, much of the time I had been lonely. And even when I had gone to work for the railways, joining some thirty other junior clerks in a lively goods office, I had remained at my own disposal. My compulsive self-reliance had set me apart from my contemporaries. Then, later, as a relief stationmaster, my mobility had denied me the opportunity to cast down roots.

At Upshott it was to be a case of 'all change', if you will pardon the pun, because at this station did everything in my life begin anew. You see, I am not urbane at heart. I have no empathy for the neoteric humbug of the cities. So this simple, highly ordered community was destined to permeate me with a sense of belonging.

Taken as a whole, the parish of Upshott was a community with no pretensions. And whilst I accept that, generally speaking, rural communities are reluctant to embrace a newcomer, in the case of a stationmaster it is rather different. A stationmaster's 'friendship' is cultivated with undignified haste due to the fact that his complicity is required in almost everyone's dealings. Yet, for all this, he does remain an isolated figure with precious few friends. By 'friends' I mean people who seek his company for genuine reasons of society. Paradoxically, were it otherwise, his authority might be compromised.

From my own standpoint, Upshott's need of a new stationmaster had come at an opportune time, for I had developed a longing to settle, and already I felt a sense of having arrived at a journey's end. But as for a lifelong companion with whom to share this lovely place, at the age of forty I understood pitifully little about the fairer sex. I fostered no notions of matrimony.

Perhaps I would continue to be happy enough on my own. Having witnessed the overcrowded towns, with their offensive skylines and windowless factories, I rejoiced in my rural surroundings. I had always delighted in the daylong melody of the birds, whose silence upon each purple sunset would herald the twisted forms of trees reaching into a starry sky, and more than once had I wondered if the cities would one day turn mankind into a plague of rats.

It seemed to me that such unnatural concentrations of people were a dreadful price to pay for progress. I dared not think what manner of growing up an industrial conurbation imposed upon the formative mind, and I reflected gratefully upon the fact that I had explored my way to adulthood in the dancing shadows of trees, not the rigid umbre of chimneys. Childhood, I reflected, should be spent learning to trap and fish, yet to ever greater numbers it was a lesson in cleaning the capitalist's machine without interrupting its deafening, profit-making frenzy.

My malady of pensiveness fled at *Lacy's* shrieking whistle. The locomotive had returned from Bessam and was passing beneath me. I glimpsed the fireman refuelling its hungry firebox, each shovelful of coal turning the engine's exhaust momentarily from white linen to dirty sacking.

With shouts and jesticulations from its footplatemen, the iron beast rumbled up to the timber trucks and crashed into them mindlessly, whereupon the coupling hook and eye were mated with the jangle of a chain-ganger's keys. Engulfing me in its glistening ivory clouds, *Lacy* reversed with its rake trucks to the headshunt and came to rest. Now, with foaming steam still curling about me and spreading away into nothingness, I watched the visiting engine crew cut short their card game and return to the footplate to run their own steed around the vans remaining on Platform One. By this manoeuvre did they make up the 8.46am Goods for Blodcaster.

The four-coupled locomotive, *Herod*, was not usually rostered for goods duties, and certainly did not look the part. More usually it was seen hauling the Royal Mail to and from its connection with the Bristol and Exeter sorting train.

I glanced at my timepiece and was pleased to note that, with *Herod* ready to depart with its truncated goods train, and *Lacy* back on the tramway, workings were almost back to schedule. *Lacy's* task now was to shunt the twenty or so timber empties to Bessam Forest for loading with pine and oak, and have them ready in time for *Herod's* return. The loaded flat-trucks were expected by an Exeter sawmill.

I would have served any railway before tilling a squire's land, turning an industrialist's wheel, or clawing minerals from a speculator's pit, if only because in railway life there was, quite simply, dignity. A sense of progress pervaded all that one did. For example, earlier in the year, word had filtered down that the London and South Western Railway Company had negotiated purchase of the Devon and Cornwall Company's new line from Lidford to Devonport. An Act of Parliament approving this change of hands was in its final stages, and this was the prelude to the London and South Western's long anticipated London-to-Plymouth railway. An alternative route west to that of the late Isambard Kingdom Brunel's broad gauge was a proposal much vaunted by the businessmen of Drake's port, not least because it would break, at last, the Great Western Railway's monopoly over the town. Trans-Atlantic passenger and freight traffic between Plymouth and the Capital would now become the target of fiercely competitive bidding.

Of more concern locally was the chaotic and inefficient business of gauge transhipment at St. Davids. The new link would also circumvent this obstacle. Once the blight of transit damage was removed, Ondle Valley could look forward to a new era of prosperity. For the time being, however, much of the valley's fine produce was failing to reach the markets of the south-west intact.

'Prosperity through trade' the South Exmoor's company crest proclaimed. An apt maxim for any railway.

A correspondent, whose name is unimportant, had commented fancifully in the *Cornhill:* 'the empire is growing muscles of iron with which mighty industry shall lift from its peoples the yoke of peasanthood.' If this was the case, then places like Ondle Valley were enjoying a somewhat unfair, if agreeable freedom from the growing pains of these 'muscles'. Whilst the railways had brought to every class of citizen the opportunity to travel faster than the pull of a beast, not a soul hereabouts had been sundered from the light of day by the foundries which cast them.

Once again the imperative of railway life rented me from my reflections. *Herod* had been delayed by the late arrival of the baton rider from Blodcaster, but was now storming the embankment noisily towards Splashgate. Its thundercloud spread through the telegraph wires and deposited a wintery fall of snow upon nearby trees before falling to engulf the cattle grazing beneath them. But never did snow thaw so quickly, for in no time had *Herod* barked under Three Arch Bridge and faded into the deep cutting at the portal of Splashgate Tunnel.

Upon reaching the far end of this tunnel, the goods train, with its short rake of vans rocking and jolting undulantly, would burst into a daylight made all the more dazzling by the glassy expanse of Splash Lake. And while tapping out its rhythm of freedom, the ensemble would continue its climb to lofty Blodcaster, reminding the hamlets of their liberation from the isolation that the tortuous highways of mud and dust had by monopoly once imposed. Reminding the people of the moors of the bandits they no longer need fear, and of their debt to that despised conqueror of the wilderness, the railway navvy.

* * *

The report from a powerful explosion bounced to and fro among the downs and died away reluctantly, leaving me unsure from which direction it had come. The birds in the trees, and the livestock in their pens, fell silent. And in that silence I heard Humphrey Milsom's words warning me of *Lacy's* sticking safety valve. My blood ran cold.

I observed a giant balloon of steam curling skywards from the trees of Bessam Forest, and began calling Humphrey. I called so loudly, and with such trepidation, that my voice cracked and failed, causing Ivor Hales to throw open his window to investigate the disturbance.

"Humphrey! " I yodelled. "*Lacy* has exploded!"

In my youth I had witnessed the aftermath of a boiler explosion, in Southampton, and consequently knew such accidents to be extremely injurious to the footplatemen. As a junior clerk I had leapt from the Goods Office upon hearing that same fragor, and had encountered a shunting engine with its middle section disembowelled in a mass of splayed boiler tubes. Everything within fifty feet had been blasted with the boiler's scolding contents, leaving at the centre of this swirling, eerie scene a lifeless driver and his mate. Both men had been twisted grotesquely by the explosion, and the sight of them had caused me nightmares for months.

I hurried down the footbridge steps to meet Humphrey, whose normally ruddy face was now drained of colour. He too had been running, so much so that the poor fellow required a moment to regain his breath before he could speak.

"What's happened Mr. Jay?" he wheezed at length.

"*Lacy's* boiler has burst! Did you not hear the bang, Humphrey? It must have been that faulty safety valve. We must organize help immediately."

Humphrey's colour returned instantly, and he began to rock with subdued laughter. His face contorted further and further until, finally, he convulsed openly. There was nothing I could do but wait patiently for him to recover from his uncontrollable hooting. Obviously I was mistaken about *Lacy*, nevertheless the matter required an explanation.

"Steady on," I cautioned the porter.

"Forgive I, Mr. Jay. Most reprehensible," he choked at last. "But they'm a blastin' over at

Splashgate Quarry today. They does it every Monday."

Humphrey started choking again, and pulled out an enormous handkerchief to blow his nose. Too flustered to speak, I returned to the footbridge to take another look at Bessam Forest. A plume of steam further along the tramway revealed that *Lacy* was still busy marshalling timber trucks at the logging station. My relief cannot be conveyed.

The echo of another blast in the quarry thudded back off Upshott Down, and I noticed Ivor Hales staring at me with a restrained grin. Such was my deliverance that I began to laugh myself, louder, even, than Humphrey.

CHAPTER SIX

SEWAGE COVER-UP UNCOVERED

I heard the clatter of wooden wheels upon cobblestones, and the snort of eager horses. The squire's coachman had returned from Bessam, so I hurried through the Booking Hall to enquire how the unloading of the cabriolet had gone. But before I could reach the daylight beyond the double doors, Jack Wheeler sprang out in front of me and blocked my way. While the clerk attempted feebly to explain his rude behaviour, I gazed over his shoulder at the splendid profile of the natural timber cabriolet and its four white horses standing upon the forecourt.

To get a better view, I stepped out into the sunshine and waited for my eyes to adjust to the light. Meanwhile Wheeler continued to dodge about in front of me with his unrequested excuses. I tutted at him with exasperation and squinted at the spectacle beyond.

Just as Humphrey had predicted, the team's fetlocks and hind quarters were caked with mud, but the carriage itself I could not see properly because of my Booking Clerk's bobbing head.

"Mr. Albury's coachman would like a word with you," Wheeler informed me fertively.

"Is the cabriolet damaged?" I enquired, with a degree of resignation as to the likely reply.

"Only slightly," Mr. Wheeler answered with a twitch.

I stepped past the clerk, and was lured across the forecourt by the coachman's angry eyes. After studying the condition of the squire's vehicle I resolved to discuss with Mr. Wheeler the meaning of the word 'slight'.

"I will arrange to have the conveyance cleaned at once," I said, mindful of the claim against the company that would inevitably follow.

"I think you've done enough for Mr. Albury today," the coachman rebounded stiffly, and took to the box. With a crack of the whip he was gone.

I was not pleased, and invited Jack Wheeler to my office.

* * *

With the exception of the arrival of the baton rider from Giddiford, Upshott Station was blissfully quiet until the return of *Herod* with the local goods train. The driver steamed *Herod* through the station slowly, to enable Ivor Hales to exchange batons from the balcony of his signalbox. I was in the box at this time, to witness Mr. Hales at work, and it amused me that a large offcut of calico accompanied him upon each trip to a lever, to be wrapped around its handle before pulling. I had seen this phenomenon before. Time-served switchmen became quite house-proud once installed in a box, and none of them would risk tarnishing a polished lever by touching it with his bare hand.

Apart from an occasional whiffle of musty air rising from the groundframe beneath the floorboards, the cabin was thick with the smell of wax polish. Increasingly it was railway practise to centralize signalling and switching apparatus, which traditionally had been distributed around the station, to protect it from the elements by placing it under one roof. Where this was done, the instruments seemed to be made only of materials which could be polished to great effect; copper, brass, teak, glass, lending the whole affair a very scientific appearance. However, I noticed that many of Ivor's instruments were new and had yet to be connected.

The location of the signalbox was such that its right-hand window overlooked the station platforms, and this being the case, I asked Ivor if he had seen an attractive middle-aged woman standing upon Platform One this morning. He had not. He had been sitting at the opposite window repairing Dr. Bentley's grandfather clock.

"It sounds as though she could have been anyone," he rambled unhelpfully. The clock chimed and he checked it against his pocket watch. "Lace is popular with the ladies. It is a cottage industry in these parts. Ask Diggory's mother. Mind you, since the government shut down the lace schools, foreign lace has become the more commonplace. I expect you don't know which she was wearing, Mr. Jay. It would be a clue. Locally produced lace is far more delicate."

"Then I believe it was local lace she wore," I reflected. "For it was as fine as a dawn mist."

"Mmm," said Ivor with a raised eyebrow. He had, I suspect, noted my romantic turn of phrase. Or perhaps, being a signalman, he was not in favour of mist as a comparison. After all, it caused accidents.

* * *

Lacy had until 10.48am to marshal the loaded timber trucks with those of the 'pick-up' goods, and be coupled with *Herod* for the 'double-headed' return to Giddiford Junction.

Rather than oversee operations, I retired to my office to deal with some paperwork, much of which was tangled inextricably in the web of Mr. Mildenhew's incomprehensible filing system. It being a sultry day I was compelled to open my window, and was thus reminded of unfinished business. The business to which I allude, of course, was that of microbes.

The smell about which nobody knew anything had become more pungent than ever, and resembled that of rotten eggs, so I stepped out onto the platform and called out impatiently:

"Mr. Wheeler, what *is* that stink?"

My enquiry was in vain.

Whilst it was not uncommon to see staff tending flower beds and vegetable patches during quiet intervals, there was a less common atmosphere of skulking abroad. Ivor Hales was raking his plot, and seemed alarmed at my interest. Within seconds he had become engaged in a struggle with a heavy sack which he appeared intent upon lodging beneath the steps of his signalbox. Wheeler pretended not to be within earshot and absconded to the coal siding while, elsewhere, suddenly no one was about. Only the Second Porter held his ground, busy as he was, mulching a bed of bright yellow flowers.

I had been unable to ascertain this particular employee's name, other than that he answered to the appellation of 'Snimple', and so I addressed him thus.

"Those are very unusual flowers, Snimple, what are they called?" I coaxed him.

The porter beamed up at me with a spotty, weathered face, and told me proudly:

"Chrysanthemums."

I had not heard of them before, but railway employees were renowned for 'rescuing' exotic items of freight which had gone astray. Indeed, employees without the benefit of a sound moral stationmaster were rather inclined to make them go astray in the first place.

"And where did they come from?" I tested him.

"China," he replied blankly. "They grow ever sno well by the railway. I think they like the snoot."

I began to understand the fellow's nickname. He was indeed simple, and troubled with a speech impediment.

"And do they benefit from that mulch?" I enquired.

"It's treated snewage," he replied helpfully.

"Oh, from the sewage farm," I jollied him.

"They give it away free," he said to my horror. "Sno we filled a chaldron truck with it. There's plenty for all if you want any?"

Perhaps there was something to be said for treated sewage, the border flowers were certainly very colourful. *Chrysanthemums?* I wondered if this was their proper name or merely Snimple's pronunciation of it. I declined the porter's offer and made off to the coal siding.

I located the offending coal truck parked against the buffer-stop on Road Five. Its cargo was humming with bluebottles and liberating a stench fit to cause nausea. I hailed Mr. Troke and ordered him to have it removed. Mr. Troke stared at me with a gappy grin and bloated white eyes, and it occurred to me that Upshott Station might be a working home for odd fellows. This set me thinking about my own appointment.

"Mr. Troke, you are the station's Rollingstock Superintendent, and I wish to see this stock rolled out of here as a matter of urgency," I remonstrated. "If this substance remains, we shall have an outbreak of Typhus. There is little point in our benefactors engineering the safe disposal of such wastes if people like you bring it back again."

"I had nothing to do with it," Mr. Troke retorted defensively.

"Its presence in this yard requires your collusion," I parried him.

"Whither shall I send it?" he whined, abandoning his hauteur.

"Dispose of it how you will," I replied impatiently.

By now it was my fervent wish to move as far away from the insalubrious truck as possible, for I could bide proximity with the sullage no longer, even if Mr. Troke was unruffled by it.

"I suppose we could wait till no one is looking and attach it to a passing goods train," Mr. Troke suggested. "You could create a diversion, Mr. Jay, while I do it."

"Good Lord, fellow!" I replied breathlessly. "Are you serious? We shall do no such thing." Mr. Troke was crestfallen at my rebuttal, making it obvious that he had intended me to take his proposition seriously. "Have it tipped into the River Ondle," I suggested hastily. "Secure the Giddiford baton when no traffic is due, and use a company dray horse to tow the truck to the viaduct. There you may tip the ghastly stuff over the side."

Had I recommended this course of action two years later, after the passing of the Rivers Pollution Act, I might have finished up behind bars. Even by this time such activities were considered highly antisocial. However, with a diabolical smell interfering with my reason, I could think of no better solution.

With the departure of the Timber and Goods train nearing, Mr. Phillips arrived with his piece of chalk for marking up the wagon destinations. About the same time, a smallholder pulling a tilt-cart crammed with vociferous geese halted a few feet away from me and began wheezing in the waft of putrefaction from the misappropriated coal truck. Being unaware of the cause of the smell, his face cockled with disgust and he fixed upon me a prolonged and knowing gaze of disapproval. I had not the least idea where I might begin an explanation, so I took flight to the Telegraph Room.

The Telegraph Room, incidentally, was barely large enough to share with a hung up overcoat, and watching the receiver chatter rapidly within its four bare walls induced in me a deep feeling of intimidation, as did most technical advances. I had once read somewhere that nothing sharpens the wits of a young lad more than a spell of duty in a telegraph office. But I was no young lad, and I felt no desire to be sharpened. Notwithstanding my apprehension, however, either I became a skilled operator or I followed in Mr. Mildenhew's footsteps.

Ironically, a still more ugly threat lurked in those telegraph wires, a threat to which I would be exposed by the very act of learning to use the apparatus. You see, prior to this invention, a stationmaster had been, as the name would imply, master of all he surveyed. He had experienced very little interference from his superiors at Headquarters where the inertia of the average administrator had been his guarantee of an autonomous existence.

Now, unfortunately, the electric telegraph was changing all that. It was bringing to every station along the line, no matter how remote, the minute-by-minute dictates of management. Not for much longer, therefore, could my blissful ignorance of Samuel H. Morse's 'clicking' and 'clacking' immunise me from this new age of accountability.

Nursing a heavy heart, I left the Telegraph Room and stood in the sunshine for a while to absorb the industry of my surroundings. Just as the sun was beginning to warm my face, however, *Herod* steamed past and blotted out the sky with its feathery coils, so I placed my hands behind my back and began to stroll.

On the parcels platform a number of fleeces were being tied in bundles and labelled with their destinations and, by the Goods shed, empty mushroom pallets were being unloaded and stacked for return to Hunt Farm.

Upon visiting the forecourt, I found one of my clerks holding back a group of children who had gathered to watch *Lacy* complete another trip over the tramway with a rake of timber trucks. Wheels grinding, *Lacy* crossed the running line and entrained a miscellany of goods vans in the South Siding before coming to rest at the refuelling staithe. While at the coal dock, the locomotive's safety valve lifted and released a tuft of steam. I turned and gazed with relief upon the hissing white feather of reassurance which had sprouted from the engine. So too did Humphrey from his vantage point upon the parcels platform. But Humphrey's interest did not last as long as mine. A second later, he was gazing at me gleefully.

"Watch out, she's ready to blow," he called.

The porter, adopting a wilfully straight face while I shrank with self-consciousness, tipped his cap politely, and I could see that I had made a mistake which I would not be allowed to forget in a hurry.

Humphrey's jibe reminded me that I had intended to challenge Driver MacGregor on the matter of *Lacy's* sticking safety valve. The fact that it was working occasionally did not mean that it was safe, and I did not want to see a comedy turn into a tragedy.

"Theer's notheng wrong wi' her," is the only comment I could educe from the Scotchman. "Ye take et from me, she's snod. Theer's notheng wrong wi' her."

MacGregor reversed *Lacy* over the level crossing, ostensibly to 'run round' the goods train, but in reality to escape my interference.

Not to be dismissed so easily, I walked to the other end of the train to greet him. Unfortunately the defiant Scotchman saw me coming and halted his charge out of earshot.

Herod, a much larger locomotive, was waiting nearby, so I took the opportunity to introduce myself to the driver who was leaning idly from the footplate.

"I am the new stationmaster here," I opened.

"How do you do," he shouted above the handsome 2-4-0's boiler rumble. "I've sent my fireman to hold *Lacy* where she is. I'd like to pull *Herod* up to the water tower and drop in the bag," he added with a grimy smile.

"You will be running late," I pointed out.

"Can't be helped," he replied. "She's got a thirst, this one."

He took the fireman's coal pick and clouted a reluctant valve with its handle. The deep rumble softened. "Mind you," the driver continued, "it's not so bad descending to Giddi'. She drinks a good thirty gallons a mile climbing up to Blod'. At one-in-forty, the gradient through Upford Cutting is the most punishing stretch on the line. Little wonder you people need a fleet of engines to work this branch."

Presently *Herod's* fireman returned and set about unhitching the locomotive for its trip to the water tower. The coupling hooks rang out sharply as the locomotive and rollingstock parted company, after which the fireman climbed adroitly back to the footplate. Here he began foraging the coal bunker to satisfy his workhorse's ignifluous belly.

"Looks as though we've a few hundredweight left over," he mumbled.

I thought the fireman was talking to himself, and since the driver ignored him, so did I.

"He's talking to you, Stationmaster," the driver chirped with a squeak of astonishment.

Since I had no idea what the fireman was mumbling about, I cleared my throat and asked: "A few hundredweight of what, Sir?"

The fireman grinned sinfully, winked, and responded:

"Oh, I understand. There's someone about who shouldn't hear." He shovelled more coal into the firebox. "Usual arrangement, is it?"

Still I did not understand.

The LSWR locomotive, in gratitude for its helping of black mineral, belched dense yellow fumes into the sky. Caught upon the breeze, this bronchial fog swirled down across the platform and enveloped me. My distress, apparently, was comical, for the footplatemen clucked with laughter.

"Filthy stuff," I reviled them, brushing the smuts from my top-hat. "Filthy!"

"Poetic justice," the visiting driver quipped. "After all, we did coal her at Giddi' on that soft Kentish slack of yours. It burns slow and, as you can see, it burns dirty. Our steed is accustomed to a diet of good Yorkshire to keep her breath sweet."

The fireman leaned from the engine.

"So it's Widdlecombe's turn this week, is it?" he joked. "You should have reminded me. I thought you were just being coy."

I frowned angrily, for the fireman's conversation continued to make no sense.

Herod's cab boomed with laughter, and the creaking locomotive pulled away to take water. With it went the smell of hot metal and oil, and the sound of sizzling tallow.

I tipped my hat self-consciously and crossed over to Platform One. Here Humphrey approached me for a word.

"Did I hear e complainin' about the quality of the coal, Mr. Jay?" he asked. "Twern't diplomatic to do so under the circumstances, if e asks I."

"Oh?" I replied. "Showering a stationmaster with soot is not diplomatic either, Humphrey."

"But... But e don't understand," Humphrey sighed with exasperation. "Didn't ol' Mildenhew tell e about the coal ration, Mr. Jay? Didn't he tell e we don't get enough house coal for the winter?"

"No?" I replied with a sinking feeling.

"Well, Sir, generally speaking, the official ration's all used up by the end of January, e see. So we gets engine coal when we can. We has an arrangement, so to speak. Builds up a stock, like."

"Oh," I said, forming the impression that I had blundered.

"When a foreign engine comes up the line and takes on South Exmoor coal, the crew don't usually wants to take the stuff back on the mainline, e see. Primarily because our coal be banned at Exeter. Residents protest about the smoke, so I hears tell. So we gets the left-overs from the tender, and Headquarters don't have a tally on her."

"When you say 'we' get the coal, Humphrey, who exactly do you mean?"

"If the engine be *Herod*, then, as a rule, Upshott. Although, if we b'aint quick enough about it, Widdlecombe gets her first."

"Then I have a feeling that Widdlecombe has beaten us to it," I said, and retreated shame faced to my office.

CHAPTER SEVEN

PECULIAR PEOPLE, AT UPSHOTT

The double-headed Timber and Goods train was departing. Its trucks percussed and separated with a caterpillar ripple as their couplings lost slack. The exhaust beat of two locomotives began to rap on Upshott Hill, a hill now dappled ominously with the rolling shadows of leaden rain-clouds. A hitherto oppressive day was freshening up portentiously, so I turned to make for the Booking Hall to give the barometer a tap. I had taken no more than a few steps when a wail emanated from the Goods Office. It blundered through my preoccupied mind and brought me to an abrupt halt.

Although I had been warned of Mr. Phillips's inclination to burst into song, I was shocked by it nonetheless, and found the noise difficult to reconcile with contentment. Apparently my Goods Clerk's passion was for the opera, his knowledge of which was sustained by the occasional excursion to Covent Garden. Indeed, since being widowed, saving up for such trips was Mr. Phillips's only use for money, and succumbing to the urge to emulate the performers he so admired was, in the meantime, his only other indulgence.

Apparently the scholarly fellow had agreed, as a result of an impassioned request, nay, an angry demand by his colleagues, to render his aria only whilst alone in his office, and then only with the windows and doors shut. But such baffles were no match for the fulminations of this clerk, so I unseated my top-hat and peered around the Goods Office door to applaud him.

Edwin Phillips's monacle dropped, and his studious, alabaster face erupted into an uncomfortable grimace upon discovering that he had acquired an audience.

"Gilbert and Sullivan," he declared obliquely and, with a curiously blank expression, awaited my response.

Regrettably I had none. I remember thinking only that any member of the fairer sex would envy his abundance of fine curly hair, although she might not require the dark beard and moustache that accompanied it.

"Gilbert and Sullivan?" I queried.

Brandishing an antique quill-pen, Mr. Phillips applied a cavalier punctuation stroke to a neat column of figures, and dipped the quill into an ornamental ink-pot before condescending to enlighten me. This pen, incidentally, had earned Mr. Phillips the cognomen 'Scratch' in certain quarters.

"My latest discovery," he told me imperiously. "You mark my words, Mr. Jay, those two gentlemen will one day be famous or there is no justice."

"Then we should do them justice," I replied vigorously. "The thunderclaps you are broadcasting in their names shall not enhance their prospects, I'll warrant."

With over-acted nonchalance, the curious fellow took up his fanciful pen and resumed scratching at his document.

The 12.32pm passenger train to Giddiford being the next disruption to my tenor, I calculated that I had just enough time to take a spot of lunch at The Shunter, a tavern across the station yard, before being required on the platforms again. Before leaving, I locked my office door and told Jack Wheeler where I could be found should anyone need me in a hurry. This taken care of, I set off for a pint of cider and a good, fat sausage.

* * *

Jack Wheeler raced into the bar of The Shunter and squealed into my ear:

"The Stores 'ut's been burgled again, Mr. Jay, and in broad daylight too. The lamp oil thief's struck."

I managed to drain my glass before being ushered away, but a distasteful break of wind prevented me from finishing my sausage.

"That's not all," Jack reminded me with his nose pressed against his fobwatch. "Everyone's gathered in the Booking 'all for to make your acquaintance, Mr. Jay. It's three-quarters Eleven gone."

Looking at my own timepiece, I did not see the need for such haste, but haste we made.

"Your watch runs wildly, Jack," I remarked.

The clerk ignored me.

As we hurried across the forecourt, I saw *Lacy* running 'light engine' through the station, heading towards Blodcaster. The term 'light engine', should this require an explanation, describes a locomotive which is not hauling a train. *Lacy* slowed down briefly at the signalbox to allow a flying exchange of batons, its presence, theoretically, putting the time at 11.50am, by which I came to realize that *my* watch was the one running wildly, not Jack's. I resolved to have Mr. Hales fettle the timepiece at the earliest opportunity.

Running headlong across the forecourt to keep up with Jack, and holding down my hat against a strengthening wind, I began to marshal my thoughts on how best to address my staff. I had been instructed by the General Manager to issue a stern warning about time-keeping, for it was reputed to be poor at Upshott. However, before I could compose a sobering discourse on the subject of punctuality, and punishment for those lacking it, I was waylaid by a delegation of angry villagers bearing a complaint. This untimely interception threatened to destroy my own good time-keeping, an example of which I had intended to set my staff from the very outset so that I might credibly demand the same of them.

Consequently I was faced with an impossible choice. Either I stopped and became a hypocrite in the eyes of my staff, or I continued and became an ill-mannered stationmaster who has no time to listen to the public. I decided to receive the delegation, and, to avoid becoming a hypocrite, omit from my speech the lecture on punctuality.

The complainants had banded together to protest over the absence of an excursion train suitably timed to take visitors to Blodcaster's Cattle and Yarn Market on Mondays. Their spokesman, a gruff gentleman by the name of Collins, stepped forward to introduce himself, and advised me that he was the proprietor of Xissington Tannery.

Mr. Collins pointed out politely that Mr. Mildenhew had undertaken to do something about the 'disgraceful' situation, yet had subsequently not acted. I reassured him, and Mrs Peabody the thatcher's wife, and the Harvey sons from the farm facing the station, that I would take up their cause without delay. I agreed with them most heartily that it was inconvenient to be limited to the regular services of 7.54am and 1.08pm on such a day. Not everyone, I conceded, was at liberty to catch the early train, and the 1.08pm was rather late in the day to be of much use.

Before I knew it, I had offered the delegation more hope than I ought to have done. The administrative inertia which strangled most railway headquarters was not something readily understood by the public. I doffed my hat and bade my seemingly satisfied lobbyists good day before they could press me into undertaking specific steps.

A miscellany of expectant faces was on parade before me in the cool gloom of the Booking Hall. Perhaps a little intimidated by them, I formalized my appointment at Upshott with as much levity as I dared without encouraging indiscipline. With the exception of Jack Wheeler, whom at first I ignored, I shook hands with each employee in turn, regardless of whether we had already made acquaintance. The reason why I did not shake hands with Mr. Wheeler was that he had chosen to witness the event from behind the pigeon-hole window through which tickets were sold. In his case, therefore, all I could do was tap on the glass and grin, rather as if passing the time of day with a goldfish.

Because Mr. Hales was anxious to return to his duties, I turned to him first and sought his formal opinion of the new signalbox. Until recently he had been required to swing the level crossing gates by hand, and to switch the points by way of cast-iron levers located around the station yard. Hostile moorland winters had made this an unenviable task.

"Its comforts are famed, Mr. Jay," he grinned

smugly. "I must turn away visitors continually if I am to go about my work."

I wondered if, by this remark, Mr. Hales was implying that my own visit had caused him inconvenience. I considered countering his discourtesy by enquiring what was in the evil smelling sack beneath the signalbox steps, but felt it better not to start life on the wrong foot with the Signalman.

Ivor was not a tall fellow, and tricked one's attention away from the fact by way of his crisp mannerisms and dapper dress, in particular by wearing a brightly coloured woolen cravat. His style of apparel did not offend me, however. Far from it. Ivor Hales, I had been informed, was consistently well turned out, and I was captivated by the way he had trimmed his moustache to a neat zig-zag. I judged him instantly as possessing the qualities of dependability found, and indeed necessary, in all signalmen.

I exchanged notes with Diggory Smith, the Junior Porter, or Porters' Boy as he was occasionally called. I was already acquainted with Master Smith's singular sense of humour, and had found out more about him by making enquiries. It seemed that he was a willing lad, if a trifle gullible, with a penchant for climbing. Apparently, the duty he relished most was scaling the tall signal posts to refill the oil lamps mounted at the top. I had learned also, by way of a secretive nudge from Humphrey, that this towering and bony young man was a 'dead shot' with the catapult, although I failed to see what constructive application this had to the railway.

The company uniform did little to mitigate the boy's scruffy nature. He appeared this day, and ever afterwards, to have dirt around his mouth, but, assuming this to be a delicate personal matter, I did not question it. Instead, trying to put the boy at his ease, I asked him an informal question or two.

"Do you live with your parents, lad?"

"There's French blood on 'is mother's side," Jack Wheeler interrupted rudely through the ticket window. His remark precipitated lewd gesticulations amongst his colleagues.

"Let the lad speak for himself," I cautioned them.

"I live with my mother in Widdlecombe, Sir," he answered at length, with a disturbingly squeaky voice. "My mother makes lace."

"So I understand. And what of your father?"

"He was the Master Farrier in the parish of Widdlecombe, Sir."

"Was he indeed," I marvelled. "But what, since you use the past tense, prevents him from practising his most laudible skills presently, lad?"

"Being six foot under, Sir," said the boy. "He expired five years ago."

I was shocked by the bluntness of young Smith's reply, and paused to clear my throat.

"I am sorry to hear that," I sympathized, delivering my words with a stridency calculated to quell a ripple of bathos.

"He died completely, Sir. Didn't have time to suffer," the boy added, as if to spare me unnecessary distress.

I was touched, and placed my hand upon the lad's shoulder, for I sensed that his bravado was tempered with a touch of bitterness. To spare myself further embarrassment, I did not delve into the cause of his father's demise. Fortunately so, as it turned out, for I learned afterwards that he had been struck by one of our trains, albeit as a result of an ill-advised perambulation in a drunken stupor.

"And how do you deliver yourself to work each day?" I enquired. "Widdlecombe is nearly three miles away."

"I walk, Sir," the lad replied sheepishly, and confessed to a breach of company bye-laws. "I walk along the railway from Widdlecombe Station."

Learning of this practice caused me unease, but I reflected upon the fact that Diggory had no need to risk his life by treading the ballast between the rails. In its wisdom as one of the line's financiers, the London and South Western Railway Company had insisted upon a spare track-bed being formed as far as Upshott, so that separate 'up' and 'down' lines might one day be laid.

"You walk the spare track-bed across Ondle Viaduct, I trust?" I cautioned the young porter with a locked gaze.

Master Smith confirmed that he did. It seemed a great pity that he could not be found duties at Widdlecombe Station but, alas, the staff complement there was minimal.

Mr. Turner, presumably still in the grip of his 'sleepy spell', seemed unable to keep his eyes open. In deference to his handicap I taxed him lightly on his personal background rather than bore him with railway matters. But as our interlocution progressed, I became suspicious that we were not reciprocating on the same topic. Indeed, abrupt proof that we were not, was to follow.

"Of course, I never knew my father," Mr. Turner told me woozily. "Although, just about everyone else in the county did."

Prompted by Mr. Turner's intimation that his

late father had enjoyed something of a reputation, I asked:

"Really, dear fellow? Who was he?"

"Some soldiers," came the reply.

I bothered Mr. Turner no more, and broke up the meeting. Next I ushered Mr. Maynard to one side. A pucker gentleman with a milky eye, Mr. Maynard satisfied me that not everyone at Upshott was idiosyncratic. The Horse Superintendent's uniform was immaculate and, as we stepped outside, I noticed gathering stormclouds reflecting in the peak of his cap. I asked Mr. Maynard to conduct me around his stables at some mutually convenient time, and he stroked his waxed moustache proudly. However, I heard no suggestion as to when this might be.

"Tomorrow perhaps?" I suggested, and waited for a reply.

Still Mr. Maynard said nothing.

I examined the fellow's gaunt profile for a clue to his silence, and noticed that his milky eye was fixed lifelessly on the distance.

"Mr. Maynard?" I tootled in his ear to regain his attention, and afterwards informed him abruptly: "I do believe I should like to see your horses tomorrow, if you will."

The Horse Superintendent broke his gaze and turned to me with a willing smile.

"I'm sorry, Mr. Jay," he apologized. "I thought you'd gone. Of course, come tomorrow." With a finger pointed to the side of his head, he explained: "Fraid I'm a trifle deaf in my right ear. Ruptured, so I'm told. Touch of artillery damage."

It must have been a direct hit, I thought.

Suddenly Mr. Maynard's face unfolded into an

accomplished smile, and he enlightened me further:

"I was a powder monkey in the Crimean campaign, don't you know. Oh yes. By the by, Mr. Jay, I should be proud to show you my draught horses. Ay, and the baton mounts too."

* * *

The 12.32pm Giddiford passenger train was due, and Jack Wheeler was issuing tickets as though they were concessionary sweetmeats. Meanwhile, with his infectious laughter, Humphrey Milsom was offering passengers a helping hand across the footbridge with their baggage. To some patrons of the railway, especially the so-called 'pillars of the community', such fraternity was considered unseemly, and these people would converse only with me. Come to that, the still loftier strata of Ondle Valley would exchange pleasantries even with a stationmaster only on sufferance, his power over their commercial affairs making it necessary. I had once overheard my vocation likened to that of a 'vulgar tradesman living above his shop'. If this was the case, then I was a tradesman without whom the community would be much the poorer.

Diggory and Snimple were carrying trunks dutifully across the footbridge to Platform Two, to assist a local gentleman bound for London. Gazing upon this spectacle, one could understand how capital bound passengers, above all others, personified the magic of railway travel, even in remote places like Upshott from which operated no regular through trains to London. It did not matter that the gentleman establishing himself amid his array of trunks on Platform Two would need to make two connections to reach the capital; one at Giddiford Junction, and the other at Exeter. His ultimate destination was the catalyst of railway 'folklore' which, to this day, explains the extra attention given to 'up' trains. You see, railway companies throughout the land have always observed the rule that when two trains cross at a station, it is the 'up' train which must receive the 'right away' first.

* * *

A gusty wind had driven Upshott Wood into wild undulations and was tossing the fleeting clatter of the approaching 12.32pm as if to make sport of its arrival. While keeping an eye on progress, I spotted the stonemason's wife, Mrs. Mitchell, among the waiting passengers. She was rocking a three-wheeled perambulator gently, so I wandered over to her and peered under its fluttering lace hood.

"How old is the mite?" I enquired politely.

"Charity will be three months tomorrow," she told me proudly. "Isn't she pretty?"

"Delightful," I sighed.

In truth, I had seen more delightful turnips, but honesty is not the policy of a stationmaster paid to spread contentment.

It was upon my first day in charge of Upshott that I became acquainted with Doctor Bentley, the village physician. He was an appointee of the benevolent Lord Lacy. The Doctor was standing betwixt his eldest son and Mrs. Bentley, grappling with a windswept copy of *The Times*. Glancing up from his tangled newspaper, and having recognized me as the new Stationmaster, his glare of frustration yielded to a somewhat artificial smile. Without hesitation the Doctor strutted towards me and introduced himself with a prolonged and savage handshake.

"We're off to Blodcaster market, Jay," he cackled with a voice of crunching gravel.

Releasing me from his clammy grip at last, Doctor Bentley stared into my eyes and produced a deep furrow of pity across his brow. For one uncomfortable moment I thought he was going to give me a penny and send me on my way.

"Doubtless you are wondering why my spouse and I are standing here waiting for the Giddiford train, then?" he tested me. "Since we are going to Blodcaster."

The puzzle had not occurred to me. Nevertheless, the pink little gentleman broke into a superior grin and revealed the solution.

"I have a nephew in Giddiford who wishes to join us," he began, "and so we are making the round trip aboard this train. My nephew will be waiting with his nanny on the platform at Giddiford."

"Bravo. An ingenious use of the railway," I commented robustly, having been forewarned of the Doctor's peculiar brand of arrogance.

Having doffed my hat to Mrs. Bentley, whom the Doctor had omitted to introduce, I prepared to move on.

As if to recapture my attention, Doctor Bentley waved his copy of *The Times* before my face.

"So, what do you think of 'Dizzy' then? If anyone can rescusitate Her Majesty's interest in State affairs, he can, what?"

"I am sure Disraeli will do as he sees fit," I responded neutrally. "Although I cannot fathom whether he is a man with a dream, or merely a dreamer." The Doctor frowned at me disapprovingly, but I continued unabashed. "Disraeli would have us overlook the many reforms which have taken place under Gladstone," I said. "However, I am unqualified to express an opinion on such matters."

"Dah! Few people are," Doctor Bentley replied boisterously. "Which is why the vote is reserved for the man of substance. Gentlemen like me, who have ventured beyond the parish boundary, and who can spell our names correctly. Never mind. You may take my word for it, Jay, Gladstone fights shy of foreign affairs. The names 'Gladstone' and 'Disraeli' may be on the nation's tongue right now, but precious few people appreciate how much it takes to sustain an Empire."

It was outrageous of the Doctor to infer that I was not equal to the privilege of the ballot box. Perhaps I should have reminded him of the fact that in Parliament a good seven years since, greater minds than his had met to confer upon all gentlemen of responsibility, and that included stationmasters, a voice at the poll. Indeed, I might have enlightened him to the fact that I had cast my very first vote only last February, having missed the opportunity to do so in 1866.

I acknowledged the Doctor with a perfunctory smile and moved on before tempers were lost. Of greater imperative, if not importance, was the completion of the platform excavations. Loose spoil and slabstones were proving perilous to passengers, and were giving rise to complaints from those it does not behove a stationmaster to inconvenience.

CHAPTER EIGHT

THE DISAPPEARING LAMP OIL

Lacy had something of a face, and an impudent one at that. Its porthole style windows, or 'spectacles' as they were known, were like alert eyes, and its tall chimney resembled an aristocrat's nose. With the regulator shut off, *Lacy's* piston rods slapped like tired feet as it trundled to a halt in the station.

The locomotive rested gratefully while my porters moved in to open the train's regiment of wooden doors, most of which had been locked. The practise of locking passengers inside their compartments was a hangover from the days when rustic folk who had never before travelled by train, and who therefore had no concept of speed, would try to alight between stations. Indeed, the South Exmoor's very first public train had been blighted by the death of a woman who, while travelling in an open Third Class carriage, had attempted to retrieve her hat from the lineside. More recently, a local farmer had stepped off a train travelling at twenty-five miles per hour to have a chat with a neighbour he had spotted standing at a crossing.

The train's two Guards handed down parcels, carboys, and cages of domestic fowl from the brake van while Driver MacGregor, anxious not to miss the starting flag, leaned precariously from the footplate to see past the milling crowds on the platform.

As soon as the passengers were aboard the train I blew my pea-whistle to clear the well-wishers and bystanders from the edge of the platform, and raised my arm to start the engine. With the trill of my whistle still echoing back from Splashgate Hill, and the starting flag fluttering in the Guard's hand, Driver MacGregor 'popped' *Lacy's* whistle in acknowledgement and opened the regulator. With its safety valve blowing off noisily, the locomotive 'woofed' softly into motion towards Fallowfield Embankment and the downhill run to Giddiford.

As the Guard rode by in his cabin at the rear of the train, I imparted to him a wooden box containing a glass jar of goat's milk and a wicker basket of eggs. These foodstuffs were the produce of the station, and I had marked them 'free of charge' for delivery to the stationmaster of Giddiford Junction in accordance with a custom begun by Mr. Mildenhew.

Now that the train had removed the outbound passengers from our midst, my staff and I were faced with a small but demanding assemblage of arrivals from Blodcaster. By the look of them, most of these people had been shopping, although others were obviously returning from an overnight stay. All of them, however, along with their parcels and trunks, required handling in strict 'pecking order' lest there be an outrage.

Among those who had stepped off the last train, having travelled in the Guard's van, was a gang of six railway labourers. When I enquired of their purpose, their foreman stepped forward and presented himself to me, handing over a job-sheet authorizing his men to dig out Platform One using tools obtained from the Platelayer's hut. With Jack Wheeler calling me urgently from the opposite platform, I was compelled to return the document without query and leave the men to their work.

I crossed the footbridge to answer Jack's call,

and found the clerk smelling as though he had embrocated himself in lamp oil.

"Sir, we'll 'ave to record one more lamp oil drum as 'aving been stolen," he informed me with mock gravity, and added with a sudden gurgle of delight. "But it aint been stolen yet!"

"What?" I returned impatiently.

"Bait!" Jack declared. "We've put out a drum where it'll be easily took. But it'll be the last one to disappear. The culprit won't come back for more. Not after 'aving 'ad a dose of this one."

"I do not think we should put company property at risk deliberately," I advised my Booking Clerk.

"This particular drum aint no good to the company no more. We've spiked it," Wheeler confided. "You did say we could go ahead, Mr. Jay."

"Regrettably, yes," I concurred, pondering the price of Jack's resourcefulness. "You had better explain exactly what you have done," I urged him.

This was a mistake. Instantly I was peppered with specious scientific twaddle of a kind only Jack Wheeler would pretend to understand.

"Simple as pie, Mr. Jay," he opened. "I read it in a book. You won't believe this, but North American savages communicate over long distances using telegraph signals made of smoke. And that's 'ow the felon who plunders our lamp oil ration is going to confess to 'is guilt. Unwittingly, of course."

"Jibberish," I snorted. "Savages would not have the faintest idea how to erect telegraph poles, even if, by some witchcraft, they could make smoke travel down the wires. You should be more careful what you read, Jack."

I waved Wheeler away, but he ignored me.

"Wires don't come into it," he advised me tetchily.

"The lamp oil will not harm anyone, I trust?" I cautioned him.

"Oh no, Mr. Jay," he came back emolliently. "Me and Tom 'ave tested it."

Boasting the complicity of Tom Turner, a man afflicted with tropical sleeping sickness, did nothing to solicit my confidence.

* * *

By the time *Lacy* was returning with the 1.08pm Blodcaster train, the workmen had reduced Platform One to the same parlous condition as Platform Two. There were ugly holes everywhere. I was standing over one of these craters, wondering what to do about passenger safety, when I saw Doctor Bentley smiling at me knowingly from a carriage window.

The practitioner's affected pleasantries did not deceive me, however, so I merely returned him an equally knowingly smile and looked away. I knew that, given the right moment, he would be asking me if it was my intention to refer to him the victims of railway accidents, and those taken sick aboard trains.

Driver MacGregor approached me and raised his tartan tammy in salutation.

"Theers a carpet o' mushrooms on Fallowfield Common, Mr. Jay," he confided. "Whurruth a veset, I'd say. Look like Blushers, they do."

I appreciated his tip, but made no plans to have someone pick them for me.

"You must be careful. Blushers are too easily mistaken for poisonous toadstools," I cautioned the driver deedily.

"Nay, theer Blushers I tell ye. Tee good te waste," he chanted.

The Market Goods was clearly going to be late upon its return trip, but it was not within my remit to warn footplatemen about picking lineside fruits. MacGregor had his own copy of the Rule Book. With a wave over the driver's shoulder, I gave his train the 'right away' and stood aside while he raced to the footplate to take the regulator. *Lacy* began barking at the gradient and, with smoke swirling around me, I fancied I could smell mushrooms sizzling upon the fireman's shovel.

The thought of fried mushrooms must have been distracting Driver MacGregor also, for his starting technique was not of the standard required to make a dignified exit from Upshott over wet rails in the direction of Blodcaster. Indeed, it was my understanding that to prevent slippage upon Upshott's adverse gradient, and to avoid wheelspin and the consequent rapid burst of exhaust so often heard from starting steam locomotives, the regulator needed to be opened and shut successively with great tactile feel. Manifestly MacGregor had lost his touch this afternoon, for *Lacy's* driving wheels lost all adhesion.

With the engine's connecting rods spinning rhythmically, the driver opened the sprinkler to apply sand, but the sand was damp and would not sprinkle, and a shower of sparks erupted from *Lacy's* chimney. Everyone on the platform scattered to escape the glowing embers floating down upon their heads, and I was startled to witness a bundle of newspapers ignite as a red hot cinder settled upon it with a genie-like puff of smoke. Ladies began to scream, and I rushed to their assistance with calming words and profuse apologies.

Despite the terror that Driver MacGregor had caused by his lapse of concentration, it was with no sense of urgency that he shut off steam to his fruitlessly chugging engine. And with equal contempt for haste did he apply the brake to check the backwards roll of his six-carriage train once the engine had been pacified. Were it not for the Guard's quick response in applying the axle-brake in the rear van, the handwheel of which took a dozen or more vigorous spins to secure, there might have been a serious accident.

Humphrey, having poured a bucket of sand over the burning newspapers, mopped his brow and examined apprehensively a scorched copy of *Trewman's Exeter Flying Post* to see whose it was.

"What went wrong?" I called to the locomotive crew. "You have been this way enough times before."

With an unlit briar-root projecting from his beard, Driver MacGregor leaned unfussed from the footplate and absolved himself of all blame.

"Ask Morgan-the-fire here," he grunted. "Yeed nay ken he hails from the Valleys wi' hes spadewurrk. The coof canny sheft coal fast enough. Tes up te hem te keep the blast from pulling holes in the firebed, nay me."

Baffled by the technicalities I was unable to comment, which, I imagine, was Driver MacGregor's purpose.

As for Morgan Jones, even had he the wit or humour to retaliate, he lacked the time just now. Cursing in his native tongue he recharged his shovel and began flinging coal into the firebox with no regard for style. Meanwhile MacGregor amused himself by casually removing a blockage from the stummel of his tobacco pipe. The Welshman knew that his mate had mishandled the regulator, but he also knew that MacGregor was a man who never admitted to his errors.

On the second attempt, *Lacy* pulled away smartly and was soon pounding Longhurdle Embankment, having left behind a number of angry citizens to be pacified. In this endeavour my staff proved invaluable. Humphrey's avuncular banter did much to calm the distraught, many of whom had been showered with sparks at the very moment they were complaining about the dangerous state of the platforms. Clothes had been scorched, and I was hectored with demands for compensation, mostly from unprincipled opportunists trying to convince me that they were wearing their 'Sunday bests' for one reason or another. Others, claiming that the apparel they wore had been ruined, could show me no evidence beyond the odd smear of ash. Fortunately the weather took a hand and drove the malingerers away.

Borne on a stiffening breeze, rain began sweeping under the canopy and flooding the platform excavations. With a heavy heart I looked about me and took stock. This was my first day at Upshott, and already my station was in a state of unbridled disorder. I was responsible for damaging the squire's new carriage, I was in receipt of a complaint about there being no special train to serve Blodcaster Market, I had been late for my own introduction to my staff, I was faced with telegraph apparatus I did not understand, and I was labelled an imbecile who has a phobia about boilers blowing up. Such a recapitulation would have broken a more intelligent man. When startled yet again by rock blasting in the squire's quarry, I confess, I uttered a curse with it all and took to the village for a reflective stroll.

* * *

For the first time in my career I regretted not having set aside a secret supply of, shall we say, something appropriately stupefying from which to take the occasional nip. Indeed, had I done so, my bottom drawer would not have been the first in a stationmaster's desk to chink with a bottle and glass. I could see now that I had been hasty in my condemnation of men of responsibility who seek refuge in alcohol. Life was teaching me fast that, in matters of morality, being right is just as easy as being wrong, and that torment is God's gift to those who are pious enough to preoccupy themselves with which is which.

Nevertheless, upon reflection, I found that I favoured a reaffirmation of my belief in the positive mind rather than the solace of the bottle. So, to commence my resurrection from the mire, I instructed the workmen, against all their protestations, to re-lay half of the platform slabstones.

"You will dig up no more than half a platform at a time," I told them. The men stared up at me with both surprise and dripping noses as the rain continued to fall. Next, pointing in the direction of the footbridge, I commanded them: "Only when that half is fit for the public to set foot upon shall you continue with this half. And before you dig up that half you will lay walking boards so that passengers may cross the line without ruining their footwear on the ballast while the footbridge is inaccessible."

The disgruntled gang began to clear up the mess at once.

I reflected gratefully on the fact that no London and South Western excursion trains were due until next month, and that, consequently, I had three hours of peace in which to recouperate. Also, at last, I was at liberty to expedite my investigation into the mysterious belle in white lace.

But patience. As a matter of priority I had first to write two letters to Headquarters. In one I would urge the company to lay on a regular mid-Monday morning passenger train to Blodcaster to accommodate the casual visitor to the cattle and yarn market, and in the other, reluctantly, I would request the services of a telegraph instructor.

* * *

With the two letters to Headquarters written and waiting in the dispatch pouch, I found myself somewhat depleted for the hour of the day and succumbed to the temptation to remain in my office for a while. The belle in white lace, I felt sure, was not about to leave the country, so I began reading a book which I had recently added to my collection. My literary taste would have surprised Doctor Bentley, for the book was Benjamin Disraeli's *Sybil, or The Two Nations*. Through this medium the learned Tory had reproved our Kingdom for becoming two nations in one land; one rich, the other poor. I believe I could have told him that.

Absorbed in my reading, I quite lost track of the time. Eventually, when I referred to my fobwatch to regain my bearings, I chanced to glimpse a lady passing my office window. She looked familiar. So familiar, in fact, that my heart missed a beat, although more from surprise than ardour. For, although the glass in my window distorted everything seen through it, I recognized the charming white lace which adorned the lady's blue dress. It was the belle! She had returned!

I closed my book with a thud and sped out onto the platform to apprehend her before she could disappear again.

"I beg your pardon madam," I hailed. "It is my belief that you wish to speak to me." The lady turned and opened her powder-blue umbrella against the slanting rain. I doffed my hat with a smile, and apologized for startling her. "Forgive me for being too busy this morning to..."

In a trice my gusto was reduced to a flutter, for the face now staring at me indignantly was not the one I had expected. Nor, come to that, was it one I would have chosen to witness.

"I think you are mistaken," the sour apparition reprimanded me frostily.

Feeling utterly ridiculous, and rendered speechless by the shock of the encounter, I bowed slightly and continued to stare.

The lady sensed my stupefication and began tutting irritatedly, at which gesture I rediscovered my tongue.

"Begging your pardon for the intrusion, madam," I stuttered feebly, and withdrew to my cloister.

This was definitely not the person waiting for me at the end of my search, for a goodly number of years were accumulated upon her face, bad ones, and I could see that anyone loitering in her vicinity long enough would take the blame for them. Back in my office, with Disraeli's help, I blotted out the uneasy hours while waiting for the return of the Market Goods train from Blodcaster.

A few minutes before the goods train was due, I heard a knock on my door. It was Jack Wheeler with, by the look of him, a weighty problem.

"Ah, Jack. Come in and sit down," I parried the clerk before he could trouble me with it. "You have a comprehensive knowledge of local people and their affairs, perhaps you can help me. I am trying to trace a lady who was on Platform One this morning at approximately 7.30."

I went on to describe the belle, as best I could, and asked Jack if he had seen anyone fitting the description.

"Blonde 'air 'ad she?" he countered me with a puckered grin.

This reaction was promising, for I had said nothing about her hair.

"Did you see her too, Jack?" I asked anxiously.

Jack sought further details before confirming: "Of about your years?"

"So you did see her," I concluded joyously.

"No," said Jack, and shook his head vehemently. "No, I never saw 'er. But I reckon I know who she is though." Jack cast his eye about my office shiftily, and began hissing through his teeth. "Is this important Mr. Jay? I was wondering if..."

"Not particularly," I interrupted him. "Well?" I jumped. "Who is she?"

"I reckon you saw Mistress Goadby," he announced confidently.

"Mistress Goadby," I repeated foolishly, and slipped into deep thought.

So the belle in white lace was married. Not that I had any notions of wedlock, of course. After all, I knew nothing about the woman apart from her name.

"She's the pig killer's wife," Jack proffered unnecessarily. "Lives in the 'igh Street near 'arvey's farm."

To this day I do not know why, but I decided to call upon Mrs. Goadby. Somehow it seemed necessary. After all, she did wish to speak to me.

"In my absence, Jack," I instructed the clerk, "I would like you and Mr. Phillips to deal with the Market Goods. And to see to it that young Diggory Smith is dispatched promptly with the Blodcaster baton once it has arrived."

"Em, Mr. Maynard always rides that particular one 'imself," the Booking Clerk corrected me plaintively. "The passenger train follows close behind the goods, so it requires a rider with a very fast turn of speed back to Blodcaster."

"Has Diggory no horsemanship?" I asked incredulously. "I was given to believe he could ride well."

"Oh, 'e can ride well enough, Mr. Jay. It's the company nags that can't," Jack complained. "Julian Maynard rides 'is own gelding, you see, Sir. Called 'Hildebrand' by name."

"Does Mr. Maynard expect payment for the use of his personal mount?" I asked.

"No, Mr. Jay. Julian's a skilled 'orseman. 'E's won cups."

"Well the company awards no cups, so tell him to go carefully over the downs," I cautioned the clerk. "The bridleways will be boggy, and I would rather a train left a few minutes late than someone should risk life and limb."

To the naked eye the distant hills were textured in velvet, but I knew their substance to be a kind of spongeous peat scoured deeply with fissures, fissures concealed treacherously from the eye by clumps of coarse grass.

* * *

With mounting uncertainty I set off to call upon Mrs. Goadby. *How can this be the woman haunting me with her loveliness?* I wondered, *with a name like Goadby, and a husband who hires himself out to kill pigs?* What did it matter? Most likely I was doomed to become a secret admirer of a Mrs. Someone, so why not Goadby? This would not be the first time I had become a distant admirer, for I seemed fated to the condition. It was the result of being in awe of the fairer sex. Anyway, perhaps Mrs. Goadby would turn out to be no one in particular.

Mrs. Goadby turned out to be someone in particular. She turned out to be the woman whom I had apprehended upon the platform outside my office, and with whose face I had not been enamoured. Upon this, our second meeting, I did not even benefit from a reprimand. When, as a result of sheer surprise and lack of ready wit, I asked her once more if she wished to speak to me, she took fright and bolted her door in my face. At the clunk of the snib I hurried away and banished myself once again to my workplace, somewhat dazed by my inability to learn. Had the pig killer been at home, there is no doubt that I would have been cured.

In riddance to the whole affair, I took to the platforms and toured at my leisure, pondering the South Exmoor Company's parsimonious methods of running a railway. The management's attitude towards capital investment was exemplified by its adherence to the curiously out-dated practise of using horse riders to ferry batons between stations. To this there was a well established alternative practise known as 'staff and ticket' which, as far as the Board of Trade was concerned, allowed perfectly safe traffic management over a single-line railway. But this would never be installed on the South Exmoor whilst a certain gentleman by the name of Crump held sway.

Mr. Crump, the General Manager, maintained that the staff and ticket system did not always prevent one train from smashing into the rear of another. It was in just such an accident, on the Screehampton and Kneeside Joint Railway, that Mr. Crump's spouse had been maimed and thereafter confined to a bath-chair. As a result, the South Exmoor's baton and horse operation was seen as the very safest way, if not the most efficient, of operating 'up' and 'down' trains over a single line.

Given Mr. Crump's constraint that there be batons, otherwise known as staffs, but no tickets, horses were undeniably cheaper to maintain on standby. Pilot engines would have spent much of their time idling in light steam, thereby wasting fuel.

The weekly overhead of each of Mr. Maynard's horses did not amount to eleven shillings. However, although the company held dear the economy of horses, occasionally it did resort to the use of a pair of pilot engines to shuttle the batons to and fro during periods of inclement weather. Nevertheless, taking everything into account, I could not see Mr. Maynard's fast horses surviving the London and South Western takeover, even should his shunting horses do so.

For all its mainline practises, timekeeping on the London and South Western Railway was notoriously bad, and it remained to be seen whether the South Exmoor's punctuality would be dragged down to the same miserable standard under its new owner. In theory, and only in theory, the branchline could look forward to an improvement in timekeeping because, at present, late retrieval of batons was the most frequent cause of delay.

CHAPTER NINE

STRANGER WITH A HANDLESS FOBWATCH

The afternoon Blodcaster train steamed into Upshott on time at 5.03pm, hauled by *Briggs*, but its departure was delayed six minutes by the late arrival of the Giddiford train. Mr. Maynard had indeed found the going rough over the downs, and had kept *Lacy* waiting for the baton. That same length of engraved wood was now back at Upshott, and, with vaudeville inevitability, Driver MacGregor was handing it to Driver Hiscox to carry with him back to Blodcaster.

Strange, is it not, that the key to preventing a railway collision lay in the relentless passing to and fro of a piece of wood. To prevent a head-on smash, only the driver in possession of the unique baton belonging to a particular section of single-line was permitted to enter that section. And whenever this baton was needed by a following train, a horse rider was required to retrieve it.

This pantomime would end only when the London and South Western Railway Company fulfilled its commitment to double the line. However, since no spare track-bed had been laid between Upshott and Blodcaster, and the boring of a second tunnel through Splashgate Hill would prove extremely expensive, I doubted that full doubling of the line would ever take place, even though the Board of Trade considered a single-line railway to be incomplete.

By Six o' Clock the rain had ceased and the village Postmaster had arrived, whistling passionately a melody which I believe he made up as he went along. As Mr. Peckham wheeled his precariously stacked handcart across the line to Platform Two, not once did he shift his eyes from Her Majesty's mail. This picture of dedication was to become as familiar to me as the trains themselves, for the Postmaster's duties brought him to the station fourteen times a week. In the prosecution of his duties, Mr. Peckham had evolved an uncanny facility for ignoring all distractions, as if hypnotized by his own trilling until the canvas bags in his charge were safely aboard the Mail Train.

Mr. Peckham's whistling ceased momentarily, filling the station with an unnatural silence, a silence accentuated by the absence of the vociferous gang of labourers that had been digging up the platforms. Without my realizing it, the workmen had departed on the last Giddiford train, no doubt treating themselves to First or Second Class seats instead of riding a swinger or jury car.

Such blessed relief from the relentless digging of holes prompted me to await the 'up' Mail in the company of the whistling Postmaster, in the hope that my society would quell his chirping. It did, and for various reasons I took an immediate liking to the gentleman. Mr. Peckham was short and thick set, with silver hair and a pink face decorated with bushy white eyebrows angled upwards like wings. His most striking feature was a permanent smile, a smile which at first one could mistake for a frown. All in all, Mr. Peckham had the ambience of a man of substance, a man who knows answers.

The level crossing gates swung open with their familiar clatter, and the 'down' disc signal changed aspect clangorously. Soon afterwards, as if in approval of these measures, a prolonged whistle tumbled from the hills, like an etude set to the wheeltap of faithful carriages, putting to flight a herd of deer on Squire Albury's estate. The Mail Train was coming.

At precisely 6.15pm, London and South Western locomotive Number 171 squealed discordantly to a halt beside me, compelling me to retreat from its deafening sibilations. Amid the foaming rapids of escaping steam, Mr. Peckham threw his sack of letters aboard the mail van and padlocked the doors proudly.

Within minutes, and with all the priority deserved of such a cargo, the London bound Mail was rolling again. The Postmaster bade me farewell and went off duty. For my own part, I would not see my strange new bed until after 11.30pm.

My next concern was to see Diggory away safely to Blodcaster with the baton received from the Mail Train, and I did not like the look of the weather. Across the valley, lingering above the now sombre hump of Widdlecombe Hill, were the vertical streaks of a downpour. A few minutes later that downpour had reached Upshott, causing my platform staff to take to their oilskins. From the refuge of these cumbersome company waterproofs my porters squinted at me meanly, as if blaming me for the bad weather.

Diggory, wearing a particularly oversized maroon cape, emerged from the station house and met Mr. Maynard who had fetched him a Company horse. Mr. Maynard held the beast steady while the boy mounted it, and the youth rode across to the signalbox to collect the Blodcaster baton from Mr. Hales.

Hunching against a howling, vitreous squall, Signalman Hales scurried down the wooden steps of his box, imparted the baton without ceremony, and returned fleet-footed to his gaslit cloister. With a sable, moorland sky now reducing the light to a menacing doomsday umbre, I urged Diggory to carry an oil lamp with him to act as a marker.

"I'll be all right, Mr. Jay," he assured me brightly. "Look, the sun's breaking through!"

The optimistic youth was referring to a silvery pool of light which had put a glaze on the railway cottages. But even as he spoke, the puddle of sunshine dissolved into a blur of driving rain. Diggory did not notice this. He turned his horse towards the village, applied the spur, and was away.

"I should reach Blodcaster in time to return on the 8.47pm train," he called back.

It was indeed customary for the rider carrying this baton to return on the 8.47pm, and since this was the train which required the baton, and therefore could not leave without it, Diggory's remark was either daft or witty. I truly had no idea which.

* * *

It was with relief that I observed Diggory stepping off the 8.47pm train in rods of rain under a worsening sky. Bruised and sagging clouds were barging overhead as if in competition to bring judgement day.

"B'aint natural, her bein' so dark," Humphrey remarked solemnly. "E mark my words, Mr. Jay, her's goin't come down in pitchers."

What did Humphrey think it was doing now?

I thanked my Senior Porter for his uplifting forecast and suggested that he carry someone's trunk. As it turned out, Humphrey was wrong anyway. A few minutes later the rain eased off slightly and so I took to the footbridge. Alone above the two trains standing in Upshott Station, listening to the steady patter of drizzle upon my top-hat, I stared at the world through a curtain of drips.

Directly beneath me was *Lacy*, simmering at the head of the Blodcaster train, and aboard its footplate, audible above the cackle and gurgle of water running to earth, were Driver MacGregor and Fireman Jones raising their voices to each other. With a humourless Welshman proud to the roots with dry steam coal and all else from the valleys, sharing the footplate with a Highlander of testing dry wit, the firebox qualified only as a secondary source of combustion.

I descended the footbridge steps and braved the exposed far end of Platform Two, to have a word with the more equable crew of the 'up' train. Here I recognized the silver hair of Driver Hiscox who was down at track level sheltering in the lee of his engine oiling the link motions. Before stepping out from behind his charge, the driver straightened up to light his pipe. Having taken a satisfying puff he pulled a forage-cap from his back pocket, unrolled it, and donned it squarely as if going on parade.

Upon realizing that he was being watched, Driver Hiscox peered upwards and gave me a sagely nod. Now he produced a mallet and stooped again to tap *Briggs's* main axles. Cocking his ear to the report, he hushed:

"Hear that ring, Mr. Jay? One dull clunk and we've a fracture."

I knew that, of course, but I acknowledged him studiously nevertheless.

"Are MacGregor and Jones always at variance?" I asked, wondering what kind of atmosphere prevailed in the engine house at Gidiford. Driver Hiscox appeared not to hear me. Perhaps he thought it ungentlemanly to speak ill of others behind their backs, even if they deserved it.

"The signal lamps need lighting," he grunted with the cadence of a man struggling against himself.

I summoned Diggory at once.

Diggory's face arched with delight, and in no time he had returned prepared for the climb up the first post.

"You won't think the duty so fine when the semaphores have been erected," Hiscox bellowed at the boy as he returned with a can of lamp oil. "Do you know what a 'Distant' signal is, lad?" Causing a shower of drips, the Junior Porter shook his head. "It's a signal they put a quarter of a mile outside the station," Hiscox told him with a mock peer through the steady drizzle. "Not quite so much fun in this weather, eh?"

Diggory remained buoyant, for the driver had overlooked the fact that servicing a pair of Distant signals would place the lad outside my jurisdiction for a while each day. It would take more than driving rain to dampen Diggory's spirit in such circumstances. The fact was written upon his face. Moreover, with modern removable lamps, he knew that filling them would be easier.

"A young man enjoys his freedom," I reminded

Hiscox with a wink, and together we watched the porter shin effortlessly up a forty-foot signal post.

Diggory was not so good at aiming a spout, however, for he was spilling as much oil as he was pouring into the lamp reservoir. With my fingers crossed, I hoped that he would not strike a lucifer and set the entire post on fire.

"These old disc signals are life expired, you know, Mr. Jay. Many of them jam," Driver Hiscox told me while waiting for the 'right away'. "We've had derailments as a result. That very signal was a second-hand purchase from Vauxhall donkey's years ago when the London and South Western declared the type obsolete."

Being by nature a gentleman, this remark was the nearest Percival Hiscox would ever get to criticizing the South Exmoor Railway Company for it's obsession with economy.

"A typical penny-saving job lot," I concurred briskly.

"Things will change, Mr. Jay. You'll see."

With this prophecy, Driver Hiscox took the 'right away' and eased open the regulator. I watched his train recede across Fallowfield Common until it had become no more than a flickering red tail lamp in the blustering rain. And when the sulphurous fog of *Briggs's* combustion had dispersed to an elusive scent, I watched the 'down' train woof into the greyness in the opposite direction, leaving the station strangely quiet.

It seemed unlikely that the light would recover this late in the day, so I set Snimple the task of lighting the platform gaslamps. Until many years later, when these lamps were converted to the incandescent mantle type, they were woefully dim and provided a fluttering naked flame no brighter than that of a well maintained oil lamp.

* * *

About 9.30pm that evening a most peculiar thing happened. I was standing under the canopy that protected a short section of Platform One from the elements, when an unfamiliar gentleman wearing a black cape and top-hat bade me good evening. Now, I grant you, there is nothing strange in this, but when I recount the gentleman's subsequent conduct, I know you will agree that there was something a trifle sinister about him. You see, at first I thought he was lost, and about to ask for directions. Then, as he drew closer, I detected in his lineaments the hint of a condescending smile, a sneer of recognition, as if the fellow had the advantage of me.

Pulling out his fobwatch, the stranger asked me to tell him the time. This he did in quite the oddest fashion, saying:

"Have you the means hereabouts to record the passage of time?"

Well, I suspected that the boorish fellow was making sport of me, and when he flipped open his silver timepiece to demonstrate that it was broken, I became convinced of it. The timepiece, though in mint condition, had no hands!

After further consideration, I revised my opinion and supposed the gentleman to be a foreigner, this accounting for his peculiar manner of speech and offensive conduct, and so decided to teach him a lesson in British civility. Matching his churlish gesture deed for deed, I pulled out my own fobwatch and showed it to him without comment.

The bounder laughed openly, at which point I decided to set him straight. However, before I could take off my hat, I was seized by an unaccountable breathlessness. Breathlessness is something to which I am not prone, you understand.

Fortunately, at this moment, Jack Wheeler came along. But the clerk's timely appearance turned out to be of no service, for Jack was as perplexed as I by the blighter's behaviour. The stranger's next remark was particularly impertinent.

"Good Heavens, that will not do," he mocked.

Wondering what he was talking about I followed the line of his finger. He was pointing at my fobwatch. The objectionable cove had the audacity to laugh at a railway timepiece, and a perfectly reliable one at that, apart from its running a trifle slow on occasions.

At this point my incredulity turned to anger and I gave serious consideration to prodding the bounder in the shoulder with the knob of my walking stick. But, being short of breath, I invited Mr. Wheeler to fight my corner for me. I nodded to the clerk, and for once saw no reason to caution him about tact when dealing with the public.

It was now that I began to fear for my sanity.

"E's right, Sir," Jack suddenly agreed with the visitor. "Watches and clocks don't record the passage of time."

"Of course not," the stranger reciprocated confidently.

I was aware that my Booking Clerk read second-hand science books, but, until now, I had assumed him incapable of understanding any of them. The stranger nodded to Jack encouragingly, and the clerk explained:

"You take anemometers, Mr. Jay. They measure the wind by being driven round by it."

"I say, Mr. Wheeler, you do take my meaning well," the stranger put in, leaving me to wonder how he knew my Booking Clerk's name. The lesson in physics was not yet over. "Likewise," he continued, "the passage of electricity is measured with an instrument called the galvanometer, which is driven by the very flow of electric current it is measuring. But what, I ask you, drives the hands of a clock? Not time. No watch was ever driven by time itself."

I tried to study the stranger's face, but I could see only a silhouette. No matter what position I adopted, poor light, twisted shadows, or the accumulation of rain upon my eye-lashes conspired to hide his identity.

With characteristic verve, Wheeler concluded:

"Clocks tell you nothing, Mr. Jay, because they're only driven by springs."

"You make me dizzy with all this scientific twaddle," I halted them, and drew the stranger's attention to the station clock behind me. "If you wish to know the time, there it is," I said.

I turned back to find Mr. Wheeler standing on his own.

"Pooh, now the gentleman withdraws without so much as a by your leave," I complained. "Perhaps Squire Albury is right about the railway bringing unwanted strangers into the valley. And I will thank you to show better style in future, Mr. Wheeler. I do not expect my staff to drag me into ridiculous conversations about clock springs with every Tom, Dick and Harry passing this way, do you understand?"

"What 'ave I done now, Mr. Jay?" Wheeler reacted defensively. "I only came to see if you were all right, Sir. You were talking to yourself."

There was a sudden roar, a cloudburst pelting the platform canopy, and it masked the approach of the evening Giddiford train coasting into the station from the gloom beyond the gaslamps. The engine's whistle gave me quite a start and left my hands too shaky to flip open my fobwatch, so I consulted the platform clock. It was 9.37pm. The train was two minutes late.

There was something amiss about this train. The darting squares of light which had become such a familiar escort to night trains since the introduction of carriage lighting, were missing.

The engine hissed through the darkness and halted stubbornly, importing a tricky problem to be dealt with by my platform staff. The First Class passengers were in revolt over having no artificial light, and, expecting no such luxury, the Third Class passengers were jeering them for their spiritless whingeing over such a minor taste of deprivation. It appeared that someone, probably a junior porter at Blodcaster, had fitted pot-lamps in the First and Second Class carriages but had neglected to fill and light them.

It was time for Diggory to go climbing again. The pot-lamps would have to be removed from their roof-top receptacles, passed down to Snimple to be filled with oil, lit, and returned to their receptacles. With rain bouncing and gushing off every surface, I could see that the higher fare payers would be drenched in their seats while this job was being done, for the pot-lamp receptacles were merely holes, each about the diameter of a pumpkin, in the carriage roofs.

I donned my cape and set off across the yard to acquire from Stores a set of pot-lamp plugs to fill these holes while the lamps were being serviced. This was when I learned that Tom Turner's sleepy spells were followed by fits of stubborness. The Stores Clerk had released a drum of lamp oil willingly, but was refusing to issue plugs because, he claimed, they were 'not readily accessible'.

Although Diggory tried gallantly to refill the pot-lamps in situ, he found that on SER stock it simply could not be done. And when I returned to the platform I discovered the lad crouching over a lamp hole in the roof of the First Class carriage, calmly shrugging off both torrent and tirade alike.

Imagine my shock, then, when I observed Diggory's cape, which had been accumulating rain-water in one of its folds, deliver a quart directly through the roof into the lap of a lady sitting below. Further, imagine my pride when I saw Snimple, with laudable sympathy and great presence of mind, rush to the poor woman's assistance with a towel, and afterwards take a footwarmer to the locomotive to have it charged with hot water for her.

Despite Snimple's good work, however, I was infuriated by this scene of bedlam. I returned to Mr. Turner with all speed.

"But I am the Stationmaster here, Mr. Turner," I beseeched him. "And all I am requesting is three pot-lamp plugs to allow Diggory to deal with each carriage in turn without passengers having to get wet".

"Someone was supposed to light the lamps at Blodcaster," he rumbled with glazed indifference.

"I'll not turn my shed upside down to accommodate other people's carelessness. That's it and all about it."

Naturally, the even tenor of Mr. Turner's life could not be allowed to take precedence over the comfort of passengers, so I gave the clerk a good verbal drubbing.

"Pot-lamp plugs are company property," I reminded him sharply. "The company needs them, and it is not within your remit to decide where, or when, things shall be done. Now fetch them at once, Mr. Turner."

To my astonishment, Mr. Turner ignored me.

"At least do it for Diggory," I resorted to pleading with the fellow.

Eventually I managed to galvanize Mr. Turner into action, but it took the threat of dismissal to do it. The clerk's black eyebrows converged miserably, and he strode away, leaving me to continue our conversation on my own.

Mr. Turner is ill, I reasoned, and resolved to submit the fellow for examination at some convenient juncture.

Of the first moment was the Giddiford train, and so I made haste back to its hapless passengers to offer them my apologies for the inconvenience they had been caused. By this time tempers were becoming frayed but, fortunately, I was spared a great deal of invective because the dry passengers, God bless them, were deflecting the anger of the wet ones by making sport of them.

A few minutes later I noticed Humphrey having a word with Mr. Turner, after which they both went to the Stores shed. I was puzzled by this, but could not investigate the development because I was engaged in attempts, however futile, to smooth Diggory's path.

The situation was becoming riotous when Humphrey, smiling broadly, returned pulling three more pot-lamps on a baggage trolley.

"I reckon spare pot-lamps be as good as the blanking plugs themselves," he announced.

The solution was obvious, and secretly I was ashamed for not having thought of it myself. I took Humphrey to one side and thanked him discreetly.

"Don't thank I," he broadcast loudly. "Twer Jack's notion. Ol' Wheeler done it again, eh?"

My eyes lowered.

Edwin Phillips, having dealt with the day's goods invoices, approached me before retiring for the night.

"There is a gentleman in the Booking Hall to see you," he said.

I went there immediately, and beheld in the pallid gaslight the silhoutte of a gentleman wearing a cape. My visitor removed his dripping top-hat and stepped out from the shadows to reveal a severe face angled at one cheek to support a monocle. His hair, being somewhat receded, was little more than a black film upon his head, and this contrasted starkly with his thin grey moustache trimmed to a neat, upturned 'V'.

With a puddle of rainwater forming at my feet, I waited for my visitor to introduce himself, hoping that he was not another foreigner with a broken fobwatch.

"I am Lawrence Albury," the stranger whirred, removing his eyepiece to wipe it.

In view of the cabriolet saga, a visit from the squire had been inevitable, but I was indisposed to wrangle with the gentleman at this late hour. Yet to wrangle was his intent. I had dealt with this sort of dignitary before. The fact that I was tired and no longer in possession of my wits would not qualify me for leniency. Indeed, in all probability, the squire had chosen late evening to launch his offensive because he knew that a stationmaster's day was more exhausting than his own.

My sin, of course, was having taken a goose in payment for a service not rendered. To make matters worse, I could not return the goose because I had given it to a widow of the alms houses. Not that this would have constituted recompense.

"I am here to register my dismay at your handling of my property," he said.

There was a rich, almost mesmeric quality to the squire's voice, but the harmony of it was spoiled completely by the clatter of artificial teeth. These would have been made of either wood or porcelain.

"The defaced conveyance is presently with the Wheelright of Upford Cross, Jay," the gentleman proceeded to berate me, "and all expenses incurred shall be your expense. Do you understand that?"

I nodded compliantly.

Plainly the squire had considered it his duty to make a personal appearance and engrave upon the mind of this newcomer his status as the valley's most inveterate land-owner. Indeed, such was the hostility of this local tyrant that he was blind to the fact that the exercise was unnecessary. The enervated stationmaster he saw before him had no desire to challenge anyone's jealously guarded unpopularity.

Yet, without provocation, the squire became increasingly incensed, all the while casting a marble eye towards the disturbance over pot-lamps on

Platform Two. Since this was none of his business, I closed the double-doors of the Booking Hall to block his view. The squire opened them again defiantly.

"Your superiors shall hear of this woeful episode," he warned me. "I will make it clear that I doubt your aptitude for this post. Personally I would take a whip to the lot of you for such incompetence."

Squire Albury had started his complaint with more dignity than he finished it. His ability to incite himself to rage merely by recapitulating his grievance was quite frightening, and I fear that my silence throughout his remonstrance, though not calculated to do so, antagonized him further. The bellicose Mr. Albury just did not allow himself time to see that I was wholly contrite; meekly awaiting an opportunity to apologize. As a result, by the time the clacking of his teeth had ceased, I was myself incensed, and felt that he could whistle for his apology.

The squire could think only to curse me.

"Damn you!" he spat, and returned to his chaise, a hoodless carriage quite unsuitable for inclement weather.

The bad tempered dignitary unleashed his surplus venom upon a wild-eyed pony and took off.

The Giddiford train eventually left twenty minutes late, its First and Second Class passengers lamplit but not amused, its spirited Third Class passengers in total darkness but highly amused.

CHAPTER TEN

FIRST DAY OVER WITH

Hauling the last train of the day, *Lacy* trundled into Upshott Station on its return trip from Giddiford, and Driver MacGregor alighted the footplate to have a word in my ear. Grinning at me devilishly, he stopped some distance away and pulled the creases from his oily waistcoat. From this somewhat protracted instalment I sensed that he was the indulgent bearer of bad tidings.

Before uttering his piece, however, the Scotchman came closer and beamed at me mischievously with two bloodshot eyes set in the margin between his blazing red beard and red tartan tammy, and scratched his nose lazily. His nose was a bulbous protuberance which had long since been ruddied to a strawberry by the heat of the fire.

"Whech of yoor orramen laid on the Chinese crackers?" he wheezed.

"Crackers?" I queried him.

"Aye, the pot-lamps, Mr. Jay. Fezzling like firewhurruks they whurr. Och, and the smoke was enough te asphyxiate ye. I should expiscate the matter ef I whurr ye."

"Very well," I responded listlessly, having no idea what MacGregor was talking about.

"Aye well, I should, Mr. Jay. 'Tes a good theng we whurr nay inside Splashgate Tunnel or we'd have had passengers breathing theer last."

"Splendid," I replied through a stifled yawn.

Driver MacGregor scratched his head and gazed

at me for a while. My docile response to his grave account had banjaxed him.

"As a matter of fact, Mr. Jay, the pot-lamps whurr sengeng wi' the skirl of the pipes," he boomed loudly in one final attempt to startle me. I was too tired to be startled. "Tes why weer running late. We'd te empty and refill all the lamps at Weddlecombe. Tesnay easy making up for lost time." My continued silence upon the matter eventually exasperated the driver, as I had intended it to, and he threw his hands in the air. "Aye, but then ye dunny noo what ahm tocknaboot, do ye?"

MacGregor was wrong. I did know what he was 'tocknaboot'. He was 'talking about' the late running of his train, and had conjured up this uncharacteristic concern for passenger safety in order to provide himself with the necessary vehicle for lodging an excuse.

"The details of your poor timekeeping are of no concern to me," I closed the subject, removing myself to the Booking Hall.

In the flickering light of the departing Blodcaster train I spotted Wheeler and Turner sloping off home. With a crooked finger I sprang across their path and beckoned them to my office to learn of their progress in snaring the lamp oil thief. It seemed more than likely that Driver MacGregor's 'fizzling pot-lamps' had something to do with Jack Wheeler's 'smoke telegraph' signals, and I decided to get to the bottom of the matter by intimidating the two clerks with a stern word or two.

Unfortunately, being gifted with no demeanour of authority, my stern words failed to cause any apprehension and I was tendered an explanation nothing short of flapdoodle. It was obvious that something had gone wrong with Jack Wheeler's plan but, the hour being late, I was compelled to postpone the hearing until tomorrow when I would be less of a pushover. The two clerks, believing that they had been let off the hook, backed out of my office deftly.

I concluded my duties with a tour of the station, shutting all the doors and windows and securing their locks, and watching the darkness follow me like ink soaking through blotting paper as I dimmed the gasses.

How relieved I was that my first day was over with. I had thought it would never end. Fatigued and demoralized, and with the unfamiliar musty smell of my new abode thick in my nostrils, I climbed the stairs to my quarters.

The station house was curiously quiet, but not so my mind. My cavernous head had become the haunt of Squire Albury's clattering teeth. 'I doubt your aptitude for this post' the porcelain incisors percussed, and I began to wonder if they were right.

I kneeled beside my bed for a while, and prayed for deliverance. I was not equipped for an alternative occupation should my career on the railways come to a premature end, and I explained to my Maker that on this, my first night at Upshott, I was feeling vulnerable in a way that I had never done before.

You will appreciate, I am sure, that when a single man finds himself in a strange place which fills him with such foreboding, not only does he lack the support of old colleagues, who would rally around him, he yearns for a domestic companion to fill the void. Someone to offer him encouragement.

For me, then, in addition to the stationmaster's inevitable isolation, there was an element of personal loneliness to grapple with. Quite a demon at times.

Yet no matter what the dint to my self-esteem, my staff would be expecting me to meet the 5.05am Mail Train on the morrow with all the stature of an experienced stationmaster, blissfully unaware that it was they who had reduced me to this ebb in the first place.

Not wishing to disappoint the trusting simpletons, all of whom I was expected to set a good example, I climbed into my bed to get some much needed sleep.

Having reclined myself, and having wriggled and squirmed until I had made the acquaintance of all the unfamiliar lumps and bumps that were to become my nightly tormentors, I snuffed my bedside candle and shut my eyes, expecting exhaustion to claim me with ease.

* * *

With so few hours in which to repose, I was not pleased at having been woken repeatedly by a rainstorm lashing fitfully at my window. Nor was I pleased by the Waiting Room sign squeaking all night like a demented bat just below my window sill. Also I could have done without the whistling of an otter seeking a mate in the stream beyond the sidings.

If I slept a total of two hours, I fared well.

CHAPTER ELEVEN

SECOND DAY BEGINS

By dawn I was back on the platforms, breathing air that was lighter than claret, and this did more to refresh me than a night spent badgered to distraction by rattles and squeaks. Without delay I took to the footbridge to savour the morning's moist redolence before the first locomotive of the day could sully it. The air was as pure as crystal, with everything keen edged and glistening larger than life. The sky, although a cold blue to the west, was in the east aflame with a new sun pulling mist from the dewy soil and stencilling long shadows down the slopes. Verily, to see the disbanding cloud-wrack of yesterday's storm was, after so many disappointments, to feel one's heart beat anew.

Before continuing the story, allow me to acquaint you with the phenomenon of Upshott's belated sunrise. This was caused by Splashgate Hill to the east of the village. When the sky was clear, the sun would lift the community from the shadow of this hill as if granting some primordial privilege, by bursting through a circle of standing stones upon the summit. It was a spectacle I found strangely stirring.

To my eye, the sun's illumination behind those standing stones transformed them into children at play, a stage-lit cameo of infancy, suggestive that only by new light is new life spawned. While witnessing this event it was easy to imagine that the 'little ones' upon the hill moved occasionally, when they thought no one was looking. No one, that is, except me, whom they appeared to regard as a friend. I was personally addressed by their charm.

This morning, standing upon the footbridge, impaled by the sun's first shards of amber, it seemed that the 'little ones' were performing a mime, a mime which allegorized with unnerving skill my doubts about myself. It was as if the dazzling circle they created in the sunshine deliberately challenged a faith which had not yet mapped itself upon my conscious mind. And elusive though was this faith to grasp, and by no means ephemeral, I knew that it represented something ominous.

To spare my eyes further glare from the sun I looked away and surveyed my more immediate surroundings, lifting my hat to my old friend nature. Whilst doing so, I was hit on the head by a slimy dollop of unidentified material. Cautiously I looked up.

Above me, in an ash tree overhanging the footbridge, was a pair of magpies chuttering and shaking dew from the branches. Thankful that the missile had been but water, and not wishing to be struck by something less pleasant, I replaced my hat and transferred myself to the opposite end of the footbridge.

From here I admired the silver railway stretching purposefully towards each horizon, and was struck again, but this time by the notion that the line looked like a frozen shooting star, down the tail of which one could slide to another world. It was, after all, a tail which spanned the chasms of both distance and culture.

Such reflective moments did much to restore my self-esteem, and through this one I had managed to rediscover my sense of novelty and pride in having become a fully fledged stationmaster.

Ivor Hales was unlocking the signalbox. He waved to me and drew my attention to a siding upon which was standing a solitary ballast truck. Across the truck was stretched a canvas sheet, at one end of which was a depression filled with rainwater. In the pool so formed were crows, as polished as boots, squabbling and scuttering for bathing space. Particularly amusing was the fact that some of the crows were waddling to the top of the cover only to slide back into the pool again, seemingly for the delight of it. I have always revered birds as nature's comics, and watching their antics around Upshott Station uplifted me wonderfully. I found that I was ready for another day.

Quite suddenly the 'down' platform was populated. Harry Peckham, whistling one of his rambling melodies, was attending his empty mail-cart amid a crescent of domestic servants. The servants, from such influencial households as the Highams' and the Lacys', always gravitated around Mr. Peckham's cart to trade their gossip and exchange pleasantries. Indeed, nearest the Postmaster was the now familiar figure of Squire Albury's coachman, having ridden up from Albury Hall somewhat better insulated than most from the damp morning air. The mist had settled upon the dark green fustian of his thick double-breasted cape and crystallized it like a sugared fruit. The coachman was, like most in the gathering, waiting to collect the London newspapers for his master.

Being short staffed, the proprietor of The Coach House, Upshott's largest though not its principal hotel, had dispatched his ostler to meet the Mail Train. This was an ugly and menacing cove who was to cause great distress to an ex colleague of mine later in the year.

Looking as wan as ever, Mr. Phillips appeared upon the platform and became irritated by the presence of the solitary goods truck parked near the footbridge, so I joined him in an investigation of its contents. Our approach sent the bathing party of crows into a spray of flight, leaving us both with glistening uniforms.

It was Mr. Phillips's misfortune to be the one to lift the cover, and, having had his curiosity satisfied with a nasty shock, he let go of the canvas smartly and pinched his delicate nose. At this point all became clear. In an attempt to deceive me, someone had moved the sewage from its long established position on Road Five, where Mr. Phillips had become accustomed to 'overlooking' it, to this new and rather stupid position outside the Goods shed. That same someone had also covered the fetid heap with canvas in the hope of disguising its unsociable nature.

It was obvious that my Goods Clerk had not been party to the ruse but I censured him nevertheless.

"I believe I requested its removal, not its relocation," I said.

"I was never in favour of harbouring this beastly stuff from the word go, Mr. Jay," Mr. Phillips pleaded indignantly.

"Who orchestrated it?" I asked him, exploiting his moment of contrition.

"Jack Wheeler," he replied, without surprising me very much.

"It will take more than a sheet of hemp to put me off this scent," I said. "Have it removed immediately."

How many more times would I have to issue this instruction before the truck finally went away?

Mr. Phillips replaced his monocle and studied me as if I were a curious surgical specimen.

"I do hope there is to be no power struggle, Mr. Jay," he sighed ominously. "There can be only one Stationmaster. I'm afraid your predecessor, Mr. Mildenhew, had no grasp of this precept, and history shows us the result."

Mr. Phillips departed for his office, leaving me to grapple with his theory. Perhaps Jack Wheeler was the real stationmaster, and I merely a figurehead?

* * *

Where was Diggory? The level crossing gates had been swung, and the air was rippling with the approach of the Mail Train, yet none of Diggory's duties had been carried out. With the station draw-well at Busy Linton having been fouled by misuse, the Stationmaster there was expecting several pitchers of fresh water to be aboard the first train of the day. When I checked the allotted pitchers, I found them empty, so I set Snimple the task of filling them at once.

Something was wrong. The driver of the approaching locomotive was sounding his whistle frantically, and no sooner had the engine reached the platform, still travelling at quite a speed, than the fireman had leapt from the footplate and was stumbling towards me waving his arms.

"There's been an accident!" he blurted, pointing towards the parcels van.

CHAPTER TWELVE

ACCIDENT ON THE VIADUCT

The Mail Train's Senior Guard threw open the double doors of the trailing van and revealed Diggory squirming on the floorboards. The young porter was manifestly in distress, and I rushed to his assistance, whereupon I learned that he had been struck by the train while crossing Widdlecombe Viaduct.

"How badly is he hurt?" I asked, taking the boy's head in my hands.

"Hard to tell," the Senior Guard replied. "According to the driver, it were a glancing blow at worst."

I instructed Snimple to fetch Doctor Bentley whilst Humphrey and I carried the gangling lad up to my private room to make him comfortable upon my bed.

"I think the young man is only bruised," the fireman told me anxiously. "But he's in a state of shock. I've come across shock, Stationmaster. I know what shock does to you."

"Indeed?" I responded.

"Ay," he replied. "I'm suffering from it myself. This porter of yours wandered straight across the line without hint of caution. It were just as if he was in one of that Doctor Braid's mystical trances." Doctor Braid, I should explain, was a pioneer hypnotist who had made a name for himself in newspapers and scientific journals by mesmerizing people. "Mark me well, Mr. Jay, there's something weighty on this lad's mind."

"The young man has mentioned nothing significant," I replied. "But then, this is only my second day in charge here."

Diggory's hair was matted with grease and clotted with blood, and so, to me, it seemed obvious that he was suffering from something worse than shock. Also his face was besmirched with the culm of his rescuers, suggesting that the muscular fireman had been the one to lift him from the line. I just hoped that the boy had not broken any ribs near his heart.

Further, I was bothered that no one had taken the trouble to recover the young porter's company cap, although quite why such a minor thing should upset me I did not know.

With Diggory's head still in my hands, I instructed Jack Wheeler to go to my office and look up the lad's home address. "Send Mr. Maynard to inform the boy's mother of the incident, Jack," I said, and added: "And impress upon Mr. Maynard the need to avoid alarming her." Jack twitched and set about it.

A little later I accompanied the London and South Western fireman back to his locomotive and thanked him for his presence of mind. Following this I had the water pitchers for Busy Linton placed aboard the train and gave the train its 'right away'.

The drumming of the locomotive faded into the hills, but the tingle of gossip lingered.

I was in my room with Diggory when Doctor Bentley, whom I noticed was wearing a night-shirt beneath his overcoat, was ushered in by Snimple. The Doctor examined Diggory thoroughly and diagnosed shock, adding that the young porter was also slightly concussed but otherwise unhurt, save a few minor cuts to the head which had bled misleadingly. There were no broken ribs, but the lad would develop some tender bruises in due course.

"It is fortunate that there is a severe gradient on the viaduct," I ventured. "As a result the train was travelling quite slowly."

"Has he been sick?" the Doctor interrupted me brusquely.

"Not as far as I am aware," I replied.

Doctor Bentley began dabbing the boy's wrists, which I knew to be cold and clammy.

"Mmm, he's sweating a little, and his pulse is weak," he observed. "Be so good as to bring me some fresh water, Jay, would you?"

This I did, and the Doctor moistened Diggory's lips carefully. The boy groaned in response.

"Perhaps he would like to drink a little of the water," I suggested. "Or better still, a tot of brandy. I believe we have some brandy in the medicine chest. I shall go and..."

"You'll do no such thing, Jay," the Doctor halted me sharply. "The patient will have a thirst, but he must not be allowed to drink while in this condition. Least of all liquor. Just keep him on his back with his legs raised like this," he instructed me, and placed my pillow under the boy's muddy boots. "Master Smith may be confused when he comes to, but the malaise will pass. Send someone to fetch me then, and I will give his lesions one last check before renewing the dressings. He'll live!"

"I am greatly relieved to hear it, Doctor," I sighed. "And so shall his mother be, I'll warrant."

Thereafter I left Diggory alone only when unavoidable. One such occasion was while having a word with Mr. Swain, the Chief Ganger, who had brought to my office an absentee reporting back for duty.

"How is your foot?" I asked the sad-eyed platelayer, exchanging a wink with Mr. Swain. "In future I should keep a sharper lookout for Mr. Albury's gamekeeper. Either that, or leave his pheasants be," I advised him.

My advice was wasted on the poor fellow, of course. The loss of a day's pay would serve only to increase his need to poach. Mr. Swain doffed his faded straw boater and escorted the limping ganghand out of my office. I returned to Diggory's side immediately.

I was gazing out of my bedroom window when someone knocked at my door. At first I did not respond, for I thought I had seen the sylphlike belle in white lace again. But with my encounter with Mrs. Goadby still large in my mind, I heeded my better judgement and ignored the urge to give chase. *You are a stationmaster now, not a lunatic* I told myself and crossed my bedroom to open the door. *Why, next you will be seeing the sylph in fat old Humphrey!*

I opened my door, and there stood Humphrey beaming at me with a friendly smile.

"Boy all right now is he?" he enquired. "His mother be here. Send her up, shall I?"

"Please, Humphrey," I replied wearily.

Humphrey clumped down the stairs heavily and invited Mrs. Smith to proceed, whereupon petite footsteps creaked their way to the landing and halted outside my door. I poised myself to greet Mrs. Smith with a few well chosen words of comfort, and stepped out onto the landing purposefully. But before I could utter a word, my composure was felled like a tree.

Facing me anxiously was the most unexpected visitor imaginable.

CHAPTER THIRTEEN

DISCOVERED: THE BELLE IN WHITE LACE

There before me stood the elusive belle in white lace. Although not in lace, she was every bit as enchanting at close quarters as I had imagined. And not only that, by jove, she was the mother of my Junior Porter! I considered pinching myself to establish the truth of the affair, for I had been troubled by some pretty peculiar dreams lately, and it was quite possible that waking up had been one of them.

It shames me to admit it, but I stared at Mrs. Smith for so long in disbelief that I must have appeared ill-bred, for her perfume had filled my head with wayside flowers and rendered me almost insensible. But not only was my tongue paralysed, my feet were glued to the floor by the woman's china blue eyes, and I could not step forward to shake her hand.

When, at last, my strength returned, I greeted Mrs. Smith with a trifling welcome which must have seemed clumsily inappropriate for such a grave occasion.

"Why, how do you do?" I stuttered politely.

Delivered with such levity, these words must have bordered on the insensitive, although I suspect that Mrs. Smith was too distracted to notice.

I thought it tactful to leave my delightful visitor alone with her son for a while, so I left the room and went downstairs. In any case, I had arranged with my Horse Superintendent to inspect the company stables.

Now, on my way to see Mr. Maynard I stopped outside the Booking Hall entrance to take a pinch of snuff, and here I overheard a conversation which convinced me that in Upshott Station there was no such thing as a normal day.

It seemed that not only I, the Stationmaster, was smitten with someone of the fairer sex. Mr. Troke, whose voice was reverberating from Mr. Phillips's office window, revealed that any scheme I might devise to acquaint myself more fully with Diggory's mother without appearing improprietous, would pale into insignificance beside the bizarre romance of one of my porters. I could scarcely believe my ears, and recall the conversation vividly.

Mr. Troke: "It grieves me, Edwin, that a fulsome woman such as Emily Higham should pick Snimple to trifle with. But then, she is a coquette who enjoys flirting with working class men. She'd give a tinker the glad eye if it passed an afternoon. Does she not realize how perilous this is?"

Mr. Phillips: "Perhaps not William, but I am bound to point out that whilst Snimple may speak a different language to the rest of us, he is quite a decent fellow. If anyone is in peril it is Snimple, I fear. However, with any luck, it is only his knowledge of horticulture which fascinates her so."

Mr. Troke: "But I've got fascinating knowledge too, and I can be discreet. What's more, I wouldn't be so daft as to fill my head with notions of wedlock. Snimple marry a Higham? Huh! It's unthinkable! Absurd! He's whistling in the park."

Mr. Phillips: "Just so. But be truthful now, William. What miffs you is that it is not you with whom this 'fulsome' woman has chosen to trifle. It is the peril Snimple is in that you covet."

Mr. Troke: "I don't covet Snimple. I just don't like waste. I'd trifle back, not talk of flowers and butterflies."

Mr. Phillips: "You would do no such thing, William. In any case, how old are you? Thirty-two? Thirty-three? Snimple may be Snimple, but he is ten years your junior, and about the same age as this Higham girl. No, I am sure the fellow does not yearn to be spliced. He has the misgiving to stay on the leeward side of the nuptuals. I say let Snimple have his day, for the poor fellow is bound to have few of them."

Mr. Troke: "Yeh? Well, unless Snimple learns to keep his assignations unbeknown, the Brigadier will be after him with his regimental sword, to make alterations."

Mr. Phillips: "You are right, of course. The ruling classes have a lamentable habit of allowing their progeny to learn of life at the expense of common folk such as you and I, and then rounding on us when the lessons prove unsatisfactory."

Mr. Troke: "You can't win. The nobs are all the same. Every each and one of them."

The inimitable Mr. Phillips demonstrated his boredom with the subject by bursting into song, and I heard Mr. Troke leave the room.

Thus forewarned, I knew that Mr. Troke would be looking to step into the breach should Snimple's love life run off the rails. Indeed, I suspected that Mr. Troke would be actively out to derail it.

Somewhat distracted by this prospect, I moved away to join Mr. Maynard and inspect the horses.

* * *

I left the stables afterwards scarcely able to recall what I had seen.

* * *

Diggory was sitting upright and complaining of a thirst, so I sent for hot drinks to revive his mother and myself, and dispatched someone to fetch Doctor Bentley. Whilst the Doctor renewed Diggory's dressings, I explained to the charming Mrs. Smith that her son would not be required for duty until he had recovered fully.

"I think we can overlook Diggory's absence for a while," I sympathized, somewhat boldly given the company's rules regarding sick leave. "Just between you and me, of course," I added confidentially.

If kept unofficial, the Junior Porter would lose no pay, and I had been told that Mrs. Smith's circumstances were meagre.

With over two hours until the next Widdlecombe train, I wondered what more immediate travel arrangements might best suit the boy and his mother. One thing was clear, Diggory was too shaky to walk or ride a horse.

Doctor Bentley came to the rescue.

"Perhaps I might offer you a lift home, Mrs. Smith," he grated. "I have my chaise outside, and I am sure I can squeeze you both in."

Concealing my jealousy, I shook the divine Mrs. Smith's hand and partook my leave. You may accuse me of wishful thinking, but I fancy I detected in Mrs. Smith's eye a twinkle which was not present for Doctor Bentley.

Even wearing a simple cotton work-dress, sans white lace, Mrs. Smith had bewitched me. Our meeting, although a brief and strained affair, and brought about by unfortunate circumstances, had at least unveiled the mystery of the belle in white lace.

* * *

Tom Turner, William Troke, and Jack Wheeler filed into my office.

"Explain," I commanded them curtly.

The torpid Mr. Turner and the mercurial Mr. Wheeler exchanged glances, seemingly unable to articulate their doubtless well rehearsed excuse.

"Come now," I prompted them. "I want no humbug, just an explanation. The fizzling pot-lamps on Driver MacGregor's train last night have something to do with your scheme to catch the pilferer, do they not?"

"What pilferer?" Mr. Troke asked stupidly.

"The one who has been stealing lamp oil," I answered him with a deedy eye.

Jack muttered something and scratched his head through his matted curly hair.

"Speak up!" I pounced.

"Me and William spiked a drum of lamp oil and put it in a prominent position to make it the most likely took," he spoke up. "Tom reckons it's the Locksmith's boy from Penpool, Mr. Jay. The Stores shed lock 'asn't been forced, and that boy comes 'ere regular to get pig iron. I reckon..."

"A bird in hand is worthless," Mr. Troke interjected with one of his maffled sayings.

"Never mind all that. With what did you spike that oil?" I interrupted.

"Well, Mr. Jay," Jack explained. "We broke open one or two of them self-detonating fog signals, and emptied out the black powder..."

"Gunpowder! I've heard enough," I halted him and switched my gaze to his accomplice. "So, in all the confusion last night, confusion which you caused, Mr. Turner, you filled the pot-lamps aboard the night Giddiford train with an explosive concoction. I can scarcely believe it, even of you cretins."

Much to my surprise, my outburst caused a degree of contrition.

Will there be disciplinary action?" Mr. Turner enquired fertively.

"I shall think hard upon it," I told him.

I had decided to leave these three fish on their hooks for a while. Although, alas, I knew I would have to throw them back eventually because my own position was more precarious than theirs. As the Stationmaster, I had been the one to authorize the laying of the trap, so, naturally, Head Office would deem me responsible for the resulting mishap.

"We may catch the weasel yet," Jack purred seductively with a hollow grin.

"Leave," I snapped with feigned disgust. I was at risk of seeing the funny side of the affair.

Before the bungling trio could get through my office door, I recalled Jack for further questioning. To unnerve him, I caught his eye and rumbled with stern brevity:

"One minute, Mr. Wheeler."

I was learning fast that economy of words gave me a psychological advantage over the clerk, and I certainly needed that.

"Sewage? I queried him.

Jack stared at me with transparent innocence.

"There are two people responsible for what takes place in the sidings, apart from myself," I began. "They are the Rollingstock Superintendent and the Goods Clerk. Yet both strangely resemble puppets. Let word filter through to the puppeteer, Jack, that only the Stationmaster pulls the strings here. Mr. Phillips seems to think there will be a power struggle, but I can assure you there will not. The puppeteer will acknowledge my authority by having that treated sewage removed, and the truck which contained it flushed out at the water tower. Will he not?"

At first Jack said nothing. In a lingering silence his face puckered convulsively and returned to its self-assured twinkle. It puckered again upon registering the continuity of my discontented stare.

"Anything you say, Mr. Jay," he acquiesced at last, but not without a defiant hint of condescension.

At this point Jack expected me to dismiss him, for which reason I detained him further. His independent spirit had yet to be dampened to my satisfaction.

"I do not expect to find the entire load of sullage spread hurriedly over the flower beds," I cautioned him after an extrinsic pause. "And take your hands out of your pockets when I am talking to you, Wheeler. Your hands are always in your pockets."

Eventually it dawned upon Jack that I was not going to release him until he demonstrated genuine subservience instead of patronizing agreement. It took a while, but in the end I gained the upper hand.

* * *

The 7.45am Blodcaster train clattered into Platform One behind *Lacy*. Driver MacGregor stepped off the footplate to consult me, pointing to a crane-truck appended to his rake of four passenger carriages.

"The swinger's for ye," he told me in a tone suggesting that its presence was a hindrance. "The Geddeford Superentendent apologizes for nay sendeng et to ye yesterday. Et wasney available then."

My stomach churned. I was taking delivery of a monument to my previous day's ineptitude.

I hearkened to the whistle of a second locomotive as the Giddiford train arrived in the opposite direction pulling three swingers of its own; a luggage van, a horse box, and a flat-truck conveying an ancient stanhope. Fortunately none of these vehicles required detaching at Upshott, so, with my teeth on edge at the clitter of the brakes bringing the 'up' train to rest, I took a deep breath and arranged for the crane truck to be uncoupled from the 'down' train.

With the shadow of the Giddiford train pulsating through the windows of the Blodcaster train and vaulting across our faces, *Lacy's* driver and I watched impatiently while the fireman disconnected the unwanted winch. And with my voice masked by the noise of the mixed traffic arrival, I turned aside and admonished myself for having omitted to cancel my request for the wretched vehicle.

The two trains departed almost simultaneously, their volumes of smoke parting like music-hall curtains to reveal the mobile crane abandoned alongside Platform One. Somewhat sheepishly, I retired to my office to deal with the day's paperwork, leaving Mr. Maynard and one of his horses to tow the two-and-a-half ton crane to a siding.

Looking at my paperwork, I discovered that I had received from Headquarters a directive concerning the installation of a 'weighing chair' at Upshott, for the amusement of passengers. My station was also to be allocated an automatic machine for vending sweetmeats. Alarmed by this, I sat down immediately and wrote to my superiors expressing my reluctance to accommodate these contraptions whilst my platforms were undergoing realignment. Indeed, I went on to make it clear that I was loth to clutter the thoroughfares of my station with them at any future time.

According to the memorandum, Giddiford Junction was to boast a 'scent fountain', and Blodcaster a 'sight-testing' machine of all things. These were the trappings of the large mainline station, not the rural branchline, and they pandered to a growing obsession with trivia.

I had also received an outrageous quarterly bill from the Company Veterinary Surgeon. His revised shoeing and general charges totalled five pounds, ten shillings and three-pence, not including retaining fee. Perhaps the practitioner was beginning to view the railway as a milch-cow, or, more probably, he was testing his luck on a green stationmaster.

Afterwards, going through some incomplete files, I discovered another of Mr. Mildenhew's tangles. It seemed that I had inherited a deadlocked dispute over a consignment of strawberries. The fruit, having come from Covent Garden, had failed to reach Blodcaster last summer because it had perished in a siding in Upshott where, allegedly, the wagon had been thought empty. A tight bundle of memoranda testified to the fact that the wrangle over compensation was interminable.

I, unlike Mr. Mildenhew, would settle the matter.

My last duty took me to the signalbox to speak with Ivor Hales. Regrettably, in line with the policy of the London and South Western Railway Company, the South Exmoor's Board of Directors had once again refused Sunday pay to members of the Signalmen's and Switchman's United Aid Society. My sympathy rested squarely with the signalmen whose 'day of rest' would continue to be, in fact, a day of unpaid labour.

Returning to my office, straining to hear the faint murmur of a train descending the far side of the valley, I detected a closer sound. That of someone clambering about on the mobile crane. I was about to investigate when Jack Wheeler popped up from behind a cog-wheel, his nose twitching like a rodent, and handed me a piece of paper. He climbed down to the ballast and joined me while studying the note, grinning readily. I did not like that grin. I ignored it and read the message.

Stationmaster Jay: When finished with the crane, please forward it to Busy Linton where it is also required. G.W.V.

Now I understood Jack's amusement. Had I left the crane coupled to the Blodcaster train, not only would the Blodcaster train have left on time but the wretched crane would have continued with it to

Busy Linton, instead of haunting me with its presence at Upshott. Thanks to my stupidity, the wretched contraption would now have to remain in my sidings until the 1.40pm ‘down’.

CHAPTER FOURTEEN

BIG STONES AND BIGWIGS

The peace of Upshott village was shattered by the approach of the bi-weekly Stone Train, bound for Splashgate.

Splashgate was a break-of-gauge transhipment point serving Squire Albury's quarry railway, situated about a mile down the line. Facilities at Splashgate were minimal, comprising a makeshift platform for quarry workers, a woefully inadequate stone hoist, and the squire's two-foot gauge rail-head incorporating mineral siding and engine release loop. No standard gauge siding had been laid by the SER.

I should explain that the railway terms 'up' and 'down', when applied to the steeply inclined South Exmoor Railway, were something of a misnomer and the cause of much mirth. You see, it is railway parlance to describe trains heading away from the capital or principal terminus, in our case Giddiford Junction, as 'down' trains, and trains approaching the principal terminus as 'up' trains. However, 'down' trains on the South Exmoor Railway were most definitely struggling upwards, and 'up' trains most definitely coasting downwards.

Bearing this in mind, you will appreciate that when in railway terminology I speak of Splashgate as being further down the line, topologically speaking I am saying that it was further up the line. Public confusion was inevitable.

To continue the story, the transhipment point to which I refer was to be found perched on a low embankment in the shadow of Splashgate Hill, and was where stone hewn from Squire Albury's quarry was transferred from the tubs of his two-foot gauge mineral railway to the four-foot eight-and-a-half-inch gauge trucks of the South Exmoor Railway.

No train clanged and crashed with more fury than the Stone Train with its battered wagons devoid of their stabilizing cargo, and each Tuesday, upon its arrival, the LSWR locomotive hauling these empties would be detached and left to fuss about the station on minor duties until relieved by an SER locomotive from Blodcaster. The empties would then be pushed by the South Exmoor locomotive to their rendezvous with the squire's mineral train, this actually being a succession of workings to be unloaded manually by an army of brawny quarrymen.

With no standard gauge siding upon which to park, the SER Stone Train would have to remain on the 'running' line while the mineral was being transhipped, thus obstructing the railway to all through-traffic for over an hour. Although no other SER trains were diagrammed to run over the line during this time, Ivor Hales would be tense, for no signals had yet been installed which could check an oncoming train in the event of an error, and the transhipment operation took place in all visibilities.

Obviously it was important not to delay commencement of this operation, and so, with repeated reference to my timepiece, I monitored proceedings from my office doorway. London and South Western locomotive *Number 222* was simmering quietly at Platform One, its fireman trimming the coal, its driver polishing the gauge glasses. As far as this footplate crew was concerned, nothing further could be done until the arrival of the SER relief locomotive which, on this occasion, was 0-6-0 saddle-tank *Exmoor*.

Unlike SER locomotives, all of which were tank engines of one sort or another, *Number 222* was a tender engine. It had been built by George England & Co. for use on the Somerset and Dorset Joint Railway, but had since fallen into the hands of the London and South Western.

I left my office doorway and wandered over to the rake of sixteen wooden mineral trucks which *Number 222* had brought with it. All were of the pointed bulkhead design, and most were owner-marked *'Amalgamated Stone Merchants'*. A few others had been roughly stencilled *'Albury Quarries (Ondle Valley) Ltd.'* while the majority of the remainder were company wagons pyrographically engraved with the SER monogram.

I expected *Exmoor* to be late, for I knew that the engine would be kept waiting for a clear road out of Blodcaster, the incoming train blocking its path being the one I had delayed while uncoupling the mobile crane which I did not need. On the South Exmoor Railway, just one oversight could set in motion a lamentable chain of delays to which there was no end.

To my great relief *Exmoor* came trundling down Longhurdle Embankment only two minutes late, and tooting its whistle as if to boast of a spritely run. There were occasions when it took presence of mind not to think of these locomotives as personalities.

London and South Western locomotive *Number 222* was steamed away to the mainline whence it came, and *Exmoor* was coupled to the rear of the mineral trucks to propel them to Splashgate. By propelling the empties instead of pulling them, the locomotive would be at the head of its train for the heavily loaded return journey.

Now, in these early days of the railways, empty mineral trucks tended to derail when pushed, and, to make matters worse, locomen engaged in such manoeuvres often could not see what lay ahead of them. This was not a salubrious state of affairs for anyone standing upon the line, which was why, as a rule, trains running backwards were preceded by someone on foot bearing a red flag.

At Upshott, this unenviable task befell Mr. Troke, he being the Rollingstock Superintendent, and Mr. Troke did not welcome the duty. You see, it was not unheard of for a 'pilotman' to be run down by the very train he was heralding, owing to the engine driver's inability to restrain his steed to walking speed for any length of time. Many people claimed that the reason why such manoeuvres were so dangerous was because there was always some fool with a flag standing in front of the train.

With the Stone Train gone, peace returned to Upshott Station and I consulted the day's traffic diagram to see what spare time it afforded me. Here I found reference to Humphrey's 'unexpected' train by which the top brass were to make their surprise visit. The schedule contained no specific details, merely a scribbled note to the effect that a 'Directors Special' would make use of a suitable 'train path', which, in plain English, meant that it might come at any quiet time.

However, my experience of junketing bigwigs told me that their round trip would be timed to allow luncheon to be taken at Blodcaster. It was axiomatic, therefore, that the Special would come through Upshott circa 11.30am. Had I the skill to decipher the chatterings of the 'electric grapevine' I would have discovered more, no doubt.

Exmoor returned at 9.35am with its brakes grinding against the massive load bearing down upon its drawbar, and this puzzled me. The Stone Train had no reason to stop at Upshott on its way back to the mainline. It was supposed to continue at speed to the exchange sidings at Giddiford. Yet, against all the coercion of a greedy squire's merchandise descending to a lucrative market, the train was indeed trying to stop. A smell of hot metal accompanied a shower of sparks from the axle beneath the brakesman's van, and wisps of wood smoke could be seen peeling away from *Exmoor's* primitive brake blocks.

The mystery was solved a second later when Mr. Troke alighted the footplate of the little black and green engine and stumbled over a keg of Leicestershire salt. The salt, incidentally, was awaiting the collection of a local potter. The squealing of brakes ceased, and the mineral train began to gather speed again. It seemed that my Rollingstock Superintendent had called upon a locomotive hauling thirty tons of mineral to provide a lift.

Was the fellow so unfit that he had been constrained to bide his time at Splashgate for over an hour in order to spare himself a one mile walk back to work? I doubted it. Applying my stationmaster's nose, I doubted it very much.

A fishing rod provided the answer. This I watched Mr. Troke fail to catch as it was thrown crazily from the footplate of the engine as the wheels bucked the worn rails. Evidently Mr. Troke considered his life of such little value that it was worth risking for an hour's poaching on the edge of

Squire Albury's private lake. Quite what I was supposed to do to prevent my staff straying in such circumstances I could not think. I hurried over and challenged the fellow about his absence.

"It's custom and practise," he proffered glibly, scraping together a gowpen of spilt salt.

"Who gave you permission to go fishing?" I asked sternly.

"Don't need permission. It's custom and practise," Mr. Troke repeated, funnelling the salt back into the keg.

Wondering what kind of glaze the potter would get using materials contaminated with platform dust, I cornered Mr. Troke and taught him something he did not know about custom and practise. Namely that stationmasters are not fools.

Mr. Troke ignored me, so I prodded him in the shoulder.

"I may be the new man here," I continued to jab him, "but I am not a sluggard. And to prove it I shall take custody of your fishing tackle. Come to think of it, any fishes hooked in company time also belong to the company, so I shall confiscate your catch too."

I looked inside Mr. Troke's kettle and saw that he had managed not a bite.

* * *

With its unfamiliar exhaust rhythm rapping on the hillside, another visiting locomotive was tackling Upford Cutting. It was 11.43am, and by 11.45am the 'unexpected' train was rolling into Platform One, hauled by a handsome Beattie express locomotive outshopped in LSWR chocolate brown passenger livery. Its train, comprising two crimson-

and-cream passenger carriages, was a spectacle to which I was completely accustomed being an ex London and South Western employee. Suspended along the sides of these carriages, one of which was a First Class saloon and the other an observation car, were roof-boards which read: 'Directors' Special'.

The locomotive was bedecked with rosettes, and featured a centre-piece which comprised a silver sash intertwining the crests of the South Exmoor Railway and its parent company. Indeed, the Special carried all the import of an inaugural train upon a newly opened railway.

In my enthusiasm I saw, gazing back at me from the locomotive's curvy mirror finish, a caricature of myself, and noticed that it was squinting foolishly. So I straightened my lapel, and myself, and cleared my throat self-consciously.

But who could blame my reflection for behaving so whimsically. Like me, it had been overwhelmed by the locomotive's lustrous copper steam dome and pipework, and was admiring the dazzling brass chimney-band and whistle. The brightwork fittings, into which had gone many hours of polishing, effulged in the midday sunshine like something from a new world.

The express locomotive's six-foot wheel splashers were caparisoned with gay tapestries portraying a valley abundant in industry and agriculture, and trains almost distorting under the weight of local produce and blandly smiling passengers. Of course, such cartoons were for the edification of simple folk, not stationmasters, but I was compelled to smile nevertheless.

The locomotive driver noticed me, and it was

clear that he shared my amusement. He nodded respectfully.

"Hey ho, what a wonderful world," I declared drolly, and tipped my hat to him.

The South Exmoor's General Manager, Mr. Benjamin Crump, stepped from the First Class saloon. Before he could spot me, I stole away to my office and had Jack Wheeler brush me down.

Not one for formalities, the affable Mr. Crump entered my office with his gloves thrown carelessly into his top-hat, and gave me a charming smile. I returned his smile and bade him good day. Sadly, this gentleman was one of a dying breed of railway captain who possessed a healthy disregard for protocol, the kind of disregard which characterized many a locally run line. It seemed that with each takeover, each absorption, and each merger, a little more of Mr. Crump's gentle era was being devoured by the sterling-hungry leviathans of the railway world.

The gentleman placed his hat on a corner of my desk.

"Well Horace," he hushed confidentially, "I am taking the trouble to stop off and have a word with each of my stationmasters today. Important changes are imminent..." Mr. Crump interrupted himself. "By the way, I have spared your horse rider a journey. I carried the Giddiford baton with me and handed it to Mr. Hales. Now, I must be brief, for I am partnering Archibald Scott of the London and South Western."

Through my door I could just make out the familiar profile of the London and South Western's General Manager sitting inside the observation car. I also noticed the erect and arrogant figure of the South Exmoor's Consulting Mechanical Engineer, a man fanciful of himself as a latter-day Brunel, with his high 'topper' and expensive cigars.

I returned my gaze to the more cheerful visage of Mr. Crump. Mr. Crump was almost completely bald, save for a tuft of silver above each ear which, when supporting a hat, gave the impression of being the extremities of a full head of hair. However, by removing his top-hat, and being blessed with a nose disproportionately larger than the petit moustache in which it nestled, Mr. Crump robbed himself of all managerial awe. Not that this bothered him, for a friendly and cultivated manner towards lesser mortals was his stamp.

"I am pleased to see that the platform work is progressing well," Mr. Crump continued with sudden gusto. "We are a year or two ahead of the London and South Western on that one. But I fear we shall experience greater turmoil than this before any South Exmoor shares are converted. However, in the interim, traffic management should become less of a nightmare with the addition of two new crossing loops, Horace. Our colleagues on the London and South Western intend operating an all year round service to Waterloo, possibly twice weekly, although it is not clear whether these trains shall stop at Upshott. What is clear, is that with fast trains on the line, signalling and communications will be of paramount importance. Incidentally, you seem very difficult to raise on the telegraph, Horace. Upshott seems to keep its stationmasters too busy to answer calls. Perhaps there is a case for employing a full-time telegraph clerk here until the system is upgraded, not that upgrading will take long now. The linesman tells me that by converting our system from metallic-return to earth-return we can have two telegraph circuits using the same pair of wires. Such a conversion would permit us to add a simple alphabetical instrument which your junior staff could operate. Now there's an economy."

Evidently my application for the tuition of a Telegraph Instructor had not come to Mr. Crump's attention.

"These are exciting times," Mr. Crump enthused. "Last month the London and South Western opened its new direct line between Poole and Bournemouth, and it also took operating powers over the recently completed Sidmouth Railway. You mark my words, Horace, these watering resorts will become increasingly plentiful sources of revenue for the railways. Indeed, in many cases the railway will create the resort."

As a rule, one did not halt a Crump dissertation, but, not knowing this at the time, I felt duty bound to remind the General Manager of his excursion partner waiting aboard the Special. Mr. Crump appeared not to understand my interruption, and continued his discourse.

"In a matter of days," he said, "the Somerset and Dorset Joint Railway Company will be opening its extension from Evercreech to Bath, and they tell me that the first sod has been turned on the Lyme Regis project. So, Horace, who says the railway boom is over?"

The question was rhetorical. I knew better than to interrupt a second time.

"And, what is more," the General Manager continued. "Now that we of the four-foot eight-and-a-half-inch camp have standardization in the bag, thanks to the Royal Commission, the late Mr. Isambard Kingdom Brunel's seven-foot gauge is losing popularity by the day. The business community cannot see broad gauge metals lifted fast enough."

Mr. Crump paused, wrung his hands, and nodded despairingly as if broad gauge had been his own personal mistake. Perhaps, like many railwaymen cogniscant of technical matters, he secretly acknowledged the gauge to be superior, and knew that it had been eclipsed by the so called 'narrow gauge' only because fewer miles of it had been laid, making broad gauge the cheaper to convert. His pensive gaze broke unexpectedly.

"I'm afraid," he said, "that when the London and South Western takes over the South Exmoor, we shall have to discontinue some of our commercially less viable services to the community. Some weekend trains may have to be axed, and Driver MacGregor will find the new management less tolerant of his antics. Antics such as abandoning goods trains in sidings to go back and shoot pheasants he has seen. Even the revered Percival Hiscox will have to forego some of his time-honoured perquisites, like favouring colleagues with nobs of winter coal plucked from Briggs's bunker in exchange for a blind eye occasionally. Oh yes, Horace, we know it goes on. Under our new masters we shall all have to make adjustments."

Perhaps the London and South Western will have more success in controlling the likes of Jack Wheeler, I thought, but doubted it. Mr. Crump collected his hat and gloves in readiness to leave.

"Your Booking Clerk will be pleased to know that his days of writing out tickets by hand are numbered," he said. "Come to that, so also are the days of bargaining with customers over season ticket prices. We are installing Edmondson cardboard ticket printing machinery in all stations. As you know, Horace, the London and South Western is a member of the Railway Clearing House, and adherance to the Edmondson standard ticket is a condition of that membership."

"No doubt I will look forward to being relieved of a good deal of arithmetic when the time comes," I predicted. "The South Exmoor's tariff is complicated enough with its seasonal and daily variations, and concessionary rates for everything from soldiers on furlough to circus animals, but the tariffs of the larger companies like the London and South Western are prodigious. Balancing the books with so many foreign tickets to account for is a sobering prospect."

"Well, Horace, in due course the Clearing House will relieve you of all that," Mr. Crump smiled with dimpled cheeks. "The clerks at Seymour Street will apportion all your inter-company takings, be they from parcels, goods, or passenger traffic. You shall think you are back with the London and South Western!"

"But I will be," I reminded Mr. Crump as he turned to leave.

"You may soon require a range of destination boards out here," he ventured, beckoning me to the platform. "How about: 'This train for Gidiford, Exeter, Salisbury, Andover, Basingstoke, Woking, Clapham Junction and Waterloo'? Who knows what will transpire, Horace? Day trip excursions from here to the South Coast are not out of the question. The perishables situation should improve also. Developments at Templecombe will soon provide Ondle Valley with a direct route to the ports of Poole and Southampton. The future is unbounded."

Under the ownership of the London and South Western Railway Company, the South Exmoor Railway was certainly likely to see a regular service between Waterloo and Blodcaster, as opposed to the occasional excursion. But as for trains to destinations other than Waterloo, not only was this unlikely, it was not even new.

Direct cross-country trains from Blodcaster had been tried in the early days of the railway, but with very little success because of what I believe is broadly termed 'boardroom politics'. The South Exmoor Company had deliberately not publicized the services. It had not even published a timetable for them. The reason being that the routes chosen had threatened the solvency of a stage coach company owned by shareholder, Lord Lacy.

With a glance at his fobwatch, Mr. Crump looked as though he might leave at last.

At this moment, however, I chanced to look towards the weighbridge house and catch sight of my Rollingstock Superintendent riding a company horse in the fashion of a postilion. In tow was a chaldron truck. Mr. Troke was looking very pleased with himself, which was never a good sign.

Now, the chaldron truck, designed to take twenty-five-and-a-half hundredweight of coal, was carrying a somewhat different cargo. To my astonishment, Mr. Troke had chosen this moment to dispose of the sewage, even though its removal to the viaduct necessitated its passing right alongside the Directors' Special.

As the sullage, now sans tarpaulin, trundled beneath the noses of the touring dignitaries, I prayed in silence that the observation car windows and ventilators were all shut. But, alas, judging by the reaction of the occupants of the car, they were open. It seemed that the gentlemen had arranged to sample the country air whilst abroad.

Mr. Troke, presumably unable to hear what was being said inside the railway carriage, appeared pleased with the invective that he had drawn upon himself from these important people, and returned his disgruntled audience a gappy grin. Snimple, who was leaning from the rear of the truck to regulate the brake, also seemed pleased, and began waving the Giddiford baton in the air proudly.

I watched in silent horror as Snimple's momentary lapse in concentration led to a corresponding lapse in regulation of the truck on the falling gradient, and closed my eyes as the treated sewage began to gather speed. Upon hearing the terrified shunting horse protest at being pursued by such an evil smelling heap, I opened one eye and prayed that the incident would go unnoticed. So far, it had.

But the poor beast of burden was all but overrun before the truck was brought under control. And I am quite certain that the animal found the odour of the cargo, which had now shifted and breached its crust, more offensive than did Snimple or Troke.

Luckily Mr. Crump had been studying his itinerary throughout and, like his colleagues aboard the train, remained unaware of the mishap. However I had now become troubled by something else. Mr. Troke's obsessive stare. My Rollingstock Superintendent's large white eyes had become fixed upon me most balefully, as if I were guilty of an indiscretion of some kind, and did not budge until distance robbed the fellow of his view.

Mr. Troke's staring had so mesmerized me that I forgot about Mr. Crump. The General Manager had by now put away his piece of paper and was ready to leave.

To recapture my attention, Mr. Crump cleared his throat loudly and wished me good luck in my capacity as Upshott's new Stationmaster. We shook hands, and I conducted the gentleman hurriedly to the observation car. It had occurred to me that I would do well to 'right away' the Special as quickly as possible, before the General Manager's attention could be drawn to the migrating microbes. Or, for that matter, before a telegraph signal could come through for one of the bigwigs. I opened a carriage door and Mr. Crump went aboard.

Intrigued by the smell of opulence, I tipped my head around the door and pried cautiously into the train's sumptuous interior. While doing so, Mr. Crump's enthusiasm for matters railway overtook him again.

"So, if this railway of ours is not to become a museum piece, we must be up and doing. Ay Horace? Block signalling next..."

"Yes, yes," I agreed with impudent haste, and tried to close the door.

"What is that smell?" Mr. Crump asked with an uncharacteristic twist of the face.

Before I could answer, someone called out to Mr. Crump from within the carriage. Reference was made to the telegraph.

"Of course, I almost forgot!" Mr. Crump exclaimed, and stepped off the train. "I was going to send word to Headquarters from here, to see if there are any messages. May I use your telegraph set?"

This was another rhetorical question. I could scarcely say no. I unlocked the Telegraph Room and suggested that I go about my duties. Suddenly Mr. Crump's arm was outstretched.

"Nonsense, you must join me," came the invitation. "My Morse is a little rusty. I may need your help." Mr. Crump placed a silk handkerchief to his nose and complained: "Do you have overdue deadstock hereabouts? Something is definitely malodorous."

I shrugged my shoulders.

Once inside the cramped Telegraph Room the General Manager stood aside and beckoned me to operate the apparatus, whereupon I took a deep breath and prepared to confess to my inadequacy. I knew that an inability to operate the instrument would not, in itself, be deemed grounds for disciplinary action, but the Board of Directors would most certainly take the view that I had deliberately misled them in order to secure my position. This, my stomach churned at the prospect, was grounds for summary dismissal, and I found myself thinking about Mr. Mildenhew again.

I must have transmitted my tension to Mr. Crump because, as the receiver started to chatter, we both jumped.

The signal was very rapid, doubtless coming from a highly proficient user somewhere, probably at Headquarters, and I froze. After all, I could not write down what was to me merely a noise. But the General Manager did not know this, and, believing my inactivity to be sheer mastery, he marvelled at my response. So impressed was he by the redundancy of my pencil in committing to memory such a long communication, and all with no hint of concentration, that his face puckered with intrigue.

When the receiver at last fell silent, Mr. Crump patted my back and congratulated me, and asked me to translate the message for him. At this my nerve broke, and I invented a coughing fit. Rather helpfully, Mr. Crump blamed my attack on the stench wafting in through the door.

"What *is* that smell?" he asked once more.

"I do not know," I spluttered with feigned incapacitation.

With the noxious load, and hence my excuse for remaining inactive, slipping further away, I knew that I would also have to feign a recovery before long. Having no idea what alternative diversion I might employ, I panicked and said:

"The smell arrived with your train."

A shadow of concern fell across Mr. Crump's face.

I resumed coughing, and pointed towards a stool in the corner of the room.

"Yes of course," the General Manager responded sympathetically, and invited me to retire.

Mr. Crump sent for a glass of water, and did not hear my sigh of relief between coughs when he took over at the telegraph set.

The gentleman's wrinkle of concern deepened over another abnormality. A second signal was coming through, this one being transmitted more slowly. As soon as the message was complete, Mr. Crump handed me the telegram pad upon which he had jotted it down.

> *FROM: Griffith* (Linton Stationmaster)
> *TO: Anyone listening in.*
> *Did you hear what happened to last night's Giddiford train? Two miles up the line from Upshott the pot-lamps exploded. Passengers had to be evacuated from their carriages at*

> *Widdlecombe. Word has it the practical joker resides at Upshott. Stop*

Underneath this, Mr. Crump had scribbled the reply.

> *This is Caxton.* (Widdlecombe Stationmaster) *Watch out what you say. The primates are about. One of them might be listening. Stop*

I read the telegram and told the General Manager that I knew nothing about exploding pot-lamps. This was not an untruth, for the lamps had not actually exploded. By all accounts they had sparkled gaily.

Mr. Crump's mask of curiosity subsided to a boyish grin, and he confided that he had not used the telegraph for quite some time. He had enjoyed working the apparatus, even though the messages made no sense.

At last the Directors' Special departed and, as the carriages swept by, I saw inside one of them the colourful Mr. Gaselee sharing a map with engineer William Beattie. Such a plum excursion did a ride on our beautiful railway make that nobody with an excuse to be on it had missed it.

However, this was another train I had made late.

CHAPTER FIFTEEN

PORTER HUNTED BY WOMEN

The midday Giddiford train arrived several minutes late, having been held up by the Directors' Special. Even so, it looked set to be delayed still further by the presence on the line of two of my staff in charge of a horse-drawn chaldron truck. Messrs. Troke and Snimple had successfully discharged the treated sewage over the side of Widdlecombe Viaduct, but were now hampering their return to the station by mishandling the horse.

To the accompaniment of Driver MacGregor's poignant commentary I watched the four-legged critter stumbling its way towards home, contending not only with a rising gradient, but the hysteria of its handlers. Indeed, the horse was becoming more obstinate with each fright. With Snimple's cowboy yodelling drifting on the wind, and a blunt Scotchman rasping at my ear, each minute seemed like an hour.

The Giddiford train eventually left half-an-hour late, at 1.25pm.

Lacy was still behind schedule with its passenger train when it returned ex Giddiford, and I delayed it further by attaching a swinger. The swinger, of course, was the unwanted mobile crane.

At this, Driver MacGregor became convinced that I was victimizing him, especially as his progress would be hampered still further by having to detach the crane at Busy Linton, and he began to badger me for an explanation. Despite my assurances that

I was not 'out to get' him, the Scotchman became ugly and told me that I owed him a rabbit stew.

At first I did not understand this strange remark, but eventually it dawned upon me that the driver had planned to harvest the lineside upon this trip. So his anger was not so much because he deprecated tardiness but because his snares would have to go unchecked. And because of the fellow's acute lack of humour over the affair, my promise to cook him a replacement stew was not well received. In fact the quip plunged us into an altercation, and a rather public one at that.

This put me in a suitable frame of mind to deal with Snimple and Troke. I summoned them to my office.

"Could not you two idiots have waited until the Directors' Special was out of the station before disposing of the sewage?" I quizzed Mr. Troke. "Would it not have been wiser to move it after nightfall?"

"Didn't think of that," Mr. Troke smarted.

"Let me see if I have this straight. You simply parked the truck on the viaduct and began shovelling its contents over the side, in broad daylight?" I asked incredulously. "You made sure, I hope, that you were directly over the river?"

"If we'd done it under cover of darkness we shouldn't have been able to tell," Mr. Troke pointed out with a dozy squint. There was, I confess, an element of logic in his defence.

As yet, Snimple had said nothing, and I had not taxed the fellow, but I began to notice in his normally ruddy cheeks the rising pallor of guilt.

"Snimple," I addressed the porter sympathetically. Snimple was always the weak link in any chain of deceipt at Upshott. "Did the treated sewage all go in the river?"

"A sntrong wind blows through the arches, Mr. Jay," he submitted meekly.

Thus I became aware that the discharge had not behaved according to plan.

"Who, or what, did it hit?" I asked without further ado.

Mr. Troke owned up.

"We think it was old Smethwick of Longhurdle Farm, Mr. Jay, Sir."

"Smethwick?" I gasped. "What was the pig breeder doing under the viaduct?"

"He grazes livestock on the common land between the piers, Sir," said Mr. Troke. "Live-stock what the master don't know about. He keeps the takings to himself, the crafty worm."

"And the sewage hit him?"

"It wouldn't have done if he hadn't got in the way," Mr. Troke complained.

"But you reckon it was Smethwick the sewage hit?" I sought confirmation.

"It was Smethwick, all right."

"Smethwick, eh?" I mused. "No harm done then."

* * *

The remainder of this warm, breezy afternoon passed uneventfully. *Exmoor* hauled the Milk Train empties non-stop through Upshott to Blod-caster, dead on time at 4.05pm. Julian Maynard rode the spare track-bed to Giddiford with the single-line baton, and I had Snimple put some tallow on the hinges of the Waiting Room sign to stop it squeaking. An increasingly gusty wind had picked up. The telegraph wires, which terminated at porcelain insulators fixed to the station house wall, had begun to howl, and it was an eerie tune they rendered. But I could do nothing about that.

By 5pm the station loop was again occupied by a pair of passenger trains crossing. In railway terminology, incidentally, the word 'crossing' applies to two trains passing each other in opposite directions. In this context, the word 'passing' generally applies to one train overtaking another, such as when a goods train is shunted into a siding temporarily to allow a passenger train to take priority.

Although my staff and I were kept busy by the two trains, everything ran smoothly with the exception of a poorly fastened saratoga trunk belonging to a London textile merchant destined for the Lacy Arms. In order to fasten the gentleman's trunk more securely it became necessary for me to have Humphrey sit on it. This the porter did, upon my signal, when the owner was not looking. Surprisingly, I heard nothing break under the strain of Humphrey's great bulk.

Later I found it necessary to admonish Snimple for leaving churns of milk out in the sun, and discovered that his knowledge of the planetary motions was a little short of complete.

"They were definitely in the shade when I left them there, Mr. Jay," he insisted. "Snomething's moved."

Beyond these two minor irritations, the afternoon was, as I have alluded, blissfully uneventful.

To avoid baton difficulties, the returning Milk Train had been combined with the Giddiford passenger train as far as Upshott, and the station yard was now befogged with the halitus of two hard worked engines; one of them marshalling dairy stock on the Tramway, the other preparing for its descent to Giddiford Junction.

Lacy's sulphurous breath cleared briefly, driven off by a veering wind, and I found Humphrey resting on a pigeon basket, the inquisitive occupants of which were blinking at the world from between his legs.

"Humphrey!" I called. "Loafing in the presence of the great British public is unseemly." I believe he knew my remonstrance to be in jest.

Together we observed a thick set young lady in her early twenties descend the footbridge steps. Her footfalls were noisy on the timber, and for some reason she tilted her head to one side periodically with a squarish smile. She was a plain girl, not by any stretch of the imagination voluptuously favoured, yet I perceived in her eyes, dark and intense though they were, a caring soul.

"Tis Miss Peckham," Humphrey advised me. "The village Postmaster's youngest."

"Big bones," I observed idly.

Perched upon the maid's head of wavy brown hair was a small, maroon bonnet, and the volumes which frothed from beneath it were by far her most attractive feature. They contracted into loose curls which cascaded prettily onto her broad shoulders.

"Amelia be in trainin' to become a nurse over at Yeovil," Humphrey grunted. "I tell e, her'll make a fearful medicine bully one day. A dragon matron."

"Really?" I replied. The young lady looked too pleasant to warrant such an appraisal. "From what I have read," I said, "we shall see nursing become a recognized profession one day, Humphrey. And Miss Peckham looks young enough to see it happen."

"Haply, but not at Yeovil," Humphrey warbled. "They'm given her a week to take a pair of scissors to her hair. Folks reckon her's refusin' to cut it short like a proper nurse because of Snimple."

"Because of Snimple?" I puzzled. "Why Snimple?"

"Don't e know, Mr. Jay? Her be after him. I reckons her goin' to snare him too, in the end. Her's a big'n to argue with."

I could scarcely believe my ears. Not for the first time this day had I heard reference to my Second Porter being the object of immodest female desires, and I began to wonder if there was another Snimple at large about the place, besides the one I had already met. Perhaps there was a Snimple in the village? The Snimple at whose feet the maids of Upshott were apparently flinging themselves would have to be chivalrous, urbane, and wealthy, not a railway porter.

"I knows what e be thinkin', Mr. Jay. Tis Snimple her be after right enough. That Higham girl be just a tease. Between e, me, and the fence post, if ol' Snimple got half a smidgen of sense, he'd sweep Miss Amelia Peckham off her feet and be done with. If nothin' else, her be wholesome. A fellow like Snimple can't be choosy."

I shut my eyes and tried to imagine Snimple sweeping a young lady off her feet, but could not. Least of all the buxom wench I had observed lumbering across Platform One. Indeed, I saw quite the reverse take place. The porter passed within a few feet of his female admirer and paid her no attention at all. Miss Peckham halted abruptly, turned, and revealed a portrait of dejection.

"Tis a case of unrequited love," Humphrey observed mournfully.

"What we have just witnessed, Humphrey," I reflected, "is not the face of determination you ascribe the young lady."

Humphrey was compelled to agree.

"Normally her comes up in red blotches and ticks him off for bein' rude," he said. "Tis a sight, I can tell e."

Personally, I thought the girl quite pretty in a singular sort of way, and I was incensed by Snimple's bad manners. I set about cornering the porter for a word, but he went to ground.

A spell later I came across a gaggle of women on Platform One, at the centre of which was the very character whose love life I was finding so extraordinary. The delicate ladies were fussing over Snimple's thumb. It was bleeding, and had been enswathed temporarily in a handkerchief. Retribution, I thought, and dispersed the gathering.

"I forgot I had a pruning blade in my pocket, Mr. Jay," he whimpered. "I'm very snorry."

"You know where we keep bandages," I railed him. "You'll make the journey without dying, methinks."

Just then, a mellifluous voice floated across my shoulder. Miss Peckham had observed the incident from the forecourt, and had returned to assist Snimple in his hour of need. It surprised me that so rugged a girl should be blessed with such dulcet tones.

"I have medication in my bag," she hushed in a broad Somerset accent and, to murmurs of approval from the other angels of mercy, pulled out a swab and miniature bottle of bright yellow salve.

Snimple cooed like a pigeon, and smiled sublimely.

"Poor Snimple," Miss Peckham responded with what I perceived to be thespian sincerity.

I guessed what was to succeed. The porter offered up his wounded limb pathetically, and Miss Peckham applied to it the unction.

A determined grin set upon the maid's face as, with her free hand, she pulled a length of bandage from her bag. Her grin, broadening fast, was now tempered with anticipation.

As expected, the medication began to sting, and Snimple yodelled with shock. Not surprisingly, he tried to retrieve his enraged thumb, but Miss Peckham held on to it. Now, with the swiftness of a loom, she wound the bandage around the enraged digit and secured it with a knot, thus preventing the porter from removing the unction to quell the fire. I could not quite see the label on the little bottle, but I fancy it read: 'Serves You Right.'

"Dutch Drops would've sufficed," Humphrey rumbled ignorantly from behind me.

Snimple had a better understanding of the medication, and looked deeply hurt by it. William Troke, on the other hand, was totally confounded and irritated by Snimple's popularity with the fairer sex. It did little to appease him that Mrs. Mitchell kissed Snimple daintily on the cheek, and breathed:

"Poor, harmless Snimple."

By now, one could see Mr. Troke visibly contemplating the rewards of being harmless.

* * *

All was peaceful. High in Upshott Wood the rooks were cawing noisily, and *Exmoor* was sizzling quietly in the headshunt. Departure of the Giddiford train had revealed the presence upon Platform Two of a cluster of milk churns and cheese barrels waiting to be loaded aboard the Milk Train after its return from the Dairy Siding. Also visible was a scullion from The Coach House. The boy was staggering towards the footbridge with a dozen hands of freshwater fish in his arms, careless that they were dripping everywhere. So, after he had gone, I instructed Snimple to scrub the platform and footbridge decking to remove the smell. There was always a nasty chore awaiting the deserving.

At 6.10pm a minor interruption to the tranquility was occasioned when Julian Maynard rode into the station jauntily with the Giddiford baton. I was applauding his efficiency when he drew my attention to a pair of crows nesting in a chimney above the station house.

"If one of those birds falls down that stack, Mr. Jay, there'll be soot all around your office before you can catch the blighter," he warned me. "Mr. Mildenhew always used to send Diggory up to clean out the pots about this time of year."

In the absence of my Junior Porter I instructed Jack Wheeler to clean them. There was always another nasty chore awaiting the deserving.

Glancing at my fobwatch, assuming it to be correct, I noticed that the Directors' Special was due back from Blodcaster, so I released my hold upon Jack's ladder and made off to find Ivor Hales for a word.

After some discussion, the Signalman and I agreed that the only way the Milk Train would reach Giddiford exchange sidings in time to make its connection with the Metropolitan Market Goods was by amalgamating it with the Directors'

Special. Knowing that the illustrious Special would be somewhat effaced by the addition of milk trucks, Ivor wished me luck in proposing the idea to the General Manager and disappeared. I did not look forward to suggesting it, especially since making the necessary arrangements might well involve a telegraph communication.

I need not have fretted. When the time came, not only was no telegraph message necessary, but Mr. Crump pointed out that having to amalgamate the Special with a milk train illustrated handsomely the need for the South Exmoor to have the line doubled, if only as far as Upshott. Thus it was that at 6.29pm, *Exmoor* and LSWR *Number 231* worked out of Upshott together with a most curious composition of rollingstock.

Many hours later, after the passing of the 'up' Mail and the evening Giddiford train, the last movement of the day pounded into Upshott Station with a crisp moon making ghosts of its steam. Humphrey began tramping the primrose squares of light cast by its pot-lamps and boomed to all and sundry: 'Last train Blodcaster. Shanks's pony to follow.'

Feeling idle, I stood aside and watched Mr. Milsom's shadow stalk him like a dumb assassin seeking an opportunity to pounce, and took a pinch of snuff. The rotund black phantom pranced hither and thither among the will-o'-the-wisps of steam and stretched elastically across flagstones to spring up walls unexpectedly.

Unfortunately I was not left alone to enjoy the spectacle for very long. Driver Hiscox had slipped away from the volcanic glow of *Briggs's* fire to speak with me. But Humphrey's bellowing prevented us from conducting a conversation, so we removed ourselves to the Booking Hall. Here the driver took my arm with a disapproving frown.

"The pot-lamp mystery remains unsolved, Mr. Jay, for I have seen another," he confided.

"Another?" I queried him. By now, Upshott had taught me the art of holding a conversation without understanding it.

"Another," Driver Hiscox confirmed unhelpfully. "I have just seen Farmer Smethwick on the bank between the cutting and the viaduct. The man was buzzing around in circles like a bluebottle with one wing, and his handlamp was sparkling. What is more, he appeared to be splattered from head to foot with mud."

"Most curious," I concurred innocently.

"Often as not, I do see Smethwick of a Tuesday," Hiscox continued. "He lingers on Ondle Common until after dark. Takes a lantern with him for the long walk home."

I refused to be drawn on the subject, and held my tongue. A somewhat bemused Mr. Hiscox returned to his hissing serpent.

Suddenly Jack Wheeler was at my side. With a platform gaslamp glimmering in his eye, he conjured a sinister grin.

"Sounds like we've identified our thief then," he grunted. "The drum containing the spiked lamp oil disappeared last night, Mr. Jay."

I stepped back. There were times when Wheeler made my flesh creep.

"We must not be hasty in our conclusions," I warned him. "Mr. Smethwick has a feudal mentality. We must not stir unnecessary nastiness."

"'E certainly could turn nasty," Jack agreed. "Nevertheless, we must confront ol' Smethwick and find out 'ow 'e came by the doctored oil."

Ex officio, it would be I who did the confronting.

The last train of the day barked into the darkness, sending a cloud of noctule bats skywards from the water tower. The bats disappeared among the stars and, a second later, reappeared as a swirl of dots around the moon. I shivered and turned up my collar. The damp night air had begun to lift from the ground the smell of coal and straw, and I was anxious to close the station and retire to my quarters.

While dimming the gases, I hearkened gladly to the day's last train distancing itself from Upshott, and began to wonder what manner of distraction had caused Diggory to step in front of a locomotive. I was also curious to know what had made the young porter leave so late for work in the first place. It seemed likely that Mrs. Smith and her son were in some kind of plight.

The next day I would ride out to Widdlecombe to see if I could be of assistance.

CHAPTER SIXTEEN

THIRD DAY BRINGS A SAD TALE

On my third day in harness at Upshott, another saga began. It scarcely seemed possible that here, in the blissful bosom of nature, far from the madding conurbations of terraces and trams, there could exist the complicated nonsense to which I was now reluctantly becoming accustomed. Yet it did. And whereas yesterday's merry-go-round had centred upon a wagonful of fertilizer, today's was to be centred upon a considerably less palpable irritant, and consequently one which was far more difficult to dispose of. A ghost!

Of this I shall reveal more later. First, allow me to relate to you the greatly unjust circumstances of the delightful Mrs. Smith, of whose ill hap I learned while visiting Widdlecombe. For the purposes of this recollection I shall set the station clock to 07.15am on the Seventeenth of June, 1874, at which time I was to be found deedily touring the platforms of my station, nurturing an ill-fated keenness to avoid trouble.

I had come to believe that I would perish, spiritually speaking, if I did not endeavour to become a little more pervious to my peaceful surroundings and make a point of forgetting about the blessed railway occasionally. To this end I tarried awhile and gazed up at the birds littering the pale blue sky. Here the great and graceful were wheeling effortlessly among the small and spritely, rather like a stationmaster amongst his porters.

While looking aloft, I was regaled by a wren which had settled upon a nearby picket fence bordering Platform One. Its rapid, energetic singing made me realize that for too long I had been allowing my worries to prevent me from enjoying the delights which surrounded me.

It was in this idle mode of gazing that my attention was drawn to the fruits of my Second Porter's labour. All around me the air was humming with bees and other insects busily working Snimple's blazing flowerbeds. But, until now, as in the case of the birds, I had not been conscious of them. Not surprisingly, the less sonorous species had also failed to capture my attention, by which I allude to the butterfly. Common Blue, Peacock, and Wall Brown were among those swirling in the scented breeze, like fragments of broken rainbow. In fact, I half expected to see Snimple chasing them with a net, for pinning butterflies to cork and labelling them with their peculiar Latin names was a fancy of his.

Elsewhere, more subtle colours pleased the eye. The cultivated lower slopes of Ondle Valley, which until recently had been uniformly brown, were now becoming a patchwork of sprouting crops. In some of the tiny oblong fields, oats were growing, in others, clover and grass for making silage, or kale and tic bean for making cattle feed. In the very bottom of the valley were several strips of wheat for milling into flour and feeding poultry.

In addition to what I could see from the footbridge, I had heard that a little barley for brewing had been sown this year, but with the railway importing quality ingredients from the fertile home counties, it seemed likely that any local yield would end up in an animal trough.

As a professional railwayman casting an eye about a district served by a railway, such diversity of farming struck me as unnecessary. With access to the metropolitan markets, a farmer no longer needed to be self-sufficient and produce a little of everything. He was better off turning his hand to bulk husbandry, producing only that which flourished in his corner of the countryside. Clearly, in Ondle Valley, the coming of the railway fourteen years ago had not inspired everyone to change their ways. It seemed that not all the producers hereabouts had the courage to break with tradition, or, come to that, the foresight to see what would become of them eventually if they did not.

Looking the other way, across the station forecourt, I could see the luxuriant boughs of Upshott's ancient trees outstretched as if to guard jealously the peaceful community which lay beneath them. And hidden somewhere beneath me, I could hear the station goat tearing up grass and chewing it industriously.

In the stables, Mr. Maynard's four horses were peering out of their stalls. The tormented creatures were nodding like a display of clockwork toys to escape the flies which swarmed to their eyes.

With the sun warming me gently, it seemed that in summer's magnificent bloom there lay an irresistible invitation to be joyous, and, in a fit of elation, I borrowed one of Mr. Maynard's nodding horses and rode away on it.

Having put the station behind me, I turned left and followed Natter Lane down to the arch beneath the Tramway. Here I slowed up, for I was without a destination, and it was rather early in the morning to go visiting.

But was it? Folk tended to make allowances for

the busy stationmaster, so I decided to go visiting anyway. I gave my mount a flick of the crop and gathered speed reverberrantly through the second arch, a somewhat more dank and gloomy one under the railway proper, and galloped back out into the daylight. Upshott Wood was now on my left, and Fallowfield Common on my right, and from here, in the company of a talkative brook, I descended the valley towards Widdlecombe to see Mrs. Smith.

My mare's ears twitched with each whisper of the countryside as I trotted her down Natter Lane towards the River Ondle, for she seemed as glad as I to be at large. Her name, by the way, was Campion, and I discovered that Campion liked to be advised about this and that along the way.

Upon reaching the river I decided to take a short-cut, and searched the shallows around Willow Island for the old ford. Campion enjoyed the splash. And having been revitalized by it she bounced jauntily across the springy turf of Ondle Common to deliver me to Widdlecombe in no time.

While tethering Campion to a fence post within reach of some succulent grass outside Mrs. Smith's cottage, I spotted Diggory sitting in the garden taking the morning air. I was glad to see that the lad's colour had returned. Indeed, were it not for his sticking-plasters and one minor bruise, one would not have known that he had been involved in a railway accident only the day before. I exchanged pleasantries with the bony specimen of youthhood, and asked:

"Are you so transported by your thoughts, lad, that you do not hear a train approaching?"

"No, Sir," he replied. "Yes, Sir," he revised his answer. "I mean, yes I didn't hear the train, but no it wasn't because I was transported, Sir."

I dare say my lack of comprehension was charted upon my face. I did not challenge the logic of Diggory's answer, however, if indeed there was any. Instead I waited patiently for him to qualify his statement.

"All I could hear was the wind rattling in my ears, Mr. Jay. It's always blowy on the viaduct."

"Quite so," I concurred.

Much as I was tempted to question the young porter about his poor time-keeping, this was not the right moment, so instead I enquired of his mother's whereabouts. At this point I discovered that we were not alone.

"Mornin' Diggory," a toothless someone whistled through the hedgerow.

"Got over yer fright yet?" another voice enquired.

It seemed that my Junior Porter was a popular young fellow in his home village. I stood aside politely while further pleasantries were exchanged, and then doffed my hat to the well-wishers, although all I could see of them were two pairs of eyes squinting through the thicket.

Upon hearing the rattle of the morning Giddiford train slowing down towards the station high upon Widdlecombe Bank, I checked my timepiece. The 'up' train was on time, it being 7.59am, and I crossed my fingers that time-keeping today would not be ruined by that troublesome new stationmaster at Upshott.

I left Diggory talking to his yokel friends and crossed the herb garden to the cottage. The door was ajar, and so I peered inside and announced my presence. Mrs. Smith called back from the kitchen where she was at the range bringing some medicinal frumenty to the boil. I was invited in.

"Please excuse my appearance, Mr. Jay," she apologized, brushing herself down frantically. "I was not expecting company."

Notwithstanding Mrs. Smith's disorientation, her appearance was, by virtue of its simplicity, perfectly charming. I espied beneath her apron a cream coloured dress printed with pale green oak leaves, and a collar pinned down with a brooch matching the colour of her eyes. Her hair was secured beneath a goffered cap of cream linen.

Naturally I removed my hat, and put her at her ease immediately.

"Will you take tea?" she asked delicately, as if risking offence.

I accepted, and a dimple of satisfaction took residence upon her cheeks.

We began talking of Diggory's accident, and of his behaviour generally, for I was deliberately steering the conversation towards these matters. I took the opportunity to express my concern that the lad had no father to guide him through the stormy passage to manhood, and Mrs. Smith explained that Diggory was indeed missing his father at the present time.

At this point I became aware of Mrs. Smith's mastery of English, for, as I understood it, she was French by birth. Her speech sounded as English to me as that of any local person, not that Upshott folk accorded the Queen's English much fidelity. However, with a little concentration, one could just detect a foreign accent surviving from childhood. But any occasional inflection giving away Mrs. Smith's native tongue did not register in the casual hearing, because it was so alloyed with the west country dialect.

When the moment was right, I taxed Mrs. Smith directly concerning Diggory's presence on the viaduct at a time of day when he should have been at his post. This enquiry, I hasten to add, I made with a good measure of caution and sensitivity.

"If I might make so bold, Mrs. Smith," I ventured. "I believe young Diggory is troubled by something. And if I am not mistaken, this something accounts for his late start for work yesterday."

"You are quite right, Mr. Jay," she responded openly. "My son is beside himself lately, and no mistake. But the explanation is lengthy."

Having made the journey across the valley to Widdlecombe, I was at pains to hear this lengthy explanation, and so I offered to bear with it in exchange for a comfortable seat. Mr. Maynard's workworn old saddle had taken its toll of my posterior and I was not ready to return just yet. In response, the charming Mrs. Smith sat me down on an oak settle and insisted upon toasting me a muffin to take with my tea.

With the refreshment set out, my hostess sat facing me and sighed deeply while pouring the drinks.

"When my husband died," she commenced heavily, "he left me penniless. So to make ends meet I turned to lace and quilt making, and Diggory abandoned his schooling to find gainful employment. At first my son worked for the rat-catcher, then, under the smithy at Upford Forge, he made good his ability to strike and shoe. Finally he found still better prospect on the South Exmoor Railway."

"But what happened to your late husband's business?" I interrupted. "Was Mr. Smith not the farrier hereabouts?"

"At Rington," she confirmed, and added bitterly: "But upon being widowed I lost the premises. A young businessman from Exeter laid claim to them, something for which I was completely unprepared, Mr. Jay. Indeed, I was no more expecting a stranger to contest my husband's will than was I expecting my husband to die in the first place. Before I knew it, the estate was in chancery, and it came to light that the business was not my husband's to bequeath. As a result, I lost the forge, the stables, the dispensary, and even the dwelling in which my husband and I had lived all our married lives. Having lost the roof over our heads, Diggory and I packed our chattels and repaired to this rented cottage."

"But how could this happen?" I asked incredulously. "Surely your husband held the deeds to his property?"

"No!" said she with a sense of shock not dulled by the years. "The business had been handed down from father to son without such documents. My husband's forebears had taken possession of the forge when its founder disappeared on a trip to Portsmouth in 1780."

"Disappeared?" I puzzled. "Mmm. The fellow was probably press-ganged." I sipped my tea knowingly. "Those who made poor sailors never survived the ordeal of going to sea, and those who made good sailors were never released ashore again."

Mrs. Smith's tea, by the way, was ghastly. Not only was it weak, it tasted excruciatingly sour. I suspected that she had bought it cheap from a street vendor. There was one pedlar in particular who sold used tea-leaves which he had salvaged from the kitchens of the big houses in the district. His trick was to purchase the expired tea from a scullery maid, dry it out, colour it with vegetable dye to make it look fresh, and sell it to folk who could not normally afford such luxury.

"So who is this Exeter businessman?" I asked, setting down the cup with a sickly grin.

Mrs. Smith did not hear my question. She was gazing distantly through the bow-window of her cottage. I watched her slim, delicately hued face contract into a chronicle of disappointment, into which broke the traces of a smile, the flicker of a precious memory.

"My pappa, God rest his soul, was a horse dealer," said she pensively. "He owned stables in a suburb of Paris, and it was on a trip with him to England that I met Thomas. Thomas was my late husband," Mrs. Smith interrupted herself. "My fate was sealed from the moment pappa decided to take advice on English Law from the same practice as Thomas," she went on. "Ironically, Mr. Jay, my fate was sealed in more ways than one by that practitioner."

"Go on," I prompted Mrs. Smith, and forced down a little more of her dreadful tea.

"Well, as I have implied, it was in this lawyer's office that I met the man who was to take me for his wife, but it was also here that the seeds of my present predicament were sown. Thomas, Mr. Jay, was not like his forebears. He did not take good fortune for granted, and when my father and I met him, although I did not know it at the time, he was looking into the legality of his proprietorship. Indeed, I did not come to know what this legal consultation had been about until after my husband's death, for Thomas thought it improper to burden his wife with business matters. After Thomas's death I learned that the lawyer of whom I have spoken had occasioned him to believe that our possession of the forge was valid in the eyes of the law, whereas, in fact, it was not."

"Upon my soul," I gasped. "So the lawyer's advice was wrong. What, precisely, did he tell your husband?"

"That by disappearing, and having no known next of kin, the founder of the business had ceded ownership of the premises to my husband's grandfather. My husband's grandfather had been employed as the senior smithy, you see, and had been left running the business in the absence of the owner."

"It is a complicated story," I remarked, and drained my cup with a gasp of relief.

Mrs. Smith offered me more tea. I declined.

"Apparently," she continued, "Thomas's father built up trade quite considerably during his lifetime, so that by the time Thomas inherited the business, albeit without title deeds, it had grown to a sizeable concern."

"To be badly represented by a lawyer is scandalous," I consoled Mrs. Smith, and joined her in a pensive silence.

While marshalling my thoughts, I surveyed the parlour and noticed a calotype hanging upon the wall above the fireplace. It seemed that Mr. Smith had been distinguished enough to have his photograph taken, and had signed his name in the bottom right-hand corner of the print. "I see you are lucky enough to have your late husband's image for company," I remarked.

"Yes, but unfortunately it is fading," Mrs. Smith replied dejectedly.

Had I been better acquainted with Mrs. Smith I might have comforted her with a pat on the shoulder, but in the lifelike and unflinching gaze of the Master Farrier, I was mindful of my conduct.

Seeing the photograph, I became curious about the late Mr. Smith. He was some fourteen years older than his spouse, or would have been had he not left this world for a better one, and I began to study his portrait more closely. Whilst at a glance it projected him as a man of fierce determination, a more detailed inspection revealed in his eyes the quality of humility, perhaps even timidity, but certainly compassion. I fancy he had regarded the uncertainties of this world as a challenge rather than a distraction, and had come to know himself rather better than most.

The late Mr. Smith certainly did not look the kind of man who needed the asylum of liquor at the end of a bad day, yet, by all accounts, he had been given to solitary bouts of drinking.

Mrs. Smith lifted her eyes yearningly to the one who, with all his faults, should never have left her. After caressing her wedding ring wistfully for a few seconds, she continued:

"The rest of the story you can piece together for yourself, Mr. Jay. Upon my husband's death, this arrogant young businessman from Exeter revealed himself to be a descendant of the founder, thereby laying claim to almost everything my husband had left behind in this world."

"And this he did while you were still in mourning," I noted disdainfully.

"He swooped upon me like a vulture," Mrs. Smith grimaced. "With no concern for my grief.

Indeed, my bewilderment must have served his purpose well. That, and the poor counsel I was receiving."

"Do you suppose he was a charlatan?" I asked. "Not a genuine descendant of the founder at all?"

"The court found him to be genuine," Mrs. Smith replied. "His lawyer, a dissolute man if ever there was one, must have advised him not to file a claim until after Thomas's days on Earth were done, in the knowledge that litigation with a grieving widow would be less fraught."

"And also that, in the meantime, the business would continue to expand by your husband's toil," I surmised angrily. "But how could a remote descendant of the founder reclaim the business after almost a hundred years?" I puzzled aloud. "The idea is preposterous. Why was justice not done?"

"Oh, but it was," Mrs. Smith replied sardonically. "You must remember that there is only one justice, and ever two or more parties laying claim to it."

Mrs. Smith was gazing through the window again. This time her eyes had come to rest upon Diggory, in whom, and only in whom, her husband lived on. I could see that her son compensated much for life's hardships.

Dastardly though this Exeter businessman's deed had been, I had yet to understand how it related to Diggory's abnormal behaviour at this far remove.

"How so does this worry your son now, after five years?" I asked Mrs. Smith.

Her blue eyes became fixed upon me steadfastly.

"I will explain, Mr. Jay," said she. "We came hither to live, finding rent of but sixpence per week payable to that same Exeter businessman, for he is the landlord of this property. Putting a modest roof over our heads to spare us a life of vagrancy was, so the gentleman would have us believe, an act of great charity. In reality, of course, he was seeking to ease his conscience. I am told that redemption in the eyes of God is not that cheaply purchased, Mr. Jay, although it would seem to be so in the eyes of the community. Naturally, the gentleman's agent, not he, collects the dues, for the businessman cannot look me in the eye. Perhaps this is why, now that the dust has settled upon the matter, it suits him to move us on again."

"Move you on again? Why, this is a nightmare!" I reeled. "All I can say is that you must stick to your description 'Exeter businessman' Mrs. Smith," I advised the poor woman, "for this bounder does not deserve the title 'gentleman' whatever may be his trappings. Whither shall you go?" I enquired painfully.

"Somewhere of still lower rent," said she, "for we are in arrears here. The railway brings cheap foreign lace into the district, you know, and this has sorely reduced my income."

"You will secure meagre curtilage for less than sixpence a week, Mrs. Smith," I observed. "The basic cottage rental in these parts is one shilling."

"Then I shall make do with meagre curtilage," Mrs. Smith advised me stiffly. "It is all I require. Thanks to the gypsies and the Hunt, I have no pigs to accommodate now."

"The gypsies and the Hunt?" I repeated slowly like the village idiot.

Mrs. Smith grimaced.

Wickedly, perhaps, I found myself suppressing a smile, for I was intrigued to know how two such diverse social entities might conspire to eliminate one's pigs.

Before I knew it, Mrs. Smith was telling me.

"The sty here is dilapidated," she explained, "and so my sow began to stray. She strayed thrice in all. On the first two occasions I recovered her from the village pound, but on the last, while soon to farrow, she was savaged by the Vellington hounds. As everyone knows, the Hunt does not pay compensation to the owners of stray livestock, so I was unable to replace her."

"You had only one pig?" I enquired.

"No, I had two," she sighed. "Which is why Diggory was late for work yesterday. He had been across the valley to recover the second pig from the gypsies. They make camp on the common this time every year, Mr. Jay, and, as if by coincidence, about this time every year livestock goes missing."

"So I hear," I sympathized. "I take it Diggory was unable recover the pig."

"He was threatened with a knife," said she indignantly, "and had the good sense to come away. So now I have only to find space for a couple of geese in my new home."

"These people are outrageous," I reacted loudly, referring, I suppose, to just about everyone who had caused Mrs. Smith grief.

"My neighbours are very good, and have offered me replacements," she smiled briefly. "But I do not go cap-in-hand just yet."

Mrs. Smith's tales of woe seemed inexhaustible, but whilst fate may have dealt her a bad hand, manifestly it had failed to cheat her of her aplomb. She had been uncommonly talkative, and appeared grateful to me for having lent an ear. She excused herself and returned to the kitchen to see how the frumenty was progressing.

Left alone to cogitate, I began to feel uneasy about the railway's part in Mrs. Smith's misfortune. First it had robbed her of her husband, and now it was robbing her of her income from lace. I felt bound to offer some assistance but, unfortunately, I could think of nothing to suggest.

Flipping open my fobwatch, I discovered that I had over-stayed my time, so I joined Mrs. Smith in the kitchen.

"Well, I must return to the station with my borrowed nag," I declared. "Or my Horse Superintendent, Mr. Maynard, will complain that I hinder him about his business. Thank you for the muffin, Mrs. Smith. I have tasted none better. None better!" I enthused gustily.

My jocularity was received with little more than a perfunctory smile, and I felt uneasy at having to leave Mrs. Smith in such low spirits. *It would be nice to tarry awhile and impart a few stories of my own,* I thought. *Cheerful ones!* But the likelihood of my being able to help Mrs. Smith at some future time would not be enhanced were I to lose my job.

While collecting my riding apparel, I decided that I would restore Mr. Maynard's mare to the company stables at once and deal only with the more pressing paperwork. By so doing, I would have time to walk to Upwater for a spot of fishing before the arrival of the midday Giddiford train. I felt I needed time to think.

"Diggory will report for duty this afternoon," Mrs. Smith assured me resolutely. "He is very like his father and cannot be without occupation."

As Mrs. Smith spoke, I detected again that fragrance which I had once thought my only clue to the identity of the belle in white lace. Indeed, I believe Mrs. Smith had applied the mischievous perfume to herself secretly whilst gone from the room. Since she had been nowhere but the kitchen, I cast my eye about the shelves to see what form the bottle took. Sure enough, I espied a miniature phial labelled 'Essence of Mirbane'. This I knew to be no herb for cooking, and made a mental note of it.

Mrs. Smith beckoned me through the back door into the garden where she insisted upon picking me some mint, for she would not hear of me leaving empty-handed. Furnished bountifully, I brushed past the thorny coils of a rambling rose which tried to cling to me as well as the brick nogging, checked my uniform for snags, and waved Diggory good-bye. No further conversation was possible now, for my presence in the garden had upset Mrs. Smith's geese, and a child throwing a tantrum could not have matched the noise.

I mounted Campion, tipped my hat, and rode away briskly from the clamour.

CHAPTER SEVENTEEN

FISTICUFFS AT THE STATION

Jack Wheeler was kind enough to lend me his rod to go fishing at Upwater, and I thanked him most profusely. He always enjoyed a big show of appreciation for his little deeds. Had I been the village idiot, I might also have thanked him for his elementary angling advice.

A scurrilous grin slid across the clerk's face as I prepared to leave for the water meadows.

"If I were you, Mr. Jay, I shouldn't bother," he confounded me. "You'll catch nothing tasty to fill your dish today. Not until you've faced up to unfinished business like a proper man." Jack began to tootle hypnotically in my ear: "*All good fortune passes by the fool who shuns the devil's eye.* You know the old saying, Mr. Jay," he said. "The one about what 'appens to cowards. Strife always 'aunts those who put off matters grim."

It may have been an old saying, but I had never heard it. To educate me, Jack repeated the couplet several times with increasing passion, and hovered about me with bated breath as if I should act immediately to avoid being damned.

"Well?" I jumped. "To what grim matter do you refer, Mr. Wheeler? I do not have all day, and I am aware of nothing outstanding. All the books are cast up and there is no traffic due."

"Smethwick, Sir. Old farmer Smethwick. *Violent* old farmer Smethwick. *Oil thief* farmer Smethwick," he chanted with affected urgency. "Your confrontation with 'im is overdue."

I frowned at Jack meanly and propped his fishing rod against my desk. My plans for dealing with the pugnacious pig breeder were well formulated and I did not require instructions from a clerk. I intended to challenge the farmer later in the day. However, before I could illuminate Jack thus, the clerk hurried away to fetch the quarrelsome peasant.

I drew breath to halt Mr. Wheler but was not quick enough, and in the wake of his lightning departure a draught rearranged the papers upon my desk. Tutting with exasperation, I redeployed my paperweights and sank into my chair to think. Quite clearly, Jack's intention was to liven up a dull day at my expense.

To my surprise and dismay, Smethwick responded to being summoned. His shadow fell across my desk while I was examining an invoice for washing soda, and when I looked up to greet him, I noticed Jack observing events through the side window of my office.

"I come my Lord," the farmer mocked, and prostrated himself.

I thought it prudent to ignore the jest, for Smethwick was clearly no cooler in temper than he had been on his last visit.

The farmer straightened himself and leered at me menacingly with half-closed eyes as he had done before. He stepped back and began to sway, but this time I knew his swagger to be stress, not the result of liquor.

"I believe you have some badly brewed lamp oil," I opened. "Perhaps you would care to explain how this came into your possession."

Smethwick would give no reply, even when I threatened him with arrest, so I tried an alternative method of intimidation. I shook my head gravely and began making notes about him on a sheet of company letterpaper. This also failed.

The reason for the miserable fellow's obmutescence, although I did not know it at the time, was that he had indeed stolen the spiked lamp oil but not from the South Exmoor Railway. Unbeknown to either of us there was an intermediate thief, from whom Smethwick had taken the oil. Incredibly, therefore, it had been stolen twice!

Consequently, from Smethwick's point of view, my involvement in the affair was both perplexing and irritating. Moreover, he was still baffled by the pyrotechnic scintillations of his handlamp last night.

"The oil to which I refer is stolen property," I told him squarely. "Railway property."

This statement precipitated a response, and the cove began protesting his innocence disingenuously, and with a vehemence which only the guilty can muster. Indeed, without provocation from me, for my keenest interest lay only in closing the matter and going fishing, Smethwick leaned across my desk and seized my lapel. A pot of ink toppled, and I watched in horror as a black puddle spread through my paperwork. The result of hours of tedious arithmetical calculations began to disappear.

The miscreant did not apologize for this, nor did he release his grip on my lapel. On the contrary, the incident seemed to amuse him, and a perverse smirk crept across his unwashed face as the last of my tabulations homogenized.

"There!" he said.

At once I called my Booking Clerk, whose nose was still pressed against my window, and watched with relief as Jack's face vanished towards my door to render assistance. But, alas, help was not on its way at all.

"Err, just...?" I stuttered as Wheeler strode past my door without stopping.

The coward was in flight.

The sickly fragrance of writing ink did not mix pleasantly with the fetor of a perspiring pig breeder. And since I was not of the strongest stomach when Smethwick pulled me against his matted beard and stared me in the eye like a cornered rodent, I blacked out.

When I regained consciousness, I was told that Smethwick had punched me in the eye. To view the evidence, I was presented with a vanity mirror. This I pushed aside, for I did not require a looking glass to feel an ache, nor to deduce that there had been no rush to my assistance after the incident. With little more than some preliminary medical attention, administered by Mr. Phillips, I had been left slumped in my chair for at least half-an-hour.

Alone again, I applied to my swollen eye a swab of iodine. While engaged in this painful but highly recommended form of medication, Jack Wheeler came out of hiding.

Offering me a tin of live bait, maggots which he had scooped from a lineside morkin somewhere, he entered my office nonchalantly and attempted to convince me that he knew nothing of the fracas.

"Do you take me for a turnip head, Wheeler?" I rebutted him, removing the swab from my eye.

Jack looked pleased. As far as he was concerned, everything had gone to plan. He now had a rattling good yarn to tell down at The Shunter.

I pushed the revolting maggots away and told the clerk to flush them under the station tap. But instead he placed the maggots back on my desk and examined my eye from the remove of a convenient distance.

"Jingo! You'll 'ave a prize black'n there, Mr. Jay," he gurgled with token sympathy, and asked a question to which he well knew the answer. "You got 'im tooth for tooth, I 'ope?"

'An eye for an eye' would have been the better analogy.

"A stationmaster does not strike valued customers," I answered Wheeler sternly. "No matter how provocative they may be. Now perhaps the venomous Mr. Smethwick will find he is able to forget the matter of his tuppeny-ha'penny pigs."

Mr. Wheeler twitched with surprise.

"Ay," I waggled my finger. "That's right, Jack. The bruise on my face has nothing to do with your blasted lamp oil, so you can forget the self-congratulations. That scoundrel Smethwick assaulted me to settle a score. Plain as a pikestaff."

Since no one else had thought to do it, I set about mopping up the spilt ink, although much of it had dried by now.

"You can tell your cronies at the public," I continued, "that Smethwick punched the Stationmaster in the eye for preventing his infected pigs from going to market, not because you arranged a confrontation over a drop of measly lamp oil."

I became dizzy, wobbled, and sat down. It did not occur to Wheeler to assist.

"Take it from me, Mr. Wheeler," I said, "Smethwick is a thoroughly nasty piece of work. He bears a grudge."

"Everyone knows that," Jack frowned.

My angry animations had set the iodine stinging again, so I waved Wheeler away. Again the clerk ignored me.

"'e didn't own up to taking the oil then?" he quizzed me snappily, indifferent to my suffering.

"What do you think?" I retorted. "Frankly, I doubt we shall ever get to the bottom of the business. As far as I am concerned, the case of the disappearing lamp oil has itself disappeared. It is best forgotten."

Jack seemed disappointed.

* * *

I allowed myself two hours fishing at Upwater, and took Jack Wheeler's advice to drop my hook downstream of the cressbeds. Jack had assured me that the biggest bites were to be had in the leat leading to the flourmill.

Needless to say, I found no fish here. But I did find the lazy splash of an overshot watermill most relaxing, and relaxation was the chief reason for my sojourn. With a Dipper for company I watched a shoal of fry hovering in the crystal slipstream, and observed in the quivering backwaters a rash of lustrous whirligig beetles circling over an inverted image of Bessam Forest. All was perfectly charming.

In contrast to the mesmeric flow of the river, the air was a frenetic swirl of martins chattering and swooping relentlessly to pick off gnats and other insects caught upon the many lambent watercourses in the vicinity. And as if this was not enough, my fancy was taken by another divertion. During my long wait for the bite that was never to come, I entertained myself searching the cloudless blue void above me to see if I could locate a skylark. Its ceaseless twittering from somewhere aloft hinted that it was hovering nearby, but its telltale speck I could not find.

Later my thoughts turned to Mrs. Smith, whose plight I began to ponder in great depth. There had to be something I could do to help, but still I could think of nothing which would not offend the widow. One thing I knew. She was sensitive about receiving charity.

I was still pondering Mrs. Smith's difficulties, and scratching my head in the manner of a classroom dunce, when my attention was drawn to the mill pond, for in that quarter the fish had begun to plop somewhat lively. Encouraged by this, I decided to put in hand the catching of my supper.

Having set up my line again, and having found a large stone with which to stun my catch, I waited for my first tug. I did not have to wait long, and I left this beautiful spot with no less than three small trout gaping ruefully from my landing net.

* * *

Diggory reported for work, if somewhat absent-mindedly, in time to assist with the 1.08pm Blodcaster train, and I thought it best to give him only one or two light duties to perform.

Immediately after the departure of this train, I located Humphrey Milsom for a brief word concerning the engagement of a woman to clean and cook for me. On my new salary of £95 per annum, and with free tenure of company accommodation, I could now afford to take on a part-time domestic servant.

"I knows just the woman e needs," Humphrey chuckled. "Young Miss Blake. Her does for all sorts when her b'aint behind the bar."

"She is a barmaid?" I queried him cautiously.

"Her father be the landlord of The Pheasant," Humphrey explained. "I'll have a word with him for e, if e likes. Tis a respectable public, Mr. Jay, used by all them commercial travellers, and Miss Blake be very reliable."

"Please do," I implored the porter, for I knew of no one else to approach, and I was falling behind with my personal requirements.

* * *

Six weeks elapsed before the domestic from The Pheasant could take me on, by which time I had become a valued regular customer of The Shunter. Although this was a dim and somewhat grimy public house, frequented mainly by labourers, The Shunter was conveniently situated by the station entrance. In the shelter of its red brick walls I had secured monopoly of a corner table at which no one else dared sit now. And such had become my relationship with the staff that I had been invited to bring food from my own larder should the house menu not suit.

This was a singular gesture, for it allowed me to make use of the gifts I received from patrons of the railway, especially since these gifts were mostly game meats. If I wanted a pheasant for my dinner, for example, I had only to deliver the bird to The Shunter an hour or two in advance, and, in return for a nominal payment, it would be plucked, pulled and cooked by the time I was ready to eat. As a result of this special arrangement, I was beginning to feel guilty about hiring a domestic, for the engagement would put to an end my patronage.

Much had happened to the South Exmoor Railway during the last six weeks. Its branchline ambience had begun to give way to that of a mainline spur. This was in no small way due to the commencement of the London and South Western's excursion trains from the metropolis.

Traffic had been increased still further by the ongoing construction of two passing loops, one at Widdlecombe, the other at Busy Linton, necessitating the frequent passage of permanent way trains delivering ballast, sleepers, and lengths of rail. These lengths of rail, which spanned several trucks apiece, were of the new Bessemer steel bullhead design, and were a vast improvement over the old Dodd case-hardened Vignoles sections which had been in use formerly. The case-hardened rails had begun to fracture at the joints.

Headquarters had designated my goods yard a temporary stacking area for signalling components awaiting installation, consequently the South Siding had become a clutter of wooden semaphore arms, signal posts, finials, steel rodding, drums of cable, pots of tallow, pulleys, nuts, bolts, levers, indeed all the paraphernalia one never noticed once installed and working.

Seen lying around loose, however, these linkages struck one as slightly absurd, and denuded the observer of any complacency he might have felt about railway travel. Try as I might, I could not reconcile this contraptionry with the blind faith put in it by the crews of trains at speed.

Sundry other items, notably tins of paint and sacks of clout-nails, were disappearing as fast as they could be delivered. But there was nothing unusual in this. Railway yards are notoriously difficult to safeguard against pilfering.

A new pair of telegraph wires had been hung, to accommodate a metallic return electric bell circuit providing communication between neighbouring signalmen. At last Ivor Hales was able to send and receive messages regarding the progress of trains, directly from the vantage point of his cabin. Although these messages were limited to simple, predetermined ringing codes, they made a busy railway a much safer place. With four wires now spanning the telegraph poles alongside the line, the South Exmoor Railway was beginning to acquire an air of importance.

So much for Mr. Crump's conversion to earth return telegraphy.

Thankfully the most bothersome improvement of all, that of relaying the platforms to the universal height of two-foot six-inches above rail level, had now been completed. On account of higher priorities elsewhere, however, the labourers had come and gone unpredictably throughout the job. My station was still recovering from the upheaval caused by these men, who had been hired from Lord Lacy's Estate.

But all my worries were the least of my worries compared to what I was about to encounter, for nothing in life prepares one for the supernatural.

CHAPTER EIGHTEEN

UNREST IN THE SPIRIT WORLD

Apropos my domestic servant, her engagement was destined to be something of a trauma. Indeed, the first in what was to be a series of disquieting developments came one Friday afternoon when I was waylaid by Humphrey Milsom and introduced to a strange woman wearing a black cashmere dress. The time must have been about 3.45pm because I remember standing back from the edge of the deserted 'up' platform to avoid the smuts from a circus special returning non-stop to Exeter.

"Meet Miss Blake," Humphrey shouted above the rumble, and presented the woman who was to do my chores.

I was somewhat taken aback by what I saw. Miss Blake was as pale-faced an icon of the female complexion as ever I had seen, but not in an attractive way, you understand, for her skin was more the texture of cabbage than alabaster. With little red eyes like an albino mouse, she emerged from the cascading smoke and stared at me as if I were her executioner. Her ears were adorned with pendulous bobs and bangles which tinkled musically with her every move, and a delicate scarf embroidered with the signs of the zodiac covered her shoulders.

Although I have indicated that Miss Blake was staring at me, upon closer inspection I discovered that she was not. At least, I think not. You see, the focal point of her gaze seemed different for each eye, one being the sky and, as far as I could tell, the other being Upshott Wood some distance behind me.

Now, as I have alluded, Miss Blake's eyes were small and red. Tiny vortexes of fire would be a fair description. But despite their intensity they had a markedly timid quality, and the incongruity of it quite transfixed me. They were the eyes of the startled.

Since the spinster wore no bonnet, I could not help noticing her hair. It was as coarse, straight, and as copper bright as the new telegraph wires glinting above the station. I also noticed that 'young' Miss Blake, as Humphrey had described her, was thirty-eight if she was a day.

The little ginger woman returned my shocked stare with a demure smile, and I reciprocated hesitantly. Remembering my manners, I doffed my hat and welcomed her to my domain, in response to which she curtsied awkwardly and uttered my name beneath her breath. This she did as if in awe of me. Truth to tell, I was in awe of her. Had the smoke of the passing circus train reclaimed her, I should not have complained.

At this point in my description of Miss Blake my pen falters because your perception of her would not be complete without an appreciation of her strange ambience. Yet whilst this ambience begs description, equally it defies it. I would merely be scratching the surface were I to say that proximity to the strange woman had a profoundly unsettling effect upon me. Going one step further, I can say that I sensed about Miss Blake an unaccountable familiarity, rather like someone half remembered from a bad dream; someone who should not exist in the cold light of day. The sensation was quite extraordinary.

Humphrey, having gone out of his way to arrange the introduction, lowered his shoulders with disappointment upon sensing the bad chemistry of it. He was further disappointed when I dealt him a glare expressing my disapproval of his good deed.

Just as I was on the point of announcing my change of heart regarding the engagement of a domestic servant, the spinster, having overcome her bashfulness, narrowed her emberlike eyes upon me and began to speak. I froze, and cocked an ear. She told me that she could not chat for very long because someone was calling her. Now, I could hear the fading rattle of the circus special, and I could hear the cheaping of sparrows upon the Goods shed roof, but I could not hear anyone calling. Consequently I was unable to comment upon the matter.

I forced a smile and waited patiently while Miss Blake struggled to remove something from her vanity bag, something which I presumed to be a reference from a previous employer. In the event, it turned out to be a hairbrush, and with it she began preening herself in lengthy strokes. While doing so, and with all the indifference of an offended cat, she quoted me her rates.

I was fortunate, word had it, to be getting the services of such a first class domestic. The 'word', mind you, was coming from the domestic herself. I also learned that because I was domiciled in a railway station, in particular, Upshott station, I ought to view Miss Blake's engagement as a very special favour.

"Oh yes, I refused to do 'ousework for Stationmaster Mildenhew," she revealed groggily, as if he had been a devil worshipper. "Yer see, trains frights I. This station frights I. But I came 'ere because Mr. Milsom be a very persuasive gent. He begged me on your behalf, Mr. Jay."

Humphrey's silver eyebrows drew together, suggesting that this was something of an exaggeration.

"Your trepidation is not unique, Miss Blake," I consoled the spinster. "Many people are still frightened of trains. There are scholars who believe that we shall one day discover a dreadful medical side-effect from travelling so fast. There are folk who claim that railway tickets spread diseases, and that passing through damp tunnels causes rheumatism. Why, I once came across a clergyman who insisted that it is only the fury of demons trapped inside the boiler of a steam engine that makes the machine work at all. Imagine that! Modern industry based upon the roasting of devils until they are forced to escape by turning a wheel. Mind you, if this is so, then the more stubborn demons would appear to become so enraged by the imposition that they prefer to explode their way out of the vessel rather than co-operate!"

Miss Blake flinched. The thought of a boiler bursting with evil did not amuse her. I adjusted my smile and continued:

"Luckily, such ignorance is no longer widespread. But then, who is to say what like of salamander breeds in the heat of these machines?"

I held my clumsy wit. Miss Blake's face had distorted badly, as if observed through a goldfish bowl. She flicked a speck of dust from my tunic, and said gravely:

"Oh don't, Mr. Jay. Tis not 'at which frights I, tis 'ere. Tis Upshott Station."

I hastened to reassure Miss Blake that my station was harmless, and quickly diverted the conversation to the matter of her hours and scope of duties. The details settled, Miss Blake left hurriedly by Stoney Way.

Humphrey took my arm to speak confidentially.

"Sir," he opened. "Have e had no enquiries on a puppydog?"

"No," I replied.

"I thinks e will then. Someone must be missin' the critter, for her fell from a train window this day. Diggory rescued the hound, and found her well enough for the ordeal, but the hungry blighter's bin drinkin' water and eatin' buns without end. Diggory b'aint got time for to be runnin' to the village to fetch buns for a stray dog, and at a penny-ha'penny a piece, I can't afford to be sendin' him."

I halted the porter.

"From which train did the dog fall?" I asked.

"Her flew out of this mornin's circus special on its way to Blodcaster. We'm had her since 9.30am."

"That was over six hours ago, Humphrey. Have there been no enquiries?"

"Tis what I be askin' e, Mr. Jay. The telegraph's been chatterin', but e weren't here to decipher it, so I don't rightly know," he complained.

I had no particular wish to see the animal myself, so I instructed Humphrey to deal with the matter.

"At 4.40pm the Brewers' Goods will be back from Blodcaster," I said. "If someone has reported the dog missing, then the Stationmaster at Blodcaster will have been trying to reach me through the telegraph. Not having succeeded, he will have instructed the Guard of the Brewer's train to pass on the message. Have a quiet word with that

Guard, Humphrey, and if no such message is forthcoming, I suggest you put the dog aboard for Giddiford, with instructions for Head Office to deal with it. If the owner cannot be found, the company veterinary surgeon will be called upon to destroy the hapless hound. This would not be the first time a member of the public has used a train window to dispose of an unwanted item." To this I added solemnly: "Be sure my instructions are carried out, Humphrey. Diggory has been taxing me on the subject of a station dog lately, but I perceive no need of one."

"Well now, Mr. Jay," said Humphrey, "with rats gnawin' darn great holes through the sacks in the Goods shed, I reckons a cat would make more sense."

* * *

At 5.50pm an unfamiliar engine arrived in the South Siding and discharged a dozen gangers from a single flat-truck. This was an unusual sight, for it was not customary for railway labourers to be given rides to and from their places of work. Indeed, it was not uncommon for gangers, switchmen and permanent way men to walk ten or fifteen miles before and after their day's toil. However, on Friday evenings on the South Exmoor, Upshott's permanent way men, if they were lucky, enjoyed the luxury of a ride home from their remote workplace by way of a locomotive going 'on shed'.

The term 'on shed', incidentally, applies to a locomotive returning to the engine shed at the end of its turn of duty. Conversely, the term 'off shed' applies to a locomotive leaving the shed at the commencement of its turn.

On this occasion the gangers had come from an isolated spot known as Chanting Bend on Lord Lacy's private estate, and it appeared that they had taken the opportunity to do some illicit shooting. The use of fowling-pieces by these men was unusual. Shotguns are rather noisy and apt to attract the attention of a gamekeeper. So only on Fridays did the men poach using firearms, this being when the steam engine was at hand to allow a quick get-away.

Encircling the jury-truck upon which they had ridden, the labourers jested boisterously over the most equitable way to split their haul. Mr. Swain, the Chief Ganger, plucked a brace of rabbit from one of the piles of limp carcases and presented it to the locomotive crew. The gift was duly hung alongside a knot of pigeon already occupying one corner of the footplate.

Having sorted themselves out, the men now threw the remainder of their day's bounty over their shoulders and repaired to The Shunter, in the hospitality of which establishment they would quench their thirsts and forget their many cares.

By the look of them, their shoot had been good this week. With eyes twinkling like diamonds in liquorice, the dirty-faced poachers set off for the public house with their tattered waistcoats appended with epaulets of hare, duck and pheasant. With much merrymaking in prospect, they had begun chaunting songs and ditties even before reaching the Tramway, and I reckoned that between them they would drain a good barrel of cider before staggering home to their wives, whereupon, incidentally, the real ding-dong would begin.

I strolled across the yard to peruse the little 2-4-0 tank engine that had delivered the gang. The South

Exmoor Railway operated four engines in all, two ancient second-hand purchases, and two locomotives of the latest design. The latter were leased long term from the London and South Western Railway Company.

The engine in the station now was one of the company's two decrepit retainers, and it compared poorly with the Beattie well-tanks. Nevertheless it did possess one or two striking features, notably a copper-capped chimney and brass steam dome, both of which were tall and curvy. But their appeal to the eye was somewhat spoiled by the upright nature of the driver's cab. This was no more than a sheet-metal box with square spectacles. However, in the Nineteenth Century, footplatemen were lucky to have any cab at all.

Designated No.2, this 40 ton piece of ironmongery from the Beyer Peacock foundry was named *Ondle* and outshopped in the South Exmoor's locomotive livery of olive-green and black. With five-foot diameter drive wheels, the four-coupled engine could doubtless manage a spritely turn of speed at the head of a light train, but it looked far from sleek with its boiler housing criss-crossed with external linkages and pipes. Further, for some reason, *Ondle's* whistle produced nothing louder than a muted gurgle.

The driver leaned from the cab, shook his head soberly, and handed me a crinkled copy of the *Daily Chronical*. I shook the newspaper straight and read the column to which he had drawn my attention. It reported the slaughter of thirty people in a train crash at Clapham Junction, caused by an inexperienced locomotive driver missing a ground signal. He had driven his shunting engine across the path of a fast 'up' train.

"Dear God," I shuddered.

The South Exmoor driver removed his cap and muttered a prayer. I could not help noticing that his supplication was not for the passengers, for whom he was sorry enough, but for the errable soul upon the footplate whose lapse in concentration had caused the smash.

"He'll be cast into perdition for such a misdeed," I heard his voice reverberate from *Ondle's* cab.

"God forgives," I remarked. "It is the driver's next of kin for whom I feel sorry. They will die of shame. I have seen it happen."

"And all it takes is a moment's distraction," came the reply.

I prayed with the driver, for such carnage was never further away than a simple oversight. Until the latter part of the century, when the introduction of mechanical interlocking equipment made it impossible to set signals and points in conflict with each other, railway safety relied entirely upon staff discipline. Nothing less than unremitting adherence to the rules would do, accompanied by sound judgement in all states of mind, all states of health, all weather conditions, and throughout all lengths of duty.

The driver snatched his newspaper from me disdainfully and tossed it into the firebox.

To improve the atmosphere I made lighter conversation, and enquired why I had not seen *Ondle* in Upshott before. The engineman dried his eye with the lining of his forage cap and replied sullenly:

"Retubing. Been away at Nine Elms."

Before I could learn more of this engine and its crew, the stoker returned from his trip to the station privy and climbed aboard the footplate, whereupon the mournful driver decided that he had no further need of my society. With *Ondle* blowing off steam at 140lbs per square inch, the crew coaxed their charge away over the turn-out and left me standing alone at the lineside.

Earlier in the afternoon I had given Miss Blake my spare latch-key, and she was now in my kitchen skinning and gutting a hare, so I remained on the platforms until 6.15pm to 'right away' the 'up' Mail. Having done this I retired to my corner table in The Shunter to steady my nerves with a malt whisky and cigar while waiting to see how good was the cook I had hired.

I had just stubbed out my cigar when Diggory flung himself through the bar door at me.

"Your dinner's ready, Mr. Jay," he shouted for all the world to hear.

With a haughty glance down her nose at me, the landlord's wife roused herself from behind the bar, crossed the room, and removed the menu from my table.

To complement my steaming dish, Miss Blake handed me a bottle of sauce and two thick slices of bread. She now bundled together some of my linen to pass on to a local woman who took in washing. I set about my meal, and discovered that the spinster could cook quite well. Despite her culinary talent, however, it was easy to see why the woman had not snared herself a husband, for her conversation was of a dreadfully morbid bias.

Also, she was given to sudden bouts of staring. For no apparent reason she would stop and stare at a window, a wall, or perhaps the door, as do cats when tormented by the presence of things not visible to the human eye, and be possessed of heavy breathing. I make no bones about it, the woman gave me the creeps.

Miss Blake spotted me placing her bottle of sauce to one side discreetly, and took offence.

"We serves that down at The Pheasant," said she stiffly, pushing the sauce back at me. Before I could think of a polite way to decline the condiment, she had uncorked the bottle and tipped a portion upon my plate. "Garn, try it Mr. Jay," she cajoled me. "I makes it special, and tis popular with them sewage workers."

I dare say it was considered tasty enough by those with a stout stomach, but such concoctions played havoc with my digestion, so I ignored her.

"Now, I be off to Parson's Farm for to collect some eggs for my mother," the spinster continued in her thin voice. "More's the pity I shall 'ave ter come back 'ere again for to clear the dishes."

Upon hearing her last remark, I looked up and discovered Miss Blake staring at something. But fortunately she recovered from the distraction and left without breathing heavily.

By the time Miss Blake returned, I had finished eating and was preparing to invigilate upon the platforms again. The domestic had scarcely begun to clear the table when she dropped a handful of cutlery and emitted a piercing shriek. Thinking that she had seen a rat, I cast my eye about the floor, but the floor was quite ratless.

"Oh, forgive I, Mr. Jay," she apologized. "I thought I 'eard a noise." She confessed: "Lor, 'ow this place do make I nervous."

"Nervous? Why?" I asked. "Are you so afraid of trains, Miss Blake, that merely being in a railway station distresses you? If so," I continued, "why did you accept this appointment?"

I have to admit that until now I had not realized just how distracted the woman was. Her uncertain eyes gathered upon me in terror.

"Truth to tell, Mr. Jay, tis this place," she blurted. "I remembers what they unearthed here when they began a diggin' the railway."

Miss Blake fell to her knees and started clawing blindly at the scattered utensils.

"Unearthed?" I asked impatiently. "What do you mean, *unearthed?*"

"Dug up," she advised me spuriously.

"Yes, yes, I know what unearthed means. But what did they dig up?"

"Remains," said she gravely, and began rubbing a fork as if it would unleash the Holy Saviour. "Human remains, they were. Found right 'ere on this very site."

Having no taste for spooky tales, I called a halt to her ghastly recollection at once.

"They were the bones of a man," she continued regardless. "An evil man accordin' to parish records. But no one would tell I precisely what the wicked evil-doer 'ad done to be denied a Christian burial in the churchyard. Still, God gave I an imagination, Mr. Jay, and if the dead man did 'alf the things I think 'e did, then tis right they buried 'im 'ere. Course, in them days, no one expected a railway to come through. This station were built on unconsecrated ground, yer see."

"Like most," I confirmed wearily.

"Twas I who found the skull," said she. "While a courtin' a navvy boy. We went among the mounds of spoil that were all around 'ere at the time, for to find some privacy for a spell, and then it 'appened." Miss Blake paused from clearing the table, and her intense red eyes narrowed upon the untouched bottle of sauce. "My, 'ow that 'andsome lad did chase I for a kiss. Oh, I ran away, course, Mr. Jay," she advised me with a seemly smile. "But not too fast, mind." She removed the cork from the bottle, savoured the spicy aroma unleashed by it, and giggled.

"This navvy boy liked your sauce?" I asked.

"Oh, 'e did, Mr. Jay," the woman purred confidentially. She flinched, and I sensed that we were back on the subject of the heathen burial. "Now, course, I wish I 'adn't run away at all, for I 'adn't gone but a few steps when I fell down a big 'ole!" she declared. "And when I opened my eyes, I were face to face with a skull! Well, I couldn't stop a screamin', so frit was I. The navvy boy slapped my face, but still I couldn't stop a screamin' for to tell 'im what I'd seen. Well, I reckon I must 'ave put 'is reputation in jeopardy, for 'e ran away never to return."

"A sad tale," I sympathized.

"Often I finds myself a wonderin' where that navvy boy be now, Mr. Jay," the spinster reflected hauntingly. "But I don't wonder where them bones is. Them's right under our feet."

"Nonsense. I have no doubt that the remains were properly disposed of," I reassured her. "There is nothing abroad in Upshott this day."

Miss Blake appeared not to hear my words of comfort. Either she was in a trance or she was listening to something unnatural, for those small, wide-set eyes of hers had become fixed in a glasslike stare from the corners of their sockets.

I decided to tolerate the woman's hysteria no longer.

"Come, come," I chaffed her. "I tell you there is nothing abroad in Upshott this day. You may rest assured of it. Your imagination is playing tricks, Miss Blake. In my time here I have experienced nothing save the creaks and groans of any building this size."

I turned away and muttered under my breath: "Why have you done this to me, Humphrey?"

Miss Blake overheard my private lamentation.

"Beg yer pardon, Mr. Jay?" she asked.

Before I could invent an answer, she twitched violently.

"Hear that?" she jumped.

"No," I replied with frail levity.

"I 'eard something, Mr. Jay. I tell you I did."

"And I tell you you did not," I retorted.

Truth to tell, Miss Blake had indeed heard something, for I had heard it too. Neither creak nor groan, it was more a bump. But unlike Miss Blake, I had chosen to dismiss the sound as meaningless.

"You heard Mr. Phillips going home for the night," I said. "That is all. The clerk is inclined to slam his door at the end of a bad day."

I, being the one who would sleep alone in the station house each night, preferred this explanation, and stuck to it. I could not afford to allow this insufferable woman to affect my judgement and have me sitting up all night armed with a truncheon.

With a wave of my hand, I discharged Miss Blake early so that I might forget the matter.

"Tweren't Mr. Phillips goin' 'ome," the scaremonger advised me while donning her shawl. "The gentleman left five-and-twenty minutes ago."

"If this station is haunted," I erupted, "then why have I not heard anything peculiar before?"

"P'raps tis my return to the scene," she speculated with a quaver. "Things are attracted to I, Sir.

Things that can't get through to normal folk. Sometimes I think a soul is callin' I from limbo; a repentant soul awaitin' a Christian burial."

"Miss Blake, I crave that in future you do not talk to me about evil spirits," I instructed her firmly. Having dealt with that, I flipped open my snuff-box and placed a small pinch of snuff upon the back of my hand. "Anyway," I said with a sniff, "if there is an evil spirit calling you, it must be doing so from the inside of a locomotive boiler. And if by being trapped there it is making restitution for its evil ways, by powering one of our trains, then I would rather you left it alone." I chuckled coldly. "Should we have a locomotive failure, then you will be called upon quickly enough to stir new life in the machine. What do you say to that, eh?"

I closed my snuff-box with a loud snap and waited for my witticism to register. This it appeared to do nicely, for Miss Blake began to cackle like a duck. But soon it became apparent that she had not heard one word of my quip, and that her cackling was not laughter. Indeed no. The spinster had heard another of her unaccountable noises, and had become hysterical.

Presently she recovered, with the aid of a seat and a tumbler of water, and her voice took on a most peculiar energy.

"I believe my coming 'ere is causing unrest, Mr. Jay," said she.

"It most certainly is," I convicted her.

CHAPTER NINETEEN

A CURSE ON THE STATIONMASTER

The following day, about noon, I was on Platform One pondering Miss Blake's macabre tale when Ivor Hales came by. Saturday was Ivor's half day, and he had transferred control of the signalbox to a relief switchman from Giddiford. Ivor was wearing green corduroys and carrying a tartan blanket under his arm, a sure sign that he was off to Upshott Hill to picnic with his family. I beckoned him to the shade beneath the platform canopy, and set about testing the authenticity of Miss Blake's story.

Expecting Mr. Hales to expose it as humbug, or perhaps a long standing joke, I discharged the details with a certain degree of levity and a barely restrained smirk, afterwards folding my arms affectedly to await his reply.

"That's about the length of it, Mr. Jay," the signalman lamented with a heavy frown.

In sheer surprise at the fellow's unexpected response, I lowered my arms, lowered my jaw, and fell silent.

Ivor laughed self-consciously.

"But these events took place well before my time here, Mr. Jay," he explained. "Have a word with Humphrey. Humphrey knows all about the curse."

"Curse?" I retorted. "What curse? This is Devonshire, not darkest Africa. We do not have curses in Devonshire. Surely you do not give credence to such nonsense, Ivor."

Ivor smiled enigmatically and stroked his zig-zag

whiskers. The fellow seemed ever to smell of bluebells, which, I believe, came from the metal polish he applied so liberally to his beloved instruments. He eyed me reservedly and grunted neutrally. I eyed him cautiously and grunted angrily.

"Well!" I chided the fellow. "It has come to a pretty pass when a man of your substance believes in the nonsense of the half-conscious. I had expected you, of all people, Mr. Hales, to pour scorn on this ridiculous ghost story."

I had been reminded yet again that education does not necessarily unshackle a country fellow from his superstitions. I was also reminded that education does, even if it fails in all else, sharpen a fellow's wit, so I studied my colleague carefully to see if he was baiting me. Frankly I could not tell.

"It doesn't signify, Mr. Jay," Ivor assured me pithily. "Folks believe what they will. Nevertheless, an Upshott stationmaster has yet to last more than twelve months, so something must be wrong."

"Just so," I concurred briskly, referring to the first of Ivor's observations. A pensive mood overtook me when the second registered. "Only twelve months?" I queried him.

Ivor confirmed this disturbing new fact and fell to a dead-eyed gaze.

"Come now," I chuckled nervously. "You shall have to do better than that if you are to get me on the go."

The Signalman grimaced, adjusted his woollen cravat, and left. I grimaced, adjusted my outlook upon the railway, and retreated to my thoughts. After this, ugly speculations began to multiply like rabbits.

I took the view that Humphrey's was the voice of sanity hereabouts, so I decided to take Mr. Hales's advice and consult the fellow. If my Senior Porter knew all about the curse, then, by the same token, he would know that it was a myth. Unfortunately, speaking with Humphrey would have to wait until Sunday morning because this Saturday was the porter's half day.

Humphrey lived a mile or so south of Busy Linton, on a small-holding managed by his two sons, and in fine weather he would walk home over the downs. By now he was probably well on his way.

Imagine my relief, then, to see Humphrey standing on the forecourt waiting for an omnibus.

"Mr. Milsom!" I called anxiously, striding towards the fellow. A number of heads turned to see such indecorous behaviour on the part of a stationmaster. To restore calm, I slackened my pace and dispensed a few bland smiles. Upon reaching the porter I observed that I was still under public scrutiny, so, to demonstrate my continued composure I opened our chat with a conversational trifle. "I see you have been shopping, Humphrey," I boomed loudly, yet casually. "Too much to carry over the hill?"

At last I was no longer the centre of attraction, but by now it was too late to stop Humphrey unleashing upon me the details of his purchases, for he had taken great joy from the fact that I should find time to make small talk.

"Arr, I be no chicken, Mr. Jay," he advised me with a laboured sigh.

Humphrey's bag had been badly packed and was bulging in all directions. Suddenly it was open, and I was invited to inspect its contents. "See here, I got some Horniman tea in one of them ingenious new packets where they puts a vacuum inside to take up the extra space," he said. "Though frankly, it be beyond me why they does such a daft thing. If a vacuum be nothin', then how does her stop the tea goin' mouldy, and why does her cost extra? T'aint cheap either, at sevenpence-ha'penny per quarter, but the missus gets this'n because her keeps fresh until we has company. And talkin' of the missus, look here, I've a tuppeny bunch of violets for to sweeten her with. Her always rounds on me, e see, for buyin' a wrong'n. But her list do say flour, umbles, and some Cornish mackerel from Cubitt's. Personally, I always reckons on pilchards myself..."

"Yes, yes. Indeed. Most laudable, Humphrey," I interrupted. "Now, what is this I hear about a cur..."

"Course, I does my best at this shoppin' lark, Mr. Jay," Humphrey resumed. "But rightly it be women's doin's. I can't be holdin' with all this idle gossip', e see. Never bin one for standin' in shop doorways chinwaggin' about what Mrs. Smicker be up to, or the price of black-leadin' and pumice stone."

"Or standing in station doorways chinwagging about what you have in your shopping bag, eh?" I teased the fellow.

Humphrey did not hear me. He was rummaging in his bag again.

"Want e a piece of ginger-bread, Mr. Jay?"

"No thank you," I replied smartly. "I would rather you told me more of this spinster woman you have loosed upon me, Humphrey. She is most unnatural, and sets my teeth on edge with tales of human remains. Why, she claims to be responsible for the discovery of a burial site beneath this station. Do you substantiate her claim, Humphrey?"

Humphrey closed his shopping bag furtively and began studying the sky.

"Well?" I barked.

"She be a fair cook, I hear," he commented evasively.

"And what is all this about a curse, Humphrey?" I enquired with a heavy heart.

My Senior Porter was not a slippery fellow by nature, but he was clearly squirming to avoid this particular subject.

"Hey ho, Mr. Jay, I see your eye's healed up nicely."

The bruise had gone long since.

"Humphrey, is there a curse?" I persisted. "Speak up, fellow. You shall not scare me with it. I do not believe in such flapdoodle."

"Then why be e askin'?" the porter turned on me with a face of stone.

I shivered.

Just then I heard the crack of a whip in Natter Lane, and Humphrey began chortling with undue excitement.

"Ah, here her comes!" he declared joyously.

At sight of a four-horse omnibus clattering over the cobbles, I gave up the inquisition and mopped my brow.

The omnibus, having turned sharply into the station forecourt, slid to rest on the gravel outside the Booking Hall entrance and brought to an abrupt end my Senior Porter's invented mirth.

With his face humourless again, Humphrey stepped out from under the station awning and handed his bag to the driver. The driver placed the bag between the legs of a railway ganger who had clambered to the roof of the vehicle to get a cheap seat.

One could see, faintly visible beneath the black and yellow paintwork of the omnibus, the words: *DIE.ET.MON.DROIT*, revealing that the vehicle had once been a mail coach. These fine conveyances had come to the second-hand market at bargain prices some years ago when the railways became the predominant carrier of Her Majesty's Mail, and nowadays were to be found in the most unlikely places. This particular coach had been acquired by the Lacy Arms for the purpose of communicating that inn with the railway station each day. Indeed, its perambulatory retirement brought it to my forecourt to meet virtually every passenger train.

To my eye, this worn but comfortable old road vehicle conjured up a picture of sedition rather than tradition, for upon its foreboot the Royal Cipher had been supplanted by the insignia of the Lacy Arms, as if the inn were the seat of a revolution.

My sense of humour further compels me to draw your attention to the fact that the arrival of this, or indeed any other omnibus outside my station at noon on Saturday, when no train was due, was something of a local eccentricity. Especially since not only did the ex mail coach run through the village to the Lacy Arms, whence it came, but continued over Upshott Hill to Blodcaster. The operator found this once-weekly extension to the service extremely lucrative because it provided transport for South Exmoor employees coming off duty for the weekend.

Now, if you are wondering why the South Exmoor Railway did not run a midday train on

Saturdays, a day which is traditionally busy, then I can furnish you with two reasons. The official reason was that of insufficient public demand. But, as a principal stationmaster upon the SER, I happened to know of a less well aired adjunct to the company's reasoning. Quite simply, it realized that there would be insufficient receipts from a train occupied largely by railway servants holding passes to travel the line free of charge.

Still more cynically, in bad weather, of which there was much on the moors, staff who could not afford to ride the omnibus, and who did not wish to get drenched walking home, would be induced to continue giving their services without pay until the arrival of the afternoon train. Their services would have to be given while waiting for the later train, you understand, because a company regulation forbade wages staff to be on the premises unless at work, paid or otherwise.

The fact that there was a lack of local demand for frequent passenger trains at the weekend might strike one as odd, but in this state of affairs, as in every other on the South Exmoor Railway, there lies a tale. Briefly, it was to do with the policies of the LSWR rather than the peregrinations of the local public. To make connections with the rest of the country, the SER passenger was dependent upon the London and South Western interchange facility at Giddiford Junction, and at weekends there were no stopping passenger trains on that section of the mainline.

On Saturdays and Sundays, therefore, the South Exmoor became an isolated railway, and, as such, was of little use to the people of Ondle Valley. Now, whereas a less community minded company would have closed its doors to the travelling public while such circumstances prevailed, the South Exmoor endeavoured to maintain a token local service. Indeed, its management was optimistic that the near future would see SER trains running over LSWR metals to Exeter at the weekends, thus also improving the service on the mainline.

Unbeknown to the likes of Mr. Crump, however, the London and South Western Railway Company had quite different plans.

Certainly I did not share Mr. Crump's optimism about the expansion of SER services in the future. This far west, the London and South Western's use of the mainline at weekends was largely confined to the movement of goods and, during the summer months, excursion trains. The latter traffic, which comprised nought but privately chartered specials visiting places like Bideford and Barnstaple, did not stop at Giddiford.

From this state of affairs sprang the SER employee's average working week of five-and-a-half days, his free time being the Sabbath and Saturday afternoon, subject to rota. Incidentally, here I must qualify the official term 'free time' by saying that it would have been more honest to call it 'unpaid time'. The hours actually worked by railway servants were vastly greater than those implied in the company's cleverly worded conditions of employment.

Before picking up the story again, let me just paint you a little more of the background to these restless times, firstly by pointing out that however deep rooted may have been this country's social and religious traditions in the early part of the century, attitudes were changing fast. Working class people seemed poised to follow the middle class into an era of increased leisure time, albeit on a more modest scale and funded institutionally rather than by increased personal wealth, and this had implications for the railways.

The introduction of the Bank Holiday in 1871 had been a direct response to this pressure, and nowhere was it more evident than on the beaches of the watering resorts. Crowds of factory excursionists and middle class day trippers were frequently so dense that one could not see the the sand or the brine upon which they had all descended.

As a foresighted stationmaster, I envisaged Saturdays and Sundays becoming quite the busiest time on some railways, certainly as far as passenger traffic was concerned. What is more, with an interesting market town like Blodcaster at the end of our line, I saw no reason why the South Exmoor Railway should not share in the bonanza.

To continue the story, we must return to the omnibus standing outside Upshott Station, aboard which we find those South Exmoor employees at liberty from noon. As you can imagine, the spectacle of an omnibus, a rival mode of transport, packed to capacity with railway workers, was one of some irony. The irony, I hasten to add, was not lost on the SER's major shareholder, Lord Lacy, for he owned the omnibus!

Humphrey's personal magnitude occupied the equivalent of two seats in the tight confines of the converted mail coach, but his conscience did not appear to be troubled by it. With a twinkle in his eye, and surrounded by resentful faces, he peered through the quarter-light at me and began mouthing words, aided by a peculiar sign language for which his stubby fingers were not sufficiently agile. Hence I could make no sense of his gesticulations. Still less comprehensible was the fact that the fellow's exertions were entirely unnecessary. The adjacent window was wide open.

"Speak normally, Humphrey," I mouthed back, jabbing my finger at the lowered glass.

Humphrey leaned towards the open window to finish what he was saying.

"... perpetual bad luck, Mr. Jay, but they found human remains here right enough."

"What was that about perpetual bad luck?" I asked.

"T'appened when they were excavatin' the drainage courses prior to tracklaying," Humphrey continued. "But bless me, Mr. Jay, all else be hearsay."

"Just a minute," I halted him. "I did not quite catch what you said about perpetual bad luck, Humphrey?"

Before my Senior Porter could say another word he was carried away by the overloaded omnibus. It swerved around the forecourt, took a right-turn into Natter Lane, followed by a left-turn into the High Street, and was gone.

I shook my head despairingly and retreated to my office to check Mr. Phillips's coal receipts. I had also to sign Mr. Hales's Train Register and deal with a mountainous backlog of correspondence.

One of the envelopes in my mail pouch bore the seal of the company Claims Clerk, and this I opened first. It contained a query regarding a claim against the company for damage done to a local dignitary's private carriage. The carriage in question was, of course, Squire Albury's magnificent cabriolet. And the damage done was a dog-hook gash in the vehicle's natural timber finish, plus several abrasions to the wheel spokes.

The report also contained a disturbingly colourful account of a 'misguided unloading operation at Bessam logging station', the reading of which reduced my stomach to a bag of ferrets. Indeed, so great were my feelings of guilt that my face, even though I was quite alone, pounded with heat and shame such as it had not done since my schooldays.

As if my unease was not enough, I was also faced with a puzzle. The claim had been submitted five weeks ago, yet for some reason it had not been brought to my attention until now. And still more curiously, I had not been brought to book over it. The explanation was to be found in the clerk's covering letter.

It seemed, fortunately for me, that Squire Albury had no friends on the South Exmoor Railway. This was no surprise, of course, but never would I have guessed that the strength of feeling against him was so great. In the words of the Claims Clerk, the squire was 'wont to claim rather too freely', and, furthermore, his claims were to be regarded as 'at best inflated, and more probably based upon an entirely fictitious event'. This being the climate of the affair, the clerk had automatically engaged the squire in a dispute over the figures, never suspecting that any real damage had been done.

To be on the safe side, however, the Claims Clerk was now writing to me to ask if I could recall seeing anything in the condition of the cabriolet which might account for the huge bill the squire had incurred in having it fettled. In a rather telling footnote, I was urged to bear in mind that it would be difficult for the squire to substantiate his claim that the 'alleged' damage had been done on the SER. It might just as easily have occurred on the LSWR or Metropolitan Railway.

By the tone of his letter, I would say that the clerk expected me to discredit the claim altogether, and since I had no wish to disappoint the fellow I drafted an evasive reply proposing merely that the squire had been overcharged for the repair.

A woolly-minded statement such as this would do nothing to clarify the situation, of course, which is why I sent it. For in such circumstances confusion is the ally of the guilty.

I had also received a letter from the company Telegraph Officer. In it he explained that he was leaving the SER to advance himself upon the Cornwall Railway, and that in the prosecution of his final duties he had arranged for me the tuition of a General Post Office Telegraph Instructor.

I was to receive two visits from this instructor. Upon his first visit he would install a dummy telegraph instrument and demonstrate how to key in the Morse alphabet, leaving me a copy of the Morse Code to learn more fully later, and upon his second visit he would test me for speed and accuracy. If I was good enough, he would award me a certificate of proficiency. The outlook was bleak.

Only when I was deemed proficient would the instructor remove the dummy instrument and leave me in peace. Until then, I would be expected to practise for no less than four hours a day. Quite where this time was supposed to come from, I had no idea.

Further, the company's outgoing Telegraph Officer had arranged for the GPO Telegraph Instructor to pay his first visit on Monday next, for which reason he had enclosed a copy of the SER's telegraphic shorthand to learn in the meantime. This was the oddest compilation of abbreviations I had ever seen. It included names like 'Hup' for

Upshott's horsebox, and 'Twinch' for the company's two-and-a-half ton mobile crane.

Frankly, with Upshott Station being referred to as 'Ups' with a gas house siding called 'Pong', I began to wonder if I had stepped into a fairy tale. Moreover, as Upshott's new Stationmaster, I had been ruthlessly compressed to 'J', which was not greatly flattering.

Looking at the length of this list of abbreviations, I predicted that I would make a poor scholar.

CHAPTER TWENTY

SPOILED BLOOMERS

To lift myself from the doldrums I put the Telegraph Codebook in my drawer and stepped out into the sunshine for a while to cogitate more pleasant matters. I was standing by the platform clock, minding my own business, when something struck my foot, exploded, and showered me with what looked like fragments of dried mud. It seemed that someone was using me for target practise.

I looked around to see who it was, expecting to find either Diggory brandishing a catapult, or perhaps Smethwick seeking further revenge, but observed nothing suspicious.

Picking up a fragment of the projectile and examining it for clues I noticed that it was curved slightly with a mottled outer surface, rather like a piece of house-martins nest, so I looked up. Sure enough, directly above me was Jack Wheeler leaning out of a first-floor window, poking about wildly with a broom handle in an attempt to dislodge the martins' nests which had accumulated under the hip of the station house roof.

Obviously it was beneath Mr. Wheeler to warn those beneath him of his activities above them, even if those below him were above him in rank, if you see what I mean.

"Who gave you permission to enter my private quarters?" I called up tetchily.

"I always do this, Mr. Jay," came the reply. "Otherwise we get bird droppings all down the wall, and a big crust on the platform outside your office. Mr. Mildenhew used to complain about it. So did all the other passing stationmasters."

What did he mean 'passing' stationmasters?

"Very well," I said, not wishing to trip over a big crust outside my office, "you may continue. But I want this mess cleaned up immediately you have finished."

I returned to my room to brush my trousers.

By the time Jack Wheeler had come downstairs to sweep up the detritus of his activities, I was at my desk counting waybills and nibbling a piece of cheese. Without knocking, Jack entered my office with a brush and pan dangling limply at his side, and began sniffing to gain my attention.

"Do you have hay fever?" I asked, without looking up.

"'Ow did you know?" Jack replied whingeingly.

The clerk pointed a finger at my lunch. Somewhat puzzled, I placed my pen to one side and took a deep breath.

"Why are you pointing at my lunch, Jack," I queried him. "Are you allergic to cheese?"

"No?"

"Well? What do you want, then?" I retorted.

"Did you know," the fellow informed me knowledgeably, "that that cheese you're eating was made by a secret recipe. It won a prize back in 1859."

"This very piece?" I queried him. "It would certainly account for the taste. Now, either tell me what you want or get out. I am very busy."

Jack did not reply. Mainly, I suspect, because he had forgotten what he wanted. He was now more interested in my figures. Craning his neck to see across my desk, he crumpled his face with workmanlike concern and advised me:

"Phew, you ought to get the microbes to do that. I've been reading up on microbes, Mr. Jay."

"Have you," I acknowledged the fellow with a dreary sigh. "Your obsession with bacteria is unwholesome, Mr. Wheeler, but if microbes can add up this lot they are certainly welcome to try."

With a lop-sided frown, my tiresome Booking Clerk paused to think.

"Yeh, but I don't reckon it'd work," he reversed his opinion. "The thing is, Mr. Jay," he snuffled, having taken on the role of station scientist, "they'd arrive at a different answer to us. Scientists are still baffled by the way microbes do arithmetic, you see." The ill-mannered oaf paused to wipe his nose with his index finger, and now used this finger to prod my papers authoritatively. "For one thing, according to what I 'eard, begad, they multiply by dividing!"

"Really?" I responded, meeting Jack eye-to-eye briefly. "I hope I am not detaining you."

Jack sighed hopelessly and left. Hard upon his heels, I followed him to ensure that he made a proper job of clearing up the mess outside my door.

The time was 1pm, and I could hear among the hills the rattle of an approaching London bound train. Since this heralded something of a special occasion, I crossed the footbridge to Platform Two to meet it.

Honouring its 'running powers' agreement with the London and South Western, the South Exmoor Company, during the summer months, allowed up to three LSWR excursion trains per week over its metals. These special excursions invariably operated out of Waterloo, although sometimes Clapham Junction, and terminated at Blodcaster. Never yet had one stopped at Upshott. It was something of an experiment, therefore, that this express passenger train should grace my station with a call.

In the spirit of the exercise I had risen early this morning and mounted an inspection of my staff. Upon lining them up, it had proven necessary to have them polish their B's, a term meaning buttons, boots, buckles and badges. Nevertheless, in the prosecution of this I found that I had unexpectedly awoken a hitherto undetected reserve of passion towards the railway, a renewed sense of unity, if you like, of the kind which only a fresh challenge can spark. After all, we stood upon the eve of a portentious occasion.

Verily, my staff's pride could not be measured. I had no sooner outlined the details of the LSWR's experimental service than they had begun to squawk like chickens about the extra work it would involve. If the intrusion of just one LSWR excursion train could unite my workforce so effectively, albeit in their resentment, then yea, dear reader, I looked forward to the day when Upshott Station would be staffed by men whose pride *could* be measured.

Having for many years been in charge of railway stations on the London and South Western network, I welcomed the occasional passing of its modish rollingstock. A nostalgic glimpse of a rake of long wheelbase carriages, lower halves crimson, upper halves cream, and windows highlighted in pencil-thin linework, made a pleasant change from the rudimentary green and white 'boxes' which lurched through this moorland backwater the rest of the time. Cocking an ear to the rhythm of a rake of four LSWR six-wheelers cruising down Longhurdle Embankment, I was instantly transported.

Because the excursion train had only just set out upon its return journey, I felt it unlikely that anyone would wish to alight it at Upshott, save perhaps the odd journeyman or commercial traveller on local business. And, conversely, since only one person had bought a ticket to board the train, a foot-soldier returning from furlough, I was at liberty to idle among my thoughts until its arrival.

Reflecting upon my staff's ill-founded complaints about the extra work, I found myself fermenting retribution. Especially since the porters and clerks whose resentment was greatest were at this moment concealing themselves behind windows, and in obscure nooks upon the platform, so that they might gaup in wonder at the excursionists without having to assist anyone.

I moved quickly upon the loafers.

"I have been giving some thought to your complaints about the inconvenience of this new arrival," I said before dispersing them. "However glamorous it may be, this excursion train is a nuisance I do realize, therefore I shall be greeting it single-handedly to spare you the trouble." With great amusement, I added: "So it will be the excursionists who do the gauping. God bless them, they will be gauping at rustic drudges going about their menial cycle of chores."

This cycle of chores, incidentally, I began arranging to be more menial than usual.

How quickly I discovered that my staff preferred to receive trains than swab floors, scrub ironwork, wash windows, trim wicks, and polish lamps in the full gaze of some two-hundred spectators. But it was in trying to find a volunteer for the final job that I encountered the biggest change of heart, the job of cleaning out the station privy with hot soda.

Strangely, I heard no more objections about the new train.

Double-headed by a pair of seven foot 2-4-0s, Fireking and Paracelsist, the express train clattered over the weighbridge loop points and rumbled past the signalbox.

Knowing that demand would be light, I made a snap decision to allow Diggory to receive the train on his own, so that I might see how he was progressing. The young porter was a little daunted by the prospect, but glad to escape the menial cycle of chores I had arranged for his work-shy colleagues.

Diggory began by labelling the soldier's kit-bag and, since he had very little time, I crouched next to him to offer a little advice and reassurance. The boy was relieved to learn that LSWR specials boasted two or three conductors to watch over passengers, and that, consequently, he was unlikely to be hailed from all directions at once. He was also pleased to learn that probably there would be a couple of Guards aboard, to protect the train should it need dividing on a steep gradient somewhere, and that these too would be on hand to help.

Although I did not envisage Diggory being taxed greatly, experience had taught me that there is generally at least one sticky moment during the reception of a long distance train such as this, especially when it is occupied by euphoric day trippers who see the outside of a factory only a couple of times a year. But this being the lad's first attempt at dealing with an excursion train I decided not to undermine his confidence with such facts. The most unsettling of which was that aboard this train was an outing of East London dye workers and their bosses, among whom would be the inevitable coterie of inflated swells demanding more lackies than had been placed at their beck and call.

The excursion train steamed into Platform Two and the Guard's door flew open, whereupon I took up hiding behind a crate of carboys. From this vantage point I would be able to observe Diggory's performance without becoming involved.

I am proud to relate that Diggory discharged his duties impeccably, and verily was he swamped with them. Impeccably, that is, until entering the Guard's 'birdcage' cabin to assist with the unloading of some domestic requisites.

In a promising show of efficiency, the young porter took off a tod of wool and three nails of calico without incident, plus some items which the Guard of the previous 'down' train had forgotten to discharge. But the lad's lack of worldliness prepared him ill for the sight that was to come, for this was to colour even my cheeks.

With laudable diplomacy, Diggory removed a weighty cask of malt vinegar for the vicar of St. Martha, making no comment that the vicarage was a peculiar destination for such a bulk consignment, and without hesitation did he also carry off a heavy box of blank booking forms for Jack Wheeler. However, when it came to handling a pair of handmade bloomers for Miss Emily Higham, his strength and diplomacy failed simultaneously.

Miss Higham, you will recall, was the Brigadier's daughter and the delicious young lady with whom Snimple was allegedly indulging in not-so-secret love trysts. For some reason her bloomers were lacking the anonymity of a wrapper, and worse, the

Guard was holding them up to himself as if to try them on.

I recoiled in horror at the lustful abnormality to which I had exposed my Junior Porter in this, his most formative time of life, and set glass chinking against glass violently as I struggled to extricate myself from the carboys behind which I had been hiding. But, alas, before I could step into the Guard's van to take over, Diggory had turned colour and developed a speech impediment.

Of course, I did not reprove the boy. I quite understood his loss of composure, for I was close to apoplexy myself. I too had never seen a Guard modelling ladies' underwear.

My unexpected appearance outside the 'bird-cage' van caused the boggle-eyed Guard to stuff the bloomers hastily into his pocket in an attempt to fool me that he was still busy handling parcels.

"Hey, you!" I called. "Just what do you think you are up to? Where is the wrapper for those... those... that item of freight you have in your pocket?" I boarded the train. "Don't try to fool me, Sir, I saw you hide that pair of unmentionables."

"It's all right, Guv, I've got the address label," the Guard defended himself. "They've not gone astray. They're to come off 'ere for a Miss 'igham."

"I dare say," I fumed. "But why are they not wrapped? Surely you realize that a personal garment of this nature should be travelling incognito?"

The Guard explained that the wrapper had disintegrated in the juice of some French plums which had been squashed in transit, venturing that the accident must have happened during gauge transhipment somewhere. Further, he boasted that he had extracted the bloomers just in time to save them from being spoiled.

Whilst I had no grounds to doubt the Guard, I did return his sudorous leer with a harsh expression of disapproval.

From this incident you will appreciate that there are no secrets from a stationmaster. I now knew that the vicar of Saint Martha was partial to malt vinegar with, perhaps, a passion for pickling unbelievers, and that Miss Emily Higham wore hand-made undergarments imported from Paris.

My own partiality, although only recently acquired, was for falling over a stack of semaphore signal arms which had been left upon Platform Two pending collection by a contractor. They had been piled so haphazardly that whilst on my way to the porters' cloakroom to coax Diggory out of hiding, I scraped my ankle on them yet again. To put an end to the matter, I called upon Mr. Troke to relocate the signal arms to the foot of the water tower.

My demise as a figure of authority was now in the making.

"Have Snimple assist you, William," I instructed the Rollingstock Superintendent.

Mr. Troke turned a baleful eye upon me and began to maunder. Maundering was a form of protest to which he was prone, so I ignored him.

"How came they to be hither in the first place?" he amplified his complaint begrudgingly.

"Just move them," I instructed him tersely.

Mr. Troke began to maunder again.

"By and by we shall be free from the flux of progress," he said. "Haply left alone to enjoy two days the same."

"If you think that, Mr. Troke, you are living in the past," I rebounded, having overheard the fellow.

Also cluttering the platform was a wicker basket containing four dozen rabbit carcases destined for Walsall. For obvious reasons it was necessary to get these away smartly, so I had Diggory pluck up the courage to put them aboard the Guard's van while I asked the driver to slow down at Exeter to allow the Guard to throw them off. Strictly speaking, this practice was not in accordance with company regulations, but drivers seldom objected.

This one did, however, but before I could persuade him to change his mind a heavy hand descended upon my shoulder and robbed me of my breath. Had this crude method of communication been applied to me any other time I would have dismissed it as the price to be paid for working with uneducated bumpkins, but, being somewhat unnerved by talk of a curse, I suffered the indignity of losing my hat. This amused the passengers aboard the train no end.

If Blodcaster was famed for its fishing, and verily it was, then news was now about to be noised abroad that at nearby Upshott there was a vaudeville stationmaster, and that LSWR excursions included a stop to see him. Keen to get value for money from this new diversion, the pasty-faced Londoners began lowering their compartment windows and leaning out. In fact, so keen were they to participate in my undoing that they squeezed their heads through the windows in such tight bunches that I thought they would be trapped there for the remainder of the journey. In this endeavour I wished them every success.

Since the offending hand was still resting upon my shoulder, I turned to identify its owner, and recognized the baggy knuckles as Mr. Troke's.

"How many times must I tell you not to punch me when you want my attention, Mr. Troke?" I nettled. "I am the Stationmaster here, not a navvy. You must not lay a hand upon me, is that clear?"

Past admonitions having failed, there was no reason to expect this one to succeed, nevertheless, for the sake of appearances I continued with the ticking off my Rollingstock Superintendent deserved.

"You have a tongue in your head," I barked, brushing his fingermarks from my tunic. "Use it!"

"It's not long enough," he replied, and smiled at me gappily.

William Troke recognized an audience when he saw one, and bulged with pride at the roar of laughter his impudence had won him. By now the excursionists, encouraged by my subordinate's unique brand of disobedience, were suggesting that we finish our act with a duet. I had a better idea. I finished our act with a rollingstock superintendent being threatened with dismissal. This proved very popular, although not with the Rollingstock Superintendent.

Disenchanted with the business of performing in public, Mr. Troke retrieved my top-hat, rather like a mummer taking his final bow, and dusted it off. Yet he did not return it to me. Instead, contemplating collecting tips in it, he inverted my symbol of authority and sallied towards the train. I checked him loudly.

Impaled by my glare of disapproval Mr. Troke thought better of the idea, and with a meek yet somehow wicked smile he came hither and restored me to full uniform.

Suddenly the clown's unnerving facial expression hollowed odiously into a slightly cross-eyed malevolence. It had occurred to him that he did not like having to pass up an opportunity to make a few extra coppers, especially since the excursionists were so delirious that they would have filled a top-hat readily.

I reseated my crooked topper, and Mr. Troke turned his evil gaze upon the grimy faces which had egged him to the brink of unemployment. Then to my horror, he spat at them.

The consternation Mr. Troke caused with this unkind gesture soon turned to anger, and so to defuse the situation I reprimanded him demonstratively for his bad form. Although, truth to tell, I was more inclined to berate him for his bad aim.

Suddenly Mr. Troke was engaged in a hasty retreat from return fire, and it looked as though a nasty incident would result. However, the ruffians aboard the train were in sufficiently good humour to confine the venting of their displeasure to within the rules of this new sport to which my Rollingstock Superintendent had introduced them. Their coarse laughter was once again rippling up and down the train.

"I seem to recall having instructed you and Snimple to remove these semaphore arms, Mr. Troke," I halted the fellow in disgust. "One wonders if you are deaf as well as stupid."

This remark precipitated another ripple of mirth among the revellers.

"Snimple's gone home to his lodgings, Sir," Mr. Troke came back miserably. "Am I to lift them thither on my own?"

There was yet another ripple of laughter. Apparently everything that happened in Upshott was funny, including a perfectly serious conversation. At this point I noticed the excursionists polling each other to see who would make the next jibe.

"Why," one of them mocked, waving his muffin hat in the air, "not only is the governer a fool, but the drudge is a weakling!"

This impertinence triggered an outright roar of mockery, and I decided that enough was enough. I stood Mr. Troke to one side and gave the excursion train its 'right away'.

As the boggle-eyed Guard swept by in his 'birdcage', he leaned from the look-out window and sniggered irreverently: "Sorry about the knickers, Stationmaster. I was checkin' 'em to see if they were cocker, that's all."

"You should have invented a different story, Sir," I called back. "Plums are not yet in season!"

With the train gone, I swivelled on my heel and instructed Mr. Troke in the manner of his future conduct should he wish to remain on the railways. Like a lamb, he sought Diggory's assistance and removed the semaphore arms.

To spare Emily Higham the embarrassment of knowing that her bloomers had been displayed in public, I went across to the Parcels Office to rewrap them. This operation I completed only just in time to avoid another embarrassing incident, for no sooner had I got the garment safely bundled into some brown paper than a servant of the Brigadier's arrived to collect them.

Before placing myself at large again, I partook of a glass of goat's milk fortified with brandy, and reflected further upon this curse.

CHAPTER TWENTY-ONE

THE WALKING HOG PUDDING

By 4.08pm, Beattie 2-4-OWT *Briggs* was busy marshalling the afternoon Milk Train in the Dairy Siding. It had not been my intention to interfere with this operation, since Driver Hiscox was methodical and thorough in the execution of his duties. However, about 4.15pm, I chanced upon two refurbished 'ticket boxes' lying beneath the footbridge steps. As an ex-London and South Westerner, I recognized these immediately. They were part of the apparatus required for the 'staff and ticket' operation of a single line railway, and it looked as though they had been earmarked for the South Exmoor. This portended ill for the company's General Manager, since Mr. Crump had always sworn that he would resign before agreeing to the implementation of staff and ticket.

At this stage in my story it might seem logical to explain how the staff and ticket system works, but I shall refrain from doing so because the principles will be understood more readily later. Suffice it to say here that the ticket referred to has nothing to do with the kind issued to passengers, and that the staff referred to is a form of baton, not the workforce.

In the staff and ticket system there did lurk ramifications for the workforce, however, and for one of them in particular the outlook was gloomy. The ticket boxes I had found under the footbridge steps heralded the withdrawal of Julian Maynard's fast horses for ferrying the single-line batons to and fro between Upshott and its neighbouring stations. Since Upshott stabled only four horses, two shunters and two baton mounts, introduction of the staff and ticket system meant but one thing. That my Horse Superintendent's responsibilities were to be halved overnight.

As one of the South Exmoor's principal stationmasters I could not understand why I had heard nothing, officially or otherwise, about this impending change in traffic management. There had been no talk of the General Manager carrying out his threat to resign, and I had seen no trace of staff and ticket apparatus until now. Indeed, the only certainty in all this was that the London and South Western Railway Company, prior to taking over the line, was empowered to demand such improvements. This precondition had been written into the contract between the two companies in 1856.

If staff and ticket operation was imminent, then it was reasonable to assume that the company would introduce it after construction of the passing loops at Widdlecombe and Busy Linton. These track improvements, combined with the more advanced signalling that was on the way, would allow the railway to be operated in four 'block' sections, and hence accommodate up to four trains on the line at once.

Manifestly, whatever was planned, further upheaval was on the way. This was no surprise, however, because despite its enviable safety record, the South Exmoor Railway had since 1860 been chaffed widely for its use of obsolete equipment and outmoded practises. In fact, the line had been built to some very diverse standards. In order to secure its long term working agreement with the London and South Western Railway, the South

Exmoor Company had been obliged to build stations of rather greater stature than circumstances warranted. Similarly, its proposal to build a frail wooden trestle bridge to carry the railway across the valley at Widdlecombe had been commuted to the building of a stout stone viaduct wide enough to take two lines eventually. And when a local squire, namely Lawrence T. Albury, had forced the second stage of the railway to be rerouted via a tunnel under Splashgate Hill, the LSWR had specified a costly oval shaped bore with at least two ventilation shafts.

In everything else, however, the South Exmoor Company had exercised absolute economy. Its mechanical signalling systems had been kept to a bare minimum, leaving most train movements to be controlled by switchmen bearing coloured flags. And even in those places where mechanical signals had been installed upon the insistence of the Board of Trade, the equipment used had been purchased second-hand.

More alarmingly, whichever the mode of signalling one found, human or mechanical, the approach of a train had first to be predicted with the aid of a timetable and an ear cocked for a distant whistle. Telegraphic communications, the infant SER had decided, were entirely unnecessary on a railway regulated by horse and baton.

As for the possibility of staff and ticket operation being introduced now, at long last, the person most likely to know what was going on at boardroom level was Driver Hiscox, and he, being in my station on the footplate of *Briggs*, became my immediate destination. Unlike most enginemen, Hiscox had moved in good society and was a company confidant.

Waiting for an opportunity to speak with the driver, I watched *Briggs* return from the headshunt and propel a rake of flat-trucks to the milk dock for loading with churns, and, when the moment was right, crossed the Tramway smartly with my eyes peeled. Since witnessing the death of a clerk, whose head had been crushed between the buffers of two goods wagons in a shunting operation, I had always made a point of negotiating parked goods vehicles as quickly as possible, with my head lowered and the soles of my feet on fire.

As I approached *Briggs*, I was encouraged to see Mr. Hiscox stepping down from his charge to oil its side-rods. Footplatemen were always more approachable at ground level. Unfortunately, before I could reach him, I was intercepted by the spinster woman, Serena Blake. She was taking a somewhat dangerous short-cut across the line to reach Railway Road.

"Be there anythin' in particler yer'd like I to get for yer dinner, Mr. Jay?" she asked.

I halted enthusiastically.

"As a matter of fact there is," I replied.

I had developed a craving for hog pudding, and advised her of it. As yet I had never tasted home-made hog pudding quite as delicious as that served from a stall at the fair, so I decided to put the spooky spinster to the test. I might overlook all manner of shortcomings in a domestic who could make a good copy of fairground hog pudding.

"I bin 'ad a word with my mother about yer noises," she volunteered. "I'll tell yer all about it later, Mr. Jay. But so's yer got somethin' ter think on, she told I tis all for to do with them standing stones up on Splashgate 'ill."

Ghoulishness must run in the family, I thought, and moved on.

By now *Briggs* had set back into the weighbridge loop. So, burdened with a sickly grin, I wended my way back through Ivor Hales's tidy regiment of vegetables and hurried towards the engine. Driver Hiscox had resumed lubricating *Briggs's* linkages, but was finishing the job and about to board the footplate again.

If I was to learn anything from this engineman, I calculated, I would first have to wheedle my way into his confidence with a little flattery, and then see if I could trade information with him. The nugget I had to offer was, of course, news of the ticket boxes lying in store under the footbridge steps. To this end I complimented Mr. Hiscox upon his mastery over the regulator in entraining the wagons so quickly in the correct order, and then serenaded him with a comradely smile. This did the trick. The normally reserved fellow smiled back at me most warmly, and I so told him all I knew.

"Well now, there's a thing, Mr. Jay," he mused, stowing his oiling can aboard the engine. Curiosity thus aroused, Driver Hiscox wiped his streaky hands and began filling his pipe with tobacco. "So you've got ticket boxes eh? That is interesting."

"Does this mean that Mr. Crump is on his way out?" I asked humbly.

"I've not heard," Hiscox replied after a brief reflection. "Mind you, I do hear there's been a wrangle at the Joint Board Meeting, and I think everyone knows that this baton rider business can't go on. But as for resignations, I've heard nothing. Nay, I should think there's been some sort of compromise, Mr. Jay. Now that we've got telegraph circuits I should think the staff and ticket system could be operated even to Benjamin's satisfaction. It's not as if we should have to go back to the old 'time interval' system of starting trains."

Driver Hiscox lit his briar and went into a trance. It seemed that I was now invisible.

Having learned nothing substantive, I returned to my office to rest my legs for a while. Here I came across the first manoeuvrings in the long anticipated cider war between the local dignitaries, Squire Lawrence Albury and Brigadier Sir Aubrey Higham K.C.S.I., the two major apple growers in the valley. Three-quarters of the rough brew from Albury Hall, which was most popular with farm labourers and railway gangers, was exported to London and Birmingham, and it seemed to me that for someone who despised the railways, Squire Albury made mighty lucrative use of them.

Truth be known, what the squire resented about railways was their neutrality in the class structure of society. He was quoted as having said that God gave us the railways to move dignitaries and merchandise, not peasants and upstarts, and that increasing freedom of movement among the masses was undermining civilisation.

Eating-apples and cider-apples, like the cider itself, were a bulk export from Upshott. But neither Albury nor Higham owned sufficient private wagons to clear his orchard during picking time, so, every year, the rival growers would hire extra trucks from the South Exmoor Railway Company to get their produce to market. This year, Squire Albury had sent my Booking Clerk an advance requisition for an extraordinarily large number of SER trucks. Indeed, my clerk had noted that the number of trucks supposedly required by the squire matched exactly the number available for hire.

This, quite clearly, was no coincidence. The old weasel had received intelligence about the SER's rollingstock disposition and was hoping to pre-empt his competitor by engaging the company's entire complement of wagons during fruit-picking time.

Mr. Albury, however, was overlooking the new stationmaster.

It was easy to see what the squire was up to. He was hoping to force Brigadier Higham, brewer of the stronger yet sweeter Xissington cider, to hire London and South Western wagons to ship his apples. London and South Western wagons were more expensive and less readily available.

Now, whilst I may not have been able to pronounce the word 'Xissington' (locally pronounced 'Sissington') without first having partaken of a glass of it, I did prefer this cider. I also preferred its brewer. Moreover, I saw no reason why Squire Albury should be permitted to waste SER company time with his shenanigans, so I decided to delay his requisition by mislaying it.

By this foolhardy venture did I become an active agent in the cider-apple war, and thereby risk drawing upon my head the fury of the party whose plans I intended to subvert. Indeed, while placing the squire's requisition slip beneath my potted Aspidistra or, to be more precise, the potted Aspidistra which Mr. Mildenhew had left behind, I heard a little voice in my head warn me that I would come to regret throwing away my neutrality. And in this conflict there was no more precious a commodity, I had been told.

But a louder voice entered my head and drowned the first with a wild chuckle. It pointed out that my neutrality would not have lasted anyway, and that if one is to enter a war it is preferrable to do so on one's own terms.

With the station quiet, I accepted a challenge from Mr. Troke to play him at the local chequerboard game Towering Battalions, for I was acquainted with its peculiar rules and confident that a cross-eyed Rollingstock Superintendent was no match for a man of my calibre. By 5pm Mr. Troke had beaten me, but, setting aside this misleading fact, I was gratified to discover that an intelligent opponent can stimulate even a simpleton to think logically.

Teased by the smell of hog pudding, and having noticed the spinster woman looking out of my upstairs window to see if I was coming, I set off to my rooms for dinner. For some reason Miss Blake was in dire haste. Having set out my meal for immediate consumption, she pumped past me on the stairs with all the wear and tear of the possessed.

"Tis on the table Mr. Jay," she gasped. "I must away to the village, for I've made arrangements to collect a pair of button boots from the cobbler, and time grows short."

I fancy it was the stirrings of my ghost that propelled her.

The hog pudding looked and smelled promising but, before putting it away, I decided to take a peek through my window. A wise stationmaster never misses an opportunity to catch his staff on the dodge. Much to my pride, everything appeared to be in order. With the exception of the spinster woman hastening along the platform, Upshott Station was a picture of reassuring tranquility.

Incidentally, I trust you will permit me use of this tautonym 'spinster woman', for it hints wickedly at Miss Blake's psyche.

The time had come to test the hog pudding. Unfortunately, with one final glance down at the platforms, I discovered that my pride in the orderliness of my station had been misplaced. The scene was not one of tranquility at all. Firstly I spotted Diggory stooping hither and thither frantically as if he had mislaid something of great importance, and secondly I spotted Mr. Troke recoiling from his duties lazily with his posterior parked upon a puncheon cask.

It seemed that because I was not at large, Mr. Troke presumed it safe to loaf. With his legs dangling uselessly like a marionette, and his jaw bouncing to and fro upon a wedge of tobacco, he had retreated to that peculiar world between his ears. Suddenly he gazed up at my window with his porcelain eyes bulging sorrowfully and heaved a sigh, manifestly unaware that I was looking back at him.

I came to the conclusion that the fellow was tormented by the aroma of my hog pudding, so, in devilment, I opened the window to strengthen the whiff of it.

"Hog pudding, Mr. Troke," I called down. "Stay where you are. I may toss you a scrap."

Mr. Troke did not see fit to laugh, nor was he shamed into returning to his duties. He simply continued to stare, so I shut the window.

As a result of the spinster woman's superstitious vagaries, I had become the victim of suggestion myself. And now, like her, I was hearing noises.

For example, I thought I heard my door creak. This was my imagination, of course. Nevertheless, out of instinct I turned to see if anyone was there, expecting to satisfy myself that there was not, and that the door was still closed. But, alas, it was open. Wide open. Just as if someone had joined me in the room. From this stemmed great difficulty because, as far as I could see, no one had.

I shut the door again, securely this time, and sat down to eat my meal. Before saying grace, I reprimanded myself for being so impressionable.

"A ghost," I chuckled privately. "Indubitably, it must have been Miss Blake's infernal heathen paying me a visit."

This was when my nerve broke, for in taking up my knife and fork I noticed that my hog pudding had gone. A tantalizing smell was all that remained of the dish. Tell a lie. Such had been the usurper's haste that the tablecloth had been splashed with gravy, and a remnant of pork lay on the floor. At a glance, one would have thought that my dinner had been snatched by a ravenous vulture.

I studied the empty plate in an attempt to understand the meaning of it, but found no answers, only pastry crumbs. And while pondering the disappearance, I heard a peculiar call, a sort of whimper, coming from somewhere nearby.

Now, I am no expert in the subject of heathen burials, but to me this sounded more like the jibber of a terrified mortal than the cry of an evil spirit being lured from limbo by Miss Blake's cooking. And I was right. Indeed there was a terrified mortal nearby. A man in black. A man of ordinary flesh and blood. A man numb with disbelief and teetering on the brink of bewilderment. A man who had seen the last of his dinner.

Still whimpering, the man descended the stairs to summon Mr. Troke.

Mr. Troke had gone, so I called Diggory. Diggory had gone, so I called Mr. Phillips. Mr. Phillips had gone, so I called *help*. It was all a waste of breath, however. Looking about me, the station appeared to be deserted. I could not even see Mr. Hales in his signalbox.

At sight of this, and mindful of the curse, I became a trifle queer and fell across the handle of a platform trolley. From this bent position I ventured another plangent cry, expecting my anguish perforce to bring assistance at last. But with the exception of my echo mocking me from Splashgate Hill, no reply was forthcoming.

However, I was not entirely alone. Like advancing Russian chesspieces, a delegation of tall shadows loomed up the wall behind me, cast by a westering sun cutting through a shifting sky. They appeared to be rallying around me to break my fall should I faint in the absence of my staff, and feeling strangely reassured by them, I took a moment to mop my brow.

But the dumb busybodies could do no more than watch helplessly as I tottered feebly across the platform to find a bench. All but one of them, that is. One shadow escorted me all the way to a seat and merged with me as I leaned against the wall.

Mr. Troke ambled out of the Parcels Office, placed a hand above his eyes, and gazed back and forth in the rubescent glow of late afternoon. Having espied me, he sauntered over and spat out a quid of tobacco to enquire why I was looking so pale. I drew breath to speak, but held my tongue. It had occurred to me that my credentials were at risk as never before. Word that my dinner had been spirited away from under my nose would do little to strengthen my authority at the station, so I loosened my collar and preserved silence.

My artless Rollingstock Superintendent was stumped. He could think of nothing to do but scratch his beard and stare at me helplessly, for he had no idea how to restart a stunned stationmaster.

Pondering the matter with a slightly clearer mind now, it occurred to me that my dinner might have been removed by an entity conspicuously more earthly than Miss Blake's wicked heathen. To wit, Mr. Troke. He had been behaving most suspiciously at the time of its disappearance.

"Do you know of any reason why my dinner should disappear?" I challenged him accusingly.

"No, Sir?" he replied with disarming innocence.

At this point we were joined by Mr. Phillips. The Goods Clerk's alabastor cheeks were carrying a rare hint of pink.

"William has been with me for some time, Mr. Jay," he sprang to his colleague's defence.

I postponed judgement and eyed William Troke's uniform deedily. There was certainly no evidence of a frenzied attack upon a hog pudding. No gravy stains that I could see. And, upon reflection, I had to admit that Mr. Troke could hardly have scoffed the dish without Mr. Phillips being aware of it. Mr. Phillips was too much the gentleman to tell a lie, even as a prank, so once more was I without a rational explanation.

"Have you seen anything?" I quizzed the Goods Clerk.

"Anything?" Mr. Phillips eructed. "I have seen many things today. What had you in mind?"

"Anything," I repeated with rising agitation. "Anything unusual."

Mr. Troke and Mr. Phillips blinked at each other as if seeking mutual inspiration.

"No," they answered simultaneously.

Manifestly my two colleagues were puzzled by my distress, but puzzled they were destined to remain, for I had elected not to explain the cause of it. One did not need a crystal ball to see that a story about a vanishing hog pudding would invoke neither sympathy nor constructive suggestion. On the contrary, it would keep the station house reverberating with laughter at my expense for weeks.

"The spinster woman is a Jonah," I snorted with disgust, and strode to The Shunter for a supper of cheese and stout.

The tap room in The Shunter was lively with gangers. Lively, that is, until a stationmaster appeared in the doorway. But I was not disturbed by this. In a public like The Shunter, any figure of authority, particularly if he represented a local employer, had a sobering effect upon the atmosphere of the place.

The silence was short-lived, and by the time I had taken myself to my corner table, the smoky room was again booming with laughter and the telling of yarns. A pretty tale I could have contributed had I been disposed to join them. Ay, and a tale not so old it had grown whiskers. But an erect stationmaster does not crave the society of gangers, for the kind of escapades such men recount while puffing their clay pipes and loosening their tongues on cider, he should not hear.

If you will permit me to place you in my confidence a little further, I did not mind my isolation, even though the very purpose of establishments such as this was one expressly of community. Far from it. Taking a glass of beer in solitude does no harm to the man with a fertile mind. Not in a world in which there is so much to ponder, such as black magic and its effect upon food.

While waiting for my piece of cheese to be cut, I took a pinch of snuff and beheld myself in a small, oval mirror hanging lop-sidedly on the wall facing me. I noticed that my hair had begun to thin since arriving at Upshott, and tried to picture myself sporting a fashionable wig. I could not, however, for I had neither the stomach nor the vanity of the swells who resided beneath such fancy hairpieces. Anyway, the chances were that any wig I could afford would differ absurdly in texture and colour to my natural side-whiskers.

Dismissing the subject, I found myself thinking once again about Julian Maynard and his future upon the railway. The Horse Superintendent was almost certainly about to lose his fast horses, and it seemed to me that at some stage in the future the London and South Western Railway Company would wish to withdraw his shunting horses too, thereby closing down the station stables altogether.

This prospect caused me to gaze out of the window and ponder the tavern sign, for it illustrated the animal after which the public house had been named, Upshott's first shunting horse. By all accounts the old Shire, alas no longer with us, had been a bit of a character, and had marshalled trucks in the days when Upshott Station was a terminus.

The inn sign showed the beast pulling a flat-truck loaded with beer barrels, and it seemed to me that should this picture survive another decade, passers by would wonder why a tavern called The Shunter should advertise itself by way of a horse. Fast growing was a generation to which a shunter was a type of steam engine.

For Mr. Maynard's sake, I hoped that this generation would find use for both forms of traction. Railway horses were Julian's life.

As a matter of interest, although no one could have known it at the time, the shunting horse era was indeed set to last. Even as I awaited my cheese, and Lord knows this was taking long enough, the London and South Western Railway Company housed in its stables at Nine Elms a vast fleet of such beasts. Indeed, in many West Country sidings, the shunting horse was to remain the most economical way of marshalling wagons until the turn of the century.

My attention was drawn to a piece of cheese and a glass of stout arriving at my table.

Returning to my quarters, I found the spinster woman in my kitchen scrubbing earthenware.

"I see yer enjoyed my 'og puddin' Mr.Jay," she chirped. "Yer didn't leave a scrap." She stooped to pick up the lump of meat lying on the floor and glanced at me disapprovingly. "Apart from this one." I received another such glance when she removed the table cloth to examine the gravy stains upon it. "Change that shall I?" she despaired with her eyes narrowed, and with top lip quivering, added: "Twer clean on this mornin' though."

As we gentlemen know, domestics never gossip. We know this because they tell us so, just as they tell each other. *'Well, Mrs. Brown, you know me, I never gossip, but I really must tell you about the new Stationmaster. He flicks his food about while eating.'* My social standing in the community was about to tumble, challenged by sneers at every street corner.

Miss Blake took up my ewer unexpectedly and announced that she was going downstairs to refill it. On her way to the door she stopped suddenly and gave me a groggy smile. I sensed from this that I was about to audience another of her blood-curdling stories.

"My mother finally told I why this location were chosen for takin' the heathen under," said she, as if this burial business was a burden upon us all.

Indeed, with Miss Blake around, it was.

The spinster woman abandoned the empty ewer beside my washbowl and set about imparting the gruesome details. In all honesty, I did not register a word, for I was preoccupied with the matter of the hog pudding. I simply could not reconcile myself to the incident.

"I be tellin' yer about the dead body, Mr. Jay," Miss Blake bullied me back to life. "Yer know? The one I found underneath the station."

"Oh, that one," I responded, wondering how many others she had found. "But I thought it was only a skull you unearthed, Miss Blake, not a dead body?"

I removed myself to a more comfortable chair, and Miss Blake followed me.

"Twer the skull of a local charcoal burner," she continued. "E came from a family as lived deep in Bessam Forest and survived by 'urdle makin' and charcoal burnin'. They were outcasts one and all, for they dabbled in strange rituals and never attended church. My mother told I these were wicked folk who always buried their dead in the shadow of them standing stones up on Splashgate 'ill. Yer see, Mr. Jay, when the sun comes up, they forms a point right 'ere on yer station. Tis on a lay line, yer see."

"A lay line?" I coughed. "My goodness! And all this time I have been deluding myself it was a railway line."

The spinster woman laughed wheezily, and begged me to take her seriously.

"Miss Blake," I cautioned her. "If you allude to devil worship, then I shall hear no more."

"Oh, but Sir, yer must," she urged me gravely, and was compelled to brush her hair.

I sighed with resignation and removed my shoes. A dose of Miss Blake's storytelling was hard enough to take without aching feet also.

Tugging at her flame red fleece, the domestic continued:

"Now, I've picked yer some wild garlic for to 'ang above yer door, Mr. Jay. Tis for yer own salvation," she assured me, and faltered: "My mother says 'e were *nefarious*."

I could see by Miss Blake's hesitant grimace that she did not quite comprehend the meaning of the word 'nefarious', beyond that it must be bad, but was too abashed to ask.

I did not assist. Instead, I told her:

"Miss Blake, you must understand something. I would sooner be haunted by your nefarious heathen than have to live with the beastly smell of garlic."

The matter was closed.

CHAPTER TWENTY-TWO

GARLIC OVER THE DOOR

That night, teased by the hog pudding mystery, I did not sleep. I laid awake listening to the shriek of a barn owl, a sound which, were I superstitious, I might have mistaken for the cry of a soul in torment. I wondered if, perhaps, my dinner had been stolen by a jackdaw or some other bird with the collecting instinct, but there was precious little comfort in this theory. Apart from the sheer bulk of the pudding, my window had been closed at the time of its disappearance, and I could not imagine a jackdaw winging its way in via the Booking Hall to make the grab.

Anyway, I thought as I tossed fitfully in my bed, *such birds take only things which shine, and the spinster woman's hog pudding was dull and lumpy*.

I was reminded of a rogue jackdaw said to live in Upshott Wood. This fanatical creature, so a wigmaker from Blodcaster had told me, was given to attacking bald heads. Strangely, no one else had ever mentioned the phenomenon, yet according to the wigmaker there was a similar bird in Giddiford, where he was now acquiring new customers. Since the gentleman had made no mention of the bird stealing puddings, I dismissed the idea.

With dozens of ridiculous theories competing for my attention, sleep eluded me, and the fight to resist believing in Miss Blake's evil spirit seemed lost. Indeed, in the absence of a plausible explanation for the disappearance of my dinner I began to feel menaced by the scratch of every mouse, the squeak of every bat, and the howl of every distant dog.

Generally speaking, rigor mortis is not a condition which one describes with the benefit of personal experience, nevertheless, rigor mortis is what afflicted me in the early hours of this morning. The condition was brought on by a loud thump and a groan coming from downstairs.

With my limbs refusing to move, and my ears pinned back involuntarily like those of a frightened animal, suddenly I was a useless object cluttering my own bed, able only to listen nervously for the next sound. And as I did so, I began to feel something peculiar happening to the back of my neck. My small hairs were trying to stand on end, but, like me, they couldn't.

Petrification is but a state of mind, of course. And just as the quiet of the night amplifies an unaccountable sound, then equally does the prospect of rising to investigate that sound diminish it. So I did not recover the use of my limbs until I had heard nothing for some while, having by this token dismissed the noise as meaningless. After all, the grounds of Upshott Station were home to enough livestock, and served as a thoroughfare to enough wild animals, to account for a bump in the night. With my limbs working again, I turned over and made a fresh attempt to go to sleep.

Presently I heard another noise, a much louder one, which resembled the scratching of fingernails upon wood, and it was followed by heavy breathing. Rented from my comforting theories about nocturnal disturbances, and straitened by the uncompromising presence of the inexplicable, my heart began to pound like a drum at a public hanging.

Determined that rigor mortis should not reclaim me, I propped myself against my pillow, flicked from my face the bobble of my nightcap, and set about lighting my bedside candle. With my hands shaking like gelatin, I did not meet with success until the very last match. Meanwhile, the noise had grown much louder.

It is only a burglar stealing company property, I calmed myself, *no matter how much it sounds like a cadaver tearing from a coffin.*

Just in case I was wrong, however, I removed from the wall above my bed a walnut rood which I had inherited as a boy, and whispered to it a short prayer before opening my door. Having opened my door very slowly to prevent its hinges creaking, and having discovered that opening a door slowly makes its hinges creak all the louder, I looked downstairs into the well of darkness below and summoned courage. I could see no flicker of an intruder's lamp, no carpet-bag half filled with stolen property, no discarded jemmy, nor any sign of a break-in, and began to wonder who, or what, was in the station house with me.

With my holy cross in one hand and my candle in the other I embarked upon the dark descent to the ground floor, reassuring myself with each exploratory step that whilst I had the cross about my person I was protected, be the intruder spiritual or temporal. For, you see, the religious artefact in my possession was weighty enough to deliver a corrective blow to the head of any miscreant I might encounter.

Alas, my stealth was betrayed by a creaking floorboard, and the station house reverberrated maddeningly with my presence upon the stairs. I halted abruptly. Creaking hinges. Creaking floors.

Upshott Station was by far the creakiest building I had ever had the misfortune to occupy.

In this place, I cursed under my breath, *one could not stalk a dead man without waking him.*

A shiver ran up my spine when I realized how apt a saying I had chosen.

Fear threatened to seize control of my limbs again, but, I am proud to relate, I did not succumb. Not even when an inexplicable draught disturbed the flame of my candle and caused a mob of shadows to dance about me like savages. With eyes half closed, I moved on determinedly.

At the foot of the stairs I stopped again to listen, but heard only the familiar wheeple of the barn owl in the ash tree by the footbridge. From here I advanced towards the Booking Hall, keeping my back to the wall, and set about searching the shadowy offices. One by one I entered them and challenged their recesses with my feeble light, but not a burglar did I find.

To complete my reconnaissance I unlocked the Booking Hall doors and stepped out into the night. Here, on the 'down' platform, the whispering breeze reduced the flame of my candle to a useless blue droplet, and chilled me as if my bed-frock was made of but lace. I walked to the east end of the platform to see if the goat or the chickens had been disturbed, but under this night's moonless sky I was unable to ascertain a thing. The darkness was total, save for a small rash of stars in the zenith and a sprinkling of glow-worms in the grass, and once again I was forced to resort to my ears for hint of what lurked abroad.

I heard nothing.

Shielding my candle from the night's fickle draughts, I moved on and cast a suspicious eye into the station yard's every nook and cranny until none was left. If there was an intruder, he was invisible.

* * *

Upon reporting for duty Sunday morning, Humphrey asked me how my new recruit was faring. He was referring to Miss Blake, of course.

"I am looking for a replacement," I told him bluntly.

"Oh? Be her a wrong'un for the job?" he asked. "Down at The Pheasant they tells I she be a splendid cook, and most reliable."

Humphrey dealt me a baffled look and began winding up his company timepiece.

"I dare say she is a splendid cook," I replied. "But I would not know about that."

Humphrey dealt me another baffled look.

Winding up my own timepiece, I explained:

"The spinster woman's presence is having a disturbing effect upon me and, as a result, I am not sleeping at night."

Humphrey blinked and smiled.

"Arr, I see," he acknowledged knowingly.

"You do?" I asked. "You have noticed it too?"

"Well, in truth, Mr. Jay, I wouldn't have known if e hadn't told I," he said, and conceded grudgingly: "But I suppose her b'aint unattractive in her own way."

"You shame me Humphrey," I gasped. "It is not what you think. All I am saying is that the woman is a disruptive influence. Upon what, I am not sure. Why, last night the dinner she cooked me disappeared, and she fetched garlic to hang over my door."

"Jingo," Humphrey replied, and fell to a perplexed silence.

I could restrain my tongue no longer, and at risk of being ridiculed, confided:

"Humphrey, I believe Miss Blake's return to Upshott Station is causing a disturbance. It seems that she, by her very presence, is arousing some kind of satanic entity. An entity which would otherwise have remained dormant." As I spoke, Humphrey's silver eyebrows began to rise. They lifted by degrees until, eventually, they disappeared under the peak of his cap. Expecting never to see them again, I concluded: "I think it has something to do with the heathen burial."

Humphrey's incredulity, it dawned upon me, was not at the notion of the station house being haunted, it was at me believing it.

"Arr, e wants to see the vicar of St. Martha," he warbled. "This be a matter for the parish church."

"I intend to," I confirmed. "Today!"

I must say, I should have felt happier had Humphrey laughed at me. Instead, he tutted grimly and wandered away to label luggage for the 10.04am Giddiford.

"Soothsay," I heard him mutter. "I always knew her'd rise up one day."

Sunday traffic was light, with but three passenger trains and no goods, and so the station was usually closed around 5pm, this being about half-an-hour after the last train. Today I decided to lock up immediately and visit the vicarage for advice.

* * *

The vicarage was a small, square house almost completely overgrown with ivy. Its frontage was concealed from the High Street by a row of mature chestnut trees and a high, mossy brick wall; and its rear was overlooked by the tower of Saint Martha. I passed through the wrought-iron gate and stopped by a garden shrub to check my timepiece and straighten my collar. Here I experienced my first twinge of doubt.

Am I really here as a stationmaster who is afraid of ghosts? I asked myself.

Wondering what the minister would make of me, I parted the powder-blue fronds of a faded wistaria and entered the porch. Here, in the cold light of day, faced with the tangible oak beams of a vicarage, and the sunny gleam of a brass bell upon a studded door, I experienced my second twinge of doubt.

Never mind being afraid of ghosts, I thought. *Am I really here as a stationmaster who even believes in such things?*

I was tempted to turn upon my heel and leave before being spotted. But instead I reassured myself that I did not necessarily believe in Miss Blake's ghost, merely that I was seeking impartial advice regarding her claim that one existed. I cleared my throat and pulled the bell chain.

Presently I was received by a chambermaid wearing a pale blue apron and lawn cap. I explained to her that, although I had made no appointment to see the vicar, I wished to speak with him on a matter of some urgency. With a sweet smile the young servant took my hat and stick and invited me to the study to wait for the minister.

Now, I am not a nosey person by nature, for I consider myself to be a gentleman, but since I was in a room called a study I took leave of my manners to study it. After all, should I be kept waiting long, a few wry observations would help pass the time.

This I should not have done, for the belongings surrounding me reflected such certainty about life that I became strangely dizzy. Now, I confess that a minister's study, in which the tenor of one's reflections is regulated by the reassuring tick of a carriage clock, and the flavour of one's senses is beguiled by the redolence of cut flowers and beeswax polish, is a curious place in which to be given over to doubt, but doubt it was. In this place, where the peace of the bible ought to have been felt as deeply as in the church itself, I became almost frightened with uncertainty.

I had not had the good fortune to travel the world, and all I knew of its troubles was that they were legion, yet it seemed to me that a tranquil vicarage, with its cultivated gardens, attentive servants, and copious stipend, was a dubious place from which to step into the pulpit with moral teachings for the poor and wretched. The vicar's little haven of security put me in mind of the words of Ecclesiastes: 'All things are full of labour; man cannot utter it: the eye is not satisfied with seeing, nor the ear filled with hearing,' and I became heavy with dread that the good Book had been read with a distorted eye.

An enclave of serenity such as this, I reasoned, *can do little to inspire practical guidance for folk whose misery stems mainly from domestic over-crowding and uncertainty of income*.

I shuddered. Perhaps Miss Blake's evil charcoal burner had possessed me to think such a thing.

The time was 5pm, and the delicate chime of the Swiss carriage clock competed feebly with the deep toll of a grandfather clock in the hall. To my worried ear, there seemed to be a hint of allegory in this sudden mechanical uproar, although, at first, I could not think what it was. But upon the fifth chime it struck me. In this grisly business of the heathen burial, I was that fragile carriage clock, and the church the dominant grandfather clock. The church would merely reinforce my own fears with a more resounding toll.

The Reverend Mr. Gittings had visited me during my first week in Upshott, to welcome me to the fold, and I had confessed to being no church-goer on account of my hours of duty. I had expected the parson of a railway parish to understand the stationmaster's predicament regarding worship, and had told him that I had learned to nourish my faith in my own way. But he had not been persuaded. I suppose a stationmaster is fair game in the building of a good congregation, and, after all, a congregation never is quite large enough. If hope springs eternal in the layman's breast, then in a minister's it must spring still more eternal.

The lethargic clunk of the grandfather clock became louder as the vicar entered the room. I was deep in thought at this moment, gazing through the mullioned window at a red squirrel scampering along the garden wall, and so my reception of the clergyman was more a flinch of surprise than a smile. Nevertheless, he greeted me with outstretched arms.

The vicar, whom I estimated to be in his late forties, cut a short figure, but was far from thin. He stared at me with eyes magnified by a pair of small, oval spectacles which gave him the appearance of a tired fish, and succumbed to an attack of rapid sniffing, as if suffering from hay fever. Scarcely had I risen to declare the purpose of my visit than the minister had taken both my hands and was shaking them so vigorously as to drive me back into my seat.

As soon as I had recovered my balance, the vicar invited me across the room to a pair of facing Morris chairs which, by the look of them, he kept in reserve for the purpose of giving private consultations.

The Reverend Mr. Gittings spoke with a lingering monotony in his voice, a penetrating drone which I imagine had overtaken him at some stage during his career after having been cultivated for delivering sermons to unattentive ignoramuses. He listened patiently and without interruption while I described the strange effect Miss Blake was having upon me, and did not flinch when I mentioned the unearthly noises which had beset my station. He did react, however, when I made reference to the alleged heathen burial. An eyebrow twitched.

Frankly, calm though the minister was able to remain whilst audiencing his parish's inexplicable happenings, I felt that his countenance was bordering upon indifference when I described the hog pudding mystery. This incident, at least, had tangible results. There was no pudding after it! Perhaps he had investigated such unimaginable stirrings in his time that, to him, a walking hog pudding amounted to nothing more than a Hallowe'en fright.

Further, after I had finished recounting events, the vicar merely emitted a long, quavering hum, and began to polish his spectacles knowingly. His demeanour was one of boredom, as though the solution was obvious.

The solution was not obvious to me, and I waited patiently while the vicar poised himself to cast judgement upon the matter. The minister could not know the extent to which my peace of mind hinged upon his reply.

The minister did not know the extent to which my peace of mind hinged upon his reply, for instead of replying, he simply stared at me through his dense lenses and erupted into another burst of rapid sniffing. This unbearable episode lasted several seconds, until, at length, it dawned upon me that the fellow's nasal nutations had nothing to do with hay fever. Indeed no. His sniffing was a form of communication, rather like Morse Code, and currently it represented a question. Unlike Morse Code, however, sniffing code was easy to understand, and I deciphered the signal roughly as follows: *Since you attend none of my sermons, by what right do you seek the benefit of my wisdom away from the pulpit?*

Having been warned of the cleric's wiles, I ignored his coded eructation and declared boldly:

"All I require is a glance at the parish records to put my mind at rest."

More sniffing followed, although this time it began to peter when I held my ground with a face of stone. Eventually the taciturn clergyman thawed and deigned to give counsel. He had realized that in the arena of awkward silences, I was equal to him.

"Hmmmya," he grinned condescendingly. "Since being the parson here I have tried to impress upon the Directors of your railway company the profanity of running trains on the Sabbath. As yet I have had no success."

What had this to do with my ghost?

To gauge my reaction to his deliberate tangent, the vicar tried his hand at another awkward silence, and seemed pleased to have foxed me at last. I could see that our duel was not yet over, and tumbled to the fact that a bargain was going to have to be struck before any advice would be forthcoming.

I had no objection to striking a bargain but, to give my adversary a dose of his own medicine, first I parried him with a neutral smile and a silence more audacious than any tried so far.

The Reverend Septimus Gittings, off balance at long last, peered over his lenses at me curiously to check that I was not a smudge upon his spectacles or an aberration of the light, and asked lingeringly:

"I trust you will do me a small kindness then, Mr. Jay?"

I could guess what this kindness was going to be, and replied cautiously:

"I am aware of your opposition to Sunday travel, Vicar, but I have a suspicion that you overestimate my influence upon the railway. Naturally I am at your disposal in the matter but, alas, the Directors of the South Exmoor Company do not seek the moral guidance of stationmasters when formulating new timetables. However," I added wearily, "I will gladly convey to the Board any protest you may wish to make."

Despite my being a railway employee, or perhaps because of it, I was entirely in favour of Sunday trains. Nevertheless, in offering the vicar my support I was not sacrificing any principles because I knew that if he succeeded in preventing the running of just one Sunday train he would become the first clergyman in history to do so.

On this score, incidentally, it might amuse you to know that a college headmaster had once managed to prevent a mainline company, the mighty Great Western no less, from operating Sunday trains over a branchline to Eton. More astonishingly, he had prevented the company from running trains to Eton the rest of the week! This feat he had first made easier by dissuading the GWR from constructing a line there. But whilst the pedagogue's stand against progress had been appreciated by the parents of the boys he feared would be killed playing upon the line, it had not been appreciated by the tradesmen of the town. Eton suffers to this day.

The vicar must have realized that his campaign to confine parishioners to their homes and church on Sundays would not be advanced noticeably by the recruitment of a humble stationmaster to act as courier. Nevertheless, it was with a mournful drone that he submitted his somewhat cryptic message to the SER Board of Directors:

"If the moral decline of this nation is to be checked, then the Sabbath must be observed as a day of rest, and set aside exclusively for the reflection of matters spiritual."

The vicar did not seem flattered that I required a pencil and paper to retain his profundity.

The truth of the matter was that the influence of the clergy was far greater upon the staff and passengers of the railways than it was upon their directors. The parishioner who took a train on Sunday was doomed to travel in the company of guilt, albeit in some cases token guilt, and trains everywhere, including those of the metropolitan lines around London, halted completely during church services. Nevertheless, the Reverend Mr. Gittings was of the school of thought that the sinner who cannot be reformed must expect his betters to place between him and his weakness an insuperable barrier. Ergo, no Sunday trains, vain hope though this was.

Our bargain struck, the vicar called for my hat and stick and offered to escort me to the sacristy to view the parish records.

We were about to leave when the comely Mrs. Gittings made an unexpected entrance and announced that the table was laid for tea. It was obvious that she had not intended or expected her message to reach the ears of the local stationmaster, for she seemed quite taken aback to find her spouse in conference at a time when there was a service to be prepared. Nevertheless, upon gathering her wits, Mrs. Gittings insisted that the laying of an extra place would be no trouble, and that to have my company would be an honour.

The vicar, seizing the opportunity to apply further moral pressure, insisted that I stay. I could do little else but accept graciously, especially as I was hungry. Relieved of my hat and stick again, I took directions for the dining room.

At first I was not sure what like of tea I had been offered, for it was a little late in the day for high tea and a little early for dinner. I was still not sure when seated at the table. Nevertheless, the spread looked pleasant. There was bread, jam, and cakes, rather like high tea, but also venison. The venison, alas not fresh but preserved in aspic, was served with various garnishings and delicacies which looked as though they had been plucked from the vicarage garden.

Among the many condiments, I noticed, was a large bottle of malt vinegar. This the vicar squirted liberally upon everything but the tablecloth while I, pretending not to notice, made polite conversation with his infinitely more sociable wife.

After the meal, I was escorted across the glebe and admitted to the church. Here, much to my dismay, studies verified both the burial of a lost soul, quote: 'on common land in the shadow of Splashgate Hill', and the subsequent unearthing of his remains during construction of the railway in 1859. The baneful outcast so buried was alleged to have murdered children, terrorized all who entered Bessam Forest and, by evil practises, to have perverted the course of justice. There was also an account of the heathen's slow, agonizing death, poisoned by persons unknown. The reading would have chilled the blood in any God fearing man.

Upon stepping out into the daylight, and whilst still digesting the meaning of what I had read, I received from the vicar a most generous and uncharacteristic flow of information regarding the heathen. Suddenly the clergyman was effusing all manner of warnings about the danger to my soul from this evil-doer.

In truth, being somewhat bewildered, I did not take as much fright as I ought to have done.

"By not attending church regularly, Mr. Jay," the vicar enlightened me, "you are as a lamb separated from the Lord's herd." Now, whilst not actually terrorized by this account, neither was I uplifted by it. "These disturbances you are experiencing," came the final pronouncement, "are the opening of the wolf's jaw, and you shall be lost at sea unless you sail into the harbour of Saint Martha without delay."

I shook hands with the vicar and said goodbye to him under the sombre overhang of a yew-tree by the cemetery boundary, and strode away pensively towards the lichgate. To reach the station as quickly as possible I decided to double back along a footpath at the side of the graveyard and connect with a short-cut through Harvey's Farm. Unfortunately, whilst on this path, I lost control of my feet. They simply collided with each other and brought me to a stumbling halt. At the same time, my head, now filled with the minister's mixed metaphors, lolloped to one side. I tell you, I did not feel at all well.

Checking that no one was about, I rested my haunches upon the low cemetary wall and mopped my brow. Here I convalesced for quite a while, for the vicar's words of comfort had made me feel a good deal less comfortable.

Feeling better, and intending to get under way again using a less rugged short-cut through the almshouses, I stood up to see if my balance had improved. Much to my relief it had. But looking over my shoulder I now discovered that the vicar had been watching me through the yew-trees along the graveyard perimeter. Among the gloomy stalks of the yews and the masonry of the tombstones, his surplice gave him too much the appearance of a ghost for my taste.

"I look forward to seeing you at evensong," he crooned with the glow of a successful commercial traveller.

* * *

Inadvisably perhaps, I did not attend church this eventide. I felt sure that the Lord understood the railway's prior claim upon my time. Closure of the station on Sundays provided me with the solitude I needed to cast up the books. The job took hours, for it involved reckoning up the week's coal and oil takings and checking that all the freight accounts were settled. In addition to this, the passenger receipts had to be tallied with the ticket stubs. If there had been any staff fiddling during the week, this was when I got to know about it.

On this particular Sunday my labours were interrupted by a suspicious character lurking among the trees behind the stables. I spotted the intruder while returning from the Coal Office with a bundle of check-sheets, and, needless to say, he did not stop when I challenged him. Rain, as predicted by the local farmers, was falling steadily and reducing visibility to a miserable few yards. The sneak took full advantage of these blurred conditions and slipped among the indistinct shadows before I could give chase.

In certain quarters, quarters which shall ever plague us I have no doubt, theft of railway property was considered legitimate sport. So, with a mind to report the incident to the Blodcaster Constable tomorrow, I made a mental note of the trespasser's appearance. Curiously, he was built rather like Diggory and, moreover, had scurried away with a similar gangling agility. Of course, the idea of Diggory stealing was inconceivable. Nevertheless, the coincidence was useful, for sight of the young lad reporting for duty tomorrow would remind me to act upon the incident. And when asked by the Constable for a description of the intruder, I would merely have to point a finger.

The hours slipped away, and I completed my book-keeping by the fitful light of a table-lamp. By now the rain had ceased, but with the humidity rising, the barometer falling, and the continuous rumble of an approaching storm among the hills, I knew that the respite would be brief.

How right I was. The inhabitants of Upshott were about to experience a most violent storm, the first of many upon the moors this summer.

Glad to have dipped my pen for the last time, my lucubrations at an end, I sealed my ink pot, applied some blotting paper to my figures, and peered out of my office to observe conditions. At first I was dazzled by the ever present whirlpool of moths which lived around the gaslamp above my door, but I needed only ears to know that a downpour was imminent. The music of the storm had already begun with the occasional ping of an empty milk churn and the growing patter of fat drops striking the platform.

I ducked under the vortex of moths, which were now sharing their pool of light with gathering glints of rain, and looked aloft again. Barging across the sky towards Upshott was a writhing black mass of cloud, at its core a snake-pit of lightning, and I could smell the muggy air becoming caustic with ozone. I stepped under the moths again and returned to my office.

Upshott village was situated about three-hundred feet above sea level, within an arc of tors reaching a further three-hundred feet. In such places on the moors the electricity in the atmosphere is palpable, and even inside my office I could feel the charge raising the hairs on the back of my hand.

I shut the door and closed the sash-window, thankful that I did not have the company of the spinster woman just now. In a storm of this magnitude one did not require the company of someone whose idea of entertainment was to spin diabolical yarns and stick cloves of garlic about the place. I had only to close my eyes and I could picture Miss Blake prancing to and fro in the lightning, laughing hysterically as puddings disappeared.

My bed seemed unusually lumpy this night, and I turned repeatedly in a fruitless search to find a comfortable position in which to repose. When I did fall asleep by some miracle, I was awoken immediately by a clap of thunder the like of which I had never heard before, and the search for a comfortable position began all over again. Worse was to come, however, for I discovered that an electrical storm gave Miss Blake the power to visit dread upon me even in her absence.

Compelled by a feeling that I was not alone, I opened one eye and peered into the flickering night. In utter disbelief I beheld the spinster woman dancing around my bedroom cheek-to-cheek with her heinous corpse, the charcoal burner. And while Miss Blake was gliding about effortlessly, as if floating on air, her partner was barely able to keep up. He, with the obvious disadvantage of being dead, was dragging his feet clumsily with footfalls which were shaking my bed.

As you can imagine, I was reluctant to open my other eye. But induced by an overwhelming desire to learn that this was not really happening, I did.

I gained no satisfaction from the extra vision. In a prolonged twitch of lightning I noticed that Miss Blake was wearing ballet pumps, and that the risen charcoal burner was wearing navvy boots. Another twitch of lightning revealed that the corpse had chosen for the occasion a somewhat stylish, if rather tattered, fustian waistcoat with matching trousers, and a gaily coloured Glengarry soft-cap.

I prayed for the images to go away, but, in defiance, the couple's circulations accelerated and began to make my head spin. Next I tried plugging my ears, for Miss Blake and her odious partner were romancing to the accompaniment of an accordion of the most jarring strains, the instrument and its player unseen. But alas, like the images, the dreadful noise would not go away.

With the benefit of hindsight, I can see that I had fallen asleep and was dreaming. Unfortunately I did not know this at the time, and being frightened I let out a yelp. In so doing, I drew attention to myself and occasioned the cadaver to turn on me. With grisly features scribbled in coarse charcoal upon a phiz of crinkled paper, the dead man glowered at me malevolently and raised an axe high in the air.

Frankly I do not know where this axe came from, for I kept no such tool in my room, but its appearance galvanized me into action and a fierce struggle ensued. A second later the axe fell upon my face and I screamed in anticipation of the pain. Now, I have no idea whether my scream was real or imagined, but it certainly woke me up with a start.

I shook my head until I had banished from my ears the sound of the accordion, and then lit my bedside candle to check myself for injuries. There was no blood, but I could scarcely believe that my limbs were my own, so cold and clammy were they.

With the nightmare couple gone, I stared across my empty room, thankful to be alive but not daring to go back to sleep. If Serena Blake could enrage my imagination to this feverish pitch, the charcoal burner would be waiting for me.

* * *

A decline towards nervous exhaustion followed

and, at one stage, I thought I had lost my reason altogether. I became convinced that certain members of my staff were behaving abnormally. Humphrey had become distant. Jack too. And Mr. Troke seemed stranger than ever, if you will accept the margin for it. As for Diggory, well, the young lad simply could not look me in the eye without conveying the feeling that something was badly wrong, something so amiss that he dared not tell me about it. At every turn I found myself interrupting whispered conversations about a curse, and in the station house each night I was kept awake by a symphony of noises; scufflings, scratchings, heavy breathings, and rapid tappings.

Most baffling of all was a remark made by Mr. Troke one morning after I had forbidden him utterance of the word 'curse' while on duty. He said:

"Don't turn a blind eye to it, Mr. Jay. I've seen Upshott Stationmasters dragged away from their sanity by pretending it never happened."

After this I was extra vigilant, and decided that the time had come to apply a little rational thought to the matter. Having put away a glass or two of beer at The Shunter, perhaps even three or four, I concluded that the station house had been colonized by rats. As a reminder to act, I made a note to myself to purchase a wedge of cheese and a vial of poison to snuff out the nonsense once and for all.

The following night, despite the rumblings of another storm, my bed seemed less lumpy, my eyes closed without persuasion and, in no time at all, my thoughts had strayed across the boundary of consciousness into the pasture of dreams.

With the blow of an axe, lightning split the darkness, thunder shook my window, and I was awake again. This night's storm was passing directly overhead, and a cloudburst had begun pounding the station roof with the roar of a rapturous audience. Above this din I heard another sound, an indescribable sound which did not, heaven forbid, come from a rat. It was more like the wail of a banshee, or the drawing of a bow across an out of tune violin. And, for some reason, the uncanny cry followed each clap of thunder. It rose sharply in pitch and fell again to become a wolf-like howl. This time I was not dreaming.

To promote consciousness I sat upright and regulated my breathing for a while, until the ringing in my ears had stopped. Next I whispered a short prayer and lit the large oil lamp which had now replaced my bedside candle. Finally I climbed out of bed and braced myself, for this dreadful thing, whatever it was, had to be faced.

Leaving every lamp in my wake at full gas, and avoiding the creaky timber which had betrayed my advance last time, I made my way to the ground floor. Here, at the foot of the stairs, a shock spectre awaited me.

A stark white face was staring out of the wall, its eyes bulging with remorse, its pupils dilated like black pebbles, and I was in no doubt that I was witnessing the manifestation of a repentant soul.

Had I not caught sight of myself in the hall mirror I would never have known how repentant I was at having resisted the idea of a station dog. An alert, four-legged friend would have been most welcome this night. But then, studying my reflection further, it struck me that my diabolical appearance was my guarantee of safe conduct, for it would ward off any intruder handsomely without need of canine assistance. Even should I come face-to-face with a hoard of marauding goblins, it would be the goblins who fled in terror, not I.

With this thought in mind, I chuckled wildly and moved on.

Being of a practical disposition, I was also ready to face adversaries of a more corporeal nature, for upon leaving my quarters this time I had collected my shotgun and loaded both barrels. Anyone showing an interest in the station safe would be administered a dose of buckshot.

The thunder was abating, and with it the awful wailing, so that by the time my search was under way, a barely audible whimper was all that remained to be traced. And most of the time even this weak sound was masked by the stampeding of rain upon the platform canopy, and the torrents of water gurgling down the rones. Eventually the whimpering ceased altogether, and once again I was compelled to abandon my foray and retire empty-handed. I began to wonder if my torment would ever end.

With every gaslamp in the house set to full hiss, I huddled beneath my blankets and reviewed the vicar's advice. I also re-examined my dislike of garlic.

CHAPTER TWENTY-THREE

MORSE CODE SICKNESS

Mondays were always busy at Upshott Station. The treadmill of events would begin at 5.05am with the arrival of the 'down' Mail Train. This was due in three minutes, and on Platform One were several enamelled pitchers waiting to be filled with fresh water for Busy Linton. I called Diggory impatiently. A stationmaster deprived of sleep soon becomes agitated, and I was mindful of the last time these pitchers had been neglected.

"Why does that boy not attend to his duties?" I snarled at Humphrey. "Where does he get to lately?"

"Don't rightly know, Sir," Humphrey sung. "Arr, but here be the lad now."

Diggory, looking somewhat red faced, emerged from the station house and began loading a luggage trolley in a feeble attempt to look busy. I transferred him immediately to the empty pitchers, for the Mail Train was whistling its approach across the valley, and there was still much to do.

The two-van train was soon climbing Fallowfield Embankment, having been spurred to a flying start by a non-stop run through Widdlecombe. In its wake were dense coils of exhaust dyed a shocking pink by the low, morning sun, and these were expanding dramatically across the watermeadows to hang like a ceiling of coarse plaster. But warm summer air quickly evaporates steam, and so the blushing canopy of mist was soon shredded into wisps and filaments of nothingness.

"Her's goin' to be a fine day," Humphrey observed cheerily, gazing upwards. "Reckons we needed that storm."

"You think so?" I replied sharply, dealing the porter a sour look.

Humphrey stared at me uneasily, wondering why I was so snappy.

"I have a telegraph instructor coming to see me today," I advised him. "So I shall not be at liberty to enjoy the sunshine. And since I am placing you in charge of the station while I am under instruction, Humphrey, neither will you."

"Why need e a telegraph instructor?" Humphrey blinked.

I did not answer him. The urgent thudding of the approaching locomotive had ceased, its regulator having been shut off to allow the train to coast into the station, and it was time to receive the mail. The hills, ever imitative of the sounds they heard, copied the thudding of the engine for a while and then fell silent also.

Twice had the telegraph instructor been forced to postpone his visit, eventually arranging to be on the 7.46am mixed timber and passenger train. Somewhat daunted by the prospect of being tutored in the manner of a schoolboy once again, I decided to retreat to my office to conserve energy.

However, before taking refuge from the world, one small matter required my attention, and it involved holding an earnest discussion with Diggory regarding his duties. Accordingly I summoned him.

"Diggory, I am worried about your perpetual absence," I opened. "Whilst I take account of your present domestic distractions, you must remember that the railway has a tempo of its own, a strict tempo which must be adhered to by all."

"Yes, Mr. Jay," the lad agreed solemnly.

"Now, boy," I continued. "You are paid a total of seven shillings and sixpence per week for your responsibilities, and presently you are not permitted to handle cash, which means that you are not supposed to sell tickets to the public. However, we both know that on occasions you do, and so have demonstrated your ability to make out tickets promptly and give the correct change. I see also that your writing is legible, even if your vocabulary requires expanding, and that you have the rare gift of being able to spell place-names correctly. Moreover, it has not escaped my attention that you frequently assist Jack with clerical work behind the ticket window. Most important of all, you have gained a reputation among my staff for being both honest and trustworthy. Therefore, I am promoting you to the grade of Junior Porter *with* cash responsibilities. I believe you will find this helpful."

The lines of Diggory's long, dimpled face rearranged themselves to form a smile.

"As you probably know," I continued, "this means an increase of one shilling and nine pence in your pay. However, I expect you to honour me by making yourself available when work needs to be done. I do not know what commands so much of your time lately, lad, but you will certainly need to reconsider your priorities if I am not to regret my decision."

Diggory's lines rearranged themselves back to a frown.

"Will I have to wait until January to get my increase, Mr. Jay?" he asked, after a little hesitation.

"As yet, the London and South Western Railway Company plays no part in staff regrading applications on the SER, so your promotion shall be effective from next week," I replied. "Now, we have a consignment of semaphore signal arms from Saxby and Farmer which need sorting into separate stacks. Some of them are 'Home' signals, while others are 'Distant' signals. You will discover which is which by referring to this."

I handed Diggory a copy of the new Signals and Telegraph Handbook, and he left my office with the lines of his face proudly rearranged to form a smile. The lad was studying the pages of the manual before he had reached my door.

By 8am I had begun to confound the telegraph instructor with my inability to absorb abstract information. At first my difficulty quite fascinated him, then the novelty wore off and he became abusive. Despite my best efforts, the dots and dashes of the universal electric telegraph system continued to perplex me. So much so that, at one stage, I suggested we forget all about Morse Code and wait until the South Exmoor acquired its Cooke and Wheatstone needle circuit. This form of telegraph, being alphabetical, could be operated by any fool.

But the instructor laughed at me and said that such a slow and out-of-date system would never be installed, not even on the SER. Mr. Crump, obviously as confused as I about such developments, had misinformed me. Like it or not, I was going to have to learn Morse Code.

The purpose of progress, it had become clear, is to make life more baffling.

During my time with the London and South Western I had never been bothered with the technicalities of telegraphic communications, mainly because I had served at stations employing skilled operators who required no assistance from me. Consequently I did not take kindly to the telegraph instructor's disparaging remarks regarding my 'luck' to have risen to stationmaster without the power of comprehension. Being called a bungler raises one's temperature at any time, but on a sultry day in August it can result in one's shirt clinging uncomfortably.

Were it not for the fact that the instructor had the means to make my life as a student even more miserable than it was already I would have struck him on the nose with the handle of my walking stick. But, the balance of power not being in my favour, I contained myself by imagining that I was sitting on the breezy banks of Upwater waiting for a bite, with nothing better to do than watch lustrous dragonflies hovering among the reedmace. This form of self-hypnosis proved effective, but it resulted in prolonged periods of absent-mindedness which irked my overseer.

* * *

With the lesson over, and the telegraph instructor shaking his head gloomily, I stepped thankfully into the cool of the evening to recover.

While boarding his train to leave, the instructor mumbled something about seven days being long enough for the intelligent man to learn Morse Code, and that he was going to allow me fourteen.

Hearing this remark, I squared my chin indignantly and insisted that seven be allowed. With a shrug of the shoulders the instructor complied, and I was left wondering why I had made such a stupid request.

The train creaked and lurched into motion, and as I stood in the turbulent steam scudding from the cylinder cocks of the diminutive four-coupled locomotive, I felt a peculiar tingling sensation creep across my face. Any other time I would have dismissed this as water spray descending from the chimney, a common enough occurrence, but on this occasion I took it to be my numbed head returning to life.

With the train gone, my thoughts turned to the dread dummy instrument that the telegraph instructor had left behind. He had installed it in a corner of the Parcels Office, complete with instructions and a note that it be left for me to practise upon until the coming Monday. After its removal, I was to commence exchanging messages with my tutor by live telegraph until my speed improved.

Now I had something to make my days as miserable as my nights.

* * *

My head was still chattering with 'clicks' that should have been 'clacks' and 'clacks' that should have been 'clicks' when I gave the 'right away' to the 10.29pm 'down' passenger, a Third Class train which, for reasons I shall explain later, was known as the 'Parliamentry'. As this train departed, I became nauseous, for locomotives burning cheap coal of the kind purchased by the SER often laid down a light grey fog smelling of rotten eggs.

Normally I was not troubled by it, but just now my stomach was easily turned.

At least the future portended favourably with regard to Miss Blake's tormented heathen, be he such, for the cadaver appeared not to have an appetite lately. My dinner had not vanished, and there was no hint of a thunderstorm by which he might wish to hold another musical soirée in my quarters. Still more reassuring was the presence of a sprig of garlic upon my door, the smell of which would keep anything at bay. True, I had not attended church, but I considered a score of three-out-of-four favourable enough for the time being.

Now, earlier this evening Diggory had been to The Shunter and returned surreptitiously clutching something wrapped in waxpaper. I had been unable to investigate the boy's unauthorized errand at the time because I was tapping out a message on the dummy instrument, but, being able to recognize mischief when I see it, I had made a mental note of the excursion. It is probable, even having made this note, that I would have forgotten about the incident had I not chanced upon the waxpaper packet while transferring the day's takings from the Ticket Office to the safe. Fat was oozing from the greasy bundle and spoiling documents on the Booking Clerk's desk.

I summoned Diggory impatiently to have him explain the contents of the wrapper. This was something of an optimistic exercise because my platform staff invariably concluded their duties and left for home directly after the last train, and the last train, being the Parliamentary, had gone. I was somewhat surprised, therefore, to discover my Junior Porter still at large about the station and apparently available for duty, in stark contrast to his colleagues who were rushing to sign off.

The boy is encouraged by his pay rise, I told myself smugly, assuming him to be occupied constructively, even though his reason for working late appeared to necessitate his skulking from nook to cranny in the manner of a sneak-thief.

Now, before delving further into Diggory's peculiar behaviour, allow me to explain briefly the purpose of the 'Parliamentary' train, for this is a most curious piece of railway history.

In the Nineteenth Century, every passenger carrying railway in the land was required by Act of Parliament to provide at least one Third Class train per day, at a cost to its passengers of no more than one penny per mile. Hence the name 'Parliamentary'. The idea was to guarantee even the poorest citizen a small degree of mobility. However, statute did not prescribe a minimum standard for this service, nor any particular time of day that it should be run. So the SER, in keeping with most other railway companies, rostered its oldest rollingstock for the duty and ran the resultant 'boneshaker'at a thoroughly inconvenient hour.

In fairness to the Company I should point out that running the Parliamentary late at night was a matter of commercial prudence rather than deliberate cussedness, for had it been provided at a convenient time of day it would have been filled to capacity with miserly folk well able to pay a more realistic fare. Such a cheap train was doomed to operate at a loss no matter how rudimentary its composition.

Many a railway company, notably the Great Western, gave its Parliamentary trains such low priority that they idled in sidings for hours on end, leaving their hapless passengers to seek the comforts of a public house in the meantime. But then, this unique institution, the Great Western Railway, seldom cared to build its wayside stations within five miles of the villages they were named after and purported to serve. The GWR's disinterest in remote countryfolk and their meagre interests was a well established fact. I was not an admirer of the so-called 'gentleman's' railway.

I summoned Diggory to the Ticket Office and drew his attention to the foul mess on the clerk's desk.

"Open that wrapper and explain its contents," I instructed him sternly.

Diggory gazed at me in silent appeal for a moment and then presented the wrapper for inspection. It contained an assortment of bones and cooked chicken, identifiable more by smell than appearance.

"Scraps?" I queried him. "So you have been to The Shunter to scrounge leftovers? Surely you are not in such straits that you are reduced to begging?"

"Spare me, Mr. Jay, I wouldn't eat this mess. I was going to put it up a tree."

I stood akimbo, and agape.

"Up a tree?" I puzzled. "This is the kind of thing lunatics do."

"For the tits," the young porter told me blankly.

I heaved a sigh of relief and lifted my top-hat to scratch my head.

"Diggory, your propensity for climbing will one day be your downfall, literally!" I jibed. "Surely you do not intend scaling a tree at this time of night to adorn it with brock? The birds have gone to roost, fellow."

"I know that, Sir." The lad defended himself, and then faltered. "I was... I was going to put it out in the morning."

Something about this business did not ring true.

"You will do no such thing," I checked the young man sharply. "I cannot allow my staff to be seen swinging about in trees clutching bags of offal. What would the public make of it? Neither can I allow you to leave slops lying around overnight. Look at this mess. You will encourage vermin. Indeed, I have reason to believe that you have done so already. Dispose of it at once, and clean up Jack's desk before you go home."

Wondering what Diggory was up to, I tutted loudly and left the Ticket Office to get on with my work.

Back on the platform, it struck me that I had forgotten to report to the police constable my sighting of an intruder last night. Upon realizing my oversight, I froze and slapped my forehead. It was too late now. The policeman had made his daily round and left by the afternoon train. I forgave myself, however, for with traumatic events rivalling each other to make my hair stand on end, it was all I could do to remember that trains passed this way.

Having observed Humphrey struggling to don his big black overcoat, I hurried towards him for a word. My intention was to discover if he knew anything about Diggory which might account for the lad's unusual behaviour lately. Humphrey moved away before I could draw his attention, but I caught up with him upon the forecourt where, by custom, he awaited his lift home. For some reason, the porter was staring intently at the sky.

"A little different to last night," I observed.

There seemed to be a conspiritorial silence about the stars this night, their purpose a secret, like pinholes of daylight escaping eternity, or a snow-storm petrified before reaching the ground. They were shining so bright and steadfast betwixt the valley's sombre horizons that one could believe one was witnessing the waking yawn of creation.

Humphrey ignored me. He appeared to be concentrating.

"You feel you could reach up and touch them," I added humbly.

"I reckons they'm a tryin' to reach down and touch I, Mr. Jay," he replied. "August be the month for shootin' stars, right enough. I've seen two on 'em in as many minutes."

"Humphrey, I would like a word with you about Diggory," I opened.

"Arr look! Her makes three!" the porter interrupted me with a stubby finger raised heavenward.

I was vaguely aware of a streak of light.

"About Diggory," I persisted.

"Funny thing," Humphrey ignored me, "most on 'ems gone in a flash, but now and then e sees a slow, sparkly one."

"Humphrey," I barked, "I have no wish to talk to your chin. If you would care to lower it, I should like to know of anything which might account for my Junior Porter's strange behaviour. Now, have you any idea what causes it?"

"Course I does," Humphrey chortled heartily. "The boy is Diggory!"

I gave up.

"By the way Humphrey," I began anew. "Are there feral dogs hereabouts? I heard a most fearful howl last night."

"S'pect the cry of a vixen's what e heard," the

porter entertained himself. "Frighten e did it, Mr. Jay?"

Humphrey's flippancy was beginning to vex me. "I have heard no fox like it," I retorted.

"P'raps twer a gust of wind in them telegraph wires, Mr. Jay," Humphrey tried to appease me. "They'm the devil's choir in a storm. I bin heard 'em emit an unearthly low hum afore now, fit to make your blood curdle."

I almost choked upon hearing this theory.

"No telegraph wire made the sound I heard," I declared with a raw laugh.

A Linton tradesman who spent most of his nights carousing in The Coach House, circled his gig over the station forecourt and brought it to a clumsy halt beneath the awning. This was Humphrey's lift home, and so, with a pat on the back, I bade my Senior Porter good night and turned away. Notwithstanding the garlic above my door, I was feeling a deep sense of loss with the departure of each of my staff this night.

CHAPTER TWENTY-FOUR

SPOOK COMES TO STAY

Walking the shadowy platform back to my office after my starlit consultation with Humphrey Milsom, I found that I could not recall the vicar making any mention of the charcoal burner's final resting place. And because there was nothing in the parish records to indicate that the outcast's remains had eventually been admitted to the churchyard, I began to wonder if I did indeed have a skeleton beneath my floorboards.

Whilst I could appreciate that an exhumation would have incited the same ugly prejudices that had surrounded the charcoal burner's burial in the first place, surely the so-called evil doer's remains had not simply been dug back into the soil by a detachment of navvies? Upon reflection, alas, it seemed likely, for had the Church been liberal enough to allow the outcast's remains to be reburied on consecrated ground, the vicar would have been only too proud to tell me about it.

Earlier in the day I had secreted a bottle of port wine in my office, and thereto I strode to partake of a measure, for I intended to sleep this night even should Beelzebub visit. Instantly I thought he had! A figure sprang out of a doorway in front of me and turned to stone upon the clashing of our eyes.

Instinctively I raised my handlamp to the intruder and sought his identity. Staring back at me in both surprise and horror, his guilty lineaments twisting rhythmically in the swinging lamplight, was a youth.

"Diggory! What are you doing here? You should be on your way home by now," I bristled.

"Mr. Jay," he stammered. To avoid me had been his intent. "I was only ..."

"Shush!" I interrupted him. "Listen. Do you not hear that noise?"

Diggory said nothing.

"Bless my soul," I breathed. "If it isn't that tapping I've been hearing at night. You must be able to hear it too."

Still Diggory said nothing.

Looking over my shoulder I saw my Rollingstock Superintendent's white eyes floating up the platform, so I called him over and invited him to follow me to the Booking Hall to conduct a search. Somewhat furtively, Diggory followed too.

Once in the Booking Hall, I led my two followers through the staff door into a short passage communicating with the various private offices. Having detected nothing untoward during this phase of the advance, I continued with somewhat greater expedition to the foot of the stairs to my private quarters and halted abruptly with a finger pressed to my lips. At this point something untoward did happen. Mr. Troke, being more concerned with a shred of tobacco which had become caught between his teeth, walked into my back. Taken by surprise himself, the oaf trampled my heels with his heavy-duty boots.

I called a halt to the fellow's feeble excuses and listened once more for the tapping.

At first I could hear only my Rollingstock Superintendent's heavy breathing, something to which he was prone whilst concentrating, but then I heard the tapping again.

"Mr. Troke, perhaps you can hear that noise," I

tested the fellow whilst dealing Diggory a withering look. "I am afraid Upshott's Junior Porter here has cloth ears. If you listen carefully, I believe you will hear a tapping noise coming from beneath the floorboards."

"Nay," Mr. Troke contradicted me with a gappy grin. "Thither it is."

Using his foot, the ill-bred fellow pointed lazily towards the Goods Office door.

Almost immediately, and for no apparent reason, Diggory began loitering beside the staircase, and seemed reluctant to move aside to allow me to advance. Confusion followed, during which the tapping grew louder and now seemed to be coming from several directions at once. In an attempt to locate it, Mr. Troke began revolving on one heel with his head cocked sideways. I took no notice of the fellow's grotesque ballet dance, for I did not envisage it achieving very much, apart from dizziness, and set about my own method of tracing the elusive noise.

Once again, Diggory obstructed me.

"Lad, what ails you?" I snapped. "Can you not see I wish to open that cupboard beneath the stairs? Stand aside. Better still," I instructed him, "fetch a spade. If we are up against a rat, we shall fare better with a bludgeon to hand. I just hope your marksmanship is as good as they say it is."

"Only with a caterpult, Mr. Jay," the rebellious young scamp corrected me sullenly.

I took no notice.

"Rats don't have catapults," Mr. Troke sniggered.

Only another Mr. Troke would have known why the fellow made such a remark.

"I'm no good with a club," Diggory sulked,

displaying a suspiciously uncharacteristic lack of enthusiasm for the job.

I stared at him meanly, whereupon the unnatural boy meandered away to the Platelayer's hut to fetch a spade.

"Hurry!" I chivvied him. "Now see here, William," I turned to Mr. Troke, "When I direct my lamp beneath the stairs to flush out this blasted rodent, you shall stamp your feet so that it is driven towards Diggory. Diggory will then club it to death." Mr. Troke chuckled maniacally in the quivering light and gave me an energetic nod of approval. "More is the pity we do not have a station dog," I added. "A little terrier would earn its crust handsomely at a time like this. What?"

"All roads lead to home, Sir," Mr. Troke agreed in his inimitable fashion, and began pounding the floorboards in a club-footed rehearsal of his part.

At length Diggory returned with a long-handled shovel, although not as long as his face, and listened miserably while I explained to him my plan of action. For a boy who had once assisted a rat catcher, he seemed extremely reluctant to participate.

"Have you no heart for this, nature boy," I teased him, and turned to Mr. Troke. "He feeds the tits, you know."

My Rollingstock Superintendent laughed and tried to pull the shovel from Diggory, but Diggory clung to it grimly.

"If you will not let William do it, then you must do it yourself," I jeered the scrupulous youth. "Rats are not tits, you know. Unlike birds, they spread disease and must be killed."

Suddenly the boy appeared to agree with me, and with Mr. Troke breathing down my neck I opened the cubby-hole door. A shard of light fractured the dark interior of the cupboard, and, as if in response, the tapping resumed. Not only did the tapping resume, but this time it was not muted. At last I knew that I had located the source of my torment.

"Rats don't tap," Mr. Troke observed succinctly, just as I was about to place my head inside the hole.

"Well, something does," I whispered back. "And whatever it is, we have it."

Unexpectedly, Diggory shouted a warning to someone and dropped his shovel. I withdrew sharply, startled by the crash, and abandoned myself to a profanity.

Shocked and angered by my outburst, I gave my Junior Porter a lambasting, although, of necessity, only a short one. For I was determined not to be robbed of the initiative in this affair. Without further ado I pulled open the cubby-hole door and thrust my lamp inside. The cupboard lit up, and I leapt backwards in astonishment.

My colleagues stared at me like wax dummies while I searched for the words to express my incredulity, but even when I had found them I am not sure that they made any sense.

With a grin prizing my cheeks apart, I stood aside to allow Mr. Troke the same remarkable spectacle. Mr. Troke's eyes bulged and whitened, and he coughed out his chewing tobacco with a wheeze of surprise. But whilst William's response was to stare with a slack jaw and slightly crossed eyes, mine was to convulse with laughter. Verily, I laughed so much that I did not regain my composure for quite some time, there being a good deal of tension to release.

Far from having discovered a corpse prizing its way out of a coffin beneath my floor, I had discovered a puppy-dog wagging its wiry tail against the joinery beneath my stairs. Blinking into my handlamp now was the cause of all my misery, a frightened little waif with luminous green eyes and a pale, speckled nose. The diminutive critter appeared far too innocent to have caused an important stationmaster so many sleepless nights, but there was no doubting his culpability, for his tail was still making the noise which had driven me to distraction. In addition, I could see the evidence of his attempts to scratch and gnaw his way out of the cupboard during the thunderstorm.

Unsure of my intentions, the four-legged chap tilted his head and barked bravely, although just the once, and made no objection when I lifted him from his gloomy prison and held him to me. Indeed, to show his gratitude, he dispensed a long pink tongue and proceeded to larrup my face with it.

"You, Sir, have shortened the sum of my days," I indicted the animal gravely, and handed him to his co-conspirator, Diggory. "This puppy is never again to be left alone," I said. "Especially during a storm. It is bad for him, and it is bad for me. Feeding the tits indeed, huh!"

Diggory hugged the creature.

"He is an English Setter," he told me excitedly.

"He is a stowaway," Mr. Troke reminded the lad.

"Praise be, at least he is not a charcoal burner!" I toppered them both. "And as for you, Master Smith, I am greatly disappointed."

"I'm sorry, Mr. Jay," Diggory apologized moodily. "I was going to put the puppy aboard the train to Giddiford like you said, but then I overheard someone saying that his neck would have to be wrung if nobody claimed him, and I couldn't do it. Can't we find him a home somewhere?" Diggory lowered his head. "I'd take him myself, but..." he foundered.

"I have heard enough," I halted him.

Whilst I was aware of Diggory's domestic circumstances, and that another mouth to feed, however small, would be beyond his mother's purse, this was not the point. Neither, for that matter, was my increasing mirth over the incident. My clear duty was to censure the young porter for his disobedience. However, for the time being, I decided to make do with a stern reminder of just how the animal had come into his possession.

"Officially the dog is lost property," I said. "Very probably he has a broken-hearted owner somewhere, perhaps a young lad like yourself, pining for him."

Diggory looked troubled by this possibility, and lifted his chin manfully to set matters straight. Indeed, with reddening eyes, he moved to rectify his misdeed on the very morrow.

"I'll put the puppy aboard the morning 'up' train, Mr. Jay," he said solemnly.

I was touched by the lad's adult sensibilities and, after a little cogitation, indulged him a minor infraction of company rules.

"No need," I said. "We shall keep the little chappie here at Upshott, and notify Giddiford of what has happened. If the puppy is unclaimed, well, I have no doubt that our Lost Property Clerk can be persuaded to endorse a solution which will spare him administrative inconvenience."

"What solution?" Mr. Troke asked stupidly.

"To wit," I ignored him, "that we offer the animal a home here. And a job! I shall put him on the payroll as a watchdog."

In a trice Diggory's eyes had lost their glaze, and he squeezed still tighter the ball of mushroom fur with its shiny black nose.

"He will be the cleverest station dog on all the railways," I was exhorted.

"If he is unclaimed," I emphasized with an outstretched finger. "Now, I must make arrangements for the poor creature to spend the night in company. No dog should be incarcerated on its own in a dark cupboard for days on end, least of all an intelligent working breed. Tomorrow we shall think of a suitable name for the little character. I do not wish to refer to him as 'the dog' while he is with us."

"He'll be no passenger," Diggory put in. "I'll teach him to do things."

"Yes, well, a dog that can sell tickets would be useful," I responded wearily, reclaiming the animal.

"We can teach him to lick baggage labels," Mr. Troke suggested, appearing to be serious. Mr. Troke worried me at times.

Giving Mr. Troke the benefit of the doubt, I replied:

"It is certainly an idea, William. His tongue is long enough to wet a dozen at a time."

I wiped my face with my handkerchief and leaned back to avoid another larruping, and to avoid the puppy-dog's unpleasant breath which, for some reason, smelled of peanuts.

With a glance at my fobwatch, I dismissed Diggory and instructed him to get off home. But being the nuisance that he was, the young porter continued to linger. I believe he was unable to wrench himself away from his new-found friend.

"I can manage from here," I waved him away.

The lad began humming a tune to himself as he wandered off into the darkness, and I crossed my fingers that I had not raised his hopes unduly. So far, all I knew about the varmint wriggling under my arm was that he liked buns and hog pudding.

Taking advantage of being alone with me while I doused the platform lamps, Mr. Troke began jockeying among the shadows as if competing with them for my attention. I was inclined to let the shadows win. I shut my ears to his gossip, but he would not take the hint.

"I hear tell Snimple spent Harvest Festival Bank Holiday with that Higham girl, Mr. Jay," he badgered me, stroking the puppy feebly. "Do you not think the humbug is riding for a fall?"

"Snimple is no humbug," I inveighed him. "And I know more about the porter's activities than you imagine, Mr. Troke. However, unlike you, I do not consider I have the right to interfere."

"She's a scarlet woman," he snuffled, blowing his nose. "Snimple'd be better off with the Postmaster's daughter."

"Good Heavens, William, what business is that of yours?" I gasped. "Snimple will return to his senses, I am sure, when he realizes that capable young maids like Amelia Peckham do not grow on trees. But he must be allowed to come about in his own time."

"All the same, it's an ill wind that doesn't blow," Mr. Troke insisted, sorting through his keys noisily.

I stamped my foot to drive him away.

"Good night, William," I called out. "We shall speak no more of the matter."

Reluctantly Mr. Troke returned to the shadows from which he had graduated.

"Oh but upon my soul, my little friend," I confided in the puppy, "how the young lady's heart is breaking."

CHAPTER TWENTY-FIVE

STAFF AND TICKET, STAFF AND TROUBLE

The telegraph instructor dismantled his dummy instrument and hailed a porter to stow it aboard the afternoon 'up' train. While the apparatus was being placed in the luggage van, the instructor retired to a Second Class compartment and made himself comfortable by a window from which, no doubt, he expected me to see him off with some degree of ceremony. I preferred, instead, to watch his exit quietly from my office doorway, relishing the fact that I would never see him again.

The four-carriage train, being scheduled to connect with a London express at Giddiford, got away smartly. With a ball of steam curling skywards, and its rear van juddering violently, it rumbled across Natter Lane Bridge and snaked over the loop points towards Fallowfield Embankment. I hurried to the edge of the platform, for the engine had left in its wake a trail of red hot clinker sizzling upon the oil-soaked sleepers. A fire had resulted, but the flames did not look likely to spread.

The telegraph instructor's departure, though welcome, had left me with a gnawing feeling of ambivalence. For whilst I was elated to have passed my telegraphy test, albeit by a gnat's whisker, I was also troubled by the expert's parting remark that lately anyone could become a stationmaster.

Taking a pinch of snuff absent-mindedly, I watched the train recede until it had almost reached Upford where, in compliance with statutory regulations, the engine's whistle was tooted to give warning of its approach to the unmanned footpath crossing on Fallowfield Common. A tuft of steam having risen from the locomotive, it always took a second for the shriek of the whistle to reach Upshott, accompanied by several echoes.

Awoken from my thoughts, I returned to my desk to see if I could repair my sock suspender. The blessed thing had snapped this morning while I was out stretching my legs in Upshott Wood.

Earlier in the week, while practising on the dummy instrument, it had occurred to me that a second telegraph operator in the station would be useful, and to this end I had made Diggory sit with me throughout my labours at the Morse key, in the hope that some of the codes would rub off on him. Theory has it, you know, that the young mind is more receptive than the old. In the event, however, this young mind had been too preoccupied with an increasingly popular puppy-dog called Spook to memorize anything technical.

With the telegraph instructor planning to tutor me at regular intervals by live telegraph, to see how I was progressing, I could no longer afford to ignore the receiver when it activated, consequently it was not long before I found myself trying to decipher a signal.

Sitting nervously at the apparatus, having over the last week developed an aversion to its peculiar smell, a pungent emission which, I had been told, was caused by an insulating material known as shellac warming upon the inductor coils, I managed to decipher only a fraction of the urgent buzzing. I did grasp that the message was coming from Headquarters, but precious little else. Indeed, in attempting to transcribe the main body of the communication, my wits were overtaken so rapidly that I was compelled to interrupt the sender momentarily by disconnecting a wire, and ask him to retransmit the signal more slowly.

After several attempts, the sender finally arrived at a speed with which I could keep pace, but by this time I was having difficulty differentiating between company abbreviations and personal abuse.

The message, when finally scribbled down, seemed to be informing me that the company telegraph system was about to be superceded, augmented, or something of the sort, by another. Frankly, by now I was entirely confused about matters telegraphic. When it came to telegraphy on the SER, everyone was predicting different developments.

But since the sender of this particular message was the South Exmoor's Telegraph Officer, it seemed logical to believe him rather than any of the other soothsayers. In so doing, however, I was binding myself to an annoying conclusion. To wit, that if the alphabetical dial-and-pointer type instrument was to be introduced after all, then I had wasted my time learning Morse Code. This left me with a puzzle. Why had I received the news from the very person who had arranged for me the services of a Morse Code instructor?

Before I could marshall my dots and dashes to make a reply, the Telegraph Officer signed off with a post script to the effect that it was people like me who had made necessary the retrograde step of a variable current circuit. By 'variable current' I presumed him to mean 'alphabetical'.

A little while later I discovered the cause of my confusion. Humphrey, who was himself something of a telegraph receiver on the rumour circuit, told me that the company Telegraph Officer had been up before the SER Board to answer allegations of equipment misuse. Apparently he had conducted some kind of illegal experiment using the Gid-diford-to-Widdlecombe earth return wire, pray do not ask me what, and now faced both summary dismissal from the SER, and legal action by the General Post Office. Consequently the scientific miscreant had become a trifle embittered and was firing parting shots at the South Exmoor Company by way of playing practical jokes upon its employees. Alas, all became clear, I had been one of his victims.

I could not understand, I must say, why the gentleman in question had not been suspended from duty pending the outcome of the enquiry, as was the usual practise. Upon reflection, I concluded that his work must be of such a technical nature that a replacement could not be found at short notice. Later an alternative possibility occurred to me, a somewhat less settling one. Perhaps the Telegraph Officer had indeed been suspended without pay, but, in the course of one of his illicit experiments, had found a way to tap into the company circuit without authorization. There were plenty of remote places along the line where a portable telegraph set might be connected.

Returning to the subject of general telegraphic developments, of which I welcomed any that would make life easier as opposed to faster, I never let my imagination run away with me. Jack Wheeler, on the other hand, was ever brimming with news of the marvels of modern science supposedly just around the corner. Yet for all his reading he was, in reality, every bit as confused as I about such things, with the difference that he did not know it.

Lately the clerk had been enthusing about an invention called the 'speaking' telegraph, which, hitherto, I had thought merely another name for the universal system. Now, thanks to Jack, I was no longer sure, and the victim of further confusion.

It all stemmed from an article Jack had spotted in *The Times*, a copy of which Doctor Bentley had discarded in the Waiting Room. The article reported an experiment, conducted in America, by which a human voice had been sent down a telegraph wire. Appealing though this idea was, and even though the venerable Doctor himself gave it credence, I found the notion hard to swallow. You must remember that in these times electricity and magnetism were surrounded by a great deal of mystery, with talk of them being able to cure diseases, induce mental telepathy, and even produce light. Wishful thinking was prevalent.

* * *

A piece of progress closer at hand than any 'talking' telegraph system, although a touch more mundane, was that of staff and ticket control. One languid Thursday afternoon I opened my mail pouch to find the much anticipated memorandum advising me officially of its introduction, and that the changeover was scheduled to take place in a matter of weeks. Staff and ticket would, so stated the memorandum, place Upshott Station at the centre of an additional two block sections between Widdlecombe and Busy Linton.

A block section, incidentally, is merely a convenient subdivision of railway line designed to make signalling easier.

Thus the time had come to explain to the employees in my charge the theory of staff and ticket working, and I knew that some of them would understand it more readily than others.

Jack Wheeler and Ivor Hales had both been employed previously on staff and ticket worked lines, so I had only to explain to them the new block section arrangements. The remainder of my colleagues, bar one, came to understand the *modus operandi* after a word or two of instruction. Not surprisingly, the one who could not grasp the theory of staff and ticket was my Stores Clerk, sleepy Tom Turner.

Mr. Turner found the subject of signalling so incomprehensible that mere mention of it torpefied him. The following day, therefore, to set matters straight with all possible speed, I peered into his hut and beckoned him to my office for some rigorous private tuition. Such was Mr. Turner's lassitude generally that he found difficulty in grasping most things in life and, at times, could try one's patience sorely. But I was mindful of my own limitations re telegraphy, and so resolved to make allowances for the dullard. After all, I had no choice but to make Tom understand the principles of staff and ticket somehow, and teaching him would make an interesting challenge. Certainly I could not exempt an employee from understanding something so crucial to railway safety as single-line traffic management simply because he was prone to unconsciousness. The rules did not permit it.

Earlier in the day, therefore, bearing in mind Tom's difficulty, I had salvaged from my waste paper basket an out-of-date picture poster and drawn upon its reverse side a large map of the railway. And upon this ingenious illustration I had placed three pencils representing trains, by which graphic I had hoped to stir into my dilatory Stores Clerk's imagination a spark of life.

So was the theory, but upon seating the clerk before me I was vexed to observe not so much as a scintilla of gratitude or excitement over my artistic efforts, efforts, mark you, which had taken up an hour of my time. To my dismay, the fellow did not even respond when I demonstrated how a pencil might be used to represent a train passing along the line; and when, to introduce a little levity into the occasion, I attempted some train noises, he merely yawned. Mr. Turner, it had become obvious by the droop of his eyelids, did not have the capacity to understand a comradely gesture, so I cleared my throat and set about recapitulating the cold facts of staff and ticket.

"The 'staff'," I began, "is a kind of baton, and should not be confused with staff as in you and I. The staff's full name, in fact, is 'train staff'. What do you say to that, Tom? Simple stuff, eh?" I jollied him. "Now, any questions?"

Mr. Turner frowned weightily, as though his studies to this point had been long and hard, and shook his head cautiously. So far so good.

"Well done," I breathed. "Now, to continue the lesson, there is one unique staff allocated to each single-line section of the railway, and possession of it authorizes a stationmaster to send trains into that section. At Upshott, therefore, there will be two staffs, just as there are at present two batons. But instead of one being valid for the line between here and Giddiford, and the other between here and Blodcaster, one will be valid only as far as Widdlecombe, and the other only as far as Busy Linton. You can appreciate, Tom, that these shorter block sections will allow more trains to occupy the line at the same time, and that shorter block sections are now possible because of the new crossing loops at Widdlecombe and Linton..."

"What will happen to the batons?" Tom interrupted me with a dull gaze. The question, though irrelevant, was a welcome sign that the clerk was still alive.

"Ah!" I gusted, trying to maintain a fizzy atmosphere. "The old batons will be discarded. They will be replaced by four new train staffs carved specially for the purpose. Naturally, only two of these artefacts will be of concern to Upshott, because from here we shall be controlling only two block sections." I paused to see if the technicalities had sunk in. "Is everything clear so far?" I asked.

The timidity of Tom's affirmative nod suggested not, and I waited in silence while he built up to admitting it. Eventually, scratching his dozy head through a heap of lacklustre curls, he reviewed his answer and smiled at me disarmingly.

I was not disarmed, however.

"Well? What do you not understand?" I snapped, losing my battle against impatience.

"Tickets," he enquired vaguely. "What are the tickets for?"

I took a deep breath, calmed myself, and forced an emollient smile.

"Oh, nothing very much," I reassured the fellow, lest he be overwhelmed by events. "Let me show you an example of one."

With gritted teeth, I went to my drawer.

The ticket was printed as follows:

SOUTH EXMOOR RAILWAY
TRAIN STAFF TICKET
Train No. ..... (up/down)
TO THE ENGINE DRIVER:

You are authorized, only after seeing the yellow Train Staff engraved U-W (Upshott – Widdlecombe section) to proceed along this section. The Train Staff will follow.

Signed................... Date..........

"These tickets," I continued, "authorize a locomotive driver to enter a particular section of single-line railway, as does the staff itself, or currently the baton. The beauty of tickets," I cajoled the clerk with a pat on the shoulder, "is that any number of them may be issued to following trains, by which I mean trains going in the same direction, without recourse to a horse rider to retrieve a baton or staff each time."

Perhaps my method of explanation was a trifle clumsy, but by now a pitiful mask of confusion had claimed Tom's face. Aware that this confusion might emulsify into catalepsy, I pressed ahead with increased speed.

"Now, as for the new telegraph protocols, I ..."

"I don't understand," Tom interrupted me. "If tickets allow any number of trains to advance into a section, why don't they undermine the purpose of having only one staff?"

"Just a minute, Tom," I poppled with irritation. "Give me a chance to explain." I ought to have recognized and nurtured this spark of curiousity, for it was borne of an unexpected insight into the affair, but by now I was working with one eye on the clock. "Only the stationmaster in possession of a particular staff can issue tickets relating to it," I continued with renewed composure, "therefore the stationmaster at the opposite end of that section cannot authorize oncoming trains. Moreover, dear fellow, a following train may proceed into that section only when confirmation has been received by telegraph that the train ahead has cleared said section. Like most clever ideas, Tom, it is very simple."

Having concluded my lecture I tore up my diagram and began crumpling the pieces of paper.

"Then how do trains get to come in the opposite direction," Tom halted me drearily.

"Ah!" I paused and applauded him. "Now that is a surprisingly intelligent question. The stationmaster in possession of the staff releases that staff to the driver of the rearmost following train."

"Oh," said Tom vacantly.

The fellow started gazing yearningly at the remains of my diagram, his interest having been aroused by the fact that a demonstration was no longer possible.

"Goodbye Tom," I nodded sharply, pointing to the door.

I took comfort from the fact that Mr. Turner, in his role as Stores Clerk, was the least likely member of my staff ever to have to issue a staff or ticket.

After my session with the torpid Mr. Turner I was rather in need of a rest, but, alas, this wretched staff and ticket business dictated that I prepare for a still more daunting encounter, and without delay. The time had come to inform my Horse Superintendent of the company's notice to withdraw his two beloved baton mounts, and it was important that I break this news before Julian could hear it through the Milsom grapevine.

Much to my consternation, and despite my most earnestly expressed sympathy, Mr. Maynard did not see fit to take the blow like a gentleman. He lost his temper and cut up rough, and my attempts to calm him served only to fuel his anger.

"You can hardly be surprised, Julian," I said. "The improvement was inevitable."

"And what precisely do you mean, 'improvement' Mr. Jay?" Mr. Maynard railed me. "My horses have served the South Exmoor effectively and cheaply for nearly fourteen years. What improvement is there room for?"

"I think you know what I mean, Julian," I parried the fellow sternly. "You cannot stand in the way of progress. It is the march of time."

"It is the march of the London and South Western!" he retorted with uncharacteristic bile. "And I shall not fall victim to it so readily. To do so would bring disgrace upon the family name. No offence intended, Mr. Jay, but I shall fight these faceless administrators of the London and South Western Railway to the bitter end. A Maynard never says die."

With this pronouncement, Mr. Maynard pulled off his immaculate SER company cap, an item of uniform which had nothing to do with the London and South Western Railway Company, and threw it to the ground. This ungentlemanly act of disgust surprised me, but the fellow's next gesture was entirely unexpected and bordering upon lunacy. He jumped upon the discarded cap with both feet and danced a grim jig of wrath. Any comedy in the spectacle quickly evaporated, however.

"Damn and curse the London and South Western," he vented. "If just one of my horses has to go, then so shall I. Touch me if I don't. What's more, I'll put a torch to this station on my way out."

I had not realized that beneath Mr. Maynard's polished exterior there festered such bitterness about the future, yet, far from being alienated by his behaviour, I was deeply distressed. In Julian Maynard I had found a valued and respected colleague, and I did not wish to see our working relationship soured, perhaps even ended, for the sake of a couple of horses.

Watching Julian saddle Hildebrand and apply the spur, I prayed that the fellow's outburst had been nothing more than a case of letting off steam. But doubts lingered as he rode away with unbecoming fury.

When the dust had settled, I recovered my colleague's crumpled cap, shook off the grit, and took it to my office. Here I gazed into its reflective peak as if seeking the wisdom of a crystal ball, and contemplated the uncertainties of the future. I saw among the twisted reflections a benevolent little railway facing the dawn of a new era, an era with harsher priorities, and noted that the casualties of this new era were going to be the very men who had taken the greatest pride in the old.

Until Next Time...

Will Mr. Maynard carry out his threat to resign? Will the cider-apple war be fought in the station yard? Will Horace Jay woo Mrs. Smith and still have time to master the telegraph? Will the Brigadier uncover Snimple's assignations with his lovely daughter?

These are some of the questions it would have been nice to answer in *Spook Comes To Stay* but, alas, Horace Jay's memoirs are too lengthy to be compressed into a single volume without losing their charm. Therefore we are forced to enjoy a second book, *Horse Race, Monkey Business*.

Not only will Book Two provide answers to the above questions, it will provide answers to questions which no one has yet asked. For example, what is the gadget that has come to Upshott? Are there Druids in Splashgate Tunnel? How does the dastardly squire's son manage to ride his horse across the sky? Will Stationmaster Jay be quick enough to prevent the company's pyrotechnic photographer from burning down the station, assuming, of course, that the Horse Superintendent has not already applied the torch?

Cast a deedy eye abroad for:

The Memoirs of H. I. Jay:
Horse Race, Monkey Business.